## DATE DUE

D105283254

*Danny as coach*

## ACKNOWLEDGEMENTS

Little did I know when I sat down at my computer on December 3, 2007, how my life was about to change. On that day I sent a letter to the editor of the *Pittsburgh Post Gazette* explaining how proud I was that my grandfather had been on the Hall of Fame ballot. The PG ran my "letter" as a quarter-page article on Page A-2 – complete with a photo of my brother and me sitting on Grandpop's lap in 1975. Editor John Allison suggested I include an email address. What a great suggestion!

Throughout the day, my inbox was flooded with emails from fans who loved Grandpop. One suggested I write a book about him. I laughed. A little while later, another suggested the same thing. I laughed again … while gently mentioning the idea to my husband. Soon a third suggested it, too. I was hooked. My husband wasn't so sure. For some reason, he thought the task might be a little overwhelming as our four kids were ages 7, 5, 3, and 1 at the time. As you can tell, I wore him down.

I've had a lot of help getting to this point. First and foremost, my husband, Brian, and our kids: Maggie, Sean, Erin, and Maura. They've tolerated the messy house, the laundry mountain, the haphazard meals, the wife/mommy functioning on three hours of sleep. Brian was also a superb editor – weeding out fluff, sharpening sentences, finding mistakes. I owe them all a bigger thanks than I can ever give them.

If this book were a baseball game, my mom and dad would get credit for a Save for helping with my kids when needed. Along with Uncle Tim, they were also the source of many of the stories you just read. Aunt Madge was my ultimate go-to source for my grandfather's early years. I'm sorry her husband, Uncle Art, didn't live to see this completed. My cousin Tim Murtaugh provided a lot of research and an initial draft for the World

Series chapters. Thank you to my brother and sister, Brian and Katie Walton, for always being there when I needed an opinion. Thank you to my brother Joe Walton for answering my baseball questions.

Sally O'Leary, the face of the Pirates' PR department for 30 years, was a true godsend. It was through her help that I was able to contact all of the former players to interview them. She also proofread my manuscript – saving me from several errors.

PJ Miller, my high school English teacher, was my other proofreader. In addition to catching several mistakes, his excitement about the book boosted my confidence as I headed into the home stretch.

Thank you, thank you, thank you to Pirate fan Steve Milman who loaned me photos of many players and several scrapbooks that appear to be my grandmother's handiwork. The scrapbooks cover my grandfather's career from high school through Charleston, WV. The first five chapters would have been sparse without these scrapbooks.

Writers Richard "Pete" Peterson and John McCollister were great sources of advice in the early going.

A big thank you goes to all of the fans who sent me their memories of my grandfather. While not all of them fit in this book, they were all treasured by me and my family. A special thank you to Steve Stake, who spent countless hours campaigning for my grandfather to be inducted into the Baseball Hall of Fame.

Many former Pirates graciously allowed me to interview them – I appreciate their time and their sentiments. Thank you to the Pittsburgh Pirates, particularly Matt Nordby, who gave me access to my grandfather's files and the team's photo archives.

Saving the best for last, thanks be to God for leading me to this opportunity and being there for me when times got tough. At every step of the way when I hit an obstacle, a way around the obstacle soon presented itself. I've also felt the Blessed Mother and my grandparents at my side throughout the process.

My apologies to anyone I missed. My only excuse is that I haven't been operating under much sleep for the past year!

*Danny Jr., who was a second baseman like his dad, gets some pointers from his favorite manager in August 1960.*

**BY STEVE BLASS**

# foreword

M y first year of spring training was 1961, the year after they won the World Series. I was 18 years old and in awe of everybody, including Danny. I always had the utmost respect for him as a person and as a manager. A lot of people thought that he was a casual observer on the bench, but I know that he didn't miss anything. He was one of those guys who, in my opinion, was never unprepared. You could walk into his office with the most bizarre situation that you wouldn't think anyone was aware of, and you'd get the impression that he'd been anticipating your visit for two weeks. It was like he had an antenna that was tuned into the people that worked with him and for him.

For example, Dock Ellis was kind of a controversial, brash guy on the ball club. He told us one day, "I'm going in there and I'm going to tell Murtaugh what's going on. I'm going to get some answers to my questions. I'm going to raise hell in there." We were all just hovering around the door waiting for him to come out. He was in there for about 20 minutes. When he came out we all said, "What happened Dock?" He said, "Damn, I forgot what I went in there for." Danny was never unprepared for a visit like that or if you came at him with an issue.

What I most respected about Danny was the fact that as a player, when you went to the ballpark, you just wanted to focus on the upcoming game – what you were going to be doing three or four hours later. The last thing you wanted was to walk through the clubhouse doors and wonder how the manager was going to be today. What kind of mood is he going to be in? Is he going to be up, down? How is he going to be? That was never the case with Danny – he was always the same and that was always really, really appreciated. You could walk in that clubhouse and get ready for your work and never have to be distracted by the manager. He did his job and expected you to do yours.

Now if you weren't doing your job, you'd hear about it. Danny had this little thing if we were playing bad and he was upset with us or not happy with the way we were playing, he would call a clubhouse meeting after a game. And he could rant and rave and get after you as good as anybody, and at the end of that rant, he'd always scan around the room, so you'd think he was looking at you. Then his eyes would move so almost everybody was included in this gaze. And he would mumble a few things so you wondered if it was you he was hollering at and then he'd walk away. And everyone would look around saying, "Was he talking to me?" and you always thought you were included in that tirade.

But if you were doing what you were supposed to be doing, you really didn't have much dealing with Danny. Why did he succeed? First of all, he had talent on those teams. But I think the fact that he treated you as a professional, he didn't get in your way had a lot to do with his success.

At the end of each spring training, after all the roster cuts had been made and he had the twenty five players he was going to have on his team, he would have a meeting before the regular season started. He'd kind of lighten the mood because we were all anxious to get going. He'd say, "Well, this is it. Look around the room, there are twenty five of you, four coaches and myself. This is it. I want to give you one piece of advice. If you get a team down and you're beating them thoroughly, don't let up, don't get it close. Because if you do, I'll screw it up at the end." Of course, we all knew better; it was kind of a self-deprecating remark. We all knew how good he was. He knew the strategy of the game. He had a sense of when to take pitchers out. He knew the strategies of the hit and run, the ebb and flow of the game and he had a gut feel.

Danny had a lot of facets to him. He was very much the professional. The professional respect he had for his players is something I still remember to this day. That encapsulated how I felt. I loved him dearly. To this day I respect him as the best manager I played for.

Danny Murtaugh is a Hall of Famer as far as I'm concerned. After reading this book, I'm sure you'll agree with me.

*Danny and his friends converted his basement into a recreation room, which was party central for the "gang" during the offseason.*

# INTRODUCTION

I f your grandfather dies when you're only two years old, you're bound to wish you had known him. If that grandfather was also a great man, you'll grow up hearing family stories about him that make you wish even more fervently that you'd known him. If that grandfather was also a legendary manager of your hometown baseball team, you'll grow up reading stories about him in books and newspaper clippings. If that grandfather was the late Pittsburgh Pirates Manager Danny Murtaugh, you'll never hear a bad word said or written about him. You'll hear what a great family man he was. You'll hear what a wonderful manager he was. You'll hear about his practical jokes, his sense of humor, his generosity, his humble nature, his devout faith. You'll hear how he retired for the fourth and final time to spend more time with his grandkids … and then died a few months later. And you'll always be very sad that you didn't know him better.

I was young when my grandfather died, but thanks to this book I now feel as if I knew him as well as anyone. The faithful husband, the devoted father, the loyal friend, the brilliant manager, the fun-loving prankster, the modest celebrity, the proud grandfather. They're all in here. If you knew him, I hope you enjoy rekindling old memories. If you never met him, I hope you enjoy getting to know him as much as I have.

*Celebrating the 1971 World Series victory. Winning pitcher Steve Blass leapt in the air with joy after the final pitch … luckily catcher Manny Sanguillen was ready for him!*

# CHAPTER ONE

# O Danny Boy

D anny Murtaugh was born on October 8, 1917. At least, he was pretty sure he was. A relative once told Danny that his birthday was really October 17. Since Danny had been born at home – without the detailed record keeping of a maternity ward in today's society – he was never quite sure of the actual date. After Danny died, a mourner at his funeral said, "I remember the day Danny was born. It was my wedding day, and Nellie [Danny's mom] couldn't come because she was having a baby." The man must have been surprised to hear Danny's daughter ask, "Oh, when was your wedding day?" Typically a woman knows her dad's birthday. "October 8, 1917," he replied. Mystery solved. And now you know how Danny Murtaugh's family found out his true birth date at his funeral.

Daniel Edward "Danny" Murtaugh was the only son of Daniel and Nellie (McCarey) Murtaugh. He had two older sisters, Betty and Eunice, and two younger sisters, Mary and Peggy. Theirs was a working class Irish family in a working class Irish neighborhood in Chester, PA, outside of Philadelphia.

Danny came from very humble beginnings. His dad worked in the shipyards, but with five kids to support, money was very tight. Nellie did her part to help keep the family afloat by taking in laundry to wash for people. She also baked pies that the kids would sell around town for her. Sometimes Danny and his sisters would walk along the railroad track looking for bits of coal that had fallen from the trains. His mom would use the coal to heat their house on cold winter days.

To call Danny's childhood home "modest" would be generous. In the dining room there was a large hole in the floor that was covered by a plank because they could not afford to fix it. Once when Danny's Aunt Tressa, whom they called the "rich aunt," was visiting she fell through the hole and landed in the cellar. According to former Pirate General Manager Joe Brown, who became one of Danny's best friends, "When Danny was a kid, he slept in a room that had practically no roof. When he went to bed he used to put up an umbrella to keep the snow off him. ... When [he] went to school he took potato sandwiches for lunch – potatoes between two slices of bread."[1]

Like many boys in his day, Danny grew up playing sandlot baseball. It was vastly different than today's world — where organized t-ball leagues, with parents and coaches guiding every step of the way, start as young as three years old. Back then, kids just played. They'd gather together in the neighborhood and head to the nearest vacant lot. Other groups would likewise assemble until there were enough kids to field some teams. They picked their own teams and enforced the rules on their own.

In 1927, when he was nine years old, Danny made it to his first professional baseball game. His Uncle Tim McCarey – known as "Unkie" to Danny and his sisters – took him to Shibe Park to see the Philadelphia Athletics. Like any young baseball fan of his day, Danny really wanted to see Ty Cobb, who was in his first season with the Athletics. Cobb played in 134 out of 154 games that season. To Danny's disappointment he happened to be at one of the 20 games in which Cobb did not make an appearance. Nonetheless, it was eye opening to witness men getting paid to play a game he loved.

Danny's first brush playing "organized" baseball came at age 10 when he played for the Chester Midgets – a group of neighborhood boys who chipped in to buy identical baseball caps. Danny was one of the lucky ones because he owned his own glove. Danny was very small for his age, so the glove was several sizes too large for him. But since it was a gift from "Unkie," he treasured it. Danny used that glove for many years, eventually growing into it as he honed his baseball skills.[2]

In seventh grade, Danny tried out for the Franklin Grammar School baseball team, which was part of the Chester Grammar School League. At first the coach was dismissive of Danny, who stood all of 4'4" and weighed a whopping 75 pounds. Danny was no quitter, though, and his determination and fighting spirit were rewarded with a trial at shortstop. That trial was all Danny needed to prove his worth, and once he got into the starting lineup, he stayed here. To his coach's delight, Danny played again in eighth grade and his aggressive play sparked the team to win the league championship.[3]

When Danny was 12, he played on the Lincoln Roses baseball team – his first time to wear a full baseball uniform. Once again he had to battle extra hard to prove himself due to his diminutive size. Danny spent only one year with Lincoln, where he played shortstop and outfield.[4] Even then, Danny was always looking to play pranks. He particularly enjoyed starting arguments and then backing away to watch the fights that ensued. One game never made it past the first inning because of a fight Danny provoked.

Danny also played baseball with the Chester Boys' Club, for a coach who saw past Danny's size and recognized his talent right away. In 1931 Danny was the captain of his team, the "Cleveland Indians." As a pitcher and a left fielder Danny led the Indians to the top of his seven-team league, earning a spot in the club's "Junior World Series." After what the *Chester Times* described as "the best played and most interesting championship series the Boys' Club has ever had," the Indians lost the matchup in the seventh game.[5]

In his teenage years Danny graduated to American Legion Baseball – where the best of the best in youth baseball came to play. Danny was the only Legion junior to play four straight years while there was an age limit of sixteen in the league. When he first made the team, Danny was smaller than the bat boy – so small that they couldn't find a uniform that fit him. The oversized one he wore made him look even smaller and younger than he was.[6] When Danny was 15, the *Chester Times* predicted, "If this pint sized athlete could add a few inches in height and a pound here and there he has possibilities for a great baseball career."[7] In 1934, his final year of Legion ball, Danny's team won the league championship and made it all the way to the state finals.

Fellow baseball legend Mickey Vernon, who rose to fame with the Washington Senators, grew up in Marcus Hook, PA, near Chester. Even 32 years after Danny's death, Mickey still choked up when remembering his friend. Sadly, Mickey himself passed away on September 24, 2008, just a few months after this interview:

> *I met Danny when I was around 13 or 14 years old and play-ing American Legion ball. I had played for the Marcus Hook Legion team one year and the following year I went up and tried out for the Chester team. Danny was the second baseman on the team at that time. Our baseball paths diverged— he made his way in the National League and I was in the American League. However, we became very good friends in*

*those years playing ball together, and we stayed friends until his untimely death.*

Life wasn't just baseball for young Danny. He was an outstanding all-around athlete and became a regular on the *Chester Times'* sports page for his soccer and basketball prowess, too. He earned a starting spot on the Chester High School soccer team when he was just 13 years old. At the time, Danny was so small that the paper called him "Little Danny Murtaugh," "midget," "tiny," and "pint-sized." However, his size didn't stop him from being a key player on a team that battled for the league championship.

In 1934 and 1935 Danny played basketball for Immaculate Heart of Mary in the local Catholic League. Even in basketball season, though, it was his baseball abilities that attracted the most attention. On February 15, 1934, the *Chester Times* noted, "Young Danny Murtaugh is just a little fellow, but he is one of the best all around athletes in the city. If the half-pint from I.H.M. adds a little beef, brawn, and height, he will be noticed by the big boys in baseball. He is developing into a Number One performer in the Catholic basketball league." As team captain in 1935, Danny often led the team in scoring and even set a league record for scoring 25 points in a single game. Danny, one of the I.H.M. stars, guided his team to first place in the league.

During Danny's time at Chester High School, the school had a soccer team and a baseball team but no football team. Since he was such a good athlete, Danny went to a football camp at Villanova University. The football coach at the time was Harry Stuhldreher, who made a name for himself in the 1920s as one of the "Four Horsemen of Notre Dame" quarterbacking for Coach Knute Rockne. Stuhldreher was so impressed with Danny's play that he offered him a football scholarship to Villanova – even though Danny had never played football outside of pickup games with his friends. Danny was not able to accept the scholarship, however, because he couldn't afford the transportation or books.

Sports aside, Danny had a very active social life during his teen years. He was just 16 years old when he started dating his future wife, Kate. In those days, it wasn't one-on-one dating or an every-day affair. They went out in groups and would walk to each others' houses. Danny came from a close-knit family in a close-knit neighborhood. His cousin Madge remembers how the old "gang" used to hang around together all the time. The "gang" included Danny and Kate, Danny's sisters and their future husbands, Madge and her future husband Art, and several friends who were also couples. They would remain good friends for the rest of their lives.

Paul Klotz was also friends with Danny growing up in Chester. His daughter Nancy remembers her dad telling stories about their Chester days: "Most were about them hanging on some corner with other young male friends, with the guys talking about the girls, and [Danny] would be commenting about such and such a game, quoting statistics, and always tossing a baseball up in the air."

After high school, with no offers to play baseball professionally, Danny worked at the shipyards like his father before him. His daughter Kathy says he probably got his job at Sun Ship in part because of his athletic skills. He played for the Sun Ship baseball and basketball teams in the Chester area semi-professional Industrial League. *Current Biography 1961* described the dangers Danny faced in the shipyards:

> *Danny followed his father into the shipyards, where he worked for 34 cents an hour as a passer boy in a rivet gang and came to know what it felt like to have hot rivets flung inside his shirt. One day he was pinned down by a metal plate that had been dropped off a crane. On another occasion two of his fellow workers were blown apart by a gas explosion fifty yards from where he was standing.*[8]

Like his father and grandfather before him, Danny also volunteered for the Franklin Fire Company in the Seventh Ward of Chester. He once carried a woman out of a burning house only to find out that she died in his arms. He became violently ill at the discovery and never forgot the incident. On several occasions Danny narrowly escaped being trapped in a burning building. Danny brought his lighter side with him to the firehouse, too, and he liked to pull pranks on the other firemen. He always wanted to be the first one in the firehouse when the alarm rang. One time the alarm rang and Danny ran out his back door to beat the other guys to the station. When he got there, he found out he'd run all that way for nothing – the fire was directly across the street from his own house.[9]

Danny finally got his chance to play baseball for a living in 1937. Although he was trading a $35/week job at Sun Ship for $65/month in baseball, Danny's mother encouraged him to go. Mickey Vernon remembers that he and Danny broke into professional baseball at the same time:

> Danny and I went away in 1937 to the Eastern Shore League. Danny went to Cambridge, MD, and I went to Easton, MD. Cambridge was a St. Louis Cardinals farm team at the time and Easton was a St. Louis Browns farm team.

> We were playing Cambridge one night. The lights back in those days weren't too good. Danny was playing shortstop and booted a ball. Somebody in the stands – some leatherlung I call them – started getting on him. After an inning or two, Danny was coming off the field and he challenged the guy to come out of the stands. Nothing happened. Around the seventh or eighth inning the manager, who was also the third base coach, sent a runner in who got thrown out at home plate. The big leatherlung started getting on the manager for pulling a boner. The manager had seen the guy's interaction with

*Danny, so he also invited the fellow out of the stands. Sure enough, this guy jumped down from the stands. The manager took one look at this big, muscular guy and then looked toward the dugout and hollered, 'Danny, I got him down here for you!' The man clobbered Danny.*

Danny may have had that "leatherlung" in mind in his managing days when he was asked about the abuse he got from fans when the team was losing. Danny responded, "Why certainly I'd like to have that fellow who hits a home run every time at bat, who strikes out every opposing batter when he's pitching, who throws strikes to any base or the plate when he's playing outfield, and who's always thinking about two innings ahead just what he'll do to baffle the other team. Any manager would want a guy like that playing for him. The only trouble is to get him to put down his cup of beer and come down out of the stands and do those things."[10]

Danny spent two years in Cambridge, posting a .297 batting average in 1937 and .312 in 1938. He got off to a rocky start with his hitting in 1937, though, and had a string of games in which he didn't produce at the plate. As Danny prepared to bat in a tight game with a man on second base, his manager told him, "Danny, if you don't knock this guy in, you'll be on the train back to Chester in the morning." Danny had no interest in ending his baseball career so soon – and no money for the train fare. He hit a single to score the runner, and he proceeded to hit in the next 22 games.[11]

A sensational fielder, Danny made very few errors. After switching between shortstop and second base in his early days, his manager in Cambridge made him a full time second baseman in 1937. A local paper had this to say about the position change: "Murtaugh looks like another ball player. He is now coming in on his grounders, fielding and throwing with a confidence seen and felt by everyone watching him closely, and don't say he can't hit."

In Cambridge, Danny was described as "snappy" and "peppery" for his enthusiastic play. Playing against Federalsburg on July 10, 1937, Danny made a remarkable play that was relayed in the local newspaper. As a ball was cracked that would have sailed over his head, Danny turned his back to the ball and raced to short right field. At just the right moment Danny turned and caught the ball over his right shoulder. "The fans gave him a big hand for this brilliant catch," the paper reported.

Danny once again switched between shortstop and second base in 1938 as players moved between his Cambridge team and other St. Louis farm teams. One local paper had this to say about Danny's proficiency in both positions:

> Murtaugh seems equally at home on either side of the keystone sack. Two years ago he broke into the Cambridge line-up as a shortstop and was later shifted to second base. ... [In 1938] he was placed at shortstop, remaining there throughout the year to become the number one shortfielder of the Eastern Shore League.
>
> The Chester boy can go either to his right or left with equal facility and has a good arm which fits in to either the longer toss from short or the snap heave from second. He covers an acre of ground and gives every ball a battle. We have seen him make plays in the [Eastern Shore League] that would have done credit to any big league fielder. In addition to helping him cover ground, Danny's speed makes him a valuable man on the base paths.

After just two years in professional baseball, Danny made the jump from Class D to Class AA in 1939. He originally tried out for the Rochester Red Wings prior to the 1938 season, but it was thought that he could use another year of seasoning before moving up. After his stellar performance in Cambridge in 1938, however, there were no doubts that he was ready for a bigger league. His hometown of Chester and his fellow volunteer firemen from the Franklin Fire Company gave him a "Bon Voyage" dinner to honor him before he left for Rochester. The dinner was reported as a "great tribute" to Danny, where "speaker after speaker praised the worth of the youngster as both a player and a clean-cut gentleman both on and off the diamond." The Chester mayor told Danny, "We appreciate what you have done to bring honor to Chester and we are for you 100 percent."[12]

The mayor of Cambridge also spoke in Danny's honor. "I saw Danny play every day, and I knew he was a ball player and some day would go places. I can understand why the people gathered here to do him honor. He gave us every ounce of his skill and strength and was in there playing every minute of the game, and playing to win, but by clean sportsmanship. I bring him greetings from Cambridge, Maryland, to your city and to Danny and extend my best wishes for his future success. … I am glad to be here tonight to bring the best wishes for success to Danny. He will make Chester proud of him, and we of Cambridge are proud of him because he got his start with us. He will make Chester go far and wide in baseball." Danny reportedly had a speech prepared for his dinner, but he was so overwhelmed by the glowing tributes of the speakers that all he could do was stammer out his thanks as his emotions got the best of him.[13]

Danny was ready to make the most of his chance in Rochester. The local paper there ran a lengthy feature on Danny in which he said, "I didn't mind going back to Cambridge in 1938, but you can make my summer address in care of the Rochester Red Wings in 1939. Nobody is going to beat me out for the job this year if I have anything to do with it – and in this case I have practically everything to do with it." The paper went on to say, "This scrappy little infielder gave the veterans a run for their money around the keystone sack. A fine pair of arms and wrists found him getting his share of base knocks and he covered acres of ground. He was shifted back and forth between second and short, fitting in nicely with all infield combinations."

Danny's manager in Rochester, Billy Southworth, agreed with the predictions about Danny's future in baseball. Southworth called Danny one of the revelations of the spring training season and noted that his hitting and fielding were above par. The experienced manager's biggest worry was that the Cardinals would decide they needed him elsewhere in the club. (Interestingly, Southworth would later be on the Managers' ballot with Danny for the Baseball Hall of Fame in December 2007. Southworth was inducted into the Hall in 2008.)

Danny made his debut with the Red Wings in grand fashion. To the delight of his hometown fans, Danny's first game was played in nearby Newark, NJ. With the game scoreless in the tenth inning, Danny doubled off the right field wall to drive home the only run of the game. His fielding was error free in the game, as it would be in the next 16 games as he bounced between shortstop and second base.

In Rochester Danny's hustle and drive once again made him a fan favorite. After one game, the local paper reported that, "Murtaugh lifted the fans out of their seats with a circus catch of Blakely's terrific smash … Danny catapulted into the air, stabbed the ball with his gloved hand and then landed on his shoulder, turning a complete somersault." He had only one fielding error with the Red Wings, which came after he was switched to third base for a short time. He also recorded a hit in all but one game, including a 14-game hitting streak that ended when he was traded to Columbus after only 22 games with the Red Wings. In a 1972 interview, Danny recalled what would be his last trip with the Red Wings that season:

*The team train stopped en route to Montreal, and there was a telegram saying to get me off the train because I'd been traded for Whitey Kurowski of the Columbus Senators. So the team trainer woke me up and told me to get off at the next stop, which was where Kurowski was playing. It was early in the morning. I was sent to a hotel and given a room key. When I got to the room, there was a blond-haired guy sleeping in the bed. I shook him awake and said, "Are you Kurowski?" The guy said, "Yeah." I said "Well you better get up because they just traded you for me." So he got up and went down to the office and I crawled into the warm bed. That was the first time we met.*

At the time, Danny was shocked by the trade. He had been playing very well in Rochester and was leading the club with a .326 batting average. Later he realized that he was a second baseman playing third base in Rochester and Kurowski was a third baseman playing second base at Columbus, the St. Louis farm team in the American Association. Since the Cardinals owned both clubs, they arranged the trade so both men could play their natural position. The move didn't work out so well for Danny offensively, as his batting average fell to .255. However, his fielding remained very strong.

Danny was on the move again in 1940, having been sent to another St. Louis team — the Houston Buffaloes in the Texas League. Danny's daughter Kathy recalls hearing one particular story from his Houston days: "One day my dad was called out on strikes by the umpire, and he got so mad that he threw his bat in the air. The umpire said to my dad, 'You owe me $50 when that bat hits the ground.' My dad didn't have an extra $50, so he dove and caught the bat right before it hit the ground."

Danny was initially brought to Houston as a utility infielder – someone to take over one of the infield spots as needed. In fact, Danny's baseball career almost came to an untimely end in Houston. In spring training, Houston manager Eddie Dyer told Danny that the league was too fast for him and he wasn't going to make the team. A more experienced teammate named Nick Cullop overheard Dyer and asked him to give Danny one more chance. Cullop worked with Danny for more than a month and really turned things around for him. Cullop's work along with Danny's natural hustle and drive landed him a starting spot at third base. The *Houston Chronicle's* sports editor, Dick Freeman, had this to say about Danny:

> *In the first four games of the season and in spring training as well, Danny has made a big hit with the fans. Third base is a strange position to him, if any infield post is strange to a man who played utility at Columbus in the American Association last year. Yet he has taken command in a large way. It is largely through hustle. He's one of the "driving-est" players I ever have seen.*
>
> *Monday night he came up with a couple of great plays, one of them with ducks on the pond, charging in, scooping the ball up with his bare hand and tossing out the runner. Again, with the hit and run on, he grabbed a sizzling grounder, stepped on third and shot the ball to first for a double play.*
>
> *And he hustles the same way on the bases. Sunday he laced a double to left, and as he rounded second, he took a quick look at the throw-in. It was a high, lobbing throw by Puccinelli, so Danny just kept on going. He slid into third head first to turn it into a triple.*

Later in the season Freeman would again feature Danny in his column – calling Danny a "real sparkplug" for the Buffs, as the Houston team was known. With an injury to the regular second baseman returning Danny to his favorite position, Freeman remarked that Danny "has brought the fans to their feet time after time with sensational plays." The article also noted, "Just before every pitch by a Buff hurler, you can hear a shrill whistle coming out of the Buff infield. The whistler is Hustlin' Danny Murtaugh, who has become a great favorite with fans here."

*The Houston Post* sports editor, Bruce Layer, had similar praise for Danny. Reporting on a game against Dallas, Layer wrote, "Brilliant fielding by Danny Murtaugh, Buff third sacker, cut off no less than three Dallas tallies. The little infielder handled seven chances and his fielding of a slow grounder in the sixth, followed by a perfect throw, was the highlight of the ball game." Danny's play helped the Buffs lead the Texas League by sixteen games at the end of the regular season.

Based on his spectacular performance in 1940, including a .299 batting average and leading the team in at bats and runs scored, Danny was widely expected to move up to the St. Louis Cardinals. In fact, Danny's hometown paper reported that Cardinals General Manager Branch Rickey himself was the source of a report that Danny would play second base for the Cards in 1941. Rickey had seen Danny play in Houston and was impressed with his hitting and fielding, as well as the fans' response to the "peppery Irishman."

As it turned out, Danny was back in Houston when the 1941 campaign began. His spring training was sadly interrupted by the sudden death of his father, who had a heart attack on March 15. On his return to Houston, Danny quickly regained his stride and was once again a leader of the team. In an exhibition game against Texas A&M on April 8, 1941, Danny homered on the first pitch. Later, he said he waited five years to find a pitcher he could slap the first pitch of the game out of the park on. He joked that he now wanted to be known as "One-Pitch, One-Run Murtaugh."

The Houston sports column "Sidelights by Andy" featured Danny's spectacular play a month or so into the 1941 season:

> *Little Dan, the hustlingest second baseman in the league, is now hitting .346 in 133 times at bat, with 46 hits. And there is a story behind that. Danny is quite a "ribber." He particularly likes to rib the sports editors. During spring training the little Irisher kept telling me that he was going to be a power hitter. "I'm changing my stance a bit. You guys'll be calling me muscles before long." Of course Danny was just joshing, but back in his mind he must have felt that he was going to hit better. Danny's batting is the only thing that can keep him out of the majors. He and Carey Selph are on a par for hustling. That goes a long way at second base. A player can loaf a half a step and miss a double play. He has to have a lot of "guts" too, because when you are no larger than Danny and run into a jam with an oncoming runner you can expect to be jolted up a bit. I've never seen "Shanty Irish" Danny back away from any play.*

By the end of June, Danny was batting .316, had scored 54 runs, and stolen 15 bases – six of which were to home plate. In a poll of Texas League owners, managers, and umpires, Danny was rated as the league's number one player. Announcing the results, league president Alvin Gardner said, "Murtaugh is a unanimous choice and I agree with them. Danny is a great team man, an amazing base runner, good hitter and a brilliant fielder."

Danny's exploits helped a group of boys from the Chester area serving in the Army at Fort Sam Houston in Texas feel at home. Private Tom Carney, of Company G, 38th Infantry, wrote a letter to the *Chester Times* sports page praising Danny's efforts for the Buffs: "Danny's playing great ball. He has all the confidence in the world, is hitting the ball solid and hustles every bit of the way. They can't keep him down." Carney included a San Antonio newspaper clipping about the All-Star Texas League baseball game. According to the article, "Most Texas League members assert that it is not Houston or its fine pitching staff that beats them, but Mr. Murtaugh. Offensively and defensively he is a very irritating young man to everybody concerned on opposing ball clubs."[14]

Danny's success in Houston earned him his long hoped for trip to the majors. After four years in the St. Louis farm system, the Philadelphia Phillies acquired him in June, and his last game for the Buffs was on June 30. The Houston fans were very sorry to see Danny go – with some even protesting the move. The Sidelights by Andy columnist chastised the fans and urged them to instead be happy for Danny:

> Danny deserves the break he got because he worked for it. Danny Murtaugh became a major league ball player because he made up his mind to be and he hustled. ... [I] have watched the little Irishman for two years. The greatest compliment I ever heard paid him was that he was a ball player's ball player. Which means that he was a constant threat out there – that he was constantly doing something to help his team. Danny was the most feared member of the Buffs because he never let up. If we are going to demand that of our ball players then we must stand up and cheer when that hustle and determination earns a player an advancement. To Danny Murtaugh we say, "Good luck, Danny, me lad, and keep up the good work."

The *Houston Chronicle's* Dick Freeman was also happy for Danny's advancement but admitted, "I'll miss him." In his June 30, 1941, Press Box column, Freeman recalled meeting Danny the spring before and asking which position he preferred to play. Danny's response: "To heck with what

I prefer. I want to play, and I don't care where it is." Freeman said he never saw a guy who loved to play baseball more than Danny Murtaugh:

> He doesn't stop one second. If an outfielder is slow on returning a hit, Murtaugh is off like a shot, stretching a single to a double or a double to a triple. If a pitcher takes too long a wind-up, Murtaugh is off for third or home. And he's just as hustling on defense. ... Now he has gone ... to the Phillies, and if he doesn't inject that needed spark into the Phillies, it's because their battery is dead. ... [The move] is a break for Danny. And I think the guy deserves it. ... Go get 'em, Danny. We're pulling for you.

Buffs Manager Eddie Dyer agreed. When the *Chronicle's* Freeman asked Dyer how he felt about the trade, Dyer replied:

> I'll tell you the absolute truth. I'm tickled to death. That kid played good enough ball at the end of last season to deserve a crack at the major leagues. He's better right now than a lot of infielders in the big time. I thought sure we'd lost him at the end of last season in the major league draft. But they missed the bus up there. ... Danny has a chance to get bigger pay with the Phillies, and that means plenty to a youngster. He was plenty happy about it. The first thing he said was: "Now, Skipper, I guess I can marry my girl this fall."

The *Houston Post's* sports editor Bruce Layer joined his fellow sports writers in praising Danny and wishing him well in Philadelphia. Layer predicted that Danny would "move in at second base for the Phils and before a week is past he will be a very popular young man with fans in the National circuit." According to Layer, "the hustling little Irishman" sparked the Buffs' to a wide lead in the 1941 Texas league race and the bosses were sorry to see him go. In the words of Buffs' president Fred Ankenman, "I hate to see Danny leave our club, but I didn't want to see him lose a chance to make the grade in the majors. He has played great ball for us and is deserving of a chance to make good in the big league."

*Early in the 1942 season, Danny was leading the league in batting.*
*Though his prowess at the plate didn't last, his hustle was always present.*

## CHAPTER TWO

# In the Big Leagues

Danny celebrated Independence Day in 1941 with his first start for the Phillies. Chester native and fellow sandlot player Johnny Podgajny had debuted with the Phillies the previous season. According to Johnny's son John, "Dad talked to Danny in the locker room before his first game and looked at his glove. Danny had a glove with a hole in it. There was a hole in the pocket of the glove. It was completely worn through. Of course, back then they didn't have two nickels to rub together. And my Dad said, 'For Pete's sake, Danny, you can't wear that.' Danny said, 'It's all I've got.' So Dad went in his locker and got him a new glove. Danny thanked him profusely and said he'd give it a try."

Philadelphia sportswriters, like those in other towns where Danny played, began referring to him as "peppery," a "spark," and a "flash." One column said Danny's "talents are lost in a bushel of ineptitude." On August 25 a headline in the *Philadelphia Evening Bulletin* read, "Danny Murtaugh Has Been Sparkplug in Phils' Improvement." Detailing the team's attempts to fill the second base slot, the article noted:

*Then came Danny Murtaugh. It seems almost incredible that a youngster, whose most exalted position was in the Texas League, could become the main drive shaft of a major league team. But he did. Danny was jittery and nervous his first week in the majors and some of the experts muttered, "Just another busher." But they didn't wait long enough. Danny suddenly got going and at this point is the brightest rookie star in the majors.*

*In the 40-some odd games he's played with the Phils he has shown exceptional judgment of pitching, has hit sharply and improved all the time, fields second like a veteran, but most of all he's a ball of fire on the bases.*

It was true. Despite playing in only the last half of the 1941 season, Danny led the league in stolen bases that year with 18. However, anyone who was at his first game would not have predicted his success in that area. In 1958 a *Pittsburgh Post Gazette* profile of Danny included a remembrance from him of his first appearance in the major leagues. Most of his old "gang" from nearby Chester had come to watch his debut in Philadelphia. Danny was called in as a pinch runner at third base, and the manager gave him the steal sign. Danny recalled, "I was a good runner then, and I took off for the plate. I got a terrific jump on the pitcher and the only thing which would keep me from stealing home would be to fall down. I did."[1] Clearly he was more careful in future attempts.

Danny's manager at the time, Hans Lobert, was one of the best base runners during his playing days. He was happy to find a player after his own heart. On Danny's first day with the Phillies, Lobert asked him what he liked to do best. Danny told him, "Down in Texas, I always liked to run." Lobert felt pretty good about Danny and told him to steal whenever he had the chance, not to wait for a signal. "Those were pretty unusual instructions for a rookie," Lobert acknowledged, "but you know the rest.

He went into bases head first, feet first and slaunch-wise; some days his body would be a mass of cuts and skin burns, but he never complained, and he wound up leading the league in stolen bases."[2] In 1972 Danny discussed his speedy play with an interviewer:

> *Nick Etten was a good hitter. I was young, and I was very fast when I was a kid. I was an outstanding defensive ballplayer. I was a good second baseman. There were a few balls hit between first and second that I thought Nick should go for instead of just running to the bag and letting me try to get the ball. So one day I said to him, "Nick, I think there are a few balls being hit down there that you should make an effort to get to." Nick was a little bit older than me, and he looked at me and said, "Son, they pay old Nick to hit. You can't hit, so you catch all those balls and I'll knock the runs in for both of us."*

Former Pirates manager Bobby Bragan also got his professional baseball start with the Phillies. He was the team's shortstop when Danny came in as a second baseman:

> *As a player, Danny was very good. Neither of us was the best hitter in the world, but we could field the ball and throw it. He was a little better runner than I. He could run, and he could steal bases. I didn't steal any bases. He could play second base. We really enjoyed playing together. The best thing to remember about him is his sense of humor. He really enjoyed life, always had a smile. He was as friendly as a person could be. He was upbeat. The greatest thing about Danny Murtaugh was not just that he knew the game and was a good player, but that he had the knack for seeing the bright side of things.*

After he became a successful manager, Danny often had the opportunity to reminisce on his early days in baseball. In 1961 he told *Delaware County Daily Times* Sports Editor Ed Gephart how he credited an unlikely mentor for keeping him in the majors for nine seasons:

> *In the minor leagues, I didn't have real good coaching in the art of making the double play. It seemed like none of the managers I had in the minors were infielders in their day. After three or four days in the big leagues, my weakness on the double play soon became apparent. The fellow who helped me a lot – and he doesn't even know it today – is Lonnie Frey.*
>
> *One day in 1941 we (Phillies) were playing Cincinnati. They had a second baseman named Lonnie Frey. I thought he was one of the greatest pivot men I had seen up until that time. During the ball game I had flubbed a double play. While running out to my position the next inning it dawned on me that I'd better get some help if I expected to stay in the National League. Frey was the first hitter that inning, and he doubled. I went over to him at the bag and said, "Mister Frey" – I called everybody Mister in those days; I was a young rookie of 23 – "would you help me to make the double play?"*
>
> *"Yes son," said Frey, then 28 but a veteran, "and when would you want me to teach you?" "How about after the ball game?" I asked, and he said, "All right."*
>
> *After the game had ended and everybody was in the clubhouse, Lonnie Frey, a big star in those days, was ready with a baseball. He and I went out around second base and he taught me the basic principles of how to make the double play. We must have worked for nearly an hour. His tips helped me to make the double play good enough so that I could stay in the big leagues for [nine] seasons.[3]*

One of Danny's neighbors, Ted van Deusen, was just ten years old when Danny broke into the majors. Ted has wonderful memories of growing up around the corner from the man who would one day become a two-time World Series Championship manager:

*Danny was my hero as a child and inspiration in my later years. He was a blur on the field, always moving, whistling, kicking dirt and stealing bases, with a head-first slide that probably started that trend. I played high school baseball and later played minor league ball, and I emulated his every action, whistling and sliding in head first.*

*Danny grew up in a duplex and we lived in an apartment right around the corner. Danny's house had the only backyard large enough to accommodate a ballgame for eight and nine year olds. Plus the street behind it was a cinder filled roadway next to the railroad with a huge stone wall behind it that kept the balls from going too far. Nellie [Danny's mom] wasn't too keen on the baseball in her backyard and shooed us more than once with her broom.*

*When Danny was home it was a different matter. He was in the Texas League when the Phillies got him and we sure were glad to see him because there were no little league fields or elementary school fields for us to use. He played with us in the yard, brought us scuffed balls and cracked bats and discarded gloves and really helped us with the fundamentals. Sometimes he even took a few of us to the Phillies games with him. We were all around ten by then.*

*Danny was a man we adored and looked up to for the rest of our lives. I certainly attribute much of my success to what he taught us as children and what I was able to emulate as an adult. I am a retired attorney and most of the kids from that neighborhood either did not survive or wound up in prison. Thanks to Danny and others like him, some of us escaped that fate. He was a generous, giving person, one who jumped up from dinner when the siren rang at the local fire department because he was a volunteer.*

Indeed, the entire city of Chester loved Danny. No sooner had Danny donned his Philly uniform than plans were underway for "Chester Day at Shibe Park" to honor Danny and teammate Johnny Podgajny. The tribute, held between games of a doubleheader on September 21, was a grand affair – beginning with a special train from Chester to Philadelphia for fans and a parade from the train station to Shibe Park. The fans chipped in enough to provide $500 defense bonds for Danny and Podgajny. The Chester contingent helped the Phillies draw their biggest crowd ever – with 10,000 fans making the trip from Delaware County to see their hometown boys.[4]

There was no bigger fan at the game than Kathleen (Kate) Clark, Danny's high school sweetheart. Danny was right when he told his Houston manager that he'd be able to "marry [his] girl this fall." On November 29, 1941, Danny and Kate were married at St. Robert's Roman Catholic Church in Chester. Danny's young neighbor, Ted van Deusen, remembers the day like it was yesterday:

*On Danny and Kate's wedding day, there was a reception at the house after the ceremony. A couple of us regular kids, poor as proverbial church-mice, were lolling on the corner by the house. Danny's Uncle Tim [McCarey], a politician who lived nearby, saw us there and invited us around to the side porch for a piece of cake and ice cream. Danny came out and wanted some pictures of us playing ball in the yard. Someone had a movie camera — a real luxury in those days — and they fin-*

24

*ished the shots of the guests and the party and took some shots of us playing ball. I saw the videos later and they were hilarious.*

Just a week and a day after Danny and Kate got married, the Japanese attacked the U.S. at Pearl Harbor. The next day President Franklin Roosevelt declared war on Japan. Three days later Germany declared war on the U.S. The United States of America was now fully involved in World War II, and every American would feel the impact. Danny recalled playing baseball during the war in a December 1972 interview:

*During the war, every time we took a trip, we had to take the train because of gas rationing – we weren't allowed to take a bus. The men in civilian clothes always felt like outcasts. At that time, practically everybody of our age was in uniform and we sort of had to sneak on and off the train. But we all knew it was only temporary because we were all going to be in sooner or later.*

*In those days, they very rarely held the cars open for us. In the past, when you traveled with a major league ball club, they usually had a car open for you and you'd go in and take over the car. But even as late as 1943, it was still on a first come, first served basis. I do know a couple of trips we took that we didn't have any eating facilities. Prior to the war we had our own eating facilities for the ball club or we had access to the dining car. There were a few trips where we went hungry until we reached our destination.*

*We all felt that we were doing quite a job, too, maintaining the morale at home. We thought that we were a necessity. I believe Congress thought the same because they didn't discontinue baseball. So even though we weren't in the service at that particular time, we felt that we were raising the morale*

✓ *of the country because so many boys did want to see baseball players. I know we had a lot of baseball games where we'd go into the army camps to play. Personally, a few times when I went over to Fort Dix (NJ) to play, I met a lot of boys from my hometown, and I'd be sort of a message bearer. They'd see me out there playing and they'd come over to give me messages to take to folks back home. That was a POE [point of embarkation] in those days, and they were getting ready to ship out overseas and they probably weren't allowed to call home. So they would write notes and I'd deliver them.*

Not everyone agreed with Danny on the value of baseball, and some people thought it should shut down as it had during the First World War. On January 15, 1942, the President sent what is known as the "Green Light Letter" to Baseball Commissioner Kenesaw Landis. In the President's personal opinion, "I honestly feel that it would be best for the country to keep baseball going. There will be fewer people unemployed and everybody will work longer hours and harder than ever before. And that means that they ought to have a chance for recreation and for taking their minds off their work even more than before." The President stressed that individual players of military age should enlist but noted that there were plenty of older players who could keep the game alive.[5]

President Roosevelt's letter was a relief to everyone who made a living in baseball, including Danny. But it didn't completely quiet the criticism. The *Sporting News* took a different approach and in April 1942 posed the question directly to men in the military: Should baseball continue while they risk their lives defending our country? The response was overwhelmingly positive – the servicemen themselves believed it was important to the morale of the troops and the country to "keep 'em playing."

To the surprise of many, that spring found Danny fighting to keep his starting job at second base. Danny was widely regarded as one of the best second basemen in the league, he led in stolen bases in 1941, and he was a great morale booster for the team. However, his hitting was weak when he moved up to Philadelphia – after batting .317 in the tough-pitching Texas League, Danny only managed a .219 average for the Phillies. In the offseason the Phillies had acquired several potential second sackers, including Alban Glossop, who matched Danny pretty well in fielding and seemed to be a stronger hitter.

On Opening Day Glossop was out with a minor injury, leaving Danny at second. He gave the fans a thrill as he led off with a single that later resulted in the Phillies' first – and only – run of the game. It wasn't enough for a win or to secure the spot at second base. When Glossop returned to duty, Danny spent several games on the bench. Less than two weeks into the season, Danny was back in the lineup – this time at third base. A story in the *New York World-Telegram* speculated as to how Danny ended up on third:

> *Though [Philly Manager Hans] Lobert is not Irish, he is favored with messages from the Small Men. One night he was awakened by a light smack on the schnozz, and he heard someone say: "Put Murtaugh at third base. He can play the position and he will outhit Glossop and May – and even you the best day you ever saw." That crack about himself got Lobert fired up and he jumped out of bed. "Just a nightmare," he said and went back to his slumbers.*
>
> *But the next day Murtaugh, the speed boy around second, was playing third. Right now he is hitting better than .275 and doing the job around the far turn about as well as anybody in the circuit.*[6]

Before long Danny was leading the league in batting. Several local papers probed Danny's "sudden success" at the plate. Key factors included fewer nerves than in his initial season, more patience in waiting for good pitches or drawing walks, and advice from his manager to stop trying to hit for the bleachers and instead shoot for holes in the infield. Danny acknowledged that he wasn't getting as many steals as he did in 1941. His explanation: "The pitchers are watching me closely and don't give me much of a chance to take a big lead. Besides, I'm hitting my way around now."

Phillies owner Gerry Nugent had this to say about Danny's play in mid-May, "Then there's Danny Murtaugh. When we were in Miami Beach and playing exhibition games on the way home, a Class B scout wouldn't have looked at him a second time. But he's our best player now. He's been going great. He's hitting well, is fast, can run the bases, and [Manager Hans] Lobert hasn't found the infield position Danny can't play. I only wish some of the others would surprise me the way he has."[7]

Danny's performance was so strong into June that there was talk in the local papers of him winning Rookie of the Year honors in 1942. Local writers also were pulling for Danny to be named third baseman for the National League in the All Star game. *Chester Times* sportswriter Bill Burk made a strong case for Danny in his Sports Shorts column:

*First of all Danny is doing a first class job with a last place club. He is a born hustler and never lets up no matter how tough the opposition may be. He refuses to get discouraged by a succession of defeats and it is a wonder to us that he hasn't pulled the Phils out of the doldrums by the sheer contagion of his will-to-win.*

*He is the top hitting third baseman of the National League, and is making fielding plays that would do credit to a Pie Traynor, Heinie Groh or a Jumping Joe Dugan. He gets balls that others wave at in passing. … As a result of his ability to get in front of these balls, Danny's body is covered with bruises and he has already been KO'd twice by smashes that hit him in the face.*

*Right now Danny is playing second base for the ailing Al Glossop, and Pinkey May is at Danny's third base station. Danny hasn't let up in his play in the shift and is covering second as he did last year when holding down the job for the second half of the campaign.*

*The fact that he is filling in at second shouldn't keep him off the All-Star team as we would rate him one-two as a keystone tender. But because of his season's performance we believe the National League owes him the third base station when the team begins firing at the American circuit's all stars.*

Despite his spectacular play, Danny was passed up for the All Star game. Philadelphians were baffled by the omission. One local sportswriter compared Danny's season with the third basemen who made the team and found Danny's batting average and fielding abilities to be higher in each case. Danny didn't let it get to him, though, and continued to hustle no matter what position Lobert had him play.

For the rest of the season, Danny remained around the keystone sack – alternating between shortstop and second baseman. When his teammate Al Glossop recovered from his ailment and returned to second base, Danny moved to shortstop. According *Philadelphia Daily News* sportswriter Ed Delaney, the two worked well together. "The best move [Manager Hans] Lobert made was the teaming of Danny Murtaugh and Alban Glossop as the Phils' keystone pair. Murtaugh and Glossop are not the senior circuit's best, but in the short space of time they've been together the two have fitted together as a combination."

Danny's prowess at the plate did not last through the season. By the end of the season, his batting average was just .241. His fielding continued to be solid, though, and he handled the moves between second, shortstop, and third with aplomb. He finished the season with 13 steals – a far cry from his 18 in half a season in 1941, but he had the sixth highest number of stolen bases in the league.

As the 1942 season closed, Danny once again found work at Sun Ship in Chester. He and several other ball players were profiled in a Philadelphia newspaper spread "From Major League Lineups to War Production Lines for Uncle Sam":

> Since the close of the past season, many major and minor league players, who are not subject to the draft because of family dependencies or other reasons, have gone into war work – helping to build ships, planes, guns, and other equipment needed by Uncle Sam's forces. Most of them plan to return to the diamond next spring, although there is a possibility that some, who are especially skilled workers and are holding essential jobs in war plants, may be 'frozen' into such employment. Shown above are a few of the many players whose names have graced big league box scores and who now are batting 'em out at war plants to help run up the score against the Axis. ... helping to win the biggest world championship battle in history.

Danny apparently wasn't one of the "especially skilled workers" holding an "essential job," because March 1943 found him once again training for the Phillies – although not in the warm, Florida sunshine. With Americans scaling back and facing rationing due to World War II, baseball team owners recognized the need to cut back as well. One primary cutback was to hold spring training closer to the teams' hometowns. To keep the railway system free for war-related shipments – including troops and supplies – the Director of Defense Transportation asked baseball to curtail its use of train travel. In response, baseball Commissioner Landis in January 1943 ordered all clubs to find spring training locations north of the Potomac and Ohio Rivers and east of the Mississippi River. The Cardinals, White Sox, and Cubs, who were outside of that boundary, were limited to Missouri, Illinois, and Indiana.

The Phillies trained in Hersey, PA, that year, as Danny recalled in a 1972 interview: "I thought the fields were pretty good [considering] we were training in the north. Being in Hersey, PA, they'd had a lot of snow that winter. They didn't have time to operate on the field and get it in big league playing condition. ... But I thought for overall training in the north it was a good facility."

Lacking the warm spring of Florida, official training started later in 1943 than was usual. Danny got a jump start on his training by working out at the Chester High School gym with teammate Johnny Podgajny and his friend Mickey Vernon, who was playing for the Washington Senators. According to a *Philadelphia Inquirer* story, Danny's main concern from the changed training schedule was the effect on his batting: "I can get into fielding shape in little or no time. But if we should miss a lot of days at batting practice it is bound to show up once the season begins. The pitchers can work out daily, strengthening their arms, but a batter must tune up his eyes in actual practice. I think everything is going to turn out all right. All the major league clubs will be in the same boat, and all the players probably will begin the season on even terms when it comes to condition."[8]

Danny's preparations worked well, and he was the Phillies' hottest hitter during spring training. His performance earned him the leadoff spot on Opening Day at Shibe Park against the Brooklyn Dodgers. Danny thrilled the fans in his first at bat – reaching first on an error, making it to third on a teammate's single, and stealing home. The Phillies lost the lead in the second inning, however, and began yet another season with a loss.

After eight games, Danny's batting average was a respectable .280. On May 5, however, he was hitless against the Dodgers. In Danny's defense, his mind was likely not on baseball that night. After the game, he hopped a train back to Chester to welcome his first son, Timmy, into the world at 8:45 a.m. on May 6, 1943. The proud papa had only a short visit with Kate and his new son – he was soon back on the train to Brooklyn for that night's game. Danny was back in town the very next day handing out cigars at Shibe Park as the Phillies began a two-week home stand.

Danny and Kate were puzzled by a gift young Timmy received from the Phillies: a pair of boxing gloves so he would toughen up quickly. Kate promptly sent a thank you note to the team, but she didn't try to hide her bewilderment: "Timmy and I want to thank you ... but no one can figure out the boxing gloves. I said I guess they didn't want him to be a ballplayer, but I surely don't want him to be a boxer."

Young Timmy was named after Danny's uncle, Tim McCarey (Unkie), who continued to be one of Danny's most ardent supporters. Unkie was very active in local politics and was well known around Chester. After his namesake was born, Unkie told the local paper he wasn't sure whether he'd make another infielder out of the new protégé or a left handed pitcher (the baby had waved his left hand vigorously). [Turns out neither position would fit Tim. He became a stand out catcher as a youth and spent several years in the Pirates farm system both as catcher and manager.]

For the first time in many years, the Phillies broke out of the basement in 1943. Fatherhood apparently agreed with Danny. According to one local paper, "Danny 'Poppa' Murtaugh is the spark plug of the team. He is playing an amazing game at second and he is an ideal leadoff batter." Another paper noted, "Dan Murtaugh, batting .328 and leading the league in stolen bases, is the spark plug." In late May the Phillies spent several weeks in fourth place – to the delight of their fans. As one local paper reported:

> Before the slightly glazed eyes of a record night crowd, the Phillies clambered into the National League's first division last evening, using the pink and mortified necks of the Chicago Cubs as stepping stones.
>
> Saluted by the hoarsely jubilant cries of 20,821 clients – the largest assortment of witnesses they ever drew after dark – Bucky Harris' incorrigibles knocked the Cubs out from under their toupees, 5 to 4.
>
> The conquest, third in succession, hoisted the Phils up to a fourth-place tie with the Cincinnati Reds and left the Cubs pinned under a heap of seven consecutive defeats.

Around this time (late May 1943), rumors began swirling that the Brooklyn Dodgers wanted to strike a deal with the Phillies to bring Danny to Brooklyn. Local sportswriter Bill Dooly wrote for the *Philadelphia Record* and *The Sporting News*. His response to the rumors was a column titled "Trade Murtaugh? Ha! Ha! Ha!":

> I don't blame the Dodgers for coveting Danny Murtaugh. … After seeing the guy in something like 22 games this year, I'll take my chances on sinking or swimming with Danny Murtaugh. There's a ground-ball hound that gets better every day, pally. … Danny, to drop into the lingo of the game, can really carry the mail. As to what he can do when they ask him to take the bat in hand and author a few basehits, well, the Giants, Reds, Cardinals and Cubs are wondering if anybody ever gets the guy out.

Bill Burk, whose column "Sports Shorts" appeared in the *Chester Times,* was equally sold on the hometown hero. Writing in late May 1943 Burk had this to say about Danny:

> *Murtaugh is like a coiled spring. He is quick in his motion, peppery in demeanor and an incurable optimist. He played with a championship team at Cambridge, MD, at Rochester, NY, and at Houston, TX. With that sort of a club he was a natural spark plug. When he broke into the Phillies' line-up in July of 1941, he lifted the club up by its boot straps and had them alive for the closing months of the year. Last year, although not assigned a regular job by [manager] Hans Lobert, Danny at one time led the league in hitting and kept running and whistling despite extreme indifference from all concerned. This year under the confidence of [manager Bucky] Harris, Danny bloomed into stardom and is once again the chained-lightning of old.*

Danny continued to play well through the summer. In late June, sportswriter Bill Dooly reported on an eight-game road trip in which Danny batted .429 and exhibited "a quite fancy brand of fielding around second base." Another local column agreed:

> *"Dangerous Dan" Murtaugh sets pace for the Phils. ... It is the consensus around the circuit that Murtaugh's all-around play stamps him as the best second baseman in the business. Not only in hitting, but his play in the field has [manager] Bucky Harris in raptures most of the time. Johnny Podjagny, now with Pittsburgh, claims that it is Murtaugh who holds the team together and is the team's sparkplug. Around Shibe Park, he is recognized as the best lead-off man the Phillies ever had and is also giving them the best second base fielding they have yet enjoyed.*

While Danny was certainly on fire, he wasn't perfect. One night, the Phillies were winning 2-1 until Danny made an error at second base that allowed the opponent to score. The Phillies lost the contest 3-2. The Phillies pitcher that night was All Star pitcher Schoolboy Rowe, and he was not happy about the loss. He was particularly mad at Danny for the error that cost him the game. In the locker room after the game, Rowe lit into Danny, told him he had no place in the majors, and called him plenty of names. Danny was already beating himself up for the error and had no response until Rowe called him an SOB. At that Danny leapt up, ready to fight. Size-wise, Danny was clearly outmatched by Rowe, but Danny had spunk and was ready to go. Teammate Ron Northey stepped into the fray, announcing that anyone who wanted to fight Murtaugh would have to fight him, too. Rowe backed down from the fight and peace ensued in the clubhouse. From that moment on Danny and Northey became great friends, and Danny never forgot the incident.

Danny's spectacular season was interrupted when Uncle Sam called. He reported to the Chester Draft Board on August 3 for his final physical tests and other examinations before being inducted into the U.S. Armed Services. The local sports pages were full of tributes to Danny. Bill Burk's "Sports Shorts" column was the first to chime in on August 5:

> *"Dapper Danno" Murtaugh ... will be sacrificing more than the average youngster who goes into the service. Having a great year with the Phillies, the Chester bell-slider could command a nifty salary for the next campaign. That is he could have under normal circumstances.*
>
> *Danny has been battling for a place in the sun. This year he achieved that spot, proving to one and all that he is not only of big league caliber, but is also a star. ...*
>
> *Murtaugh will make a good soldier. He has a way of putting*

*everything he has into his job. That is a trait that has stood him well in industrial ranks (he is very popular at Sun Ship), and in baseball. It will serve him well in the Army.*

*The contribution Danny has already made to the morale of the boys in the services has been excellent. Chester and Delaware County boys under arms boast of his feats ... Many of those lads in the service are personal friends of [Danny] ... Thus Danny has a background of service before he dons a uniform.*

Danny's last game before reporting to duty was on August 19 – dubbed Danny Murtaugh Night by the Phillies. The *Philadelphia Evening Bulletin's* Ed Pollock noted that fans and baseball officials would pay tribute to Danny "with cheers and high praise, and perhaps a gift or two." However, Pollock emphasized that while Danny's entrance into the service prompted the timing of the testimonial, it was not the reason for it:

*The reason is he's a hustler and that has made him a popular ball player. Who can help loving a guy ... athlete or not ... talented or not ... who's always putting out everything he has?*

*That's Danny Murtaugh. He has been with good clubs and bad, but whether his team was in first division or last place, the quality and quantity of his efforts remained constant. He has always been in there fighting for basehits and runs, and extending himself to physical limits on defense. ...*

*[Danny is] a great fellow for any ball club because his spirit will lift team morale and keep others fighting when, as last year, there wasn't much to fight for and little to fight with. A great fellow for the Army, too. The war will be won by men with his sort of spirit.*

For his part, sportswriter Bill Dooly wasn't sure who would miss

Danny the most – the Phils, the fans, the sports reporters, or those who have played against him around the league. "Danny is one of those kind of people that when you see them approaching you feel better for it, for he is a guy you like to have around when there is time to kill. He has also made the Phillies' pitchers feel pretty good seeing him shagging grounders behind them. ... [Danny] plays with all he has, on good days or bad. ... There's no need to worry about Danny making good in the service. He's been a good soldier right along."

Before heading off to begin his time in the service, Danny got five days at home with Kate, young Timmy (now almost four months old), and the rest of his family. At this time, Danny and Kate lived with Danny's mother, his sister Mary, and his sister Peggy in the family home. Most of the family lived in the immediate vicinity. Kate and Timmy would remain with Danny's family throughout the war. Many of the men from their old "gang" were also in the service – including Mary's husband Bud (Danny's brother-in-law and good friend) and Art, another good friend who was married to Danny's cousin Madge. Living very close to each other was a godsend at this time, as the women all stuck together and helped each other while their husbands were overseas.

CHAPTER THREE

# ᴅuty calls

"**M**urtaugh. I'm looking for a guy named Murtaugh."

Danny hadn't even made it into the reception center at Camp Meade when he heard a colonel bellowing his name. "My gracious," thought Danny, "I've only been here an hour – I haven't done anything wrong yet that I know of." It turned out that he was being sent to New York to participate in the War Bond Game on August 26, as Danny recalled in a 1972 interview:

> *There was going to be a benefit ball game up in New York at the Polo Grounds. It was a mixed team of the Yankees, the Dodgers, and the Giants. They were going to play an All Star Army team. Since I was just heading into the Army, Larry MacPhail [a baseball executive who was doing PR work for the Army] thought of me right away. He got the Colonel down in Ft. Meade to ship me up north to play the game.*
>
> *I think they made $800 million in war bonds from that game. I got my wife a seat for $10,000 that was given to me – I didn't*

*have that much money. They had box seats in the Polo Grounds that had sort of a horseshoe effect from first base to home, and they sold those for $1 million a box.*

*Before the game there was a five or six hour show by all the leading celebrities in Hollywood. In those days, the show Yankee Doodle Dandy came out with Jimmy Cagney, and he had the whole cast there and they put on a great show – we sure enjoyed it.*

Danny was back for his processing the next day, and he was amazed at how quickly the Army put him through the "assembly line." As his identity became known, a crowd gathered around him. He recalled for the group his final game with the Phillies – Danny Murtaugh Night, where thousands of fans from Chester came to see him off. According to the Army paper *In the Service,* Danny said he played "awful ball" that night. "Like every other ball player on such occasions, I should have been good, but I was terrible. Sun Ship gave me $300 in War Bonds, their best wishes, and a great sendoff. What do you think I did? Messed up. Went hitless among other things, and how I wanted to hit that night."

Once in the armed forces, Danny dreamed of being a pilot instead of in the infantry. *In the Service* reported he had a reason for wanting to be in the Air Corps. "This war is going to last at least a couple of years, perhaps longer. When it is over, I want to come out of it with something … something I can do when I get out. People don't realize it yet, but after the war is over, the day will not be far off when Philadelphia vacationers, or anyone else, can be driven to the city airport and take planes for Moscow, London, Paris, Rome, and other foreign centers and be there in a few hours. … I expect to go back to the Phillies when this is over, but I'd like the Air Corps training to fall back on when my baseball days end."

Danny's request for the Air Corps was granted, and he was transferred to Buckley Airfield in Colorado for training. Danny played for the Buckley Airfield's baseball team and had great success there. His batting average was .440 and he led the team in singles, doubles, triples, stolen bases, batting average, RBIs, and runs scored; he was second in home runs.

Unfortunately, after a few months at Buckley, the Army tested Danny and realized he was colorblind — which automatically disqualified him to be a pilot. He was moved to the ground force of the Air branch and had a chance to remain at Buckley to play on the baseball team. However, Danny decided that playing baseball wouldn't help much in the war, so he went into the combat infantry. His son Tim believes his time in the infantry took a lot out of his baseball because one of his big assets was speed. "A couple of years in the infantry walking across Europe in 1944 and 1945, especially those cold winters, took a lot out of his legs. He probably just lost a step when he came back and it shortened his career. He had a bad knee which really ended things prematurely."

Tim's not alone in believing the years in the war significantly lessened his dad's baseball career. Gerry Nugent was the Phillies owner who acquired Danny from St. Louis in 1941. Nugent originally signed Danny because *Chester Times* sports writer Frank Johnson assured him that thousands of fans would come from Chester to see Danny play. Nugent never regretted the move. In addition to Danny's obvious success with the Phillies, Nugent appreciated the estimated 40,000 Chester fans who flocked to Shibe Park just in Danny's first week. Nugent would later say that it was Danny's two years in the service that prevented him from being one of the all-time major league greats.

✓ Tim recalls that it was hard to get his dad to talk about the war. "There was one story he told about a time when they were pinned down in Germany or eastern France. It was a bitterly cold winter. Dad was out on patrol and there was a sniper who kept shooting at him. The sniper was getting really close and they couldn't find him. He said to himself right then, 'If I get out of this alive, I'm never going to worry about anything the rest of my life.' He sort of lived by that. He didn't get too depressed or too excited. He was very even tempered and I think that's why – from his war experiences." And the sniper? According to Tim, "My dad and the other men waited as long as they could. Eventually it just got too cold for them, and they had to get back to their unit. Fortunately, they didn't encounter the sniper again on their route."

As a foot soldier in the 97th infantry in the 1st army, the sniper experience wasn't Danny's only brush with danger. In all, Danny's outfit got three battle stars, proving their valor. *Chester Times* sportswriter Matt Zibitka got Danny to open up a little about his war experiences as detailed in a December 5, 1957 column:

> It was back during the heavy fighting of World War II in Europe. The Allies had just invaded Europe and were trying to secure positions. One night, an officer in the 97th Infantry Division asked for "volunteers" (Army style – you, you, you, and you) to go on a very dangerous mission.
>
> The job was to infiltrate the heavily guarded German lines to secure information, which was very vital prior to a giant offensive. As the small band of serous-faced G.I.s started out on their dangerous mission one of the members, a fuzz-faced youngster, got so scared that to send him out on this important job would have proved detrimental to the safety of the others.
>
> Another G.I., who wasn't included in the patrol team, noticed the quivering lad, and he felt very sorry for him; so sorry that he himself volunteered to take the lad's place. This G.I. [Danny, of course] then went with the others on their special journey through the German lines, knowing that every step they took could be their last step on earth.
>
> Through the grace of God, the patrol made it through the

*German lines, got the necessary information and en route back
captured several Germans. The captured Nazis told the patrol
that they saw the G.I.s crossing the line earlier and could have
machine-gunned each and every one to death – but somehow
chose not to do so. ...*

*This episode was just one of many brushes with death that
Danny experienced in the ETO [European Theater of Oper-
ations]. And it's one facet of his colorful life that has rarely, if
ever, been revealed to the public.*

When the war in Europe ended, Danny was sent to the Pacific to be
part of the occupation force in Japan. His unit was one of very few to serve
in both the Atlantic and Pacific theaters of the war. Staff Sergeant Merle
Kalp served with Danny in Tokyo. Kalp recalls that Danny was placed in
charge of re-building the athletic facilities at Stateside Park in Tokyo.
These facilities would have held the 1940 Summer Olympics had the war
not interfered. While there, Kalp says that he, Danny, and the other soldiers stayed in the Meiji Hotel, which had been built for the Olympic athletes who would have competed in the 1940 Summer Games. The
accommodations were certainly an improvement over his experiences in
Europe.

During this time soldiers could accumulate Victory Points to try to
get home early before their service was up. The Victory Points were based
on length of service, what type of combat the soldier had seen, and various
other factors. Periodically the soldiers would sit down with a superior officer and go over their records looking for Victory Points they had missed.
When Danny got to Japan, he was anxious to go home so he could get to
spring training. He asked his Sergeant to check his Victory Points to see
if he could go home. The Sergeant told Danny he had to see the First Sergeant who was around 30 miles down the road. Danny somehow got a
jeep and drove down to see the First Sergeant. When the First Sergeant

came to the door, Danny saw that it was one of his good friends from Chester, Arky Kraft. Needless to say, Danny got his Victory Points pretty fast.

Danny began the 1946 season with the Phillies after being released from the Army just 15 days before spring training began. Danny's fielding was top notch that spring, although his hitting eye wasn't there immediately. As Opening Day approached, Philadelphia Manager Ben Chapman indicated he planned to stick with Danny as long as he could because he "like[d] his spirit" and the way "he pivots that double play." Apparently Chapman wasn't the most patient manager in the world; after playing in just six games, Danny was traded back to St. Louis. Danny recalled this time with an interviewer at his Woodlyn home in December 1972:

> When I reported to spring training with the Phillies in 1946, I had forgotten how to play baseball. I still recall that when I batted in spring training, I thought that every ball the pitcher threw was going to hit me right in the head. I knew there wasn't any way that I could play good enough to stay in the major leagues. After about a week of the season, they sent me to Rochester. I had the same trouble for two or three weeks. Then one day I walked out on that field and it seemed like about thirty pounds just dropped off me all at once. I could run and field and I could see the ball from the pitcher. I was on my way back again. It was an unusual circumstance, and I don't know how to describe it, but in just one day it happened – just over night. It all came back to me.

Danny spent the remainder of the 1946 season back with the Rochester Red Wings, one of his teams from 1939. Danny had a clear goal in mind at Rochester: making it back to the big leagues. He didn't lose confidence in himself when the Phillies sent him packing. He believed they made a mistake by not giving him more time to get into the swing of things after his time in the service. At one point during the 1946 season, Danny was batting .396. His success at the plate was matched in the field, and Rochester's combination of Danny at second and Eddie Joost at shortstop was considered the best in the league.

Danny's determination and spirit once again endeared him to the fans in Rochester. However, this time around he also had more experience, which made him even more valuable to the team. In the first game of a doubleheader against the Toronto Maple Leafs, Rochester Manager Burleigh Grimes and Shortstop Eddie Joost were kicked out of the game in the second inning. Danny stepped into several gaps that night: taking over at shortstop, as field captain, and as manager. Danny coached at third, made eight player switches – including five pitching changes – and still managed a double and a single at bat. In the closing game Grimes and Joost were back in action. Danny, now able to focus more on his own play, hit three for three and scored four runs. Almost two months into the 1946 season, Danny was leading the International League in hitting with a .360 average. He finished the year with a .322 average in 541 times at bat. He had 11 stolen bases and 62 RBI. The Boston Braves took note of Danny's success in Rochester and in November drafted him from the Cardinals' farm system.

As Danny prepared to join his new team for spring training, he and Kate were getting ready for another big change. On February 2, 1947, their second son, Daniel Edward Murtaugh, Jr., was born. Two weeks later, Danny arrived at spring training in Ft. Lauderdale to find a familiar face at the helm: the Braves' manager was Billy Southworth, who had managed Danny in Rochester in 1939.

Unlike the stereotypical Irishman and the stereotypical baseball player, Danny wasn't a drinker. However, he enjoyed playing cards, going to the horse races, and other social activities. One night during spring training, Danny and his roommate were out late and broke curfew. They went right to the ballpark in the morning, showered in the clubhouse, and headed out to the field ready to go. Southworth came up and asked Danny how his night had been. Danny assured Southworth it had been fine, "Got to bed around midnight and never even turned over." Really, wondered Southworth, "Not even when that big trailer crashed into your room?" It turned out a truck had lost control and plowed through their hotel room while they were out enjoying themselves. Danny battened down for the rest of spring training, determined to make the most of his second chance in the majors.

When Opening Day rolled around, Danny was still on the Braves' roster. Unfortunately, however, he was not in the lineup. Nor would he be for the next month. He knew he was still on the team – he kept getting his paycheck – but he didn't know how long it would last without a chance to prove himself. Back then a team could keep 28 players until May 15, at which time the roster dropped to 25. Kate always waited until after May 15 before joining Danny for the season. Once the deadline passed and it appeared Danny had made the cut with the Braves, Kate joined him in Boston with Timmy and newborn Danny Jr.

Finally, in the second game of a May 18 double header against the Cincinnati Reds, Danny got his chance to play. While he didn't register a hit in the contest, his defensive prowess earned him the "Play of the Day" spot in a local newspaper. Danny's six put outs and two assists helped save the game for the Braves, who won 3-1 after losing the first contest 2-1. After appearing in just two more games Danny was sent to the Braves' minor league team, the Milwaukee Brewers.

According to General Manager John Quinn, the Braves were one over the limit and had to drop somebody. They had enough infielders already on the roster, and they felt Danny could help the Brewers in their American Association. Danny was very disappointed in the demotion. The one bright spot in the move was that Danny was reunited with Nick

Cullop, his former Houston teammate who saved Danny's baseball career by intervening with his manager and helping improve his hitting. Cullop was now serving as the Brewers' manager.

Danny was as determined as ever to make it back to the big leagues – in part because when the Braves sent him down he learned that he only needed 28 more days in the majors to reach the five year mark and become eligible for a pension at age 50. With a wife, two young boys, and a widowed mother to support, this was a powerful incentive. Like always, though, the love of the game was enough of a motivator for Danny. In Milwaukee as in other towns, Danny was a great spark for his new team. The locals began calling him Whistler – in recognition of his trademark whistling – as they happily noted that the Brewers' infield finally had some life to it. *Milwaukee Journal* sportswriter Sam Levy noted that the fans had even started whistling along with Danny.

It wasn't just noise that Danny provided for the Brewers' infield. His skill at second base played a key role in the team breaking the .500 mark for the first time that season. In his first 18 games with the Brewers, he handled 109 chances without a single error. He also had 48 putouts, 61 assists, and was involved in 17 double plays. But it was his .404 batting average a few weeks into the season that was the talk of the town. Soon the headlines on the local sports pages read, "Brewers Ride Murtaugh's Bat … to 7-3 Win," "Murtaugh Sparks Brews to 3 Straight Over Birds," and "Murtaugh Sets American Association Afire with Great Performance."

By mid-summer, rumors were swirling that Danny would be traded to the Philadelphia Athletics, managed by baseball legend Connie Mack. The team's shortstop at the time was Eddie Joost – Danny's partner at the keystone sack with the Rochester Red Wings the previous year. Speculation was rife that the Athletics were looking to reunite Joost and Murtaugh to shore up the infield and make a run at the first division. Major league scouts who watched Danny play agreed that he was out of place in the minors. For his part, Danny would have loved to be back in the big leagues, but he preferred playing daily in the minors to warming the bench in the majors.

The rumors were partly true – the Athletics sent scout Harry O'Donnell to follow the Brewers around for two weeks in an attempt to acquire the star second sacker. Despite being offered up to $50,000 for Danny, the Braves management said, "No Deal!" The Braves were battling for second place in the National League, and one of their utility infielders was out with an injury. Braves Manager Billy Southworth couldn't afford to let Danny go in case he needed another infielder down the stretch.

Danny was naturally frustrated that no deal was made because it would have led him back to the majors and back to his hometown. Nevertheless, he continued to shine with the Brewers. In July, Danny broke a 22-year-old American Association fielding record by going 42 consecutive games before committing his first error. Prior to his July 6 error, Danny handled 231 fielding chances, including 191 putouts and 139 assists. He factored in 36 double plays as well. No one was surprised when Danny was named to the American Association All Star team. By season's end, Danny was sporting a .302 batting average and had recorded seven home runs (his highest ever in one season), 49 RBI, and 96 runs. His .988 fielding record with only nine errors set an American Association fielding record for second basemen. Danny was a key factor in Milwaukee beating Syracuse in the Little World Series – the Brewers' first win in 11 years.

Despite his success in Milwaukee, Danny was happy to see the season end. He and Kate purchased a new row home on Chester's Kerlin Street. Danny was eager to get settled with Kate, Timmy, and Danny, Jr. The connecting houses in the row belonged to Danny's sister Eunice and her husband George, his sister Mary and her husband Bud, and his cousin Madge and her husband Art. Danny's mother, Nellie, would remain in the family home on Barclay Street with her brother Tim (Unkie).

A new son, a new major league team, a new minor league team, a new home ... 1947 was certainly a year of changes for Danny Murtaugh. The end of the baseball season would bring another change for Danny – one that would affect the course of his life forever. As the 1947 season came to a close, the Boston Braves traded Danny to the Pittsburgh Pirates. This was one trade the Pirates would never regret. After playing for nine teams in nine years, Danny Murtaugh had found his baseball home.

*Danny's baseball career would enable him to meet all sorts of interesting people, including the legendary Bing Crosby. This 1949 photo shows broadcaster Bob Prince interviewing Crosby, who was part owner of the Pirates, as Danny looks on.*

CHAPTER FOUR

# the whistling irishman

The "Whistling Irishman" was Danny's nickname during his Pirate playing days. Pittsburgher Martha Shanley lived in the same Squirrel Hill neighborhood where Danny stayed his first season with the Pirates. "We were bleacher-ites. There were four of us who never missed a Sunday game or a Friday night game or a Ladies' Day game. One of our great reminiscences is his whistle from second base. [She mimics his whistle.] That let us know everything was all right. It was kind of like 'Okay, let's go get them.' It was always when they were all in position waiting for the next pitch that he would whistle. It was very reassuring."

Pittsburgh sports attorney and baseball historian Sam Reich vividly remembers watching Danny play for the Pirates:

> *The Pirates of 1947 were a pretty sad outfit. They came in dismal last place and second base was like a deep hole. They tried at least three different guys to fill the position including the manager, Billy Herman, who is in the Hall of Fame [as a*

*player]. It was just a bad team. Nobody had any expectations in 1948. Then they brought [Danny] into camp, and he made the team as a second baseman. He had a remarkable season. Danny finished ninth in league MVP voting that year. To me that's a very significant distinction.*

*Danny and [shortstop] Stan Rojek led the league in double plays in 1948. It was fun watching Danny and Rojek — they were the best double play combination the Pirates had in years. I remember on Labor Day they were playing a big game against the Cardinals and the Pirates turned six double plays. Danny was involved in five of those, which tied a record set in 1905. As for his hitting, Danny batted .290 and his 71 RBIs were second only to Ralph Kiner.*

*That was a magical year for Pittsburgh sports fans because that was the only year after World War II that the Pirates did well in their division until 1958. From 1946 till 1958 they were dismal as far as the standings were concerned. It's hard to describe what fun we all had in 1948 because going into September the Pirates actually had a chance to win the pennant. It was a four team race and it was very close among the four teams. They really gave it a good run, and Danny was a big part of their success.*

The *Pittsburgh Sun Telegraph* chronicled the Pirates' successes and failures throughout that glorious 1948 season. Based on the news coverage, it appears that Danny really caught fire during the second half of the season. Danny is described as "a National League sensation," "one of the reasons the club is where it is," the team's "spark," and "brilliant at bat and afield." After the Pirates swept a double header against the Boston Braves on August 29th, the *Sun Telegraph* included this account:

*The brightest star of the afternoon was scrappy Danny Murtaugh, the best clutch hitter Pirate fans have applauded since Glenn Wright left the Oakland scene.*

*The first battle scarcely had been under way before Danny and Stan Rojek threw the stands into an uproar with their fielding, but it takes runs to win ball games and Murtaugh's five hits — a triple, a double and three singles — were deep in both wins.*

*Murtaugh's double in the early game paved the way for the winning run. After the Braves had scored twice in the first round of the afterpiece, Murtaugh put his team in the game with one of those two-out singles with a runner in the scoring zone. That is one of his best numbers.*

*The Pirates drove for four runs to win in the seventh and it was Murtaugh's single, the fifth hit of the inning that put on the finishing touch.*

Throughout the 1948 season, the *Sun Telegraph* ran a Pirate Star of the Day contest. After each game sportswriter Chilly Doyle would pick one or more stars from the game. They kept a running count, and at the end of the season the player with the most stars won $500. The player with second highest number of stars won $300. Third place won $200, and fourth and fifth each won $100. Danny received the second highest star count, with only Ralph Kiner ahead of him.

Frankie Frisch, a former second baseman who was elected to the Hall of Fame in 1947, saw Danny play in 1948. Frisch had spent 1940 – 1946 managing the Pirates, so he was very familiar with the team. He was also extremely impressed with Danny:

*Murtaugh is the 'glue-man' of the Pirates. He's the fellow who has kept those Pittsburghers in the race, with all due respect*

51

*to Ralph Kiner, Frankie Gustine, Elmer Riddle and all the others. He's a steady man at second base and a handy man at the plate. Murtaugh has the kind of spirit out of which ordinary teams become good and good teams become great.[1]*

By all accounts, Danny did have a career best playing year in 1948. As previously mentioned, he and Stan Rojek led the league in double plays that year. This was particularly impressive considering that they were up against future Hall of Famers Pee Wee Reese (SS) and Jackie Robinson (2B) of the Brooklyn Dodgers. Danny also led the league in putouts and assists that year. For the first time since 1938 the Pirates placed three men in the top ten in Most Valuable Player balloting in 1948. Danny placed ninth – with just three fewer votes than teammate Ralph Kiner, who placed seventh. Danny's double play partner Stan Rojek rounded out the top ten. The Pirates would not fare so well in MVP balloting until 1960, when four of Danny's World Series Champion players made the top ten.

On September 9, 1948, the *Sun Telegraph* ran an article that Manager Billy Meyer wrote for the International News Service. In it Meyer tells why the Pirates were the season's "surprise club of the major leagues." Meyer wrote, "It's hard to single out any one individual on the squad as being most responsible for our success. At present, I can narrow the count down to three men — the keystone combination of Stan Rojek and Danny Murtaugh and the great work of [pitcher] Bob Chesnes."

The Pittsburgh skipper was not surprised that Danny was one of his star players. Meyer had spent the previous year managing the Yankees' minor league team in Kansas City, where he had seen Danny playing second base for Boston's minor league Milwaukee Brewers. He had pushed to have the Pirates bring Danny on board, and he was happy to have his choice succeed. Danny likewise had tremendous respect and affection for

Meyer. He would later say that he learned much of his managerial style from Meyer.

When Danny's former teammates are asked about him – 60 years after that magical 1948 season – it is his personality that they remember. Most mention how well he played in 1948; some mention that he was one reason that the team was in the pennant race until the end of the season; some mention the whistling. But every one of them remembers him as a "great guy." Even though it's been 60 years since they played together, you can hear the smile in their voices as they talk about Danny Murtaugh. Baseball aside, that's a nice legacy to leave behind.

Like Danny, former catcher Ed Fitz Gerald also joined the Pirates in 1948. Fitz Gerald was on the team for Danny's entire four years, and they remained friends beyond their Pirate playing days. Fitz Gerald has good memories of their time together:

> Danny had a good year in 1948, I think, because he got there and he was just ready to play. He was really the veteran on the team in terms of time in the majors.
>
> Our families were close. Betty Ann [my wife] and Kate were good friends. We used to play bridge together – there were four couples. It was Betty Ann and I, Danny and Kate, George Strickland and his wife, and Bob Chesnes [and his wife]. We all took turns hosting the bridge nights. Danny was also good friends with Monty Basgall; they were roommates when we were on the road.
>
> Kate and Danny were godparents for my second daughter, Nancy, who was born in January 1951. We had her baptized in Pittsburgh. Danny and Kate always sent presents to both girls over the years.

*Danny and Kate were two of our favorites. Even when he was managing and I was playing for Washington, I'd go to the park early when the Pirates were in town just to talk to him and agitate him. He was really a nice man. A real good man. He had a lot of good qualities. You couldn't say anything bad about Danny.*

"Oh, Danny Murtaugh. Danny Murtaugh. You're talking about a fine person." Former Pirate Wally Westlake played with Danny from 1948 until 1951, and he is clearly emotional when reminded (out of the clear blue) of his old buddy:

*We were good friends on the field. I thought the world of him. I called him 'The Monk' – we used to joke about which one of us was the ugliest. It was a tough decision. We just enjoyed one another. There's nothing I could say indecent about Danny Murtaugh.*

*I really enjoyed playing with him, especially in 1948. He was just a different type of person on the field. We both played the same way: 'I'm going to kick your [butt].' He and Stan Rojek put in a hell of a year [in 1948]. He was a hell of a guy – a real pleasure to play with. He walked out on the field and there was one thing on his mind 'I'm going to kick your butt, dude.' I always wished I'd still been there when they won the championship.*

*There was nothing flashy about Danny. Nothing phony or make-believe. He just let you have it, which I liked. He was his own man. We all enjoyed him.*

If you're ever on the game show Jeopardy with baseball history as a category, there's a chance that one of your clues could be: "The baseball player who lost his starting job with the Dodgers in 1947 to make room for Jackie Robinson." Thanks to this book, you will be able to hit your buzzer and confidently answer "Who is Ed Stevens?" One year later, in 1948, Stevens became the Pirates' first baseman. He and Danny worked well together and became good friends:

> When Danny first came up he was an exceptional fielder, but his hitting was a little weak. As he went along, he changed his batting style – he choked up a bit – and he started to make good contact.
>
> I remember one of the few times that Danny ever got upset with me. I wasn't playing this particular ball game and Danny was playing second base. He had already had a couple hits and drove in a run or two. Around the eighth inning, Danny came up to bat again. I was sitting on the bench, and the manager [Billy Meyer] said, "Ed, I want you to hit for Danny." Well, Danny really got upset. Even I couldn't see why they were going to have me hit for him when he was having such a good day. But Danny got upset and threw the bat against the grandstand and sat down. As it happened, I hit a home run that put us ahead to win the ball game. After that Danny told everyone, "I'll never question Billy Meyer again for letting Ed hit for me when he can hit like that."
>
> Danny could hold his own, though, he didn't need help. He was an exceptional fielder and a good team man. He wasn't an outstanding star, but he was a consistent every-day player that could help a ball club. He kept the bench stirred up and encouraged everyone to keep going. He'd cheer us on with good baseball talk. All in all, he was just a good team man.

The 1948 season stands out for long-time Pirate fans because the team had performed so poorly in the previous years. The one bright spot for the Pirates during the 1946 and 1947 seasons was home run king Ralph Kiner. He was on the team for all of Danny's four years, and the two men were good friends:

*We had a good team in 1948 – the only good team the Pirates ever had when I was there. We had a chance to be in the pennant race until the last month, and then we ran into some problems. Danny was an outstanding fielder and a great guy to have on the team. He was a big part of that 1948 team. He was a big guy on the infield, and we had a good infield. One of the weak spots in 1947 was second base – we had all kinds of guys playing second base. Then in 1948 we got Danny from the Boston Braves, and at shortstop we got Stan Rojek from Brooklyn. Danny had a good year for us.*

*We all liked and admired Danny. He was a funny man, and we got a lot of fun out of the pranks that he pulled. Danny was always a trouble maker. He'd speak in this doubletalk [gibberish mixed with some real words] with the reporters and he'd throw in a player's name. Then the reporter would have to go find the player and ask him what was going on. You didn't know what he was saying with the doubletalk.*

*Danny always had something going on. He was a big tobacco chewer and he could spit tobacco juice better than anyone I've ever seen. He liked to spit it on your feet. You had to protect yourself when he was around. He was something else. He was very serious when he played baseball, though. It would be on the bench that he would institute [pranks] like that.*

*Danny was just part of a nice family community back then. He had a whistle that you could hear all over the ball park – he did it himself, it wasn't a tin whistle or anything like that.*

*It's so different today. The game has changed considerably. You don't really see things like that go on anymore. It's not part of the game. It's much more commercial – players just don't have the fun that we used to have. It's quite a bit different. Not that I'm complaining, but it's one of the changes we've had over the years in baseball.*

Former catcher Joe Garagiola played for the Cardinals during Danny's playing days with the Pirates. Garagiola had a brief career with Pittsburgh and later went on to be a popular baseball announcer and television host. Although they never played together, Garagiola has strong memories of Danny from playing against him:

*Danny was a scrapper. He came up in the Cardinal organization – I had heard about him when I was with the Cardinals. He made the most out of his baseball abilities, there's no question about that. But he also had a great sense of humor. If there was an All Humor team, he'd either be playing regularly or managing that team. He always had something funny to put a smile on your face. There was a lot of bench jockeying in those days. He and Walker Cooper got into it one day. Cooper said to him, "Why don't you shave your neck and walk backwards – you'd be better looking." You couldn't say that these days without getting into a fight. There was more good humor back then.*

*I remember one game when I was catching for the Cardinals and Danny was at bat. The umpire, Jocko [Conlan], called Danny out on a high pitch. Danny turned around and argued with Jocko, and Jocko threw him out of the game. Danny pointed around and said to Jocko, "Are you going to throw me out? Take a look at this infield. First base, Musial, he's*

*Polish. Second base is Schoendienst, a German. I don't know what Marion [the shortstop] is. On third you've got Kurowski, another Pole. On the mound you've got a Frenchman, Pollet. Behind the plate you've got a spaghetti-bender [that was me]. There are only two Irishmen on the field and you're going to throw half of us out?" Jocko started laughing and let Danny stay in the game. That doesn't sound too politically correct these days, but Danny was so good natured that no one took offense. He didn't mean any insult by it.*

It's probably no secret that sports figures – especially those who become popular sports announcers – embellish their stories a bit. Garagiola shared another story about Danny that he likes to tell at speaking engagements:

*One time we were in Pittsburgh and we had a beanball contest. Stan Rojek had been beaned in a game. The next night Rip Sewell was pitching, and he knocked me down. When he came up to hit, he and I had some words. Nothing happened then, but when I was up next he knocked me down again. When that used to happen, people always said to bunt the ball down the first base line and when the pitcher covers it you can collide with him and go at it. I bunted down the first base line. Rip Sewell started to first base, but he was a little smarter than I was and he threw a block into me. He practically knocked me into the Pirate dugout, which was on the first base side. I was laying there and all I could see were Pittsburgh uniforms. Murtaugh said to one of his teammates, "You grab the right leg and I'll grab the left, let's make a wish."*

In a profile in the *New York Times* on March 29, 1970, Danny shared some amusing stories from his many years in baseball. His "eyes were twinkling" as he recounted the Garagiola tale. According to Danny, he and Rojek decided to teach Garagiola a lesson when he got to second base: "When he slid in, I leaped 10 feet in the air and came down on him." Danny noted that Garagiola had "embroidered" the story with the "make a wish" line. (There was no mention as to whether Danny's claim of jumping 10 feet in the air was also an exaggeration.)

When standout Pirate pitcher Vernon Law first arrived in Pittsburgh, Murtaugh was second baseman. "We got to meet him early in life and had a good relationship with [Danny and Kate]. As a matter of fact, the way Danny got his job is the way a lot of athletes got to be known. Someone got sick and couldn't play. When Danny got his opportunity to play at second base he got a couple of hits the first time. That continued and then the original second basemen lost his job because Danny played well. That happens to a lot of athletes. When you get your chance you have to go for it."

Vernon's wife VaNita also has fond memories of Danny and Kate. "Kate and the kids didn't come to Pittsburgh until school was out. In Vernon's first year with the Pirates, we didn't know where to live. [The Pirates] put us in Ma Daniel's boarding house. Some of the players stayed there when the wives couldn't come. But she had the bedroom so if the wife came they could stay. They let us stay there until we could find a house. I remember Kate and Danny's kindness in trying to help us find a place to live. That was the start of our being close to them."

The two families would remain friends over the years and frequently got together for family meals. Law was nicknamed The Deacon because he was an elder in the Mormon Church, and Danny's daughter Kathy recalls her family having dinner at The Deacon's home one night. "When we had dinner at our house, if my dad called your name it was your turn to say Grace [the prayer before meals]. We sat down to dinner at the Law's, and there were rolls on the table. I reached out for a roll – I didn't know that was bad manners. My dad said, 'Kathy!' and I began our

Catholic Grace 'In the name of the Father and of the Son ...'" The Deacon still chuckles at that story.

As a player, Danny never again matched the success he had during the 1948 season. His daughter Kathy was born on February 22, 1949. However, she insists that she was not to blame for Danny's poor 1949 season. Danny's second son, Danny Jr., had reached the Terrible Twos that year. Danny Jr. didn't sleep much, so neither did his parents. This, according to family lore, was the cause of Danny's lackluster performance just one year after he was hailed a "National League sensation." In reality, it was injuries – including a broken ankle, a back injury, and arm trouble – that held Danny back in 1949.

Danny rebounded in 1950, posting a .294 batting average and 85 double plays. Tragically, on August 30, Danny was hit in the head by New York Giants pitcher Sal Maglie and suffered a linear fracture of his skull. Maglie was known as "Sal the Barber" because of his "close shaves" – his use of beanballs to brush back batters. He defended his pitching in later years, claiming he would not have succeeded as a pitcher without using the brushback. Recalling the incident with Danny, however, he said he nearly vomited when he went to the hospital after the game and learned that Danny had a cracked skull. Danny was in the hospital for ten days and was expected to be out for the rest of the season. The tough little Irishman surprised everyone by re-joining the team in late September and pinch hitting in a few games.

During this time Danny was also involved in a bit of a stage career, as it were. He would often perform at baseball writers' dinners using his doubletalk. One skit had Danny interviewing Manager Billy Meyer on the team's prospects. However, the skit didn't last long because Meyer was laughing too hard at Danny's sallies and couldn't keep it up. One night in 1950, Bob Hope had a show at the Syria Mosque, and he was joined by a quartet from the Pirates: Danny, Ralph Kiner, Wally Westlake, and Bill Werle. Danny had the entire place laughing, and some of his gags even managed to fool Bob Hope, who chimed right in with Danny once he caught on.

In April 1951, Danny's teammates elected him as their representative. But Opening Day found Danny sitting on the bench while Monty Basgall played second base. By the end of May, Danny had made an appearance in about half of the Pirates' games, and his hitting was a lackluster .220, although he was error-free in the field. His mediocre play didn't stop the fans in Milwaukee from giving him a rousing welcome when the Pirates played the Brewers in an exhibition game on May 24. Fans there still remembered the thrills Danny gave them when he helped lead the team to victory in the Minor League's Little World Series in 1947.

By June 5, there was talk of replacing Pirate manager Billy Meyer, and Danny was mentioned as a possible replacement. At that time, the Bucs were 16-27 and had won only two of their last 16 games. Meyer wasn't being blamed – many pitchers were having arm problems and they had two outfielders (Kiner and Westlake) playing the infield. But some expected new General Manager Branch Rickey to try to placate the frustrated fans by making a change at the helm.

In the end, Meyer kept his job for the entire season. But everyone could see that Rickey was grooming the "Whistling Irishman" for a future managerial position. Rickey had watched Danny come up through the Cardinals farm system – a system that Rickey started and which would later be copied by every major league team – and he liked what he saw in the plucky infielder. As for Danny, perhaps the only bright spot he had at the plate in 1951 was when he homered against "Sal the Barber" Maglie on June 1. His appearance in just 68 games and his anemic .199 batting average were enough to convince him his future in baseball was not on the playing field. Danny asked Rickey for a managerial position in the Pirate system. Rickey suggested a player-manager role in New Orleans, and Danny accepted the job.

After the season was over, the new manager went to Deland, FL to serve as an instructor with the Pirate Training School. Danny also found time that fall to join forces with Boston coach Jimmy Brown in choosing members of an All Ugly team for the National League. Since they named themselves to the team – Brown as manager, Danny as a coach – none of the members took too much offense. Joe Garagiola, then a new Pirate, was named catcher for the team. He called it a "pretty fair team," but claimed he wasn't on it until he threw off his hat while arguing with an umpire and Brown spotted him. Garagiola joked, "We're going to get a game with the American League All-Uglies, captained by Yogi Berra, of course. The proceeds from this game will pay for a plastic operation on the face of one player from each team."[2]

When he finally made it back home, Danny told the *Chester Times* he considered himself "darn lucky" to get a manager post that high (AA) in organized baseball. No doubt Danny's fan club in Chester considered New Orleans "darn lucky" to have him.

# eaRly managing Days

In January 1952, Danny headed south to attend a reception welcoming him as the New Orleans Pelicans' new manager. The Pelicans at the time were coming off a 14-year stretch in which the team had been skippered by twelve different managers. The team, which competed in the Southern Association, had not won a pennant since 1934, and the fans were clamoring for some success. Pirate GM Branch Rickey hoped that Danny would be a stabilizing influence for the club.

At a sports banquet near Chester before the season started, Danny was asked about his new team. There's only one position in the lineup that is set in stone, Danny told his questioner, "I'm playing second base." For Danny's family, one bright spot was that the Pelicans played all night games. That gave Kate and the kids more time to spend with Danny than if the games were in the middle of the day.

Danny's new post also enabled him to return a favor to an old friend. In March, the Pirates named Arky Kraft to their scouting staff on Danny's recommendation. Kraft was the Chester friend who helped Danny tally up his Victory Points and get out of Japan in time for the 1946 baseball season. Kraft's new job was to follow through on prospects that the home office named possible future big league players.

Danny arrived in New Orleans to high hopes. Writing in the *Times-Picayune*, Bill Keefe noted, "Danny Murtaugh, new Pelican manager, looks like the best player on the team to those who have watched the Pels go through a fine season of spring training. ... Murtaugh is the big cog in an infield that looks good. ... Murtaugh's pitching staff is nothing to brag about right now. The Pel manager is hoping for help from Pittsburgh, however – and not too late." Danny's pitching staff was one of the youngest and most inexperienced in the league.

Harry Martinez, sports editor of the *New Orleans States*, was also optimistic about the Pelicans chances under Danny:

> *Murtaugh has established himself as an outstanding player. He is tackling his first job as manager after 15 years of brilliant major and minor league playing. His first job in the majors was with the Phillies where he remained from 1941 until 1944 when he entered the service.*
>
> *When Danny got out of the service, he rejoined the Quakers in 1946, only to be sent to Rochester, where he hit .322. The Braves purchased him for 1947 but optioned him to Milwaukee. He helped spark the Brewers to the American Association championship and victory in the playoffs and Little World Series. For the year, he had the remarkable fielding average of .988, and at one stretch went through 42 consecutive games without an error. In addition, he hit .302 to insure himself of another chance in the major leagues.*
>
> *The Pirates obtained Murtaugh in a trade with the Braves*

*and in 1948, as a Buc, he led the National League second basemen in putouts, assists and double plays. He suffered a setback in 1950 when "beaned" by one of Sal Maglie's pitches. Last year, injuries kept him on the bench much of the time.*

*Bill Meyer, under whom Danny played at Pittsburgh, predicts he will have great success as a manager. Tackling a job in a double A league like the Southern with no managerial experience is a large order but Danny believes he is capable of meeting the challenge.*

The Pelicans opened the season on Saturday, April 12 with a 3-1 victory over Birmingham — in a game that was stopped five times for rain and then finally called at the end of the sixth inning. Danny introduced himself well to his new teammates and fans as he compiled four putouts, two assists, no errors, and a hit that drove in one run. Pitcher Norman Morton allowed Birmingham only one hit in the game. The next day, the teams split a double header, with the Pels winning the first game 6-5 and losing the second 5-1.

The *New Orleans Item's* sports editor Hap Glaudi encountered Danny in the team locker room after the April 13 double header. The Pelicans were 2-1 at this point, and Danny was mighty chipper, "How did you like us? Okay, eh?" While Glaudi was "smitten with Danny's play at second," he apologized to Danny and admitted he didn't think the players were experienced enough to compete in the Southern Association. However, Glaudi was impressed with the hustle and drive that Danny inspired in his players. One week later, as the Pelicans came off a 6-2 road trip, Glaudi's column implored, "If it's not asking too much, Danny, keep 'em flying!"

The *Times-Picayune's* Bill Keefe believed that Pirate GM Branch Rickey was undercutting Danny's efforts by refusing to send him enough good pitchers. "It looks as if another young manager is being pushed out on a plank, expected to make a good showing in a fast league with a pitching staff that other managers would not even try with." However, he, too, was impressed with the spirit of Danny's Pelicans:

> If there are any members of the 1952 Pelican team who like to take things easy and do their stuff along the lines of least resistance they're going to find themselves very unpopular not only with the fans but with their own teammates. With Danny Murtaugh as the sparkplug and with most of the other Pels anxious to emulate their well-liked little leader in fire, zip, and derring-do, no lazy man can fail to attract attention, and it will be the wrong kind of attention.

> Apparently there is no member of the team who doesn't want to play in high gear; they all dash out on the field as if eager to start fielding; and they dash in from the field as if champing on the bit to get to the bat.

> That's the kind of spirit fans like. It's the stuff that makes critical patrons skip over errors – even boners. True American sportsmanship excuses mistakes if the competitor makes those mistakes because he is trying very hard. ...

> Murtaugh has been instilling into his men the advantage of playing the game without cognizance of the stands. Any athlete is better off if he can forget the stands and perform just as if no one was watching him. ...

> It probably will be expecting too much of some of the 19- and 20-year-old Pelicans to make the grade in this league. ... But they're trying, and trying hard.

Joe L. Brown was the New Orleans General Manager at this time. The son of a popular comedian, Joe E. Brown, Joe L. got his start in baseball with the Lubbock Hubbers in 1939, then a Chicago farm team. Like Danny, Joe L. was a World War II veteran, having spent 3½ years in the Air Force. The two men met when Danny came to New Orleans, and they would remain close friends and baseball associates for the rest of Danny's life.

Brown came to New Orleans in 1951, so he knew well what Danny was up against with the team he inherited. Thus, Brown was thrilled with the success the team was having in the early days of the season. He admitted to the *New Orleans States'* sportswriter Harry Martinez that he was having a hard time keeping his feet on the ground. "Nobody knew just how Danny Murtaugh would fit into the managerial job, but he really has a way of getting the confidence of young ball players and, by setting an example of all-out effort and by smoothing over the mistakes and settling the kids down, he's doing a perfect job. I surely hope the boys can come home on top."

New Orleans fans were thrilled to see their team holding the top spot after so many years. One headline pointed out that the standings were "Not a Typographical Error" lest fans were worried that the Pelicans were listed first because it had been printed upside down by mistake. Boasting a record of 9-5, the team returned home to a warm welcome after their first road trip of the year.

Lacking depth in the pitching staff, Danny's Pelicans were unable to maintain their first place position for long. However, Danny's keen management of his young talent kept the team near the top of the heap. Danny looked forward to May 15, when Branch Rickey would be trimming players from the Pittsburgh roster. On an earlier visit to New Orleans, Rickey told Murtaugh and Brown that the Pelicans would be getting some pitching help when he made the Pirate cuts.

The Pelicans were able to remain competitive despite the lack of pitching because of strength in other areas. Danny's outfield, including Paul Smith, Frank Thomas, and Stan Wentzel, was considered one of the best in the league defensively. Frank Thomas, Dale Long, Stan Wentzel, and Felipe Montemayor were all hitting well as the season began.

Danny himself was considered the team's best infielder, despite the fact that he was playing with an injured leg. On Opening Day, Danny tore a muscle in his right thigh, and he aggravated it in a game against Little Rock a few days later. The team doctor told Danny that rest was the only way to heal his injury, but when Jim Rice, his backup at second, sustained a rib injury, Danny was forced back into the lineup. Sports editor Martinez put Danny's dilemma to words:

> It makes a big difference when Murtaugh is playing. He keeps the club together and is more helpful to the young pitchers. Besides, he gives the Pels that strength down the middle, which is so essential. Danny is a slick double-play maker and a most formidable clutch hitter. He has been nursing a bad Charley horse. Otherwise he would be playing every night.
>
> For a player who had never managed a ball club before, Murtaugh has shown more poise than most managers the Pelicans have had in recent years. He has had the team up in the fight from the start – even in first place once – and has done a good job juggling his pitchers to get the best out of them.

When x-rays revealed the extent of Jim Rice's injury, it became apparent that Danny's rest would not come soon. According to the *New Orleans States* on April 29, "Manager Murtaugh, whose thigh strain badly needs rest and repair, is going to have to carry on at second. X-rays reveal Jim Rice broke a rib when hit by a thrown ball in Sunday's Mobile game. Danny still looked plenty spry in starting a zippy double play that got [pitcher Lenny] Yochim out of a jam in the seventh."

Despite "a knot on his right thigh the size of a fist," Danny continued to play and manage well. Shortstop Gair Allie credited Danny with improving his batting, "He showed me how to meet the ball instead of trying to knock the hell out of it. And you know what, it works." As the *New Orleans Item* recounted, Danny finished out April by "playing a sparkling game at second and whopping home three runs ... on a bum leg, too."

While Danny was able to play on a regular basis, the Pelicans were the best team in their league. Despite a warning from the doctor that he'd have problems for life if he didn't rest his injury, Danny wrapped his leg tightly and kept on playing until he could hardly walk at all. The doctor was right, though, and Danny's leg sometimes gave out under him in later years. His niece Betsy recalls a memorable moment:

> When we were little we always got milk, eggs, and juice delivered to the house. The milk and juice came in glass bottles. The milk man would make Christmas Eve deliveries for some of his favorite customers. One year, the milk man brought over a big crate full of milk, eggs, and juice to last through the holidays. Uncle Danny saw him unloading the crate from his truck and said, 'Here, let me carry that for you.' On the way up the front steps, Uncle Danny's leg gave out and he dropped the crate – breaking the glass bottles and the eggs. The milk man said, 'Heck, I could've done better than that.'

Though Danny played through his pain in the spring of 1952, Joe Brown knew he needed a break for his leg to heal. He arranged for shortstop Johnny O'Neil to be transferred from the Pirates' Hollywood team to New Orleans to relieve Danny at second. Brown told the *Times-Picayune* that O'Neil was an experienced player who led the Pacific Coast League in fielding the previous year. He predicted O'Neil would be a steadying influence on the infield in the same manner that Danny was.

Brown also expressed his pride in the Pelicans' play to date [May 6] and said he was more than pleased with the way Danny had been handling the team. He pledged to keep the wires hot trying to round up players so the grass would not grow under the Pelicans.

Meanwhile, the local sports pages continued to praise the "spunky" manager. Phil Johnson's column, "Phil the Pel Sez," suggested a "Medal for Murtaugh" in recognition of his gutsy play while injured. *New Orleans States'* Martinez took note of Danny's role in the Pelicans' early season successes:

> *Danny Murtaugh, in his first year as manager, has shown rare ability handling a staff of young Pelican pitchers. In spite of four straight losses – two to Atlanta and two to Birmingham – Danny called on "rookie" Clarence Lafayette Richardson last night to end the Pels' losing streak in Birmingham, and he performed like a veteran. He stayed in there the full nine innings and gave the Birds a 5-3 victory. This gave the Pels undisputed possession of second place as Memphis beat Chattanooga, 3-1. ...*

> *Taking the attitude that you can't tell what the young pitchers can do until you give them a chance, Murtaugh gave Richardson a tough assignment last night. He held the Barons to eight hits in their home park. Incidentally, he became the eighth member of the Pel staff to win at least one game. ...*

> *The Pel manager hasn't four top pitchers to work as starters. He's still experimenting and it's paying dividends.*

Even without Danny in the field, the Pelicans stayed in the thick of things all season. Danny discussed the end of the season with *Chester Times* Sports Editor Bob Finucane, "What a race. It was so close that if we had won our last game and the teams ahead of us had lost we'd have finished second. We lost and they won. As a matter of fact, all we had to do to clinch a playoff berth was win one of our last four. So what happens? We lose all four."[1] The Pelicans ended up in fifth place.

The season over, Danny and his family happily headed home to Chester. With nearly 15 years of professional baseball under his belt, Danny was by now a fixture on the local banquet scene. He was often joined by his good friend Mickey Vernon, who was still pounding out hits for the Washington Senators. The pair was well fed that winter as they made their way from banquet to testimonial to luncheon. Frequently Danny was the speaker at an event honoring Little Leaguers. At one such affair, Danny emphasized to the boys that the professional teams give the kids every chance in the world to prove themselves:

> *Take the Pittsburgh organization, for instance. Every so often Pittsburgh will call in all its farm managers for a meeting – all 12 or 13 of them. They all sit down in front of a huge chart on which are the names of every ball player in the Pirate system. Then they go down the list – starting with the roster of the parent club.*
>
> *Switches are suggested. One player will be pushed back from Double A ball to a Class B league. Another player will be moved up. And when they get to the lowest league in the chain, someone may be released. But if 12 of the 13 managers say they don't think a certain boy can make the grade, the boy isn't dropped. He's kept.*
>
> *As long as even one manager thinks the boy has what it takes – even though he's been slow to show it – that boy won't be cut.[2]*

Baseball managers, on the other hand, were frequently let go. Danny himself was the thirteenth New Orleans manager in 15 years. In 1952, his mentor Billy Myers was fired from the Pirates, who had once again finished in last place. Because of the impressive job he did in New Orleans – taking a club that finished in last place in 1951 and keeping them in contention for the whole 1952 season – Danny was mentioned by sportswriters as a potential replacement. However, since he had only one year of minor league managing experience, Branch Rickey decided it was not Danny's time.

When Danny arrived back in New Orleans in 1953, he saw a doctor about some soreness in his left leg. The doctor told Danny that he had several small broken bones in his leg and he'd have trouble if he played. Danny made brief appearances in just three games as a pinch hitter.

Danny gained a lot of managerial experience that year, and the Pelicans had a brief span of time where it looked like they might compete for a playoff spot. But the team couldn't keep pace and again finished in fifth place. Danny and his family headed home not knowing what the future would bring.

After the 1953 season, Danny was called upon to do some coaching closer to home. There was a new team added to the local Suburban Major Basketball Association: the Chester Buffs. Danny was recruited to coach the team when he could fit it into his banquet speaking schedule, which was still heavy.

Danny's wife Kate also recruited Danny that offseason, for a very different job … painting their house. Danny joked with local sportswriter Matt Zibitka that it was hard to get any painting done with all the well wishers who kept calling and stopping by – although he clearly loved the interruptions. On December 3, Danny learned that he had been retained by New Orleans for the 1954 season. That news, coupled with the start of the Christmas season, was enough to make the entire clan happy indeed.

Tragedy disrupted their joy on Friday, December 18, 1953. Danny's brother-in-law, Air Force Capt. Bennie Dale Wilson, died in an airplane crash in Utah, where he was stationed. Danny wanted to fly out immediately to bring his sister, Peggy, and her young children home. Back then, of course, 24-hour ATMs were non-existent and banks weren't open on weekends. Danny didn't have enough money on hand to buy a plane ticket.

Fortunately, his cousin Madge and her husband Art had been saving money at home to buy their son a bike for Christmas. They insisted he take the money, and he got on a flight that very night. Madge remembers this time vividly, "Danny was always helping everyone else – he wasn't used to receiving help. As soon as he was back home and the banks were open, Danny got out the money to pay us back. But he never forgot that – even years later he would say how much he appreciated our help."

To Peggy and Dale's children, Uncle Danny nearly walked on water. Daughter Betsy was seven years old when her father died:

> When my dad died, Uncle Danny flew out to Utah and picked us up. My first memory of him was when I came down the stairs the next morning and he was sitting in the rocking chair. Then he cleaned everything up and took us back to live with him. We lived with them for quite a few years. Uncle Danny was always such a big part of my life after my dad died. He was the most generous person, but he always did things quietly.

The expanded family made it through Christmas together. Soon it was baseball season again, and Danny, Kate, and the kids headed back down to New Orleans. The Pelicans were in the race from day one – always at or near the top of the heap. Danny spent the season coaching third base – his playing days were done. The Pelicans finished in second place that season with a 92-62 record. The fans, however, were not satisfied with second place. Danny – and his family – endured a lot of harassment.

Danny and Kate decided they'd had enough, and Danny retired from managing New Orleans at the end of the 1954 season. During his three seasons with the Pelicans, Danny led the team to 248 wins and 215 losses – a very respectable .535 winning percentage. The second place finish in 1954 marked the Pelicans last good season. In 1960, the franchise was sold to Little Rock, and New Orleans was left with no baseball team.

The primary factors underlying Danny's decision to retire from the Pelicans were his children's ages and the long distance from home. The school calendar dictated Kate's schedule, forcing her to wait for summer vacation to head south. With Danny already ensconced in New Orleans, Kate was on her own for the trip. Traveling to New Orleans for the summer with three young children – and no highways – was very difficult. According to Mapquest, the trip from Philadelphia to New Orleans on the highway system of 2009 would take almost 20 hours. On the roads of the 1950s, the trip would have been even longer (not to mention the lack of air conditioning in the car). For Danny's first season with the Pelicans, his mother traveled with Kate and the children to "help" them. Truth to be told, though, it was like having a fourth child in the car. Kate would later joke about sneaking out in the middle of the night in order to make the trip with just Timmy, Danny, Kathy, and herself.

While the New Orleans position wasn't ideal, Danny wasn't ready to be done with baseball altogether. After talking it over with Kate, he applied for a job managing the Charleston Senators, an American Association team in West Virginia. The Senators were thrilled to have a manager of Danny's caliber and experience, and Danny was thrilled to stay in baseball. Talking to the *Charleston Daily Mail* Sports Editor Dick Hudson, Danny noted that the club president Danny Menendez was sincere in wanting to give the fans a "real good team." Danny pledged "I'll give the job everything I've got in an effort to please the fans." For his part, Menendez had much praise for his new skipper:

> I consider Murtaugh the best man available for the job. Throughout his baseball career, which spans 17 years, he has established himself as a pepper-pot with a lot of spirit and hustle. I believe the Senators fans will like this colorful type of aggressive leadership. He has a winning record as a manager and he worked for Branch Rickey three years, which is a good recommendation in itself. Baseball men will tell you that Danny Murtaugh always has been a hard worker along with his colorful play on the infield. I'm sure we have landed a good man.

The hiring of Danny as manager of the Senators was met with approval by the fans. The Senators Stalwarts and Auxiliary, a group of Charleston baseball promoters, met shortly after the announcement. They voiced approval of Danny's "pepper-pot aggressive reputation." Group member Dick Frampton was designated to wire a welcome greeting — signed by all 40 of the members present at the meeting — to Danny at home in Chester:[3]

> Dear Danny:
>
> The Charleston Senators baseball boosters club is more than pleased in Danny Menendez's selection of you as manager. We want to welcome you to the biggest little baseball town in the United States. With a first division club, we will be selling standing room in advance.
>
> Wishing you the best of luck,
>
> – C.R. Frampton

In early March, Danny and Kate went to Charleston for a "Meet the

Manager" party in his honor. The affair was sponsored by the Stalwarts and was attended by 200 fans anxious for a chance to chat with the new skipper. Danny spent a good bit of time taping radio broadcasts and answering questions for the local sportswriters. After spending the weekend in Charleston, Danny and Kate returned to Chester so the new manager could arrive at spring training in Fort Pierce, FL on March 13.

The Senators and their fans weren't the only ones who looked forward to the Murtaughs' move to Charleston. Young Timmy had acquired a reputation as an excellent Little League baseball player, skilled at catching, pitching, and hitting. One local paper noted that the family had yet to find a house for the summer and suggested that Timmy might want to play for the person who offered them the best proposition on a home.

Danny and the rest of his team had high hopes for the 1955 season. When asked by the *Daily Mail's* Dick Hudson how good the Senators themselves thought they were, Danny replied, "By golly, they think they're pretty darn good." Unlike his crew in New Orleans, Danny's team this time had plenty of experience and many had played on good clubs in the past.

From the outset, the Senators had good spirit and camaraderie as a team. In the *Charleston Daily Mail,* Dick Hudson's Warming Up column highlighted this aspect of the team after their last pre-season practice. Luke Easter, the team's first baseman, was in the sausage business in Cleveland and had prepared sausage sandwiches for the team. A local judge, who was scheduled to swing at the mayor's first official pitch on opening day, was there for the celebration. The judge admitted that he hadn't swung a bat in 55 years. Danny, always the jokester, facetiously asked, "Say, Judge, didn't you used to play with Ron Northey?" (Northey, Danny's old buddy from the Phillies, was a Senators outfielder with several major league seasons under his belt.) Northey laughed and shouted, "Hi, Judge, how've ya been?" One of the pitchers chimed in, "Wasn't Murtaugh on that same team?" To which a fellow pitcher replied, "Naw, he was in the Little League then."

Danny took the club's cohesiveness as a good sign and began the season optimistically. He repeatedly stated that the team would not finish last, which was a logical goal considering the Senators had been dead last each year since moving to Charleston in 1952. In New Orleans, Danny had taken the Pelicans from last place to fifth place in one season and on to second place two years later. First baseman Luke Easter – the sausage guy – typified the team's response to the new manager, "Danny's doing a good job of keeping us together."

After his team won their season opener, Danny reminded sportswriters, "Like I've said before, this club may raise some hell before the season's over." While the contest was tight, Danny found much to be happy about in the 1-0 win against Omaha. His team had gotten out of three tight spots with well-timed double plays. Danny was also happy that nearly 5,000 fans turned out for the game despite wet weather. The next two games in the series were quite different, with Omaha beating Charleston 10-6 and 8-0.

Next up on the Senators' schedule were the Denver Bears. After losing the first game 8-0 – two 8-0 games in a row! – the Senators came back 6-4, 5-2, and 17-7. In the third game of the series, outfielder Bill Antonello went down, saying he was hit by a pitch. The umpire ruled it a foul tip and said the ball hit the bat and then hit the batter. Antonello argued the call and was removed from the game. Danny came out to take up Antonello's case, and the game was delayed for a bit while Danny and the umpire "discussed" the matter. The extended debate was to no avail, as the ump's ruling stood, but it made good fodder for local sportswriter Don McClure:

(SCENE: Two American Association umpires are seated in

*the waiting room of Dr. Horace P. Skutnick, noted psychiatrist and tracer of lost nerves):*

*1st umpire: (Unable to pull his eyes away from 2nd Ump, who is gulping aspirin tablets between furious drags at a king-size cigarette) — Just worked the Charleston series, eh?*

*2nd Ump: (mutters incoherently, with the words "Murtaugh" and "Charleston" vaguely discernible).*

*1st Ump: Do they still open the games by playing "Three Blind Mice" instead of the national anthem?*

*2nd Ump: (chain-lighting another cigarette) No. They decided that was unpatriotic.*

*1st Ump: (hesitantly) Uh – have any trouble with Murtaugh?*

*2nd Ump: (turns pale, shudders) I thought Guadalcanal was bad. That Irishman goes after umpires like McCarthy after General Zwicker.*

*1st Ump: What about the fans?*

*2nd Ump: (pulling his tie loose) They're with Danny. Between games of a doubleheader I heard a mother tell her three-year-old kid that if he didn't behave, he'd grow up to be an umpire. You shoulda heard the brat scream!*

*1st Ump: (lighting up a king-size) Well, the players …*

*2nd Ump: Listen. You talk about the Yankee uniform doing things … why, the Senators have players who haven't opened their yaps at an umpire in years. Soon as they pull on that Charleston uniform they want to steal his whisk broom.*

*1st Ump: (wiping brow) Maybe we should see Doherty about hazard pay.*

*(The door to Dr. Skutnick's inner office opens and the doctor walks out, leading a pale, gaunt figure wearing a dark blue uniform and cap.)*

*Dr.: You'll be alright. Just lie in a hammock and sip prune juice – and don't listen to any baseball games.*

*(Blue-clad figure stoops, brushes imaginary broom over imaginary plate, and departs.)*

*Dr.: (shaking his head) Strangest case I ever saw. Umpired in the Southern Association all last year. Keeps muttering something about New Orleans ... and a guy named Murtaugh. Piteous case ... Now, what can I do for you gentleman?*

Danny was once again very popular with the fans ... and not just for his baseball abilities (or for arguing with the umps). A local attorney sent one of the newspapers a note expressing appreciation for first aid rendered to his nine-year-old granddaughter by "Dr. Danny Murtaugh." His granddaughter, Anne, and her mom were in a car accident that left Anne with a big knot on her head and an injured right shoulder and arm:

*Two little boys standing nearby rushed up and said we have a real good doctor here at the ball park, Dr. Danny Murtaugh. So Anne was rushed over to the office of Charleston Senator's Manager Danny Murtaugh who very kindly made a first aid examination and found that there were no bones broken. He put an ice pack on her head, which by this time had a knot as large as a hen egg. Anne thought it quite a thrill to have the manager of the Charleston Senators give her this much attention, and asked me to bring her up and see some of the games which I promised to do.*

The Senators left for St. Paul on their first road trip of the season sporting a 4-3 record. The team had a rough time on the road, including losing all four games in the series against Minneapolis. Their 1-7 record on the trip left them at 5-10 on the season. But the season was still young, and Danny continued to insist the team could finish in the first division.

The first home game after the dismal road trip was against St. Paul. The Saints were managed by Max Macon, a familiar face to Danny from their days playing against each other in the big leagues. A local paper relayed that Danny and Macon had traded friendly jabs in spring training. "If all the pitchers in the big leagues were like you were, I'd still be playing up there," Murtaugh ribbed. "Yeh, and if all the hitters up there were like you were, I'd still be pitching," Macon responded. The Senators came out of this series on top, putting the teams at 3-3 against each other for the season so far.

Unfortunately, as the season went on, the Senators proceeded to lose more often than win. In several of those defeats, the Senators took an early lead only to lose it in the late innings. In one series in Louisville, Charleston lost all four games in the last inning. By mid-May the Senators were in seventh place out of eight teams. In late June the team was once again in the cellar. Sports Editor A. L. Hardman, of the *Charleston Gazette*, said Danny had been a "real soldier during [the team's] collapse":

> *As the Charleston Senators ventured into the West yesterday with nothing but sad memories haunting them after their most disastrous home stand since they joined the American Association three years ago … the guy who probably felt like getting a fitting for a strait jacket was Skipper Danny Murtaugh.*
>
> *The fiery little Irishman, who never knew the word quit, has been hurt more than anyone knows over the poor showing of his club. But he hasn't complained and he hasn't tried to alibi. He has expressed disappointment, yes, but never in a bitter manner.*

*"I just can't understand why we don't get some hits," he has said over and over again as his team went down in defeat. "Our pitching has been real good at times but we simply couldn't get enough runs to win."*

*Not once has Murtaugh singled out any one for criticism. Instead he has tried to pick the few bright spots, such as Forest Smith's fine play at third base, the steady improvement of Catcher Earl Battey, the sure-handed fielding of Joe Torpey, etc.*

*Yet we know the little fellow's ulcers jump all over the place when someone fails to come through in the clutch. The Senators have left a lot of runners on the sacks.*

*Then there isn't much anyone can do about the team's lack of speed. But it has hurt the club tremendously. And, oh, that awful handicap of not having a relief hurler of some stature.*

*There's many a thing which hasn't jelled as expected. But the thing we want to point out is that Murtaugh has shown plenty of intestinal fortitude during these trying days. And our fans are proud of him.*[4]

The club was also in a financial bind and operating with a significant deficit. Team president Danny Menendez attempted to sell the team in June, but he received no offers. He then launched a $25,000 ticket campaign, but it only realized $5,000. In desperation, Menendez sold or traded several of his best players, including outfielders Clyde Vollmer and Ron Northey, infielder Chico Ibanez, and pitcher Floyd Melliere.

Despite these moves the team continued to lose money. Finally, Menendez felt he had no choice but to release Danny. The players, fans, and sportswriters were shocked by the announcement. The Senators' 27-

year-old catcher Vernon Rapp, who managed a bit in the Army, was named the new manager. Menendez called the decision "one of the hardest moves I ever had to make." He emphasized repeatedly that it was strictly a financial decision and praised Danny's managerial abilities.

Danny realized the Senators' financial plight and said he understood Menendez' decision. "It's a necessity of baseball. If releasing me from the job will help, I've got to be for it 100 percent. My association with Danny [Menendez] has been the best and I leave here as a good friend of his." Danny also thanked the people of Charleston for being so nice to him and his family. On the bright side, Danny noted, "my family and I can take our first summer vacation since 1937." Danny stressed that he would be rooting for Menendez, Rapp, and the Senators while he and his family were relaxing at the sea shore.

After leaving Charleston, the family headed to Wildwood, NJ, for two weeks of fun and sun. They stayed at a family friend's place. Danny's kids were thrilled to finally take a family vacation. Kathy, who was seven at the time, remembers thinking that getting fired was the best thing that could happen to a person. Tim's memories are a little more troublesome – that vacation marked his first bad sunburn and his first experience with sand-filled swimming trunks. To this day, Tim is not too fond of the beach.

With the Charleston experience fresh in his mind, Danny resigned himself to life outside of baseball. In August the Chester Recreation Department hired Danny to teach baseball fundamentals to Chester youth. Danny loved the job and was always amazed at how well the kids picked up the tricks he taught them. However, he needed something more substantial to take care of his family. Since Danny had worked in the sporting goods department at Sears for several off seasons, a friend proposed that he and Danny open up a sporting goods store in Chester.

Danny still felt the pull of baseball, though, so he was relieved when Joe Brown – now General Manager for the Pirates – called and offered him the managerial post with Williamsport, PA in the Eastern League. Williamsport was a Class A team that had a working relationship with the Pirates. While it was a step down from New Orleans, Danny was happy to be able to stay in baseball, and the close proximity to home would be easier on his family. After talking it over with Kate, Danny happily accepted the job.

He never made it to Williamsport, though. In February 1956, as Danny prepared for Spring Training, he received another call from Joe Brown. One of the Pirate coaches had left the team, and Brown needed to find a replacement. Was Danny interested in the position? He jumped at the chance.

# Back to Pittsburgh

W hen Danny arrived in Pittsburgh in 1956, there were several familiar faces there to greet him, including: Manager Bobby Bragan, who played for the Phillies with Danny in 1941 and 1942; pitcher Vern Law, who had joined the Pirates when Danny was a second baseman; and infielder Frank Thomas, who played for Danny in New Orleans. The Pirates of 1956 were longtime basement dwellers – consistently finishing seventh or eighth out of eight teams in the National League. The team had only finished at or above .500 once since 1946 — in Danny's stellar 1948 season the Pirates were 83-71 and wound up in fourth place. They were not so fortunate in 1956; their 66-88 record landed them in seventh place once again.

The 1957 season did not look much better. After the first two weeks of the season, the Pirates never rose above seventh place. Joe Brown recalls, "The talent that we had was not very good, and the ones who were good were inexperienced." The fiery Bobby Bragan knew baseball and was a good field manager. However, he wasn't able to build up the confidence of the young players enough for them to succeed. In August Joe Brown decided he had no choice but to fire Bragan. The team was in Chicago at the end of a four city road trip. Before Brown could get there, Bragan had a highly publicized skirmish with the umpires on August 2. Nearly 50 years later, Bragan vividly remembers the incident:

> I had an argument with the umpire, and he ejected me from the game. I went back out on the field with a soft drink and was talking to the umpires on the mound. I told them I'd only been ejected four times and that it was this crew each time. I asked if they wanted a sip of my cold drink while we talk it over. There was a picture taken of it and it was all over the papers.

Most people assumed that the soft drink episode was what led to Bragan's firing, but Joe Brown maintained that the decision had been made before the incident. Brown first approached the Pirates' more senior coach, Clyde Sukeforth, to discuss the managing job. Sukeforth wasn't interested, but he thought Danny would be a great choice. Brown agreed, although he stressed to Danny that it was only an interim position. After accepting the managerial post — with its temporary status — Danny remarked, "Joe, I'm a much better manager than you think."

Danny was named manager on Saturday, August 3, which was an off day. It was trial by fire for Danny the next day: he had to deal with a double header in Chicago his first outing as manager. The day seemingly got off to a good start. As he did every Sunday, Danny headed first to Mass. On this day the priest happened to be named Father Murtaugh. Danny took that to be a good omen … until the team lost both games of the double header. However, Danny didn't lose his confidence. *Pittsburgh Post Gazette* Sports Editor Al Abrams had a chance to interview Danny for an August 7 column:

*"You know something," Danny Murtaugh said, "I got fired in mid-season when I was managing Charleston a couple of years ago, but I consider that the greatest experience I ever had up to that point."*

*"You mean getting fired was your greatest experience?" [Abrams] asked, shifting tongue from cheek to cheek.*

*"Naw," Danny laughed. "I mean managing Charleston. I learned the hard way what it is to be a manager that year. You gotta bear down and manage hard with a last place club. You get smarter that way."*

*The grinning Irishman left himself wide open here. [Abrams] couldn't resist the impulse to crack: "Well, boy, you're going to be a lot smarter that you ever were handling the likes of the Pirates."*

*This brought another laugh. "Oh, I don't know," Danny said. "This Pittsburgh club isn't as bad as you and the others think it is. We'll get straightened out. We may even play .500 ball the rest of the season. This club is capable of it."*

*[Abrams] was ready to say, "Wanna bet?" when [he] decided to go easy on the newly-appointed Buc pilot. Let him dream, peacefully.*

Despite his optimism, Danny did hedge his bets a little. In the same interview, Abrams asked if Danny planned any personnel changes, particularly in the coaching ranks where he left a vacancy. Danny paused before answering, "No, I'm not planning any changes. I'm not going to add another coach to the staff." Then, with a big grin he added, "I'm going to leave that position open. You know, I might need that job back next year."

Pirate Coach Clyde Sukeforth did not expect Danny to need his coaching job back in 1958. In the August 15 issue of the *Chester Times*,

Sukeforth predicted that Danny would remain the Pirate manager for a "long, long time." Sukeforth also denied that the position had been offered to him, "Brown called me on the phone after he fired Bobby Bragan and said he wanted to talk about the club," Sukeforth said. "The job never was offered to me and, while talking, I told Brown he wouldn't find a better manager than Murtaugh."

As Sukeforth saw it, Danny was good for the players' morale because he didn't lash out when they lost and he was quick to pat them on the back when deserved. Sukeforth also pointed out that Danny previously managed many of the players in New Orleans and knew them well. Sukeforth finished, "This business of playing the infield back – or pulling it in – almost every manager employs the same tactics on the field. The difference between managers is their ability to handle men."

Danny's family was very happy for him. Talking with the Women's Editor in the August 4 *Pittsburgh Sun Telegraph*, Kate'e eyes "sparkled" as she discussed how she felt about Danny being appointed manager. "The decision is his. Whatever he does is okay with me," she said, as she noted that being a manager was Danny's dream. "He'll have more worries now," she noted. "But I don't think he'll spend much more time with the club than he always has. I think – in fact, I'll vouch for it – that he always was the first man in the ball park every day."

Kate actually found out about Danny's promotion from a Chester sports editor. In the same *Sun Telegraph* article Kate said that Danny called her later in the day: "He just sort of laughed and asked me what I thought about it and how the kids felt. As for the kids – Timmy and Danny [Jr.] think 'It's okay.' Kathy is worried because she explained 'We can't go to Kennywood anymore.'" [For the record, as Kathy's daughter I was amused – but not surprised – to hear her reaction. My whole life I heard my mom say that she couldn't go to Kennywood once her dad became manager because so many people would stop him for autographs. Even today, when people ask her what it was like to have a famous manager for a dad, she usually mentions not going to Kennywood.]

One sports reporter asked Kate if Danny got a raise along with his promotion. Kate was unusually forthcoming in her reply, "I can't say we've ever really been in the clear. Danny never was a big money player. We always felt the years Danny spent in the Army would have been his best playing years. He never did get into the big money. I don't even know whether he got a raise now from the Pirates. We talked on the phone, but there were so many people here I didn't get a chance to ask him."[1]

When asked about the challenges of being married to a professional baseball player, Kate acknowledged some drawbacks – such as having a husband and father who is away much of the year and moving the entire household for the summer. However, she said the advantage of having him do something he loved was worth it because it made the rest of life happier.

Fortunately for Danny, his whole family also loved the game of baseball. It would have tough otherwise, because their lives revolved around it. Both Timmy and Danny Jr. played backyard baseball and in various youth leagues. Timmy, 14, was the catcher in the Munhall Pony League when Danny was named manager. Danny Jr. liked to play second base – his dad's position in his playing days. Kathy played shortstop "when the boys let her."

Pat Friend, wife of Pirate hurler Bob Friend, first met Danny and Kate in 1950 when her husband joined the Pirates. Pat believes she knows at least one secret to Danny's success. "Kate was so supportive of Danny and I think that was key to a lot of his success. There was great love in the Murtaugh family. Danny and Kate were fantastic people. Kate was so supportive of the wives, too – she knew what the life was like. She was always there for us."

The popular former second baseman was well received as the new manager. However, reaction to the whole situation was strongly mixed among Pirate fans. *Pittsburgh Sun Telegraph* sportswriter George Kiseda was very blunt two days after Bragan was fired, "It is my opinion that Joe L. Brown fired the wrong man. He should have fired Joe L. Brown." Kiseda figured that the Pirates' losing record had more to do with the quality of the team assembled by Brown than with Bragan's managerial style.[2] According to Kiseda fan reaction was 10-1 for Bragan and against Brown in response to his column.[3]

Danny wasn't bothered by Kiseda's low expectations. In fact, as he had with the *Post Gazette's* Abrams, Danny once again predicted that the team would play .500 ball for the remainder of the season. Only this time, Danny backed up his prediction by betting Kiseda a steak dinner.

On August 13 the Pirates made their first road trip to Philadelphia with Danny as manager. His hometown crowd made big plans for the event. The Franklin Fire Co., where Danny spent so many hours as a volunteer fireman, sponsored three buses for fans to take to the game. The Chester police color guard, the Chester Elks band, and the acting Mayor were also there to honor the hometown hero. The acting mayor issued a proclamation marking the occasion, which ended on an eerily prophetic note:[4]

> PROCLAMATION: *Two hundred and seventy-five years ago, William Penn first set foot upon the soil of Pennsylvania, and at the place where first he trod the City of Chester came into being.*
>
> *In all the years since that historic date, Chester has contributed greatly to the welfare of this Commonwealth and the glory of this nation, but never until the present time has it produced a manager of a major league team in the great American sport of baseball.*

*Danny Murtaugh has brought great honor to our community, not only by becoming manager of the Pittsburgh Pirates, but also by exhibiting, for many years, the qualities of character which make men truly great.*

*He has displayed great courage and true integrity. He has been loyal to his friends and humble before his God. He has lived cleanly, played the game cleanly, and has been a real gentleman all his life.*

*On behalf of the people of the City of Chester, I do proclaim the great admiration and respect which we, his friends and neighbors, feel towards Danny Murtaugh and declare that we are truly proud of his achievement. I express our fervent wish that someday he shall guide the baseball champions of the world.*

*Clarence G. Smedley, Acting Mayor, City of Chester*

When Danny took over for the Pirates, the team's record was 36-67. After the unfortunate doubleheader that served as Danny's welcome to major league managing, they fell to 36-69. He had better luck in his first game in Pittsburgh, beating the Philadelphia Phillies 5-3. Danny managed to steady the team. In a September 24 article in the *Pittsburgh Sun Telegraph*, Joe Brown discussed the Pirates' "Hope for the Future":

*Murtaugh has rebuilt individual and team confidence in the Bucs. In order to become a champion in any sport, it is necessary for the player to have confidence – to believe in himself and his team – and this is particularly true in baseball, which is both a team and an individual sport. Sometimes young players without experience gain their initial confidence from an outside source, and under the wise handling of Murtaugh, the youthful Pirates have developed confidence in their ability and assurance in their future.*

Under Danny's leadership the Pirates were 26-25 – proving Danny was right when he predicted the team would play .500 ball the rest of the season. Sportswriter George Kiseda tried to buy the new manager a steak dinner to make good on their bet, but Danny refused. Prankster that he was, Danny preferred having something to hold over Kiseda's head.

As the 1957 season drew to a close, Joe Brown put to rest Danny's concern that he "might need that [coaching] job back next year." Brown admits to being as surprised as anyone that Danny ended up being the man for the job:

> *I knew Danny had a good baseball mind as soon as he started to manage [in New Orleans]. But to start with he didn't have as much success as his abilities because he was too mindful of the effect on the players if he took a pitcher out of a game or didn't play a player. He knew everyone wanted to play, so he hurt for the guys who were sitting on the bench. After 1954 he went to Charleston, WV, to manage. His team didn't have much talent, so he learned that in order to have a chance to win you have to play the best players available. You can't worry so much about their feelings. In order for the team to be successful you have to put the players in a position where they can be successful.*
>
> *When I asked Danny to be manager after I fired Bobby Bragan, I knew his abilities. But I didn't know his experience had changed his approach. He took over a team that was playing well below .500 (36-67) and he managed a game over .500 (26-25) for the rest of the season. He was originally named "interim" manager, but he showed how good of a manager he was on the major league level, so there was nothing to do but hire him for 1958.*

Second baseman – and future Hall of Famer – Bill Mazeroski gives Danny a lot of the credit for the team's turnaround in 1957:

> *I thought [Danny] did a great job. He was good for me, I know that. … Everything was in turmoil with Bobby Bragan. … Once Danny took over, he just solidified things. He got people and put them out there and let them play. There wasn't much hullabaloo about it, not hollering at anybody or screaming or yelling. He just let us play and we turned out to be pretty good ball players.*

Not surprisingly, Chester was bursting with pride over its hometown hero. The Chester Junior Chamber of Commerce sponsored a Danny Murtaugh Testimonial Dinner on December 12, 1957. The main speaker for the event was six-time All Star Yankee pitcher Lefty Gomez, who refused even travel money for coming to the event, saying he was glad to honor Danny. In all, nine speakers spent around an hour paying tribute to the new manager. Danny had a four-page speech written for the event, but by the time he got a chance at the microphone he was too choked up and could only say, "I consider myself a very lucky man. I don't know how I could express how I feel about what the City of Chester – and the county – has done for me and my family. All I can say is thanks." Danny's mother, Nellie, was also there and said her only regret was that her brother Tim – Unkie – hadn't lived to see Danny so honored.[5]

In 1958 Danny opened his first spring training camp. To get his players in top notch condition Danny asked Ray Welsh, a Pirate scout and former track coach, to devise an intensive running program for the team. This conditioning likely helped the Pirates stay relatively healthy throughout the season, which was essential to their success.

*Pittsburgh Post Gazette* sports writer Jack Hernon watched Danny in action that spring and was impressed with what he saw. According to Hernon, Danny didn't make himself the focal point. He could be seen talking to players in the infield, hitting ground balls in the outfield, or just standing with his hands in his back pocket observing the club. Danny delegated to his coaches and listened to their assessments of players and positions, but he made the final decisions himself – much like his former manager Billy Meyer. Listening to Danny talk after a practice game, it was obvious he hadn't missed much. In his "Roamin' Around" column on March 7, 1958, Hernon shared some of what he had heard from Danny in spring training:

> "Don Osborn, Jack Shepard, and Clyde King handle the pitchers," [Danny] answered to a question. "They teach them. Bill Burwell, one of the best, is taking care of the younger fellows. Teaching them a new pitch if the others feel the fellow needs it.
>
> "Frank Oceak has the word to keep his eye on the infielders, as does Lenny Levy. He and Sam Narron also are to watch the catcher's actions. George Sisler and George Detore handle the batting instruction.
>
> "If my pitchers aren't in shape, I'll just point to Ray Welsh. His job is conditioning and he handles it well. Rex Bowen charts our daily workout.
>
> "I particularly want to point this out to you newspaper guys," he kidded his inquisitor. "During the season if the pitching is lousy, you can blame Burwell. If someone on the infield doesn't do his job, it's Oceak's fault. And if one of the fellows doesn't hit when we need it, blame Sisler. Levy and Narron are responsible for the catcher's mistakes. I'm just a coordinator, so don't blame the manager for all these things."
>
> How about a bad throw from the outfield or one of them throwing to the wrong base? Who gets blamed for that? "I'll think of an answer when the time comes," [Danny] said.

Danny didn't limit his interview availability to sports editors at major papers. In February, he was interviewed by the newspaper for St. James Catholic High School, where his son Timmy was a freshman. The student reporter asked Danny some basic questions about his baseball career and the upcoming season. Danny was noncommittal when asked how the Pirates would finish in the league that year, although he did predict that Milwaukee and the Yankees would win the pennant.

The young reporter finished the interview by asking Danny what advice he would give to any boy who wants to become a major league baseball player. Danny responded, "You have to practice the things you don't do well in, don't smoke or drink, always be in good physical condition, get the highest education you possibly can, and last but not least, attend church because there just isn't room for atheists and agnostics in professional sports. It may sound tough, but I can certainly say, 'It's worth it.'"[6]

Danny no doubt said, "It's worth it," when the Pirates started the 1958 season on a high note, beating the Milwaukee Braves 4-3 in the 14th inning. They struggled a bit during the first half of the season, posting a 36-41 record at the halfway mark. But while they spent some time in seventh place (out of eight teams), they were not in last place at all that season. Under Danny's steady leadership the team caught fire in the last half of the season.

While the Pirates were clawing their way into the first division, tragedy struck Danny back home in Chester. After battling an illness for several months, Danny's mother Nellie passed away on July 25, 1958, at his sister Eunice's home where she had been living. Eunice told the *Chester Times* that Danny's success made Nellie "the proudest mom in the world."[7] Danny arrived in Chester from Pittsburgh first thing in the morning on July 25 and stayed through her funeral on Tuesday, July 29. He left the Pirates in the capable hands of longtime Coach Bill Burwell, and the team was 2-1 against the San Francisco Giants in his absence.

By the time the Giants left Pittsburgh, the Pirates had pushed them out of first place. The Bucs, meanwhile, had inched their way into third place. On August 8 the Pirates were in second with the Giants in third. Homerun powerhouse Frank Thomas had played with Danny in New Orleans and was on the Pirates when Danny became manager in 1957. Leading the team in homeruns (35) and RBI (109), Thomas was a key part of the Pirates' success in 1958. His efforts were rewarded by fans and peers with his fourth place ranking in MVP voting and his appearance on the NL All Star Team. Thomas really enjoyed playing for Danny:

> He was the best manager I ever played for, and I played for a lot of good managers. Danny had a way about him that he would get the best out of the players. If you did something good, he'd pat you on the back. If you did something bad, he'd kick you in the fanny. That's the way it should be.

> If you did something wrong today, you'd still be in the lineup tomorrow. He didn't put you in the doghouse. He also stuck up for his players. If there was an argument with an ump, he'd argue to the fullest extent to keep the player in the game. He said, "If I get thrown out, it's not going to hurt anything. If the player gets thrown out, it hurts the club."

> Danny let us play. That's the thing. Some managers are calling all the shots. Let the kids play. That's what makes a manager good. Each player has his own personality, his own characteristics. You have to know what players to pick on to get the best out of them and which ones you don't have to. That's what Danny did – he had a knack for that.

Danny was extremely popular with his team. On August 22, 1958, a headline in the *Pittsburgh Press* read, "Hiring Murtaugh for '59 Gives

Pirates Shot in Arm." Joe Brown had a special meeting with the team before a game in Chicago to formally announce the hiring. Brown had planned to make the announcement in Pittsburgh, but he thought it might be the spark the team needed just then. The team responded with an ovation – and an 8-2 victory over the Cubs. They proceeded to win 20 of the next 33 games and finished the season in second place.

After his remarkable success in leading the Pirates, Danny was the clear front runner for Manager of the Year honors in 1958. The Pirates sent out a press release promoting Danny for the honor:

> *Murtaugh's leadership has had as much to do with the Bucs'*
> *development this year as any other factor. A tough battler in*
> *his playing days, Danny has exhibited an innate quality of*
> *patience and a display of confidence in his men – which was*
> *thought to have been a thing of the past, insofar as baseball*
> *managers are concerned. ... Perhaps Danny's big asset was*
> *his ability to handle the men in general and the pitchers in*
> *particular. ... [Danny] has taken virtually the same club that*
> *finished in a tie for seventh place last year and has come on to*
> *give the Milwaukee Braves a run for their pennant money.*

The newspapers were full of articles dissecting Danny's success in turning the Pirates around. Danny acknowledged that he had adopted many managing techniques from his former Pirate manager Billy Meyer. In his last year playing for the Pirates Danny would often sit near Meyer in the dugout, and Meyer would explain every strategic move he made. According to Danny, Meyer always kept his temper until the next day – gave it 24 hours to simmer down.

Like Meyer, Danny was very patient and even tempered. He had a lot of confidence in his team, and he managed to build the confidence of his players. Not surprisingly, Danny tried to deflect credit for the Pirates' success in 1958. Most observers – including the voters for Manager of the Year – disagreed with Danny's assessment.

Former Pirate pitcher Bob Friend was one of those who disagreed with Danny on his importance to the team's success, "Danny knew how to handle people. He was the best manager I played for and he was a friend." Asked if the team's turnaround was related to Danny's managing, Friend doesn't hesitate in his response:

> *I think [our success] was [a function of Danny's managerial style]. The team wasn't doing very well. Bragan, who'd been a good manager at one time, was kind of having a bad year himself. When they brought Danny in, no one was sure what to make of it. Danny went around and talked to each player individually. He said he was going to keep us going.*
>
> *He was my favorite. Danny did more good for me than any-body in baseball. I had a terrible year in 1959, but he stayed with me until I came out of it. I still had a bad year, but if he'd stopped pitching me I doubt I'd have had the year I had in 1960. He had good instincts, and he liked the way I threw the ball. I pitched every third or fourth day for him.*
>
> *I remember how he used to make the pitchers run from one end of the outfield to the other. He'd hit fungos [balls hit from a practice "fungo" bat] and put the ball just out of your reach so you had to run and get it – that's how he got us in shape. He had good quality coaches, too.*
>
> *Danny never showed up his players in press, he always took any blame, he always put the players out front. He was never looking for publicity, and he got the best out of his players that way. The best managers do that. He knew enough about the game. As far as technical parts of the game, he was as good as*

*anybody. But it's how you deal with the 25 men on your team
that counts. He was a good disciplinarian. If you had it coming, he let you have it. But he didn't do it in front of the team.*

*Danny was a good leader – he was a natural leader and he'd
been in the war. He always kept everyone loose. Joe Brown
made an excellent choice with Danny. They were a great combination – producing those championships like that. Championships aren't easy to come by.*

Pirate All-Star shortstop Dick Groat, who would go on to win the
NL MVP award and batting title in 1960, agrees with Bob Friend. Before
he became manager, Danny worked closely with Groat and Bill Mazeroski
as infield coach:

*He was the best manager I ever played for. He got the most
out of the twenty-five players. He handled people extremely
well. Whether you're managing a company, a baseball team,
a basketball team, whatever it is, getting the best out of your
players is really what it's all about. Danny did a better job of
that than anybody I was ever around.*

*For example, the minute he became manager, he came up and
said Mazeroski and I were his shortstop/second base combination. He never took Maz out for a pinch hitter early in a
game like Bragan did. We were able to relax and play better
because we weren't always worried about losing our spots.*

Despite trying to deflect credit away from himself, Danny collected
a number of prestigious awards after the 1958 season. As expected, he
won the Associated Press Major League Manager of the Year title in a
landslide – Danny received 149 votes and the runner up received six votes.
This was even more impressive considering it was the first year with a joint
ballot for both leagues. In prior years, there was separate voting for the

National League and the American League. Danny responded to the honor in characteristic fashion:

> *Actually, a manager doesn't have too much to do with where his team finishes. The players do, and this honor should have gone to them. A majority of players reached their expected potential this past season and that is why we finished as high as we did. I think a lot of the rival clubs will worry about us next year.*[8]

According to an Associated Press sportswriter, however, "what he did with his mixture of callow youth and grizzled veterans verged on a baseball miracle." The writer noted the team effort put forth under Danny and added, "The youngsters, under the understanding and intelligent guidance of the stocky Irishman, gained poise and confidence. They were unawed by the reputations of their opponents."[9] Even the *New York Times'* Pulitzer Prize winning sports columnist Arthur Daley opined that Danny "did a superlative job with the material he had" and was the only choice for the Manager of the Year award. Daley provided evidence of Danny's effect on the team:

> *Ron Kline had a 2-15 record as a pitcher when Danny took command of the club. The big right-hander's confidence was shattered. When he fed a three-run home-run ball to Harry Anderson of the Phils, Kline looked fearfully at the bench in expectation of a fast hook.*
>
> *Murtaugh walked to the mound. "You all right, Ron?" asked Danny, instantly communicating his own calmness and serenity to the jittery pitcher. "Sure," said Kline eagerly. "Stay in there," said Danny. "We'll get those runs back for you." The Pirates did, and Kline, his confidence restored, won nine of his next ten games. ...*

> *As a manager, he moved into the assignment in a rather unob-*
> *trusive fashion. He didn't push himself or pretend to be a*
> *know-it-all. However, it soon became evident to the Pirate fol-*
> *lowers that this quiet man steadily was gaining the respect of*
> *his players. Soon they were going to him for advice, the unmis-*
> *takable sign that he had it made.*[10]

After the unexpected success of 1958, everyone had high hopes for
the Pirates in 1959. In spring training, Danny again instituted the running
program that he used in the year before to ensure all of his players were
in top shape. He also took the time to give shortstops Dick Groat and Dick
Schofield and third baseman Harry Bright pointers on playing second
base in case anything should happen to Bill Mazeroski during the season.

The team was full of confidence, although some outsiders speculated
that the 1958 season had been a one-shot deal. The players bristled at sug-
gestions like that. "Not one of those boys out there thinks last year was a
fluke. They're not going to beat us before we get to the ball park," was
Danny's response to the critics.[11]

The season got off to a very disappointing start, with the Bucs losing
their first five games. By mid-May they had clawed their way up to playing
.500 ball, but they were still in a disappointing sixth place. On May 21,
frustrated by a three-game losing streak and a perceived lack of focus by
his team, Danny gave the team what reporters called a "tongue lashing."
Dick Groat, who was team captain at the time, remembers that meeting
vividly:

> *Danny called me on the phone in our hotel St. Louis and told*
> *me to come to his room. He told me he was going to have a*
> *meeting in the clubhouse that night, and I wasn't to pay any*
> *attention to whatever he said. He said he was going to beat*
> *me something awful, and he thought by beating me up it*
> *would help turn the team around. Sure enough, it worked.*

When the Pirates went on to win that evening's game – and the next four in a row – Danny wondered why he hadn't done it sooner. The five-game winning streak came to an end on May 26, the most remarkable game of the season. The Pirates were kicking off a road trip with a three-game series against the Milwaukee Braves, two-time defending league champions. Pittsburgh hurler Harvey Haddix made history that night as he pitched a perfect game through not nine, not ten, not eleven, but twelve innings of baseball. As he took to the mound in the bottom of the thirteenth inning, the score was knotted at 0-0 and Haddix had retired an unfathomable 36 consecutive batters. A fielding error allowed the first Milwaukee base runner of the game. With the perfect game ruined, Danny had Haddix intentionally walk slugger Hank Aaron. The plan didn't work, however, as the next batter drove the only run of the game across the plate. Harvey Haddix had pitched perfect baseball for twelve innings and lost the game.

The Buccos would continue to battle, and by early June they were in third place and only three games back. Unfortunately they weren't able to keep it up. A nine-game losing streak in late July, which included a five game sweep by the Milwaukee Braves, sent the Pirates back to fifth place. Once again the Bucs battled back, winning 15 of 18 games in a 2½ week home stand in August. After winning eight of 11 games against the top three teams in the National League, the Pirates entered September just four games out of first place. Another long road trip – the first 15 games of September were on the road – proved to be too much for the Bucs. When they limped back home, they were 7½ games out of first after going 5-10 on the road. They finished the season a disappointing fourth place.

One local sportswriter, Frank Ramsden of the *New Kensington Daily Dispatch*, wrote in October that he never believed the 1959 Pirates had a chance:

*The Mighty Buccos, never more than a fourth placer in our book, were one big flop from the start. The team just didn't have it – and sportswriters and Pirate tub-thumpers were wrong in attempting to sell the fans a bill of goods. ... The whole thing was a farce and should never have been foisted on the unsuspecting public. ... And that brings us to one Danny Murtaugh and 1960. It seems a good bet, they say, our Mr. M will be asked to manage the Pirates again in 1960 – with the actual signing to take place following the World Series. But, and here goes our pipe dream exploding again – maybe Mr. Murtaugh won't be brought back.*

*All the undercover talk keeps hinting that Leo Durocher is not really interested in Cleveland, Milwaukee, and the various other franchises in the Major loops, but has a coveting eye on Branch Rickey's vacated stock and Murtaugh's managerial reins. And wouldn't that be something. Just how long do you suppose Mr. Durocher would put up with the stand pat business as usual attitude put forth in recent years by the Pirates. In fact, it would be downright nice to have a Durocher around to pump some life back into a club that has been near dead for a couple of decades.[12]*

Fortunately, Joe Brown didn't hold Danny responsible for the Pirates' poor showing. Asked about it, Brown said that Danny did as well as possible considering his players had been plagued by injuries. In late October the Pirates announced that Danny would lead the team again in 1960. His salary at the time was believed to be around $30,000, although neither he nor the team confirmed that number. Whatever the amount, Danny would certainly prove his worth the next year.

# the Bucs are goin' all the way

At just after 3:30 p.m. on October 13, 1960, Bill Mazeroski walked from the Pirates' dugout to home plate with his bat in his hand and only one thought in his head: make contact and get on base. Yankees right-hander Ralph Terry waited on the mound, kicking the dirt, hoping to make quick work of the Pirates so the Bronx Bombers could get back to the plate and score the winning run. It was the beginning of the bottom of the 9th inning of Game Seven of the 1960 World Series and the score was tied 9-9.

Few in the sporting world had expected the series to last as long as it had. The Yankees were prohibitive favorites in the early speculation, featuring seven past, present or future American League Most Valuable Player Award winners. Indeed, to that point in the series, the Yankees had outscored the Pirates 55-26, outhit them 91-59, and had amassed a team

---

*Tim Murtaugh, oldest grandson of Danny Murtaugh, co-authored this chapter.*

batting average that was superior by 82 percentage points. While the Pirates had eked out three wins by three runs or less, the Yankees had taken their three victories by scores of 16-3, 10-0 and 12-0. Nevertheless, the deciding Game Seven was tied at nine in the ninth inning and there was still work to do.

The announced crowd at Forbes Field was 36,683. Years later some would jokingly observe that there were millions of people on hand in the ballpark, if one believed everyone who claimed to have been there. Indeed, former President George W. Bush would make a similar observation upon meeting Danny's daughter Kathy at a White House Christmas dinner in 2007. According to Kathy's recollection of her brief conversation with the president the exchange went something like this:

> "I know you are a baseball guy, so I wanted to tell you that my father was the manager of the Pittsburgh Pirates for years," said Kathy. "He won the World Series twice."
>
> "Oh, yeah?" the president said. "What years?"
>
> "1960 and 1971," Kathy replied.
>
> "Danny Murtaugh," President Bush said. "Let me ask you a question about that. What was the attendance in 1960 when Bill Mazeroski hit that home run?"
>
> "I don't know, thirty or forty thousand, maybe," Kathy said. "Forbes Field wasn't that big."
>
> "Nope," said the president. "About two million – if you count everyone who claims to have been there."

With the actual souls in attendance buzzing with nervous energy, Terry wound up and delivered a fastball, which Mazeroski decided was too high and let go past for ball one. The pressure increased. Spectators in the stands and television viewers and radio listeners across America waited expectantly for the next pitch. Before he came to the plate, Maz had been sitting on the Pirate bench remembering how the Yankees beat his favorite boyhood team, the Cleveland Indians, year after year. "Those damn Yankees are going to do it again," he thought to himself.[1] Or could Mazeroski stop them?

While the Thursday afternoon audience observed the unfolding drama, it was clear that this Pirate team on the brink of baseball history had made a tremendous journey in a remarkably short period of time. And it was due, in no small part, to the skillful handling by Manager Danny Murtaugh, aged 43 years and five days, with only three full seasons as the Pittsburgh skipper under his belt. Years later, catcher Smoky Burgess would have this to say about Danny: "I know there are a lot of great managers around. But I've never seen a manager in the same category as Danny Murtaugh. He studied everything and got the most talent out of his players. You had to treat a Dick Stuart or a Dick Groat or myself differently. Danny did. He'd go to each of us and get the most from all of us."[2]

Heading into the 1960 season most of the "experts" predicted a third or fourth place showing from the Bucs based on their 1959 performance. And for good reason. Spring training in 1960 revealed a team that was nearly identical to the team that finished in fourth place the previous year. Despite the low expectations Danny expressed confidence in a column for the Associated Press:

> Last year Pittsburgh finished fourth because of (1) injuries, (2) several players having sub-par seasons, and (3) lack of another long-ball hitter and a right-handed hitting catcher. I look for this year's club to be better because (1) I don't look for another injury siege like the last one, (2) fellows like Bill Mazeroski, Dick Groat, Bob Skinner, and Bob Friend are bound to bounce back, and (3) we have come up with a good offensive right-handed catcher in Hal Smith. Our club still needs a long-ball hitter to go along with Dick Stuart.

*As our team now stands, we have a very good defense, adequate team speed, and pretty good hitting. If the boys play up to what we know they can, we feel we must have a fighting chance for the pennant. I feel the trades we have made this winter have improved our club. First we acquired a good catcher in Smith to go with Smoky Burgess. Second, we acquired a good all-around outfielder in Gino Cimoli. Bob Oldis, another catcher, should help us. The departure of Ronnie Kline leaves us an opening in our pitching rotation. Friend, Vernon Law, and Harvey Haddix are our first liners but we'll have a number of candidates in camp trying for the fourth job.*

*Offhand, I'd say Joe Gibbon, a left-hander who pitched for Columbus last year, and Jim Umbricht, a right-hander from Salt Lake City, have a good chance. … Our outfield is intact. It includes Skinner, Bob Clemente, and Bill Virdon, with Roman Mejias a valuable fourth man. We have good reports on a rookie from Denver named Hank Mitchell.*[3]

The Pirates kicked off the 1960 season on April 12 with a loss to the Milwaukee Braves, a team that nearly won the NL pennant in 1959. The bright spot of the game was that Bob Friend, who dropped from 22-14 in 1958 to 8-19 in 1959, gave up only seven hits in seven innings. By April 24 an AP headline read: "Pittsburgh's Bob Friend Looking Like Old Self!" after the pitcher recorded two straight victories and helped bump the Bucs into first place. The Pirates held onto first for two weeks and dropped to second for the next ten days.

On May 18 the Pirates hosted the St. Louis Cardinals at Forbes Field with Vernon Law on the mound. The Pirate ace threw a shutout until the ninth inning, when he gave up two runs. The 4-2 victory marked his sixth complete game and his sixth win (against one defeat) for the season. By the end of the night the Bucs were 20-10 and had climbed back into first place. Except for two days the following week, the Pirates would hold onto first place for the rest of the season.

Danny and Joe Brown knew they would need more help in the pitching department to stay in first. Friend, Law, and Haddix were their core starting pitchers, but they needed another mainstay if they wanted to go all the way. On May 27 Brown addressed that need by acquiring 1959 All Star lefthander Vinegar Bend Mizell from the Cardinals. As part of the deal, Brown traded minor league second baseman Julian Javier, who would eventually become a two-time All Star and appear in three World Series with the Cards. Announcing the deal Brown said, "I'm giving up one of the most brilliant prospects in the minor leagues, but I'm shooting everything for this year."[4] Brown's gamble paid off as Mizell contributed thirteen wins (against five losses) during the 1960 season.

On July 10 the Pirates were in Philadelphia holding a five game lead over Milwaukee. Although the Bucs and Phillies split the series 2-2, Philadelphia manager Gene Mauch was full of praise for the Pirates and their leader, Danny Murtaugh. "The more I see of them, the more I like the Pirates," said Mauch. "The Pirates have the healthy approach to togetherness and they're hungry for the pennant."[5]

The Pirates were headed into the All-Star break with a lead in the National League, and the baseball world was starting to notice. Longtime *New York Times* sports reporter Louis Effrat noted, "If the other teams do not start taking the Pirates seriously, they may be in for a shock. Much credit for the [Pirates'] superb showing so far belongs to Murtaugh, the square-jawed squire of Chester, PA. Most of Danny's calls have been right."[6]

Characteristically, the even-keeled Danny didn't get too excited, and his team followed suit. While a five-game lead at the midpoint was nice to have, there was no guarantee that it would hold up. Effrat reported that neither Danny nor his players would talk pennant, which one (unnamed) opposing player called a weakness: "If I were a manager, I'd want my players talking pennant every minute of the day."

Danny admitted to Effrat that even he did not foresee his team being in this situation halfway through the season: "'I certainly didn't,' Murtaugh said. 'But the boys have been great. Bob Friend, Bob Skinner, Roberto Clemente and Bill Mazeroski have made strong comebacks. Smoky Burgess and Hal Smith have been producing in the catching department, and, mainly, we haven't been beating ourselves.'" Danny wouldn't say whether his team would remain in first; according to Effrat: "[He didn't] need to say it. One could read the answer in his eyes. He just wasn't talking about it."

Danny was right not to count on holding his five-game lead. Milwaukee got hot in mid-July, and by July 24 the two teams were tied for first. The never-say-die Bucs kept at it and regained their lead over the Braves. Following a win in Cincinnati on August 20 the Pirates had a 7½ game lead, but Danny kept his cool, as Myron Cope reported in the *Pittsburgh Post Gazette* the next day:

> Recently an out-of-town newspaperman came away from a dugout interview with Danny Murtaugh muttering purple oaths. "What's the matter?" another newspaperman said.
>
> "We're just gonna take them one game at a time," mocked the out-of-town writer. "One of these days Danny may give us a sensational quote by saying, 'We're just gonna take them two at a time.'"
>
> Daniel Edward Murtaugh, who one game at a time is rapidly managing the Pirates to their first pennant in 33 years, is a successful paradox – two people – a split personality – a Will Rogers one moment and a Cal Coolidge the next. Danny Mur-

taugh the man is a fun-loving, garrulous practical joker with a firehouse wit that makes him charming company in the dugout, at social gatherings, or over a plate of his wife Kate's roast beef at their home in Chester, Pa.

Danny Murtaugh the manager, on the other hand, is a great stone face who steadfastly follows a policy of grim reserve. If one of his players made three errors, got picked off base twice, went 0-for-5, and wound up the night by breaking curfew, Murtaugh would have no comment to the press.

By the same token, a brilliant performance by one of his players evokes little more than mild praise, if that. Last Wednesday, when Clem Labine emerged from the ranks of baseball's unemployed and pitched hitless ball for three and two-thirds innings of relief work, Murtaugh was asked if Labine had surprised him. Replied Murtaugh: "That's hard to say. I put him in because I thought he could do the job." ...

Why is it, [Joe] Brown was asked, that Murtaugh cannot bring himself to wax enthusiastically over outstanding performance by his players? "One reason he doesn't blow up one man is that he wants team play. If you've got three or four stars and they get all the credit you may have trouble. When credit goes to the team as a unit, when the manager acts like we win because we're a team, then he fosters and nurtures the very spirit with which our team is where it is. ... You certainly cannot criticize Murtaugh for lack of success."

In the same article Brown noted that Danny always had a reason for everything he did. Brown echoed that belief in a 2008 interview:

Before each game, Danny used to go into his office and sit there for an hour all by himself in his big rocker with his spittoon.

*He'd rock back and forth. I asked him one day, "What do you do in there for an hour?" He said, "I play the game." I said, "What do you mean you play the game?"*

*He said, "I know what pitchers I have available on my club. Not just the starting pitcher, but also my relief pitchers. I know who has pitched recently. I go through every situation. If my starting pitcher gets knocked out in the early innings, I know who I'm going to bring in. If the reliever has problems, I know who is coming in next. If we have a lead and I look on the wall and I see that the third or fourth hitter in the inning is Musial, I know whether I'm going to leave that pitcher in or bring in somebody. And I not only know if I'm going to make a change, I know who I'm going to bring in based upon past success of the pitcher, how much he's been used lately, if his arm's tired, and so forth.*

*"The same thing with us at bat. If we've got a situation in late innings and they bring in a different pitcher, I know whether or not I'm going to pinch hit and if so who it will be. I know whether or not I'm going to bunt. I go through all of the conditions that are present for the game. I not only go through our game, I go through the other team's game – who they'll bring in when we've got them in a pinch. So nothing is new to me when we're in the game – I've already gone through it."*

*Maybe other managers do something like it, but I don't think they do it to the extent that Danny did. He did it every day before every game. So all of his managing, all of his thinking had already been done before the game even started.*

*Initially, players who played for him didn't recognize how keen a baseball man he was until they'd been there long enough to* see what he was really doing. Because he made managing look easy, people underestimated the depth of his knowledge and his control of the players on his team.

On September 25 Danny's team approach paid off as the Pirates clinched their first National League pennant in thirty-three years. The *New York Times* the next day called it "a solid team victory" and noted "no one man can take all the bows":

> Not even Dick Groat, the Pirate captain and shortstop and leading candidate for player of the year honors. Not even Vern Law, the Bucs' 20-game winner, nor ElRoy Face, the superb little relief artist, nor Don Hoak nor Roberto Clemente.

> Danny Murtaugh, the unobtrusive manager whose sound guidance and undemonstrative masterminding has been the steadying influence, can't take all the credit. Nor can Joe Brown, the 42-year-old general manager, whose shrewd trades and behind-the-scenes activities have been highly instrumental in the team's success.

> If ever a team jelled as a unit, with every able-bodied man contributing his bit, this was it. It's a team with no dynamic star of the caliber of Willie Mays or Stan Musial, but a squad of hungry players who get along well.

> Groat is the inspirational leader, Hoak the take-charge guy, Bill Mazeroski the defensive stalwart, Clemente the runs-batted-in boss. Bob Skinner and Dick Stuart are the long-ball hitters and Bill Virdon, Smoky Burgess, and Hal Smith are steady performers.

> Another big factor has been the Pirates' strong but unspectacular pitching. Law, enjoying by far his best season, and Bob Friend, the old-timer of the staff, have been the mainstays. But

*Face and a couple of southpaws, Harvey Haddix and Vinegar*
*Bend Mizell, have made major contributions, and lesser lights,*
*Fred Green, Joe Gibbon, Tom Cheney and, a late arrival,*
*Clem Labine, have also helped. …*

*In the final analysis, it was the Pirates' determination, their*
*supreme confidence, their refusal to wilt under pressure that*
*drove them to Pittsburgh's first pennant in thirty-three years.*

Milwaukee Braves pitcher and future Hall of Famer Warren Spahn, who saw a lot of the Pirates in 1960, disagreed a bit. Spahn told *Pittsburgh Post Gazette* Sports Editor Al Abrams on October 2 that he didn't think Danny got enough credit for the Pirates' World Series appearance: "'What a marvelous job he's turned in!' [Spahn] said in admiration. 'There's a guy that got the most out of his ball club. Very few thought he had the best team in the league when the season started. He showed them otherwise. I think he should get all the credit.'" Spahn, unlike most in the baseball world, predicted the Pirates would defeat the Yankees in the Series.

Forty-eight years later former Pirates and Yankees recalled the 1960 World Series matchup in the *Pittsburgh Post Gazette* on June 22, 2008:

*"We were underdogs in the media's mind," Pirates center*
*fielder Bill Virdon said. "In our minds, we felt like we had a*
*chance. I don't think there's any question about the level of*
*talent on the two clubs. I think they had the best talent overall."*

*"You have to remember we were an absolutely unique baseball*
*team," [Dick] Groat said. "We kind of believed we weren't*
*supposed to lose – that we were invincible, that we were a team*
*of destiny."*

*Still, these were the Yankees.*

*"Man for man, if you matched up by position, it looked like*
*we had the better team," Yankees shortstop Tony Kubek said*

*in an interview. "But teams are reflective of their manager and
I knew Danny Murtaugh was scrappy. They were a team that
was going to be extremely competitive."*

The Pirates were lucky. In 1960 the National League team had the
home field advantage, so Game One, on October 5, was at Forbes Field.
The Buccos got off to a 3-1 lead in the first inning and never let go. Vernon
Law held the Yankees to two runs in seven innings. Reliever ElRoy Face
gave up a two-run homer in the ninth, but he put the brakes on and the
Pirates came away with a 6-4 victory.

Game Two, on October 6, was also at Forbes Field, but the similar-
ities ended there. Starter Bob Friend gave up three runs (two earned) in
four innings – and he had the best night of the six pitchers that Danny
sent to the mound. By the time the game finally ended, the Yankees had
scored sixteen runs to the Pirates' three. The front page headline in the
*Pittsburgh Post Gazette* the next day read:

PIRATE SECOND VICTORY slightly delayed

BEAT 'EM, BUCS, NEXT TIME!

No such luck for the Pirates. On October 8, Game Three took them
to Yankee Stadium, The House that [Babe] Ruth Built. It was Danny's first
time in that storied baseball stadium; it was also his 43rd birthday. It
would be a memorable one, to say the least, as the Pirates got clobbered
again. Yankee pitcher (and future Hall of Famer) Whitey Ford threw a
four-hit shutout that ended in a 10-0 rout of the visitors from Pittsburgh.
"That wasn't a very good birthday present, was it?" Danny asked Myron
Cope after the game. After acknowledging that the game didn't make him
feel any younger, Danny said, "We'll celebrate tonight. The Irish always
celebrate birthdays happily. You never know whether it's your last birthday."[7] Daughter Kathy, eleven at the time, recalls hearing that her parents
saw a play on Broadway that night in an attempt to salvage the day.

The Pirates were down, but not out. In a special to the *Pittsburgh Post Gazette,* third baseman Don Hoak sounded upbeat heading into Game Four: "Well, Vern Law is pitching. The Deacon has great control. If he can't get ahead of those Yankees, then I'll admit we're in deep trouble. Meanwhile, don't dump us in a grave yet. We're going to bring this series back to Pittsburgh and when we get the Yanks back home we'll be awful tough on them. The past two games have been pretty sickening, but our boys didn't behave like zombies even when we were ten runs behind today. If you quit on the Pirates now, there's a very good chance you'll have to eat your words in a few days."[8] There wouldn't be many hungry sportswriters when the Series ended.

Hoak was right to pin his hopes on the Deacon for Game Four. As John Drebinger put it in the *New York Times* the next day, "Pittsburgh's spunky Pirates fought their way back to even terms with the Yankees at the Stadium yesterday by winning the fourth game of the World Series, 3 to 2." Despite a sore ankle, Law went 6 1/3 innings and gave up only two runs. He was relieved by ElRoy Face, who retired the remaining eight batters in a row. The Pirates had faced the mighty Yankees on their home turf and won. The Bucs had ensured a return to Forbes Field for Game Six and possibly Game Seven. Things were looking up.

Game Five. Harvey Haddix was set to take the mound on October 10 for the first time in the Series. His normal spot in the rotation would have given him Game Four. If the Series went to seven games, Danny knew he would need Vernon Law in that final contest. To ensure Law had sufficient rest between games, Danny put him in Game Four and Haddix in Game Five. It would prove to be a wise move. Like Law the day before, Haddix held the Yankees to two runs in 6 1/3 innings. In the bottom of the seventh, with two on base and one out, Danny called his star reliever from the bullpen once again. ElRoy Face came out and delivered his third save of the Series. The Pirates, who appeared doomed just two days earlier, were heading back to Pittsburgh with a 3-2 lead in the Series.

The Pirates arrived at the Greater Pittsburgh Airport around 8:30 p.m. on October 10 and found a jubilant crowd of around 10,000 there to greet them. The Yankees had arrived – with much less fanfare – an hour earlier. According to the *Pittsburgh Post Gazette,* Yankee Manager Casey Stengel remarked, "I understand we've made a lot of people happy here and that they're glad to see us back. Personally, I'm not so happy to be back." Danny, of course, was quite happy to be there. Asked if he'd ever given up on his team Danny replied, "We always bounce back. You people oughta be used to that by now."[9]

Pennsylvania Governor David Lawrence praised ElRoy Face and had this to say about the Buc skipper: "Danny Murtaugh's superb judgment in the last two games has been uncanny. He knew just when to lift Harvey Haddix and send in Face to put out the fire in the seventh inning. Again in the ninth inning he made a smart move, sending Joe Christopher in to run for Smoky Burgess. It paid off when Ryne Duren cut loose with a wild pitch to set up our Pirates fifth run, a nice piece of insurance in any cliff-hanging game."[10]

After a day off, the Pirates and Yankees took to Forbes Field on October 12 for Game Six. A Pirate victory would mean the first World Championship for Pittsburgh since 1925. Bob Friend, who won eighteen games during the regular season but got clobbered in Game Two, was on the mound for the Buccos. For the Yankees, six-time (to that point) All Star Whitey Ford would do the honors. Ford's regular season record in 1960 was just 12-9, but he'd been responsible for the Game Three shutout.

As Yogi Berra might have said, it was like déjà vu all over again. Ford pitched another shutout. The Bucs used six pitchers, just as they had in the previous two losses. The difference this time was the Yankees scored twelve runs instead of ten. *Pittsburgh Post Gazette* reporter Mel Seidenberg overheard one fan explain the game's outcome: "Don't let that score worry you. That's the same strategy as Murtaugh used last week and it works – Let the Yankees tire themselves out running around the base paths; then we'll take them."[11]

Had he heard the fan's comments, Danny undoubtedly would have approved. After the shellacking the Bucs received in Game Six, Danny reminded *New York Times* writer Joseph Sheehan: "The last time I checked the rule book, they were still settling the World Series on games won and lost, not total runs. The standings show the Yankees have been beaten three times, too."[12]

October 13. Game Seven had arrived. Vernon Law was on the mound for the third time in the Series. He'd been pitching on a sore ankle, but all Danny asked was for five strong innings. Law could – and would – deliver. To start the game he retired the top of the Yankees' lineup – three powerhouses – in order. The Pirates followed with two early runs. After Bill Virdon flied out to left field and Dick Groat popped up to shortstop, Bob Skinner reached first base on a walk from Yankees' starter, right-hander Bob Turley. Rocky Nelson followed with a two-run homer. Roberto Clemente popped up to second base to end the inning, but the Pirates had grabbed an important early lead.

*Pirates 2, Yankees 0*

Second inning. The next three batters in the Yankee lineup were future Hall of Famers Mickey Mantle and Roger Maris and team batting leader Bill Skowron. Once again Law took them out in order: three up and three down. First up for the Bucs was Smoky Burgess, who delivered a lead-off single to right field. Yankees manager Casey Stengel decided Turley, who had only faced six batters, did not have the correct 'stuff' in the all-important deciding game. Casey pulled Turley and brought right-hander Bill Stafford to the mound. Stafford promptly walked Don Hoak, moving Burgess to second base. Bill Mazeroski followed with a single, loading the bases with none out and the Pirates leading 2-0.

Pitcher Vernon Law batted next and grounded one back to Stafford, who threw home to catch Burgess. Yankees catcher Johnny Blanchard – behind the plate that day for New York with Yogi Berra in left field – tagged home plate and fired to Bill Skowron at first base for the double play. With two outs and Mazeroski and Hoak on second and third, the Yankees were desperate to get out of the inning while the Pirates hoped to push more early runs across. Bill Virdon came through with a single to right field, scoring both Mazeroski and Hoak. Dick Groat grounded out to end the inning.

*Pirates 4, Yankees 0*

Third and fourth innings. Law retired the first two batters – the Yankees had yet to get a guy on base. Leftfielder Hector Lopez was brought in to pinch hit for the pitcher and reached first base. But Bobby Richardson flied out to Skinner in left field to end the inning. Former All Star, former MVP, and eight-time Golden Glove pitcher Bobby Shantz took the mound for the Yankees and retired the Pirate batters one-two-three. With one-third of the game over, things were looking good for Pittsburgh. The fourth inning went just as quickly with neither team recording a run.

*Pirates 4, Yankees 0*

Fifth inning. First baseman Bill Skowron led off with a homerun to break the ice for New York. Three straight outs later and the Pirates got another chance to widen their lead … to no avail. Shantz retired Law, Virdon, and Groat with no one reaching base. Shantz had gone three innings with no hits and no runs. Law had allowed only three hits and one run in five innings. The fans were glued to their seats.

*Pirates 4, Yankees 1*

Sixth inning. Richardson led off with a single and shortstop Tony

Kubek, who would feature prominently in the game shortly, was walked. Danny came to the mound to remove Law from the game. In spite of his sore ankle, Law had done what Danny had asked of him – kept the Pirates in the lead through five well-pitched innings. As he had in Games One, Four, and Five, Danny called on his ace reliever, ElRoy Face.

Face induced Maris to pop up to Don Hoak for the first out, with men still on first and second. But Mickey Mantle followed with a single to center that scored Richardson and moved Kubek to third. Yogi Berra, appearing in his eleventh World Series, stepped to the plate and slammed a home run. Suddenly the Yankees were ahead 5-4 and the Pirates faithful had the air taken out of them. Face retired Skowron and Blanchard, but the damage had been done. New York had scored four runs on three hits and now led the deciding game of the Series by one run headed to the bottom of the sixth. Although the heart of the batting order took to the plate, the Pirates went three up and three down to close the inning.

*Yankees 5, Pirates 4*

Seventh inning. With Face returning to the mound, the Yankees managed a hit but no run in the top of the seventh. Same story for the Pirates in their half – one hit, no run. After a leadoff single, catcher Smoky Burgess was lifted for pinch runner Joe Christopher. Hoak lined out to Berra in left and Mazeroski hit into an inning-ending double play.

*Yankees 5, Pirates 4*

Eighth inning. The stunned Pittsburgh crowd would see the Yankees draw more blood. Face made it past Maris and Mantle unscathed. With two outs and no runners on base, Face walked Berra. Skowron hit a single and moved Berra to second base. Catcher Johnny Blanchard also delivered a single, scoring Berra and moving Skowron to third. The next shot, a double by Clete Boyer, sent Skowron home and gave the Yanks a

7-4 lead. After a merciful fly out from pitcher Bobby Shantz, the Pirates finally got a chance to get back in the game.

In the bottom half of the eighth, Gino Cimoli pinch hit for Elroy Face and singled. Up next, Bill Virdon hit a screaming ground ball to Tony Kubek at shortstop – what looked a sure double play that would clear the bases for the Yankees. A play-by-play sheet from the game will show that Bill Virdon is credited with a single, but the ripped ball was bigger than that in this contest. Routinely described as a "vicious" ground ball, Virdon's missile hit a rock or a bump in the infield, jumped up, and struck Kubek in the throat. The shortstop fell down in a heap. The players recalled the incident in the *Pittsburgh Post Gazette* on June 22, 2008:

> When I hit it, I said, 'Uh, oh' — well, maybe not in those words — 'double play,' "[Bill] Virdon said."It was automatic. Hard hit and hit right at him."

> "He hit it, and I thought, 'That's it. That's the double play,'" [Tony] Kubek said. "My only thought was, 'What do I do after I catch the ball? Do I run over and take it to [second base] myself or toss it to Bobby [Richardson]?' Well, it never happened."

> The ball struck something just before it got to Kubek and slammed into the shortstop's throat. "I couldn't get my hands up [in time]," Kubek said recently. "If it had hit me in the chest, I pick up the ball and we at least get one [out]."

> Richardson picked up the ball as the Yankees rushed to Kubek's aid. Yankees manager Casey Stengel kept yelling: "Give him air! Give him air!"

Joe DeMaestri took Kubek's place at shortstop and the inning continued. Instead of two out and no one on base, Shantz was facing runners on first and second with no outs. Groat singled to left, scoring Cimoli and sending Virdon to second. Stengel decided Shantz had done all he could do and took him out for right-handed starter Jim Coates. Danny called for a bunt and Bob Skinner delivered a sacrifice bunt that sent Virdon to third base and Groat to second. After a Rocky Nelson fly out, Clemente came to the plate and knocked a slow grounder toward first base. Coates failed to cover first base on the play, so Virdon scored and Clemente got a single instead of ending the inning.

Hal Smith came to the plate, having replaced Burgess behind the plate in the top of the eighth. He came through in a big way: with a three-run homer that would – in the hysteria that followed the end of the game – be somewhat lost in history. But his teammates widely acknowledged it as a one of the most important hits of the game. Ralph Terry replaced Coates on the mound and got Hoak to fly out to left. The Pirates had scored five runs and suddenly jumped ahead with only one inning to play.

*Pirates 9, Yankees 7*

Ninth inning. "But still the battle raged," is how the October 14 *New York Times* described the atmosphere heading into the final frame. It was Bob Friend's turn on the mound and the first two batters he faced made it to base. With runners at first and second and no outs, Danny sent Harvey Haddix to relieve Friend. Haddix allowed only one hit, but the Yanks scored two runs off the runners that Friend had left on base.

Historic Game Seven of the 1960 World Series was headed to the bottom of the ninth inning, with the score tied at nine apiece. Ralph Terry would end up facing only one batter that inning: Bill Mazeroski. The rest, as they say, is history:

> *"There's a swing and a high fly ball going deep to left. This may do it! Back to the wall goes Berra. It is … over the fence!*

# the bucs are goin' all the way

*Home run! The Pirates win! Ladies and gentlemen, Bill*
*Mazeroski has just hit a one-nothing pitch over the left field*
*wall to win the 1960 World Series for the Pittsburgh*
*Pirates ..."*

*– Chuck Thompson, play-by-play, NBC Radio,*
*October 13, 1960*

Yogi Berra was playing left field as Maz's shot flew through the air. Thinking the ball would remain in play, Berra turned to see where it would land. Instead photographers captured the image of the Yankee great watching the ball sail over the fence. In a 2009 interview, Berra acknowledged that he wouldn't have turned to watch it if he'd known it was going over. Nearly fifty years later, he still sounded surprised: "I thought it was going to hit the fence. I really did."

"Every Pirate is a hero," said Danny following the game. "What a terrific way to win the Series. It was just typical of my ballclub – a fighting ballclub all the way. ... When Bill Mazeroski hit that ball in the ninth I doubted just for a moment that it would go over the wall. When Yogi Berra stopped I knew we had the World Series, and my one thought was – I'd like to kiss my wife."[13]

Danny's wife Kate had good reason to doubt Danny's claim that she was the one he wanted to kiss. Kate would tell people that she'd never seen her husband as happy as he was right after the victory. Danny agreed with her assessment and added, "[If] you had been standing on one side of me, and Mazeroski on the other side, and I had to kiss one or the other, it wouldn't have been you."[14]

To this day, there are hundreds of dedicated Pirates fans who converge every year on October 13 to remember that glorious day in 1960. While Forbes Field is long gone, a portion of the old wall still stands – a hallowed spot for these pilgrims as they listen to a recording of the original

NBC radio broadcast. The organizers try to time it to end as close to 3:36 p.m. as they can – the approximate moment that Mazeroski's ball cleared the left field fence at Forbes Field. The exact spot is marked by a plaque on what is now Roberto Clemente Drive.

One of the organizers, Herb Soltman, of Greentree, Pennsylvania, says that listening to the tape of the old game gives him the sensation that the events are just happening at that moment. "You sit there and listen to it and you're still not sure they're going to win."[15]

The post-Series reviews were just as aghast and shocked by the outcome as the Series previews had been kind to the Yankees.

"Danny Murtaugh and his Pirates, generally expected to finish third or fourth in the National League, ran roughshod over all opposition to win Pittsburgh's first pennant in thirty-three years," wrote John Drebinger in the *New York Times* on Christmas Day. "Taking on Casey Stengel and his Yankees, the Pirates then outscrambled the Bombers in a thrill-packed seven game World Series. A ninth-inning home run by Bill Mazeroski sank the Yanks 10-to-9." It is still the only World Series to end on a home run in the bottom of the ninth inning of Game Seven.

A *New York Times* editorial would be more amusing, accusing Danny and the Pirates of thievery of the most degenerate nature. "Dear Danny Murtaugh," wrote James Reston on October 14, 1960. "I call your attention to Article I, Clause 10 of the Constitution of the United States, which states that "The Congress shall have the power * * * to define and punish piracies":

> *Accordingly, you are hereby charged with diverse acts of piracy in and around the city of Pittsburgh against the persons and property of the New York Base Ball Company, particularly on the afternoon of October 13, 1960.*

# the Bucs are goin' all the way

*The general charge against you is as follows: That on this day a group under your direction widely known as the Pittsburgh Pirates did willfully and with malice aforethought appropriate without authorization a valuable and deadly device known as the long ball or home run, conceived, invented and owned by the New York Base Ball Company, and that this said device was brutally used to destroy its rightful owners.*
*...*

*First, it is said that in a raid of unusual ferocity, at a time when the representatives of New York Association were [frolicking] peaceably on the green, a Pirate identified as one William Virdon felled a visitor from New York named Anthony Kubek striking him unconscious with a fast-moving projectile. ...*

*Second, it is charged that shortly thereafter, and while the visitors were thus incapacitated, another Pirate, by the name Smith, a refugee from Kansas City, overwhelmed the visitors with a murderous blow that shook the entire metropolis of New York.*

*Finally, it is asserted that, having revived the visitors momentarily and encouraged them to believe that they might get off with their lives, a bull-mouthed ruffian named William (Big Bad Bill) Mazeroski suddenly appeared out of a hole in the ground with a large wooden club over his shoulder and wiped out the New York aggregation with a single blow.*

*These are serious and felonious acts, Mr. Danny Murtaugh, and cannot be taken lightly. This nation has a long opposition to piracy. In 1815 and 1816 the United States was forced to wipe out the Barbary pirates. Shortly thereafter, it took action against the pirates operating along the Cuban coast (they seem to have come back lately).*

*We have not labored thus for hundreds of years to defend ourselves against Sir Francis Drake, Sir John Hawkins, John Cavendish and Captain Kidd in order to tolerate Flatfoot Skinner, Rocky Nelson and Captain Groat.*

*Is it true that after your fateful raids you and your men repaired to in the clubhouse in the dungeon of a place called Forbes Field in Pittsburgh and there reveled in the melancholy plight of your victims? That you laughed and scorned the mighty? ...*

*Is this true, Danny Murtaugh? Did you sing ... while the Yankees mourned? If so, you are forgiven, for it was the best darn ball game since Abner Doubleday pirated rounders from the English.*

In the weeks following the hubbub of the World Series, quieter times found Danny and Kate sitting at home alone together in the living room of their modest house on Kelly Avenue in Woodlyn, Pennsylvania. Kate was sitting in her favorite chair doing some knitting while Danny sat in his familiar location reading a sports page account of himself in the local newspaper.

"Kate," Danny asked his wife. "How many really great managers do you think there are in baseball?"

Kate, not looking at Danny, paused a beat before answering: "I think there's one less than you do."

And thus, even at home – perhaps especially at home – Danny was never anything more than the local boy from Chester.

# CHAPTER EIGHT

# Rough Sailing for the Pirate Ship (1961)

January 19, 1961. A blizzard couldn't keep Danny's fans away. As a snowstorm dumped a foot of snow on Chester, four hundred of Danny's closest friends and admirers gathered for a testimonial dinner. While fierce winds blew the snow into three and four foot drifts, TV and radio announcers urged people to avoid driving unless absolutely necessary. To the relief of worried organizers, Danny's supporters deemed the event necessary and braved the snowstorm to get there.

And what a night it was for those who made it. Pirate radio announcer Bob Prince – who was also the team's biggest cheerleader and a good friend of Danny's – was the main speaker for the event. Prince used his trademark humor to delight the crowd, filling his talk with lively anecdotes about Danny and the rest of the Pirates. He turned serious, though, as he reminded the crowd of what Danny had accomplished in 1960.

*Here is a man who took an enigma like third baseman Hoak,
a quiet guy who doesn't speak above a whisper at shortstop, a
phlegmatic second baseman like Mazeroski, a quiet guy in
centerfield like Virdon, a donkey on first base like Stuart, [the
lumbering Skinner] in leftfield, a high-pitched showboat like
Clemente in rightfield, one catcher who only likes to hit,
another catcher who can't hit, and a couple of nervous pitchers
and molded a championship team.*

*And he did it because he possesses that certain something that
all great champions must possess. Murtaugh has the ability
to give it everything he has – and just a trifle more.[1]*

There was one thing Danny didn't have the ability to do – make it
through his own speech that night without getting choked up. The *Chester
Times* provided detailed coverage of the dinner, including Danny's emotional, albeit short, speech:

*"I've had many thrills in my twenty-five years of baseball,
including last fall's World Series," said Danny, "but this tops
them all. The thrill of being honored by people who you were
born and raised with is a thrill which all men dream about
but which rarely happens. All of us think about the Hereafter
and we like to feel that we can leave something behind by
which we can be remembered." Danny's voice became gripped
with emotion as he continued. "I feel what you have done for
me tonight will be remembered long after any material thing
you might have given me. I've been a very lucky man," said
Danny, as his voice broke. "I... I just don't know what to say."[2]*

While none meant quite as much as the Chester testimonial, Danny
was honored at numerous events that off-season. In January alone he
headed to sportswriters banquets in Boston, Chicago, Philadelphia,

# Rough sailing for the pirate ship (1961)

Milwaukee, New York, Harrisburg, and Houston. The Milwaukee event was particularly poignant for Danny, who played for the Milwaukee Brewers in 1947 when they were a minor league team in the Boston Braves' farm system. By 1961 the Brewers were gone and the Boston Braves were now the Milwaukee Braves. The Milwaukee baseball writers still claimed Danny as one of their own, though, and presented him with the newly created Distinguished Alumnus Award. Danny began his remarks by requesting the audience to stand for a half minute of silence. The crowd was solemn until Danny explained: "That was in memory of the Braves' 1960 season."[3]

Danny did not receive adulation everywhere he went. Former Pirate Director of Scouting Murray Cook recalls a story Danny told about spring training in 1961: "At the winter baseball meetings in Miami in 1961 I am the lion of the hour. I am the manager of the champions of the world. My pal, Mickey Vernon, and I go to a night club and I discover that the chanteuse is a gal I went to school with. I invite her to join us and we go through the remember this and remember that bit. Then she turns to me, the toast of the sports world, and says something that really puts me in my place. 'By the way, Danny,' she says very sweetly, 'what line of work are you in now?'"

Danny's last banquet before spring training was the Dapper Dan in Pittsburgh. Danny told the crowd he was tired of being on the go so much but admitted there were perks to it: "I haven't paid for my dinner in ten weeks. That's one of the joys of being invited out so much!"[4] As always, Danny particularly made it a point to attend local events whenever possible to give back to the community that was so supportive of him. Some days he would attend two or three events and, characteristically, he never accepted a dime for his presence.

Danny's players were also enjoying the afterglow of the World Series during that offseason. Bill Mazeroski, whose dramatic ninth inning homer in Game 7 decided the series, and 1960 MVP Dick Groat were in the highest demand and each attended 80-90 dinners during the off-season. Bill Virdon, Bob Skinner, Roberto Clemente, Bob Friend, Vernon Law, and Elroy Face attended so many banquets that sports writers speculated the team would be too fat and happy to repeat in 1961. But they reported to spring training in decent shape and ready to defend their title. When asked about it, Danny quipped, "I'm happy we had so many dinner engagements last winter. Our guys got exercise pushing themselves away from the table that they wouldn't have had otherwise. Take a look around – see there's not a fat stomach. And you can take my word for it, there are no fatheads either."[5]

The Pirates had extra incentive to succeed in 1961. Throughout the winter various Yankee players had made disparaging comments about the Pirates, claiming that the better team did not win the World Series. Don Hoak was the most vocal Pirate to respond to the Yankee charges. One day Danny asked a spring training visitor, "So, do the Yankees still think they won the World Series?" Hoak overheard the question and came out with both guns blazing.

> I understand they've been crying all winter that the better team lost the Series. Well you can tell them for me they're not only the worst World Series team I ever saw, but the poorest sports. They're cry babies. We played some of our worst ball all year, but we won. We'd have won it in four straight if it weren't for injuries.
>
> Vern Law pitched with a bad foot, Bob Skinner missed most of the Series because of a thumb injury, and Dick Groat played with a sore wrist. Sure they took a couple by lop-sided scores, but we won all the tough games with the pressure on. If they win the AL pennant again this year, we'll beat 'em again. I

# ROUgb Sailing foR the piRate sbip (1961)

*don't know about them, but we'll win again. You can bank on*
*that.*[6]

At a banquet before spring training began, Dick Groat and Danny, along with Yankee outfielder and American League MVP Roger Maris, were being honored by baseball writers in Boston. Maris was the first to speak, and he belittled the Pirates 1960 World Series win. Groat followed him at the podium and, after thanking the writers for the honor, decided to answer Maris right there. Groat told the crowd that some teams may have had more ability than the Pirates in 1960, but none had more desire to win. He also pointed out that the team wasn't playing at the top of their game in the World Series because of several injuries. After the dinner Groat told Danny he was surprised that fiery Irishman had not responded to Maris. The manager assured his shortstop that if Groat had not fired back, then Danny would have taken care of it.[7]

Sick of all the snide comments, the Pirates were raring to go when spring training opened. Danny was pleased with what he saw, particularly from his hitters. The team was perceived to be weak in terms of power hitters, but Clemente, Mazeroski, and Dick Stuart were all hitting well in spring training. The Pirates won their first four games in the Grapefruit League, which added to the confidence felt by the team. The sweetest victory, though, came on March 31 when the Bucs beat the Yankees 4-2. It was just a spring training game, they knew, but it was a good answer to the Yankees' disparaging comments.

The 1960 World Championship team was largely unchanged as the 1961 season opened. One addition that Danny was very excited about was Bobby Shantz, a left-handed pitcher who was acquired in a trade with the Washington Senators. Many observers believed Pittsburgh got a substantially better deal in the trade – with some speculating that Danny's friendship with Mickey Vernon, the Senators' new manager, gave him a negotiating edge. Danny maintained that the trade benefited both clubs since they both had very different needs in terms of players.

The headline of an April 8 Associated Press story noted, "Pirate Mound Staff has Rugged Spring." The article continued, "Just when they should be getting a sharp edge, pitchers of the World Champion Pittsburgh Pirates are being bombed. Only Bob Friend has been consistently in command, and Manager Danny Murtaugh already has tapped the big righthander as his opening day pitcher against San Francisco Tuesday. But the way the other frontliners on the staff have been belted of late is enough to make Murtaugh swallow his chaw."

The Pirates opened their season on April 11 in San Francisco. The game was almost as dramatic as Game 7 of the 1960 World Series. With two out in the ninth inning, Bill Virdon hit a three run homer and propelled the Bucs to an 8-7 victory – a gutsy kick-off to what would become a tough follow-up season. Two days later, Danny left the game in the first inning due to the flu and coach Bill Burwell took over at the helm. The Pirates suffered a 6-5 loss in twelve hard-fought innings.

Two weeks into the season, the race was about as tight as it could be. The Pirates were in a three-way tie for second place and just one game behind the leader. The seventh place team was only two games out of first. As May began the Pirates were in first place by a half a game, but it would be their last time all season to hold that lofty perch. As the team struggled through May, Danny noted, "We haven't been bunching our hits as a unit. When we do, we'll start to win games. Our pitching has been pretty good and our relievers have done an exceptional job. It's not their fault that we haven't been winning."[8]

By the end of May, the Pirates had dropped to fourth place. After losing both games of a Memorial Day doubleheader in Chicago, Joe Brown expressed his continued faith in the team, "I feel very confident and positive. It's just a question of getting out of a rut. The team just hasn't been playing ball. All we've got to do is to win a few games and get some momentum. Right now the team has momentum in reverse." Danny agreed as he acknowledged the Pirates' sloppy fielding, "Players and teams go into slumps in the field just as they do at bat. They'll just have to fight their way out of it, that's all."[9]

It certainly didn't help that four Pirate fielders were injured at the time. In one game Danny was forced to use first baseman Dick Stuart and utility infielder Dick Schofield in the outfield due to injuries. Stuart – a first-rate power hitter – had earned the nickname "Dr. Strangeglove" for his error-prone fielding. Danny treated Stuart's fielding woes with his trademark humor. One night Danny heard the Forbes Field announcer give his usual pre-game warning, "Anyone who interferes with the ball in play will be ejected from the ball park." Turning to one of his coaches, Danny quipped, "I hope Stuart doesn't think he means him."

Entering June, the Pirates were still in fourth place, but they were just three games out of first. Danny hadn't given up on his team, and he still expected a six-team pennant race in the National League. He didn't anticipate much competition from the Phillies or Cubs because, he noted, they were in rebuilding years. Danny predicted that once Vernon Law was up to snuff "we'll make our presence known."[10] The right-handed pitcher, who recorded twenty wins in 1960, tore the rotator muscle in his shoulder and was not in the regular rotation throughout the spring. As of June 21, 1961, Law had three wins and four losses – compared with ten wins and two losses at the same point in 1960. In July Law was put on the disabled list for the rest of the season.

The All-Star break in July came as a welcome relief to the beleaguered Pirates. As the manager of the 1960 National League pennant winner, Danny managed the National League All Star team in 1961. Casey Stengel, manager of the 1960 AL pennant winning Yankees, had been released after the 1960 World Series. Baltimore manager Paul Richard was chosen to lead the American League All Star team in his place. There were two All Star games scheduled: July 11 and July 31.

Back then the players voted for the All Stars (other than pitcher), and the top vote getters at each position were the starters. The manager chose the pitchers and the alternate position players. It was customary for the managers to pick the first runner up at each position as the alternate. Danny followed this custom in choosing four infielders, four outfielders, and a catcher. Danny also named his starting pitcher and first two relievers, including ace Pirate reliever Elroy Face.

Richards stirred up quite a bit of controversy by not following these traditions with the American League team: "I'm going to keep my starters in the game as long as I can and make changes only when it means winning the game. Heck, if we're not out to win, then we should discontinue the All Star game. ... All I'm interested in is winning. That's why I didn't stick to the custom of selecting the runners-up in the player voting. I picked the men who would give me a balanced squad. I know All Star managers in the past observed the theory of playing every available man. This theory may be in vogue again next year, but not while I'm managing. Players will only get in if they can help us win."[11]

Danny took a different approach: "Naturally, our prime objective is to win. But I believe we owe it to the people to use as many All Star players as possible. I appreciate Richards' thinking, but he has different ideas on the subject. I believe the National League has boys with recognized ability and regardless of how they came out in the voting, we won't weaken the team no matter who we play."[12]

When the National League won the game 5-4 in the tenth inning, Danny's decision was vindicated. Roberto Clemente drove in the NL's winning run and later said, "When I got that big hit in the tenth inning, I felt better than good. What made me feel best of all is that manager Danny Murtaugh let me play the whole game. He paid me quite a complement, and I didn't let him down, no?"[13]

Three weeks later, the second All Star game was tied 1-1 when it was rained out in the ninth inning, but Danny had made it through with no defeats. Unfortunately, he did not have similar success with his own team. The Pirates' record between the two All Star games was an abysmal 3-13. Talking with *Pittsburgh Post Gazette* Sports Editor Al Abrams, Danny admitted he was disappointed in the World Champions' near total collapse that season:

> *My pitching is the big reason. Good pitching would have won us a lot of games we gave away. The loss of Vernon Law was the big blow. It threw both my rotation and spot pitching plans all out of whack. The fact that a couple of others aren't pitching up to potential didn't help either. We have a few players who are having bad years in the field and at bat. But we had some who didn't play up to their potential in 1960 and we won the pennant and World Series, didn't we?*[14]

The Pirates never managed to get any upward momentum throughout the season. Their longest winning streak was just four games, and it occurred in April. However, they had three five-game losing streaks and one four-game losing streak. Danny's fans – both in Pittsburgh and in Chester – were pretty fickle to the man who was a hero the year before. In 1961, when the Pirates came to Philadelphia, there was no bus caravan from Chester to witness the game. His close friends and family, of course, were there to show their support. But it was a big change from the previous year.

In Pittsburgh things were even worse for him. Les Biederman of the *Pittsburgh Press* wrote an article in *The Sporting News* detailing the disgraceful treatment Danny was receiving from fans. Danny's son Tim remembers it was a very difficult time:

> *The fans were giving everybody a hard time – not just my dad, but the players, too. It was sad, because they were pretty much the same players, the same coaches, and, of course, the same manager as the year before. My dad felt bad for the players – the effort was there and everyone was working hard, they just couldn't get it going. He felt bad for my mother and us kids, too, because we had to listen to it when we went to the games.*
>
> *He didn't mind it so much for himself. He'd been around a while and he knew how to take it. He preferred the razzing to be on himself than on the players. In one game one of his pitchers was getting hit around pretty good and the fans were booing like crazy. It was a young pitcher, and my dad was trying to let him pitch through his troubles to get his confidence up. He went out to the mound once for a pep talk – with the crowd hissing and jeering him.*
>
> *The pitcher continued to have trouble, so my dad went out to the mound again. He was trying to get him through the inning so he could take him out later for a pinch hitter. He got out there, looked at the young pitcher and said, "Don't feel too bad. They're not booing you – they're booing me for not taking you out sooner."*

The sportswriters at the *Delaware County (PA) Daily Times* (formerly the *Chester Times*) stuck up for the hometown boy. Sports editor Ed Gephart and writer Matt Zabitka took turns pointing out to their readers that it wasn't Danny's fault the Pirates' ship was sinking. In addition to having Vernon Law on the disabled list, Gephart noted that 1960 MVP and batting champ Dick Groat's average had fallen to .266 as of early

# Rough sailing for the pirate ship (1961)

August and the Pittsburgh defense had collapsed. Zibitka agreed, and added Bob Skinner to the list of Pirate woes, citing his 1960 stats of 15 homers and 86 RBIs compared to two home runs and 12 RBIs in 1961:

> Perhaps it was complacency, or maybe it was too much off-season celebrating. Or it could have been just a natural let-down after a most fabulous year when everyone clicked at the same time. Whatever the reason, the fact remains that it wasn't Murtaugh who dumped the Pirates into sixth place. It was the players themselves who fizzled. After all, a manager can't hit, field, or run for his charges.[15]

By the time the Pirates made it to Philadelphia on August 7, the team was in sixth place out of eight teams, where they would remain for the rest of the season. When October finally arrived, the Bucs had won only 75 games and lost 79. They were 18 games behind the first place Cincinnati Reds.

There was a bright – if bittersweet – spot for the Murtaugh family that fall. Tim was headed to the College of the Holy Cross in Wooster, MA. Back in his Charleston days, when money was tight, Danny often told people that he hoped Tim would one day earn a college scholarship through his baseball abilities. Danny's wish came true, and Tim was offered nearly a full ride through baseball and academic scholarships. By 1961, though, Danny's financial situation was much improved. He wrote a note to the college president saying he felt fortunate that he could afford Tim's tuition and asked that the scholarship go to someone who could not afford it.

With baseball season over and Tim off to college, Danny settled into his offseason routine of winter meetings, banquets, and family time. It was widely expected that the Pirates would make some significant changes during the offseason that year. Joe Brown had other ideas, as *Pittsburgh*

*Press* sportswriter Les Biederman reported in a special to the *Delaware County Daily Times* on December 28, 1961. The article's headline summed it up well: "Brown Won't Push Panic Button: Pirates Will Stand Pat for '62." Apparently Brown still believed in the '60 team:

> *I don't like to make trades just for the sake of changing faces. I could have made a dozen deals. There's a great deal of interest in some of our players, but I feel that this is a good team. I feel that the decline of the Pirates last season had something to do with Vern Law's injury. There was a sub-conscious letdown when we lost Law. Yet if some of the players would have taken up the slack, we could have made trouble. I believe we had a better team than Cincinnati.*

Law shared Brown's faith in the team, "If we can come through in 1962 like we did in 1960, we won't need any trades. Some of us had bad years but can bounce back. We did it before." By December Law's arm was feeling good, but he still wasn't allowed to throw a ball until spring training. January brought encouraging news from three doctors who examined Law's shoulder. "The x-rays the doctors took looked encouraging," said Law, "but I still have to throw a baseball. I haven't done any throwing since last summer, and the best way to tell is to get out there and pitch. I certainly have faith in myself."[16]

Danny pauses for a lunch break while working at Sun Ship in Chester during the offseason in February 1943.

Danny and Kate started their new life together on November 29, 1941. This wedding photo shows "Unkie" (Danny's Uncle Tim McCarey), Kate's sister Betty, Danny, Kate, and Kate's dad Frank Clark.

Dannys' first son, Timmy, was born May 5, 1943. Two months later, Danny was drafted into the Army. Kate brought young Timmy to see Daddy play in his last game with the Phillies before he reported for duty.

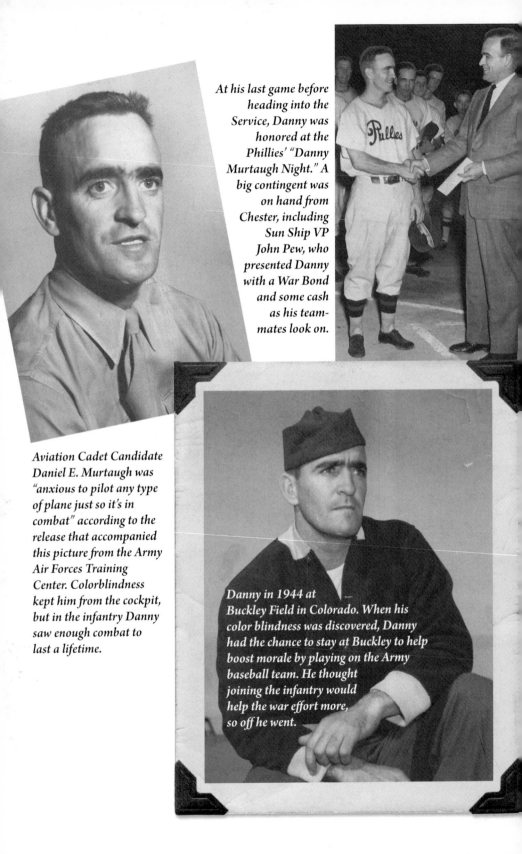

At his last game before heading into the Service, Danny was honored at the Phillies' "Danny Murtaugh Night." A big contingent was on hand from Chester, including Sun Ship VP John Pew, who presented Danny with a War Bond and some cash as his teammates look on.

Aviation Cadet Candidate Daniel E. Murtaugh was "anxious to pilot any type of plane just so it's in combat" according to the release that accompanied this picture from the Army Air Forces Training Center. Colorblindness kept him from the cockpit, but in the infantry Danny saw enough combat to last a lifetime.

Danny in 1944 at Buckley Field in Colorado. When his color blindness was discovered, Danny had the chance to stay at Buckley to help boost morale by playing on the Army baseball team. He thought joining the infantry would help the war effort more, so off he went.

*Danny rounds third while playing for the Army Air Corps team at Buckley Field in Colorado.*

Throughout his career, Danny was known for his daring slides – head first, feet first, whatever it took. "Just kick up a good cloud of dust," he told the neighbor kids. "That way the umpire can't see if you're out." Looks like he took his own advice.

*Danny dives for a catch while playing infield for the Phillies.*

*Danny in action during his Pirate playing days.*

In 1948 the Pirates' combo of Danny at second and Stan Rojek at shortstop led the league in double plays – even beating out the Dodgers' future Hall of Famers Pee Wee Reese and Jackie Robinson.

Danny chats with Pirate legend Honus Wagner in the dugout of Forbes Field

Danny often said he learned many of his managerial techniques from his former Pirate manager Billy Meyer.

Danny got his managerial start in 1952 with the New Orleans Pelicans, a Pittsburgh AA farm team. In three years with the Pels, Danny compiled a .535 winning percentage and took the team from last place to second. It was in New Orleans that Danny and Joe Brown began their long association.

*Real or just a pose? While he was never a strong enough hitter to be in the cleanup position in a game, Kate assured fans that this shot of Danny in the cleanup role at home was real.*

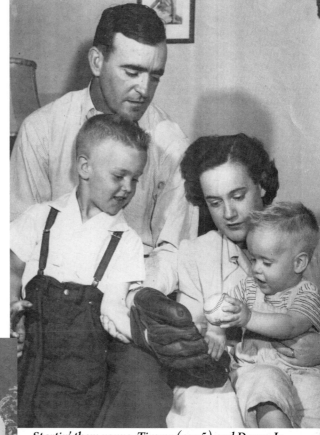

*Startin' them young. Timmy (age 5) and Danny Jr. (age 1) in an early game of "catch" during Danny's first year with the Pirates.*

*Danny, Kate, Timmy (8), Danny Jr. (4), and Kathy (2) in 1951.*

*Just days after Danny became Pirate manager in 1957, his family lined up in the dugout to give him some tips.*

*Danny and Yankee Manager Casey Stengel chat before Game 3 of the 1960 World Series, held in Yankee Stadium on Danny's birthday (October 8). The Buccos were crushed, 10-0.*

*Danny opens his first spring training camp in Ft. Myers, FL in 195*

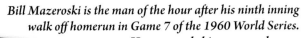

*Bill Mazeroski is the man of the hour after his ninth inning walk off homerun in Game 7 of the 1960 World Series. He sure made his manager happy.*

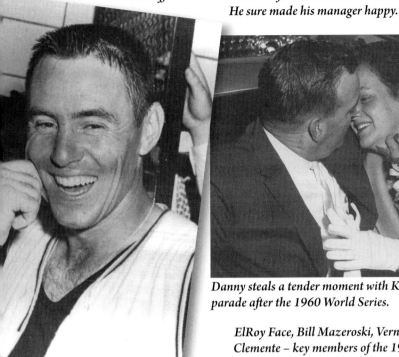

*Danny steals a tender moment with Kate in the victory parade after the 1960 World Series.*

*ElRoy Face, Bill Mazeroski, Vernon Law, Roberto Clemente – key members of the 1960 World Series Championship team.*

Dick Groat and Danny admire the Silver Bat that Groat won as batting champion in 1960.

During the 1960 World Series, Danny met with former Pirate Manager Bill McKechnie at Forbes Field. The 1960 victory was the first World Series title for the Pirates since McKechnie's 1925 team took the crown.

Comedian Joe E. Brown, father of Pirate GM Joe Brown, brought some laughs to Forbes Field when he visited in July 1961. When Danny was young, he used to save his coins to watch Joe E. Brown shows at the local theater, so it was quite a thrill to meet him as Pirate manager.

Danny first met Joe L. Brown in New Orlean in 1952. The two became as close as brothers throughout their long association. It was larg loyalty to Brown that would bring Danny ba to the Pirate dugout time after time.

*Danny celebrates the 1960 World Series Championship with catcher Hal Smith. In the bottom of the eighth, Smith's three-run homer gave the Pirates a 9-7 lead over the Yankees heading into the final frame of Game 7. The Yankees came back to tie the game at 9 apiece, leading to Maz's dramatic finale.*

*Danny and Mickey Vernon met when they were 13 year olds playing American Legion baseball. They remained close friends for the rest of their lives. Danny asked Mickey to be a coach for the 1960 Pirates. In the last month of the season, Danny activated Mickey as a player and had him pinch hit a few times, giving Mickey the rare achievement of playing in the majors in four separate decades.*

*With the Phillies in early 1940s.*

# "Some things never change."

*Pirate manager in early 1960s.*

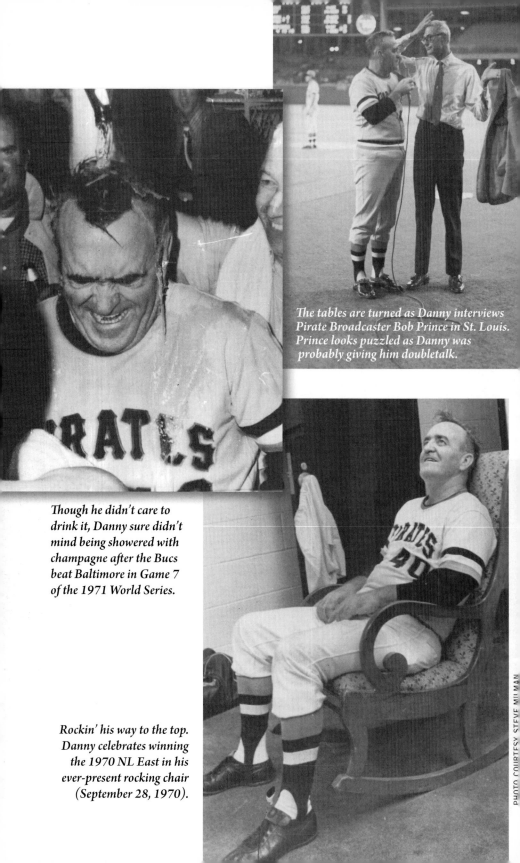

The tables are turned as Danny interviews Pirate Broadcaster Bob Prince in St. Louis. Prince looks puzzled as Danny was probably giving him doubletalk.

Though he didn't care to drink it, Danny sure didn't mind being showered with champagne after the Bucs beat Baltimore in Game 7 of the 1971 World Series.

Rockin' his way to the top. Danny celebrates winning the 1970 NL East in his ever-present rocking chair (September 28, 1970).

PHOTO COURTESY STEVE MILMAN

*The Lumber Company powered the Pirates to NL East Championships throughout the 1970s. Pictured here (L-R): Manny Sanguillen, Rennie Stennett, Richie Hebner, Al Oliver, Richie Zisk, Willie Stargell, and Dave Parker.*

*Danny and then-coach Bill Virdon share a laugh in the dugout.*

Danny's success never changed him, as evidenced by this modest house in Woodlyn, PA, that he bought in 1957. He lived there the rest of his life despite winning two World Series titles and having numerous offers for more lucrative positions.

Danny doted on his only daughter, Kathy. When she got older, Kathy was a tour guide at Three Rivers Stadium. If she and Danny arrived at the stadium together, the guards often recognized her and not him. She'd say, "It's okay, he's with me," to get Danny past security.

Like father, like son. Danny's son Tim followed in his footsteps for many years. In 1976 Tim was managing the Charleston Charlies (a Pirates' farm team). Looks like he's trying to teach his dad a thing or two.

Danny loved being a grandfather and was thrilled to give Timmy a tour of Three Rivers Stadium when he came to Pittsburgh.

*When the Pirate caravan rolled
through western PA in 1975,
Danny got a special treat:
a visit from his grandchildren.
Joey (3) and Colleen (1)
lived near Meadville, PA,
and met the caravan there.*

*Danny strategizes with grandson
Timmy before the Buccos take
the field.*

# the 1960s

After the disappointment of 1961, Danny was once again worried about the state of his pitchers, particularly Vernon Law. Despite the good reports from doctors who examined Law's arm, both Joe Brown and Danny were very cautious. They knew the real test would be when the pitcher tried to deal with the physical reality of major league pitching. The *Delaware County (PA) Daily Times* ran a column written by Danny on February 15 in which the Pirate manager discussed Law's impact on the team:

> *Vernon Law is the key to our pennant hopes. Our chief weakness last year was not having a capable replacement for him. Naturally, when you lose a 20-game winner, it's got to hurt.*
>
> *If Law's arm is sound again, we'll be right up there with the contenders. We have so many strong clubs in the National League that it is impossible to select the one which should be favored. I've always considered the defending champion the team to beat, so Cincinnati will be the target.*

*The rest of our pitching staff shapes up pretty well. Bob Friend is a mainstay. So is Elroy Face in the bullpen. Joe Gibbon should be a star pitcher and Al McBean showed me a fine arm last summer. Tom Sturdivant knows how to pitch and I figure he'll be a big help.*

*Our strong points are up the middle. In Bill Mazeroski and Dick Groat we still have one of the best double play combinations in the league. We have one of the best defensive center fielders in Bill Virdon. There is also the batting champion Roberto Clemente in right field, Dick Stuart at first base and Don Hoak at third. We don't expect Bob Skinner, our left fielder, to have two bad years in a row. The same applies to Groat. They were two of our outstanding players when we won the championship two years ago.*

*We're bringing a couple of young catchers to spring training to back up our regular, Smoky Burgess. They are Gary Rushing, the most valuable player in the Sally League in '61, and Elmo Plaskett. I'm planning one major change and that's using Harvey Haddix exclusively as a relief pitcher.*

*Basically, we have the same club as last year. The improvement will have to come from better years for the players we had last season.*

*I don't want to predict where the Pirates will finish, but we have high hopes this year will be a more interesting one for Pittsburgh fans.*

Danny was impressed with the physical shape of his players when they arrived for spring training; he told sports writers it was the best he'd seen since becoming manager in 1957. His own health was not so impressive. On March 18 Danny took advantage of two days off to check himself into the Lee County Hospital for a checkup and rest. He claimed to have been suffering with recurring flu ailments since arriving in Florida for spring training. Only his doctor and those closest to him knew it was really heart trouble. However, after a complete check up and some rest, he was deemed healthy enough to be back in the dugout for the rest of the pre-season action.

Opening Day was on April 10 when the Pirates hosted the Phillies at Forbes Field. Bob Friend, who won 18 games in 1960 but lost 19 games in 1961, was the starting pitcher. The game began with the same lineup that won the 1960 World Series, which was also the same lineup that fell to 6th in 1961. The Bucs won the game 6-0 and went on to win the next nine games to kick off the season with a mark of 10-0. This was even more impressive considering that Vernon Law was still not pitching because his shoulder continued to bother him. There was some good news on the pitching front, though, with Bob Friend winning four of five decisions in April.

After their ten-game winning streak, the Pirates lost four of their next five and by May 2 had dropped to third place. From April 24 to May 5, the Pirates played a dozen games against the San Francisco Giants and the Los Angeles Dodgers. The Bucs' won only four of those twelve games, with a 2-2 record at home and 2-6 away. They had a couple days off, and then they were on the road again. A loss in Milwaukee on May 9 put Pittsburgh in fourth place. By this point Vernon Law had only pitched one inning all season. For the next month, they bounced back and forth between fourth and fifth place. *Pittsburgh Post Gazette* Sports Editor Al Abrams focused on the Pirates' trouble in his Sidelights on Sports column on May 16:

> *"If you can't hit," Danny Murtaugh growled into the telephone, "I don't want to talk to you!" This was before last night's game with Milwaukee. The reporter was taken aback*

*by the greeting. But not for long. "You mustn't be talking to anybody on your club then," he shot back. "Ain't it awful?" Murtaugh sighed. "Up until Sunday's game with the Reds we weren't getting much hitting at all. I know these guys can hit. They'll snap out of it. And, I hope very soon."*

*Without making it sound like an alibi, Murtaugh went on to say that Roberto Clemente hasn't hit up to average since "his bout with the flu;" Billy Virdon has been hobbled by injuries; Dick Stuart hasn't "hit at all." Murtaugh pointed out the Pirates' desperate need for Stuart's powerful bat. "We need his hitting," he said, worry tingeing every word. Just as quickly he brightened to add: "Stuart will shake out of it. He's too good a hitter to be kept in check this long. So are the other guys. Once they get hot again we'll win a few games."*

*Meanwhile, Danny is worried. A manager would have to be nuts or will be that way in due time if he doesn't worry while watching his team throw away one game after another.*

*Murtaugh could have further alibied the loss of Joe Gibbon, a potential 20-game winner, Don Hoak being out of the lineup with injuries, and Vernon Law's status as a regular up in the air. All he would say was this: "I don't think any club can lose pitchers of the caliber of Law and Gibbon as we have these past two seasons and not feel the effect."*

By mid-June the Battlin' Bucs had climbed back into third place. Coming out of the All Star break on July 12, Pittsburgh was only 4½ games out of the lead. Rival managers had begun talking about the Pirates as a threat. On July 19, after winning 22 of their last 27 games, the Pirates were still in third place, but they were only 2½ games behind the leader. A headline in the *St. Petersburg (FL) Evening Independent* on July 20 read "Starting to look like '60 Again" with the Pirates on their way up and the Yankees leading the AL. As fate would have it, that same day the Pirates started a thirteen-game road trip that kicked off in San Francisco and included time in Los Angeles and Cincinnati. By the time they limped back home, the Pirates had won only three of the thirteen games, leaving them in fourth place and eleven games out.

As for Vernon Law, the injured Pirate ace had one outing in spring training when he pitched three innings and allowed three hits and two runs. While Danny was pleased with the outing initially, Law reported a twinge in his arm afterwards and sat out the rest of spring training. Law returned to the rotation in May, and he finished the season with ten wins and seven losses. However, his shoulder continued to bother him, and he was unable to pitch a complete game. In the *Delaware County (PA) Daily Times* on August 23, Danny praised Law's efforts:

> Law has been pitching on nothing much more than courage. The Deacon doesn't throw a single ball without it hurting and his arm starts acting up after six or seven innings. That leaves us without the real stopper the Deacon was in 1960, when he opened so many series, practically all important ones, including the World Series. Because I couldn't be sure of Law this season, I banked heavily on Joe Gibbon, the big left-hander, to take his place. You can imagine how I felt when Gibbon pulled up with a sore elbow in the spring. Later Joe injured a finger sliding in a game against the Mets. We have had him for no more than four or five starts and then he hasn't been right.

The Pirates stayed in fourth for the rest of the season and finished 7½ games behind the leader. As the season drew to a close, the September 6 edition of the *St. Petersburg (FL) Evening Independent* ran an article titled "Family Reaction":

*How does the family of a baseball manager react to victory and defeat? "Our children never say a word to their father when the Pittsburgh Pirates lose a game," says Mrs. Kathleen Murtaugh. "It was more noticeable when they were young," adds Danny Murtaugh. "When my team won, they'd greet me at the door and climb all over me. When we lost, they weren't anywhere to be seen."*

The offseason after 1962 was markedly different than the previous year. In the space of ten days in November, Joe Brown traded three-fourths of the 1960 World Series winning infield: Dick Stuart, Dick Groat, and Don Hoak. Only second baseman Bill Mazeroski was left. Asked if the trades would produce a pennant contender, Joe Brown replied, "We finished eight games out of first place last season, and we think we have made noticeable improvement [with these trades]. Are we a pennant threat again? Draw your own conclusion."[1]

In January 1963 Vernon Law was still having problems with his shoulder. When Joe Brown sent him his '63 contract, Law called and gave the Pirates a chance out of it because of his problems. Brown assured the hurler that the Pirates still wanted him. Nonetheless, when Danny would discuss pitching staff, he always put Law in the questionable category because of his arm troubles. Pitcher Joe Gibbon was also considered uncertain.

With former team captain Dick Groat now playing for the Phillies, Danny named Bill Mazeroski as the new team captain. Entering the final two weeks of spring training, the Pirates' lineup was still considered unsettled. As of March 27, Danny had only nine more exhibition games in which to firm up his starting lineup for the Pirates' April 8 season opener with Cincinnati. Up to that point, what was expected to be the regular lineup still had not played together as a unit because of injuries that sidelined various players. Roberto Clemente, Bill Virdon, Bill Mazeroski, Bob

Skinner, and Bob Bailey all missed quite a bit of spring training action due to injuries. The bullpen had not been selected yet, and there were still four men in the running for two back up positions in the outfield.

*Delaware County Daily Times* sports writer Rich Westcott previewed the 1963 season in his April 8 Sports Scope column, "Trades hurt Pittsburgh. With apologies to Danny Murtaugh, the Pirates don't seem to have it this year." The Pirates managed to stay competitive for the first month of the season. On May 6 they were tied for first with a 14-8 record. It quickly went downhill from there, though.

The Pirates were admittedly trying to instill some youth in the team in 1963. In the *Post Gazette* in late May, Joe Brown told sports writer Jack Hernon of his recent unsuccessful attempts to get a big hitter for the team – only older players were available. "The program we started on this year is to get a young club together again. We would be defeating our purpose in this direction if we traded for older players," noted Brown.

On August 7, the Pirates sat in eighth place with only the New York Mets and the Houston Colts behind them. *Pittsburgh Post Gazette* sports editor Al Abrams "put Joe Brown on the witness stand" to quiz him about the Pirates. Abrams asked point blank if Murtaugh was to blame for the Pirates' poor showing. Brown dismissed the idea:

> *Danny Murtaugh is one of the best managers in baseball. He proved it while we were riding high. He's just as good a manager now as he was then. The thing I like best about Danny is he doesn't panic. He plays his best players regardless.*
>
> *As to injuries, I've never made it a point to alibi the loss of key players. ... [But] aside from catchers and pitchers, Murtaugh hasn't been able to use his regulars 34% of the time because of the hospital list. ...*
>
> *... Our fielding has been disappointing at times and our*

*hitting miserable in the clutch. We've lost more games because
of our failure to hit with men on than for any other reason.*

The pitching staff performed well in 1963, compiling an overall 3.10
ERA for the season. The Pirates' were fourth in the NL for number of hits
and fifth for combined batting average, but only the Mets and Colts ranked
below them in runs scored. These statistics seem to back up Brown's explanation for the team's failure to compete – it's not enough to get on base,
the team needs to score runs. The Pirates' opponents outscored them 595-
567 for the season.

Don Cardwell, the right-handed pitcher the Pirates acquired in
exchange for Dick Stuart, lost six of his first seven decisions in 1963.
Danny had his pitching coaches work with Cardwell to increase the type
and speed of pitches in his repertoire. Cardwell responded well to his
coaches, and posted a 12-9 record for the remainder of the season. Unfortunately, it wasn't enough. Bob Friend's 17-16 record made him the only
starting pitcher to have more wins than losses in 1963. One of the bright
spots for the 1963 Pirates was reliever Al McBean, who finished the year
with a 13-3 record.

In the spring, when Danny was asked where his Pirates would finish
the 1963 season, he replied, "In San Francisco, on September 29." He certainly never expected his team to be in eighth place by the time they got
there. Despite the disappointing finish, no one was surprised when Joe
Brown announced that Danny would be back the following year.

However, Danny was still plagued by health issues. An Oregon
newspaper, *The Bulletin,* reported on April 24, 1964, that Danny "privately
has confided that this is his last time around" – although no one else seems
to have picked up on the comment. The injuries his team suffered surely
did little to help ease Danny's troubled heart. In his June 10 Roamin'
Around column, the *Post Gazette's* Jack Hernon recounted a key issue that
Danny faced:

*These days Danny Murtaugh is never sure how many pitchers will be available for work until he has a roll call before a game. The Pirates are going through a year like that. It all started with Don Cardwell back in the spring at Ft. Myers. The injuries among staff members made it rough going in the early part of the season. And the hurlers are having the same woes again. … Pitching was to be the big thing for the Bucs this season. Potentially it was there. Injuries and some ineffective work, where it should have been otherwise, have ruined what the brass thought was a top-flight staff.*

In 1964 the team continued to struggle, bouncing between third, fourth, and fifth place most of the season. The Bucs were still in pennant contention in the middle of August until they plunged to sixth place by losing ten out eleven games in one stretch. The season ended with a road trip to Cincinnati and Milwaukee, during which the Pirates got to play the spoiler by beating the Reds and knocking them into second place.

After the second Cincinnati game Danny shocked his players and fans by announcing that he was retiring at the end of the season due to health concerns. Throughout the season he frequently suffered from what he called the flu or stomach trouble. The truth about his ailments – including a likely heart attack – was a well-guarded secret. Like most people, *Pittsburgh Post Gazette* sports writer Al Abrams was surprised by the announcement. But in retrospect, he acknowledged, "We should have known":

*When a major league manager resigns his position as Danny Murtaugh did without warning Wednesday morning, the usual wild rumors and conjectures are sure to follow. Most of the initial reaction to the surprise move centered on the question: "Was Murtaugh asked to quit?" The answer is no. Danny is leaving his field duties because of ill health.*

161

*Only his family and close friends know the Buc manager has been bothered by a heart condition for a little more than two years. While doctors do not consider it serious, Murtaugh wisely made the decision that health and family came first. It was not until last Sunday that Danny, after due deliberation and talking the matter over with his wife, Kate, and Joe L. Brown thought it best to chuck the tension-ridden duties of a manager for a front office post the Pirates will give him. Murtaugh's move came as a complete surprise. Only a month ago Brown indicated that Danny would return as manager in 1965. ...*

*Last July, I visited with Danny in the Forbes Field clubhouse following an illness which kept him at home a couple of days. He looked peaked and tired. "It's acting up a little," he said, pointing to his heart. "Nothing serious," he added, quickly. Naturally, nothing was mentioned in print. All his newspaper, TV and radio friends have the utmost respect for Murtaugh and maintained his confidence because he leveled with them.[2]*

As Abrams indicated, Danny was not leaving the Pirate organization altogether. He remained on as a scout and advisor to Joe Brown, who in a 2009 interview described Danny's position:

*In essence, he was the assistant to a man who he knew a lot more than ...*

*Danny became my right-hand man in discussing trades and discussing the team. He'd go out in the minor leagues and talk to our managers. And of course they knew him well. They knew the depth of his knowledge of baseball, and they would pay more attention to him than they would to me – even though he couldn't fire them and I could. They recognized and appreciated his knowledge, so he could talk to managers, talk to players, and come back with reports on various players.*

*He would go out during spring training and spend a lot of time in the minor league camps. Of course he'd go to the major league camps, too. But he would go to the minor league camps and work with them a lot. He was a great instructor. Particularly of infield play. He always said, "See, I'll tell you how much I know. I made Mazeroski what he is today."*

Danny worked from home in his new position, traveling as needed. The family enjoyed the extra time they got to spend with him. Danny appreciated that when he traveled he now stayed in one spot for a longer period of time, so Kate often went with him. This worked out nicely for Kate, because Danny Jr. had joined Tim at Holy Cross in Massachusetts that fall. Having her husband around more made up for the loneliness of her boys leaving. Kathy was a junior in high school and stayed next door at Peggy's house when Kate was gone.

Danny enjoyed his time as a scout, a job he called "the golf tour of baseball." *Pittsburgh Press* sports editor Les Biederman wrote a column on March 10, 1967, with the headline "Danny Enjoys Life Outside Limelight." Biederman said that two years after his retirement, Danny did not miss managing. The columnist noted that Danny had never sought the limelight. In 1960, when the press clamored for interviews, Danny directed them to the players instead so they could earn some extra money. According to Biederman, "He [also] turned down a regular radio show and a weekly TV program, because he felt managers should be in the background." Regarding his baseball career Danny said:

*This is what I like and any man doing what he likes is wealthy. Baseball has been good to me and my family. I saved my money and never spent it foolishly. I hope baseball is half as good to my son, Tim, as it was to me.*

Tim shared his dad's hopes, having signed with the Pirates in 1965. While Danny was talking to Biederman that March, Tim was in spring training preparing for the 1967 season with the Pirates' high A farm team in Raleigh, NC. The Pirates, meanwhile, were preparing for a season in which they were widely expected to be pennant contenders. They had finished in third place the year before, just three games out of first. The team was plagued with problems, though, and just couldn't get it together. They spent part of May in second place but went downhill after that.

There was speculation that manager Harry Walker wouldn't be around much longer, but Joe Brown spoke up for Walker in early July and said he didn't blame the manager for the team's poor performance. Just a few weeks later, on July 17, Brown called an unscheduled press conference to announce that Walker had been fired and Danny was "reluctantly" coming back to finish out the '67 season.

According to local sportswriter Chet Smith, Walker was replaced because he "unsettled" the Pirates. Smith said the team had been bothered by "one irritation after another" through the season. Other reports cited dissension and unrest within the club and said Walker's frequent pre-and post-game team meetings had become a joke around the league. Smith likened Danny to a tranquilizer brought in to calm the frazzled nerves in the dugout.[3]

Unfortunately, Danny's presence wasn't enough to turn the hapless team around. Danny inherited a sixth place team playing .500 ball; by season's end, they were still in sixth place and had an 81-81 record. Danny later acknowledged that he wasn't mentally prepared to manage a team at the time and said he was more of a cheerleader than a manager.

In case anyone doubted Danny's determination to step back down from the managerial post, the Pirates announced before the season ended that he was being named Director of Player Acquisition and Development.

In this role, Danny would supervise the Pirates' farm system and scouting organization. In mid-October, the Pirates announced that Larry Shepard would take over as the Pirate skipper.

In 1968, the Pirates were again expected to be a pennant contender, and once again they were floundering. By late July the Bucs were in eighth place as they headed to Atlanta on a short three-game road trip. There were rumors aplenty that Shepard would be replaced.

As luck would have it, Danny was scouting near Atlanta and had an open day on one of the Bucs' game days. He decided to take advantage of the chance to see his old team in action. When he got to Atlanta, it occurred to Danny that the manager always had a two-room suite. He realized he could save the Pirates some money if he crashed with Shepard instead of getting his own room. After all, he was only going to be there one night.

Always the prankster, Danny decided to have a little fun with his successor. He found out Shepard's room number, went up unannounced, and knocked on his door. When Shepard opened the door and saw the man who had replaced two previous Pirate managers mid-season, his jaw dropped. "What are you doing here?" he stammered. "You mean Brown didn't talk to you yet?" Danny asked, looking embarrassed. Then he burst into laughter and Shepard realized he'd been had. The Bucs ended up sweeping that series.

The team continued to struggle, though, and once again finished the year in sixth place. Despite the disappointing season Shepard was rehired a few weeks after Danny's prank. Danny, meanwhile, got back to his scouting and troubleshooting duties. In 1969 Danny happily accepted another duty: grandfather. To his and Kate's delight, Tim and Janet gave them their first grandson on July 10, 1969. It would not be the only big change in Danny's life that year.

The 1969 Pirates got off to a strong start, winning five of their first six games to keep them tied for first place. Their last day to sit at the top of the heap was April 13, and they gradually dropped further and further behind most of the season. By the end of August, the Pirates were bouncing between third and fourth place and they were often at least ten games behind the leader. Shepard began to suspect he might get the ax for real this time.

On Saturday, September 20, Joe Brown and Larry Shepard had dinner in New York after the Pirates beat the Mets. Shepard asked Brown if he was planning to change managers at the end of the season, and the GM would not commit one way or the other. Brown later explained, "[Larry] said if there is going to be a change he'd like to know so he could look elsewhere for a job. I realized that [he] had a good point."[4]

Until that dinner Brown had planned to wait until the end of the season to announce the change in managers. Once Shepard indicated he'd prefer to know sooner rather than later, Brown decided to make the announcement. He arranged a meeting with the soon-to-be-former manager on September 26 to inform him that he was being fired. Shepard told the *Pittsburgh Post Gazette's* Charley Feeney, "I thought I was prepared for it, but I wasn't." Addressing the media later, Shepard said it felt like his stomach dropped out when he heard the news.[5]

Pirate Coach Alex Grammas was assigned the manager's role for the last five games of the season. Brown stressed that he had not yet decided on a manager for 1970. The Pirates finished the 1969 season in third place, twelve games out of first, and with an 88-74 record. Joe Brown had a big decision to make, and he had to make it quickly. Not surprisingly he discussed the situation with his closest advisor:

> *I was trying to make up my mind between three different fellows [for the manager post]. Danny and I were both down in*

*Florida at our training base where we had [an instructional league] going on every fall. I talked to him about the individual candidates. We talked until 11 at night. Then he went to bed. He had a room we called the Murtaugh Suite because it was always held for Danny.*

*About 7 o'clock the next morning there was a rat-a-tat-tat at my door. It was Danny. He came in and said, "What's the matter with me?" I said, "What are you talking about?" He said, "You talked about those three guys last night, what about me?" I said, "Danny, you know you can have the job any time you want. But first you have to have a clearance from your doctor and second you have to have a clearance from Kate."*

*He came back a few minutes later and said, "I already have a clearance from my doctor. I just talked to Kate and she said it's fine." I said, "Okay, you're the manager." That was a memorable time because I wasn't even giving him any consideration.*

Danny and Joe were both a little surprised by the turn of events. They decided they might as well surprise everyone else with the announcement. Joe Brown called a press conference aboard a Gateway Clipper boat on the Allegheny River. He doesn't think a managerial announcement has ever been done like that before or since:

*We knocked them dead. I said, "Here is our manager for 1970." Danny walked up the stairs, and they all turned and looked at him and said, "Okay, here's Danny, but where's the new manager?" They were so used to seeing him in Pittsburgh. I said, "You're looking at him." Everyone was shocked.*

In his December 10, 1969, Roamin' Around column, *Pittsburgh Post Gazette* sportswriter Charley Feeney discussed Danny's "Urge to Return."

He noted that when Danny took over for Harry Walker in 1967 his doctor told him not to get too excited during the game. "It was frustrating," Danny acknowledged. In the early part of 1969, Danny had a more positive report from the doctor: "Danny, you're in good shape. You can do anything you please." After that, Danny said, he began to think about managing again. As Feeney reported:

> Murtaugh said, "… I thought I was kidding myself. I used to say to my wife, Kate, 'Better treat me good, or I'll go back to managing.' She never took me seriously and I didn't take myself too seriously."

> Murtaugh said he had no intention of telling Joe Brown that the urge to manage had returned. "I figured Joe had a man in mind to replace Larry Shepard," Murtaugh said. "I figured Joe would mention who he had in mind and that would be it. I wasn't about to suggest myself. When Joe met me in Florida … I could see he was undecided. It was then that I asked him to consider me."

> When Danny Murtaugh puts on his baseball uniform next spring, he will be a lot different than the Danny Murtaugh who was the interim manager for the last half of the '67 season.

> "You'll see me bounce out of that dugout if I think the umpire has blown a play," Murtaugh said. "The players will find that I'm healthy – and maybe a bit wiser, too."

*Pittsburgh Post Gazette* sports editor Al Abrams visited the Pirates 1970 spring training camp and reported on it in his Sidelights on Sports column on February 25, 1970. Danny told him, "I feel like I'm at my first spring training camp." According to Abrams, "Danny had the boys going all out today – and liking it. This is the secret of a superior boss – having the men putting out and happy to do so."

One of those men happily putting out was Maz. The *Rome (GA) News-Tribune* headline "Bill Mazeroski Makes the Team" would not have been out of place in the 1950s, but it was pretty surprising on April 19, 1970:

> *"I had my doubts whether I'd make it when I went down to spring training this year," [Mazeroski] confesses. The reason he had those doubts has to do with some kind of mysterious muscle tear in his upper thigh which severely affected one of his legs two years ago and the other last year when he sat on the bench for most of the season and it began to look like curtains.*

> *"I don't know how I did it," Mazeroski says about his muscle tear. "All I know is I couldn't go through another year like last year sitting on the bench." … He appeared in only 67 games [in 1969] … and he was considered finished at the ripe old age of 32.*

> *He wasn't quite sure of [being finished], so what he did was go down to the Pirates' training camp at Bradenton, FL, on January 5 and give it one more try. It wasn't the usual one more try. Mazeroski ran four miles each day. That only got him warmed up. Then he'd go out in the Gulf of Mexico and swim for about an hour, lying on a kickboard and kicking both legs to stretch the muscles.*

> *When the rest of the Pittsburgh players reported for spring training, Maz hadn't gotten rid of his doubts. They were still there the second week of March just before the club was due to make a four-day exhibition trip to Mexico City, at which point Manager Danny Murtaugh decided it was a good time for a little talk.*

*"Maz told me he wasn't seeing the ball coming off the bat too well," Murtaugh says. "As an old infielder myself I knew that would be the last thing to come around and I told him that."*

*Mazeroski listened. He accompanied the club to Mexico, and that's where the whole thing turned around for him. "I started moving real good again down there," he says. "I can't actually explain what happened but whatever it was, happened there. It feels good to make it again."*

Danny's boys continued to go all out once the season started. It was a close campaign in the National League Eastern Division, with the reigning World Champion Mets as the team to beat. The Pirates got off to a bit of a slow start, but no team really took charge throughout the season. The first place team never had more than a five and a half game lead all summer. For the bulk of the baseball season there were no more than three or four games separating the top three teams: the Pirates, Mets, and Cubs.

On July 11 the Pirates established themselves in first place, a position they would relinquish for only two days the rest of the season. Less than a week later, on July 16, the Pirates played their first game in the brand new Three Rivers Stadium. The final game at Forbes Field had taken place on June 28, two days before the sixty-first anniversary of the first baseball game played there.

In honor of the new stadium, the Pirates published a Souvenir Book that detailed the team's new state-of-the-art facility: the all-weather, all-purpose Tartan Turf; larger, "unusually comfortable" theater-style seats; the "scoreboard [that] does everything;" the advanced lighting system; and the enhanced eating options. The Souvenir Book also took a look at the Pirates of the day and the past, including a feature on Manager Danny Murtaugh written by *Pittsburgh Post Gazette* sports editor Al Abrams:

*I was glad Murtaugh was back. … There is something about*

*Murtaugh which denotes greatness. For one, baseball people, especially the opposition, hold him in high regard. Number two, and even more important, is his ability to handle men. This is a requisite every leader in any business must possess or he'd better give up. … [Murtaugh] has his own unique way of keeping his players and all those about him happy. He jokes with everyone, yet at the same time he lets all know he is in complete command.*

In late August the Pirates were in California for a nine-game swing through Los Angeles, San Diego, and San Francisco and they lost seven of the nine games, dropping their lead to one game over the Cubs. Former Pirate All Star Al Oliver remembers Danny "was a very low key manager – he didn't do a lot of screaming and hollering and carrying on." He recalls only one exception – that California road trip:

*We played terrible. We had a meeting in San Francisco. He came down on us and said he was going to send us back to the minor leagues if we didn't start playing like Pirates. Here I am, a young player, on my way to a strong career. I said to myself, 'I'm not about ready to go back to the minor leagues. … I wonder if he means guys like Roberto and Stargell?" I really think that if we hadn't started winning, he would have done that. I'll never forget that meeting. After that we took off and we started rolling. We went on to win the division.*

Danny's talk certainly had an impact. After posting a 70-63 record up to that point (.526 winning percentage), the Bucs went 19-10 the rest of the season (.655 winning percentage). The Pirates were plagued with injuries all summer long, testing Danny's managerial skills as he juggled position players and pitchers to deal with each problem that arose. UPI sports writer Joe Carnicelli noted on September 19, 1970, "It seems as if the more the Pittsburgh Pirates hurt, the better they play." Danny agreed,

"That's the story of this team all season. We've been hit hard by injuries but it seems that the player we put in always does better than the man he replaces."

After winning the NL East title, the Pirates were swept 3-0 by the Reds in the National League Championship Series. Heading into the season, though, they weren't even expected to compete for the pennant. When *Pittsburgh Press* sports writer Bill Christine previewed the 1970 season in a column on February 15 he noted, "The oddsmakers have ... listed the Pirates as 12-1 in the National League pennant race. Three teams in their own Eastern Division – the Cardinals, Mets, and Cubs – are given better chances of winning. So are four clubs in the West – the Braves, Giants, Dodgers, and Reds." Those were the odds Danny faced with a healthy club, which he had anything but. The Pirates summed up Danny's accomplishments in 1970 in a press release promoting him as Manager of the Year:

> *If one were to ask baseball people the qualifications of a good manager, most would include (a) handling players, (b) manipulating the pitching staff, (c) being a strategist, and (d) devotion to the job. Danny gets a good report card in every category.*
>
> *The 1970 Pirates were a loose ballclub, thanks to Murtaugh's low-key approach. A bad performance one day never resulted in a benching for the following game. Danny had no "doghouse"; yet he played no favorites. Win or lose, he never lost his sense of humor. When injury after injury crippled his ballclub, especially his pitching staff, Danny utilized his full bench to maximum advantage; and young pitchers saw action in clutch situations. All season long he built the confidence that paid off in September.*

*"I hope he comes back next year," said Pirate star Roberto Clemente. "This has been a happy ballclub."*

*The aforementioned injuries necessitated drastic revisions in what Murtaugh originally considered his starting rotation. With Bob Moose, Steve Blass, and Dock Ellis all sidelined for extensive periods totaling more than 100 days during the course of the season, relievers Bruce Dal Canton and Luke Walker were evicted from the bullpen. The Pirates won four of the six games started by Dal Canton, and Walker went on to become the big winner on the staff with fifteen victories. Up from Columbus came Fred Cambria, John Lamb, Gene Garber, and Dick Colpaert, and acquired in late season deals were George Brunet and Jim "Mudcat" Grant. Each made his contribution to the Eastern Division title.*

*Danny's ability to make the right moves was acknowledged by his peers. Late in the season Buc Coach Bill Virdon explained it this way, "With the pennant race coming down to the wire, I would say that we are in good shape because Danny gives us a bit of an edge over the other managers." In one game at Shea Stadium in the crucial series at seasons' end he used four relief pitchers and received perfect performances from each.*

*As for devotion to his job, Danny set the example in the Pirate clubhouse. The first one in and the last to leave – that was Murtaugh all season long.*

*The 1970 Pirates may not boast of a batting champion, a Cy Young winner, or a home run titlist, but they certainly have a top candidate when it comes to selecting a "Manager of the Year."*

The Pirate Public Relations Department was right. In 1970 Danny won *Sporting News* Manager of the Year, AP Manager of the Year, and the Dapper Dan Award. According to the *Pittsburgh Post Gazette* on November 25, Danny's players cheered his selection as the Dapper Dan winner. Ace relief pitcher Dave Giusti said, "It couldn't happen to a more deserving person. Danny kept us together all year. He made the difference in our winning the division." Thinking back to the 1960 triumph, Giusti could not resist adding, "I just hope Danny's success doesn't run in decades." He would soon find out it didn't.

*It's a happy group surrounding Danny in November 1970 as he announces he'll be back in the dugout in 1971. From left: Joe L. Brown, Willie Stargell, Danny, Richie Hebner, Dave Giusti, Dock Ellis.*

## CHAPTER TEN

# Beat 'em Bucs!

"I hope I'm just as smart in 1971 as everybody thought I was last year. ... I hope I have as good a club out there as [Joe] Brown thinks I'll have. That would make it easier." With his characteristic Irish wit, Danny was a big hit as he accepted the 1970 Dapper Dan Award on February 7, 1971. The crowd of 2,100 hailed Danny for leading his "scrappy" Pirates to the NL East Championship in 1970.[1]

This would be the last chance for Danny to revel in the success his team enjoyed the previous year. Spring training was just around the corner. The Pirates were heading into the season as the team to beat. Winning the NL East in 1970 had only whetted the appetites of Danny and his players. They were hungry for more ... hungry for a World Championship ... ready to end the drought that the Bucs had endured since that magical 1960 season.

The 1971 season got off to a slow start for the Pirates. By the end of

*Tim Murtaugh, oldest grandson of Danny Murtaugh, co-authored this chapter.*

April, their record stood at an unspectacular 12-10. They were tied for third place, just a game and a half out of first. They spent the spring bouncing around between first, second, and third places. Although they weren't where they wanted to be, the Pirates would not panic. Until May 20 that is.

On that day a shockwave hit the entire Pirate family. Prior to a game against Sparky Anderson's feared Reds, Danny was stricken with chest pains and was whisked to Cincinnati's Christ Hospital for tests and observation. Despite Danny's history of heart troubles, the cardiologist could find nothing wrong. He was kept in the hospital as a precaution.

Four days later Danny was transferred to Presbyterian University Hospital in Pittsburgh for further testing. With his future as a baseball manager seriously in doubt, Danny responded to press inquiries only by saying that he felt fine. He would not speculate as to whether he would ever return to uniform. It was later learned that he had confided in friends and family the previous week "these games are tough on my boiler."[2] Meanwhile, hitting coach Bill Virdon continued as interim manager.

After a combined two weeks in the hospitals, Danny was released at the beginning of June. Because of the thoroughness of the tests he underwent, he was advised to take a week off at home to relax. Luke Quay, sports editor of the *McKeesport (PA) Daily News,* talked to Danny while he recuperated at his Mt. Lebanon home: "I took a long walk yesterday and I'm going to take another one today. That's what they suggested I do to strengthen my body. They put me through some pretty tough tests in the hospital and I do feel weak." While the doctors hadn't given him an official report, Danny thought being tired and rundown helped bring on his troubles.

Danny returned to the dugout on June 6, ten pounds lighter after his prolonged hospital stay. He came back to a ballclub that had gone

9-7 in his absence and dropped to second place. The team celebrated the popular skipper's return with a 9-8 victory over Houston at Three Rivers Stadium. Four days later, the Bucs snuck into first place with a 3-1 win over St. Louis. They stayed on top the rest of the season.

By September 1, 1971, the Pirates had a five and a half game lead over St. Louis with the post season looming in the distance. The Phillies were in town, and Danny was preparing for the last game of the three-game series. He filled out his lineup card, handed it over to home plate umpire Stan Landes, and hung a copy on the clubhouse wall. The historic lineup, twenty-four years after Jackie Robinson had broken the color barrier, was:

> Rennie Stennett, 2B
>
> Gene Clines, CF
>
> Roberto Clemente, RF
>
> Willie Stargell, LF
>
> Manny Sanguillen, C
>
> Dave Cash, 3B
>
> Al Oliver, 1B
>
> Jackie Hernandez, SS
>
> Dock Ellis, P

The fans awaiting the start of the game had no idea they were about to witness history in the making. For the first time ever, a Major League Baseball team fielded a starting lineup that consisted entirely of minority players. While the crowd sat unaware, the players in the locker room sure knew what was happening. Thirty-eight years later Manny Sanguillen laughs delightedly remembering when the guys saw the lineup on the wall:

*We looked at each other and started to laugh. We loved it. We [the minority players] were making fun of everybody and we said "We have it now."*

*We were playing the Phillies; we said, "We're going to kill them." Of course the biggest mouth was Dock Ellis. He was screaming to the Phillies, "You guys don't have a chance." Woody Fryman was pitching for Philadelphia and they scored two runs in the first. We scored five runs in the first. It was unbelievable. After the Phillies scored the first two runs Dock was still telling them, "We're going to get you." And he was right – we won 10-7.*

*People started to wonder if Danny did it on purpose, but he just wanted to win the game. He told us, "Listen, I don't care who plays. As long as you play to win the game, I'll put you in the lineup. I prepare you guys to play every day."*

First baseman Al Oliver agrees: "When he sent the all-minority team out there, I don't think he was back in his office making out his lineup and saying, 'I'm going to send nine brothers out there tonight.' He was just looking at which nine players could win that night." Pitcher Steve Blass reminisced about "that wonderful time on September 1, 1971," in a 2009 interview:

*The baseball writers all rushed in [after the game] and said, "Danny, do you realize what happened?"*

*"What do you mean?" Danny asked.*

*"You had an all-minority lineup for the first time in the history of baseball."*

*"Oh. When I made out the lineup card I just thought I put in the nine Pittsburgh Pirates that I had the best chance to win with tonight."*

*He just diffused the whole thing. He treated it with the respect it deserved, but didn't act like it was as big of a deal as they were making – he just put out the nine best Pirates and didn't care if they were white, black, Latino, whatever. It was a tremendous response to that whole thing, which was a big deal.*

Meanwhile, the Pirates were keeping busy – winning the National League East for the second year in a row. The San Francisco Giants clinched the NL West in the last game of the season, and the stage was set for the National League Championship Series (NLCS).

The best-of-five NLCS opened at San Francisco's Candlestick Park on October 2 with Pirate ace Steve Blass facing the Giants' Gaylord Perry. After two scoreless innings the Pirates struck first with two runs in the top of the third. The Giants immediately responded, and after three full innings the scoreboard read: Pirates 2, Giants 1.

The fifth inning was an entirely different matter. The Pirates were blanked – three up, three down. Then the Giants erupted. A pair of two-run homers, by Tito Fuentes and the great Willie McCovey, put the Giants ahead 5-2. Though the Bucs would score twice in the seventh inning, Game One went into the books as a 5-4 Giants' win. Perry went the distance for the win, while Blass took the loss after pitching only five innings.

The next three games would be all Pittsburgh.

Game Two was the Bob Robertson show. The muscular first baseman went 4 for 5 with three home runs, a double, and five runs batted in. Pitcher Dock Ellis gave up five hits and two runs in five full innings. Bob Miller relieved Ellis in the sixth with two runners on base and no outs. He made it out of the jam, and by the end of six the Pirates led 4-2.

In the top of the seventh the Pirates ripped open a six-run lead. Dave Cash scored on a Clemente single, and Bob Robertson brought Al Oliver and Clemente across the plate with a three-run homer. Robertson bumped the lead up one more with a solo home run in the ninth. Willie Mays answered him with a two-run homer in the bottom of the inning, but it wasn't enough. Dave Giusti relieved Miller in the final frame and sent the rest of the Giants packing. Final score: Pirates 9, Giants 4.

The NLCS came to Pittsburgh for the third game, with Juan Marichal facing Bob Johnson on the mound. It was a pitchers' duel. The Pirates drew first blood by scoring in the second inning with yet another Bob Robertson home run. That lead held until the sixth inning when the Giants scored on a Richie Hebner throwing error. At the end of six, the game was tied at one apiece.

In the eighth inning Hebner atoned for his earlier error by launching a solo home run off Marichal to give the Pirates the lead once more. The score was now 2-1. Bob Johnson had gone eight innings with no earned runs. Dave Giusti replaced Johnson for the ninth and retired the Giants in order to preserve the 2-1 victory.

Game Four, on October 6, was a slugfest in the early going, with the two teams scoring a total of ten runs in the first two frames. As in Game One, Gaylord Perry was on the hill for the Giants against Steve Blass, who would last only two innings. At the end of those two innings, the game was tied 5-5.

There would be no more scoring until the sixth inning. With two outs and Dave Cash on second base, Clemente hit an RBI single that sent Cash home. The Giants' Jerry Johnson came out of the bullpen and replaced Perry on the mound as Willie Stargell stepped into the batters' box. The catcher flubbed a pitch and Clemente made it to second. An intentional walk to Stargell brought Al Oliver to the plate. Oliver ripped a three-run homer and the Pirates held a substantive four-run lead (9-5).

That lead would hold. The Pirates were heading to the World Series.

"I can't compare this team to our 1960 championship club," said Danny after the game. "I never compare clubs. It wouldn't be fair. This team's character ... well, call them wonderful. It's a hitting ballclub with a strong bench."[3]

After besting the San Francisco Giants, it was safe for Danny to talk about the upcoming World Series. The Pirates would face the Baltimore Orioles, who had beaten the Oakland Athletics in three straight games in the American League Championship Series. "Sure, Baltimore has good pitching," said Danny. "Four 20-game winners isn't bad, is it? But if you look back, we had some pretty good pitching in our division. Like Ferguson Jenkins, Bob Gibson, Tom Seaver, Bill Stoneman and Rick Wise. We still won it all, didn't we?"[4]

And so the World Series would begin.

## THE WORLD SERIES

Previewing the upcoming World Series, the October 9 *New York Times* sports page described the Pirates as "having lost the Series on paper." Danny was familiar with being cast as the underdog – from his childhood, to his playing days, to his previous endeavors as the Pittsburgh skipper. He seemed to relish the role.

"Baltimore has a good club. We respect them," Danny said. "But we fear no one. If they have any sense, they'll respect us. I don't think there's a team stronger than Pittsburgh."[5] The cavalcade of media leading up to the World Series seemed to suggest that the Bucs cave in before the Series even began:

> The Pittsburgh Pirates wondered today why they even bothered showing up for the World Series. ...
>
> "From what I'm reading in the papers we shouldn't even have bothered coming here," said [Willie Stargell]. ... "We've lost

*it already. But we're not going out there with the idea that they have a superior team. They have to prove it." ...*

*"Everybody says they are going to win," said the immortal Roberto Clemente. "The way everyone talks, we're much inferior. We should be playing in the Little League. Sure, they have a good team. But so do we."[6]*

Indeed they did, and Clemente was a key part of that "good team" – as he would soon show the world. In Danny's early years as manager, there was some friction between him and Clemente. After discussing the situation the two had come to understand each other. By 1971 Roberto served as an intermediary for Danny to the Latin American players. Whenever a problem arose, Danny would talk to Clemente. Within a few days the problem would invariably be solved. When questioned by reporters on his relationship with Roberto, Danny answered with his trademark wit: "I'm old enough, I'm intelligent, and I think I'm smart enough to get along with anybody on our ballclub – especially if he's a .350 hitter. ... Clemente's the best player I've ever seen."

Manny Sanguillen was one of Roberto's best friends on the team. He agrees that by 1971 Danny and Roberto had long gotten over any troubles they once had: "I never saw him and Clemente argue. Their communication was so great, that's why the team was so good. Whatever one said, the other agreed with it. We [the other players] loved that. I remember Clemente always said, 'You guys take me to the World Series and I'll take over.'"

"Danny played Clemente like a violin," is how former Pittsburgh sportswriter Bill Christine, who wrote a book about Clemente, describes their relationship:

*Clemente was a great ballplayer, but he was a guy who danced to his own drummer. I'm sure he must have been a difficult guy to manage. ... I know Danny had to play it close to the vest with Clemente. ... The bottom line to me on Clemente was he didn't want to play when he was hurt. He had a legitimate back injury and some other injuries that came into play. He didn't want to play when he was hurt because he wanted to give his all and didn't want to embarrass himself. I don't think he [Clemente] ever realized that Clemente at eighty percent was better than anybody else they could put out there at 105 percent. As a result, he sat out a lot of games.*

Not the World Series, though. As Clemente would later say, "When you're playing in a World Series, nothing bothers you. There are only seven games. And I would play them on one leg or standing on my head because there is so much at stake for all of us."[7]

The Series kicked off on Saturday, October 9, the day after Danny's birthday. While many sportswriters were kind enough to wish Danny a Happy Birthday, they were less generous with their assessment of Pittsburgh's chances against the mighty Orioles. Danny's daughter Kathy recalls one Baltimore sportswriter predicting the Orioles would win the Series in three games. Impossible, of course, in a best-of-seven contest, but it emphasized the Pirates' status as underdogs.

"Sorry, Danny," wrote Arthur Daley in a *New York Times* birthday message. "There seems to be no way this can be arranged by the little creatures who direct man's destinies from some never-never land. Beating the Orioles is such a monumental assignment that it might be beyond the powers of the head leprechaun that Murtaugh, a County Mayo man, has been known to import from Ireland on occasion." Still, Daley allowed for the possibility of some Murtaugh magic:

*It might be a mark of wisdom for Earl Weaver, resident*

*genius of the Orioles, to watch the beguiling Mr. Murtaugh with suspicion. In World Series play, Danny is not to be trusted. A discovery that Casey Stengel made to his intense dismay in 1960.*

*Stengel's Yankees scored twice as many runs, 54 to 27. Who won the World Series? Murtaugh's Pirates. Dauntless Danny did it with mirrors or something, especially in the seventh game, in which the lunatic touch ran rampant.*

*Even to this very day, diehard Yankees fans hold fast to the conviction that supernatural forces interposed to do them dirt. They had to be Murtaugh's imported leprechauns. There is no other explanation. And neither Weaver nor the Orioles should be fooled by the look of innocence on Murtaugh's map-of-Ireland face. ...*

*I find the temptation severe to pick the Orioles in four straight. I resist it because it flouts all laws of probability. So the pick here is the Orioles in five games. Sorry about that, Danny. Happy Birthday, anyway.*

## GAME ONE

Right-hander Dock Ellis took the mound for the Pirates in the first game of the Series. "I'm ready to go," he told the *New York Times*.

So were the Orioles.

Calling it a "virtuoso performance," sportswriters raved about Orioles starter Dave McNally's effort in Game One. Having won twenty-one games during the regular season and beaten only once since May, McNally was a fierce competitor for the Bucs to encounter.

After a scoreless first inning, the Pirates batted in the top of the second. Slugger Bob Robertson led off with a walk, and a McNally wild pitch moved him to second base. Manny Sanguillen ripped a ground ball to the left side of the infield. A throwing error allowed Robertson to score and Manny to reach second. After a groundout, Sanguillen was on third base with one out, bringing up Jackie Hernandez.

Danny called for a suicide squeeze play that scored Sanguillen and yielded a bonus: Orioles catcher Ellie Hendricks threw badly to first base, allowing Hernandez to reach second. Dave Cash followed with a clean single, scoring Hernandez. After two innings the scoreboard read: Pittsburgh 3, Baltimore 0.

It would go downhill from there.

The Orioles settled down and held the Pirates scoreless for the rest of the game. McNally completed the game, allowing only three hits and the three (unearned) runs from the second inning. The Oriole bats did the rest. Home runs from the usual suspects – Frank Robinson, Merv Rettenmund and Don Buford – gave the Orioles a 5-3 lead by the fifth inning. There it would stay. Final score: Baltimore 5, Orioles 3.

"We had a bad inning," observed Baltimore manager Earl Weaver. "But not a bad ball game."[8]

"We respect the Orioles," said Danny. "But we're not intimidated by them. We'll be back tomorrow."[9]

## Game Two

A rainout on Sunday, October 10 postponed what would be a Baltimore rout in Game Two. The Orioles took the field on Monday and banged out 14 hits – all singles – as they crushed the Pirates 11-3. The Pirates used six pitchers in the game, starting with Bob Johnson, who lasted three and a third innings and gave up four runs on four hits. His support staff did not do much better, allowing seven more runs over the rest of the game.

Brooks Robinson, Baltimore's venerable third baseman, managed to achieve greatness once again by reaching base five times in the game – three singles and two walks. Only Babe Ruth and Lou Brock had done the same in a World Series game. The lone bright spot for the Pirates was Richie Hebner, who nailed Oriole ace Jim Palmer for a three-run homer in the eighth inning. Those were the only runs Palmer would give up in his eight innings. By the time the Birds let up, the scoreboard read: Baltimore 11, Pittsburgh 3. As the Series headed to Pittsburgh, the Orioles were up two games to none.

## GAME THREE

"The world has yet to see the real Pittsburgh Pirates," declared Danny. It was clear after two games that Earl Weaver's Orioles were every bit as good as they had been billed. They had schooled the Pirates twice – with pitching, power, and regular hitting. To that point in time only five teams in the 68-year history of the World Series had lost the first two games and gone on to win. It appeared to be Baltimore's World Series to lose. Danny's Pirates weren't so sure.

"Nobody gave us much of a chance except Danny and our team. He never let us lose confidence in ourselves. He knew that we were going to play better baseball when we got home," recalls second baseman Dave Cash. Danny was a big influence on the players, according to Cash. Because of Danny, "We still believed we had a chance."

Manny Sanguillen caught both games in Baltimore. Through the years, Danny had taught Sanguillen how to read the batters and know what pitches they were hitting. He'd taught him to know when a pitcher had the right "stuff" and when he didn't. In turn, Danny trusted Manny's judgment. Manny vividly remembers arriving back in Pittsburgh:

> We had a scouting report that said to pitch to certain Baltimore players certain ways. They killed us the first two games

*in Baltimore. When we got back to Pittsburgh Danny said, "Manny, come early to the ballpark." I went to his office and he asked me, "What did you think about the scouting report?" I said, "I don't like it." He said, "You what, Manny? I don't either. We're going to have a meeting and tell everybody 'Forget the scouting report. Play like Pittsburgh Pirates."*

*So he called a meeting in the clubhouse and he held up the scouting report. He said, "This stuff is no good. We don't need it. Let's go play like the Pittsburgh Pirates." He ripped up the scouting report and threw it in the garbage. The clubhouse erupted in applause. And that's when the games changed. We started playing like the regular season. We played with no pressure. We played like Pittsburgh Pirates.*

October 12. Danny's daughter Kathy recalls reading her dad's horoscope that morning – it said he would have good luck in the next three days. He sure needed it. Another loss would leave the Pirates facing a 3-0 deficit – something no team had ever overcome in the World Series. The Pirates did not want to try becoming the first. Dependable Steve Blass, who led the Buc starters with a 2.85 earned run average, was on the mound for the Pirates.

Game Three would be a tale of strong pitching from Blass and timely – and in one instance, somewhat accidental – hitting.

In his pre-series report on the Pirates, Baltimore scout Jim Russo warned, "They come out swinging. They hit the first ball."[10] Dave Cash would prove that to be true when he doubled down the left field line on Mike Cuellar's first offering. Two batters later Clemente sent Cash home to give the Pirates a 1-0 lead in the early going.

Neither team scored in the next four and a half innings. A lead-off double from Manny Sanguillen in the sixth brought Jose Pagan to bat. In this, his fifteenth major league season, Pagan had become a utility infielder. In a 2009 interview, Al Oliver credited Danny's skillful managing that kept Pagan fresh throughout the season and enabled him to get key hits. It paid off. Pagan drove Sanguillen home with an RBI single to left. At the end of six innings, the Pirates led 2-0.

A Frank Robinson home run in the top of the seventh was the only run Blass allowed all afternoon. It was only the second hit surrendered by Blass, but it cut the Pittsburgh lead in half. Two strikeouts and a ground-out later, the inning was over. The Pirates clung to a 2-1 lead heading into the bottom of the seventh.

Clemente began what would be a pivotal seventh inning for the Pirates by reaching first on the Orioles' third error of the game. A Stargell walk brought Bob Robertson to the plate with two on and no outs. On a one-nothing pitch, Danny gave Robertson the swing sign but the slugger fouled the ball off.

Noting the arrangement of the infield, Danny decided to change strategy. "We saw that Brooks Robinson was playing him deep at third, so we decided to bunt," Danny said after the game. At second base, Clemente saw the sign and was unsure if it was accurate, so he waved his arms in an attempt to call time out. Stargell at first base had seen the sign as well. Robertson did not.[11]

Instead of laying down the bunt, Robertson launched the Cuellar pitch to right-center field for a three-run homer to blow the game open and give the Pirates an imposing 5-1 lead. As Robertson rounded the bases, he was unaware that he had missed a bunt sign ... until he crossed home plate and was greeted by Stargell. "That's the way to bunt," Stargell said.[12]

"It was the first time I've missed [a sign] all year," Robertson said. "If I had seen it, I would have bunted." When Robertson got to the dugout he approached Danny, who showed no emotion on his face. "I guess I fouled up," Robertson said. "Possibly," said Murtaugh.[13]

Pittsburgh now held a four-run lead. Steve Blass rolled through the Orioles' lineup for the last two innings. Final score: Pittsburgh 5, Baltimore 1.

Following the game much of the talk was about Blass' impressive performance. He had gone the full nine innings, giving up just three hits and one run. Blass would later say that he thought that he was just a handful of pitches away from throwing a no-hitter that day. Asked if it had been the best performance of the year he said, "How about of my life?"[14]

There was plenty of chuckling about Robertson's non-bunt, which had cemented the win for the Pirates. "No, there'll be no fine," said Murtaugh, regarding Robertson missing the bunt sign. "But there won't be any bonus, either."[15] The Pirates had cut their deficit in half and were ready to come back to work for Game Four. It appeared that playing like Pittsburgh Pirates worked a lot better than following a scouting report.

## GAME FOUR

On October 13, 1971, the Pirates and Orioles took to the field for the first night game in World Series history. The significance of the night start was pretty much lost on the Pirates, who thought only about winning the game to even the Series. "We were so consumed with the immediacy of winning the World Series, not the social significance of the first World Series night game," said Steve Blass years later.[16]

"It never even occurred to me," said pitcher Bruce Kison when asked if he felt a part of history. "I had no idea. I didn't think about it until afterward. ... All we knew was that day game, night game, home game, away game – didn't matter, we had to win that game."[17]

The game would not start well for the Pirates. Left hander Luke

Walker was on the mound and encountered trouble immediately – giving up three hits and three runs in the first inning. Danny emerged from the dugout to remove Walker. In a surprising move, the Buc manager put rookie Bruce Kison on the mound. The lanky 21-year-old had gone 6-5 in eighteen games in 1971. Kison quickly retired Davey Johnson to end the Pirates' misery. After just a half an inning Pittsburgh was down 3-0.

On the mound for the Orioles was Pat Dobson, who had gone 20-8 with a 2.90 earned run average on the season. Back-to-back RBI doubles by Stargell and Oliver closed the gap with the Orioles. As an estimated television audience of 60 million watched, the eventful first inning ended with the score Baltimore 3, Pittsburgh 2.

In the third inning, Richie Hebner scored to tie the game at three each. It was still tied in the bottom of the seventh when pitcher Bruce Kison was due at the plate. The rookie had performed wonderfully in relief, going six and a third innings and giving up only one hit and no runs. But the Bucs needed some runs of their own. With two outs and runners on the corners, Danny selected Milt May to pinch hit.

The twenty-year-old May was in his first full season with the Pirates. He was the son of former major leaguer Pinky May, who played in Philadelphia with Danny from 1941 to 1943. Milt ripped the second pitch into right center for the biggest hit of his young career, scoring Robertson and giving Pittsburgh an all-important one-run lead.

Dave Giusti – whose 30 saves had led the National League – entered the game and would slam the door on Baltimore. He worked perfect eighth and ninth innings, getting out the Orioles' two-through-seven hitters. The final score was Pittsburgh 4, Baltimore 3. The Pirates had evened the Series at two games apiece.

Giusti was thrilled to have been able to pitch at night. "I remember I was glad it was a night game because, in my way of thinking, my stuff was better at night. I thought it was harder for the hitters to pick up the spin on my palm ball at night than in the daytime."[18] Others were also aware of the novelty of the night game:

> "It was kind of different," Pirates third baseman Richie Hebner said. "It was the first night World Series game. National TV. You were the main event that night. And, if you didn't have an alarm clock, you were not going to work the next morning. Everybody was there."
>
> Including an elderly gentleman who sat next to Hebner's parents in a box seat behind home plate.
>
> "The guy never stopped talking," Hebner said. "He never shut up. I think he was talking to everybody who'd look at him. And with 50,000 people there, no wonder he never stopped talking."
>
> And no wonder people looked at the guy. Turned out Hebner's parents sat next to Casey Stengel.[19]

## GAME FIVE

Heading into Game Five, it appeared to be a mismatch on the pitching mound. Orioles' pitcher Dave McNally was coming off his fourth consecutive season with twenty-plus victories. In Game One McNally had limited the Bucs to just three hits. Nellie Briles, on the other hand, had never won twenty games in a season. In 1971, Briles had a respectable 8-4 record and 3.04 ERA, but he wasn't an "ace" pitcher like McNally. Luckily the game was played on the field, not in the stats books.

The Pirates put the first runs on the board in the second inning. Bob Robertson started the fun with a lead-off homer. Manny Sanguillen followed with a single and then stole second when Jose Pagan struck out. McNally made it two in a row by striking out Jackie Hernandez. Nellie

Briles came to the plate with two outs and Manny on second. Briles took the opportunity to help his own cause as he rapped a single that sent Manny across the plate. A grounder from Dave Cash forced Briles out at second, but after two innings the Pirates were ahead 2-0.

In the third inning Briles again made short work of the Orioles: three up, three down. McNally took the mound again and promptly walked Gene Clines. Clemente hit a ground out that sent Clines to second. After Stargell flied out, Bob Robertson made it to first on an error while Clines advanced to third. Manny Sanguillen was next up for the Bucs. He happily stepped aside for a moment to allow Clines across the plate when McNally threw a wild pitch. Manny struck out, but the Pirates had increased their lead to 3-0.

Innings four, five, and six were quick for the Oriole batters, as Briles retired them in order each time. In the Pirates half of the fifth, Clines led off with what the *Post Gazette's* Charley Feeney described as "an ordinary double [that he] ran into a triple." Clemente sent Clines home with a single – his only hit of the game. At the end of five innings, it was Pittsburgh 4, Orioles 0.

There the score would stay. Briles plowed through the Orioles lineup in order in the sixth, seventh and eighth innings. After retiring the first two batters in the ninth, Briles walked Don Buford and threw a ball to Paul Blair. With Oriole powerhouses Boog Powell and Frank Robinson waiting their turns at bat, Pirate pitching coach Don Osborn rushed to the mound. "Hurry up," he told Briles. "We have to catch a plane to Baltimore." Briles complied and retired Blair to end the game. Final score: Pittsburgh 4, Baltimore 0. The Bucs made the flight on time.[20]

"Briles Blanks 'Em; Bucs 1 Up" read the front page of the *Pittsburgh Post Gazette* the next day. PG sports writer Charley Feeney was unabashed in his praise of the hometown team: "Those incredible Buccos are one victory away from a world championship. Instead of being buried by the Orioles at Three Rivers Stadium, the Pirates came alive. Now it's the Birds from Baltimore who must do the chasing ... The Pirates have turned [the Series] around with some fantastic pitching which held the hit-happy Orioles to nine hits in three games at Three Rivers. ... The Birds [have begun] to wonder just what could stop the Pittsburgh machine which suddenly has a well-oiled pitching staff, home-run power, and a bag of base hits in the bat rack."

It was Nellie Briles' third time pitching in a World Series – and his first World Series shutout. He allowed only two hits in the game. Briles discussed the win with the *Post Gazette's* Jimmy Jordan: "This game today meant the most to me of any game I've ever pitched. I had to be sharp. The Series was tied and a win here would mean so much to everybody before we returned to Baltimore. It was most gratifying."[21]

## GAME SIX

As the Pirates headed back to Baltimore for Game Six, *McKeesport (PA) Daily News* sports editor Luke Quay caught up with Roberto Clemente to get his thoughts on the Series:

> *Roberto Clemente wasn't surprised that the Pirates took three in a row from the Baltimore Orioles at Three Rivers Stadium and now hold a 3-2 edge in the World Series going into tomorrow's sixth game here. The Great One practically predicted it was going to happen after the Bucs dropped the first two games of the series. ...*
>
> *Clemente has hit safely in every World Series game in which he has played – twelve straight including seven in 1960 and five this year. And he has a shot at the record of 13 hits in a seven-game series ... But he isn't interested in setting any personal marks right now.*

*"I would be satisfied to go 0-4 as long as we win," Roberto said. "Everybody said that Baltimore is the best team in base-ball. But we think that we are the best. And the only thing I want to prove is that we are better than the Orioles."*[22]

And prove it they would ... but not in Game Six. After a scoreless first inning, future Hall of Famer Jim Palmer – one of those pesky 20-game winners – was back on the mound. Palmer had to cancel golf plans to pitch that day – plans he made when the Orioles had a 2-0 lead in the Series and expected to finish the job quickly in Pittsburgh.[23] Al Oliver led off with a double to right field and was sent home by a Bob Robertson single. Palmer made it through the rest of the inning with no more runs.

A homer by Clemente was the only Pirate hit in the third inning. The Bucs held a 2-0 lead. Neither team would score again until the bottom of the sixth. Pirate pitcher Bob Moose had kept the Orioles off the scoreboard through five innings. Don Buford's leadoff home run in the sixth narrowed the Pirate lead to one run. Two batters later Moose was in a bind: runners on first and third, no outs, and clutch-hitter Frank Robinson heading to the plate. Danny sent pitcher Bob Johnson to the mound to replace Moose. Bob Johnson retired the next three batters, leaving Davey Johnson and Powell stranded. At the end of six the scoreboard read: Pittsburgh 2, Baltimore 1.

Bob Johnson didn't last long on the Pirate mound. In the bottom of the seventh inning, with two outs and runners on first and second, Danny felt it was time to bring in reliever Dave Giusti. The first batter he faced was Davey Johnson, who hit an RBI single. Suddenly the game was tied: Pittsburgh 2, Baltimore 2.

The Pirates failed to score in the ninth inning, bringing the Orioles to the plate with a chance to finish off the Bucs – and force a seventh game. Giusti recorded one walk, one strikeout and one hit in the ninth inning –

but no runs. Game Six of the 1971 World Series was heading into extra innings.

Weaver had put a pinch hitter in for Jim Palmer in the ninth inning. For the tenth, the Orioles manager just plucked another of his 20-game winners from the bullpen. This time, the honors went to Pat Dobson. Leading off for the Pirates was Vic Davalillo, who lined out to second. Dave Cash followed with a single to right field. As Hebner struck out, Cash stole second base and was now in scoring position. Clemente and Stargell were the next two batters in the Pirate lineup.

Manager Earl Weaver decided he'd rather face the slumping Stargell than Clemente. He had Dobson intentionally walk Clemente, which also set up a force out at all three bags. Weaver brought lefty Dave McNally to the mound. McNally walked Stargell to load the bases as Oliver headed to the plate. To no avail. Oliver flied out to centerfield and the Bucs left three on base.

In the bottom of the tenth, Bob Miller headed to the mound for the Pirates. Boog Powell led off with a groundout, but Miller then walked Frank Robinson. Merv Rettenmund singled and sent Robinson to third. Brooks Robinson stepped to the plate with one out and runners on first and third. He delivered a sacrifice fly to centerfield that scored Frank Robinson. Final score: Baltimore 3, Pittsburgh 2. The Orioles had tied the Series at three games each. The Game Seven showdown was coming.

## GAME SEVEN

Heading into the biggest game of 1971, the two rival managers shared their thoughts with sports writers. Orioles manager Earl Weaver harkened back to childhood: "When I was a kid of six or seven, I always dreamed about going into the seventh game of the World Series. But in those games, I came to bat and won the game with a base hit. Here I am in the seventh game of the World Series and can't even pick up a bat."[24]

Chewing tobacco and talking to reporters before the game, Danny recalled his feelings from the same moment in 1960. "No different," he said. "I remember I chewed four packs of tobacco that day and didn't spit a lick. I wonder where it all went."[25]

Game Seven featured a marquee pitching matchup at Memorial Stadium in Baltimore: Pirate ace Steve Blass vs. Orioles star Mike Cuellar. The first three innings were a wash. In the Pirates' fourth, Dave Cash lined out to second base to start the inning. Gene Clines was thrown out attempting to bunt. Roberto Clemente was up next with two outs, no runners on base, and no runs on either side. Cuellar tossed a pitch to Clemente and The Great One pounced, launching a rocket that landed in the seats in left-center field and gave the Pirates a 1-0 lead. It was Clemente's twelfth hit of the series – one shy of the World Series record. While it was a slim lead, with Blass on the mound the team felt confident.

There was no more action on the scoreboard until the eighth inning. With the score still Pirates 1, Orioles 0, Willie Stargell approached the plate. After going 0-4 in Game Six, Stargell hit a leadoff single to left that would be pivotal. Jose Pagan followed with a double to score Stargell. Suddenly the Pirates were ahead 2-0. Although the Pirates would go down in order from there, the two-run lead seemed huge in the pitchers' duel that was underway.

Ellie Hendricks and Mark Belanger began the Orioles' eighth with consecutive singles. They were moved to second and third after a sacrifice bunt from Tom Shopay, who was pinch hitting for Mike Cuellar. Don Buford grounded out to first base, allowing Hendricks to score from third. With two outs and a man in scoring position, Davey Johnson approached the plate. A solid hit would tie the game. Instead Johnson hit a grounder to Hernandez at shortstop to end the inning. The score was Pirates 2, Orioles 1.

Pat Dobson took the mound for Baltimore in the top of the ninth and coaxed Clines into a groundout. Clemente stepped into the batters' box for what could be his last chance to notch a record thirteen hits in a single World Series. He struck out, but his fourth inning homerun had kept his streak intact: he'd hit safely in fourteen consecutive World Series games.

After Bob Robertson and Manny Sanguillen both singled, Dobson was pulled by Weaver. With no Game Eight to worry about, there was no reason to save arms for the next day. With two on and Stargell at the plate, Dave McNally entered the game. Once again McNally silenced the slugger's bat as Stargell grounded out to second. The game went to the bottom of the ninth inning with Pittsburgh holding a tenuous one-run lead.

Blass took the mound again to face the Orioles' three, four and five hitters – Boog Powell, Frank Robinson and Merv Rettenmund. Ground out, pop fly, ground out. Then Steve Blass leaping in the air. The Pittsburgh Pirates were World Champions again.

Steve Blass had faced three twenty-game winners in a single game and won. He went the full nine innings and gave up only one run on four hits. He struck out five and walked two.

Final score: Pirates 2, Orioles 1.

Roberto Clemente was named the Most Valuable Player of the Series, having hit safely in all seven games – 12 for 29 in all – for an average of .414. He had two home runs, two doubles, a triple, and four runs batted in. It was Clemente's – and Blass' – World Series. "Clemente, as great as he was, didn't finally beat us the way Blass did. Murtaugh did an excellent job," said Orioles' Manager Earl Weaver.[26]

Danny's daughter Kathy's fondest World Series memory came after Blass recorded that last out: "When the Pirates won Game Seven, my mother, my brothers, my sister-in-law, and I were sitting to the right of the dugout along the first base line. My dad came over to hug and kiss us before he went out to celebrate on the field with the team. It was a very touching moment for me."

Pittsburgh General Manager Joe Brown was ebullient. "This is the biggest thrill of my life, by far," he said. "And one reason is that the team we beat is such a great team. There is no doubt they are a great club."[27]

## AFTERMATH

On the Sunday that the Pirates beat the Orioles the city of Pittsburgh erupted in celebration, but it wasn't like the 1960 celebration. Tens of thousands of Pittsburghers flooded the streets, and the scene quickly turned bad. Police went into full riot mode. "We're just fighting a holding action," a police sergeant said. "So far, we definitely aren't holding them."[28]

Fire hydrants were opened, store windows were broken, automobiles were overturned and set ablaze. The crowd created such a standstill in downtown traffic that even police and emergency vehicles could not pass. "This is one hell of a mess," shouted one policeman over the radio. "We can't move."[29]

Danny's daughter Kathy was five months pregnant with her first child during the 1971 World Series. She recalls riding with Danny and Kate in the parade from the airport into the city when the team arrived back in Pittsburgh:

> We were riding in a convertible. The man who owned the car and his son were in the front. My parents and I were sitting in the back. When we got into town, my dad sat up high on the back of the car so he could wave to people. The crowd starting getting crazy, so he moved down to the seat. It got even crazier, so we put the roof up on the car. People started climb-

*ing up on top of the car and the roof started to cave in. My
mother and I were kneeling on the floor with our heads on
the seats.*

*A young guy climbed on top of the trunk and was trying to
get people away. My dad was worried about me since I was
pregnant – but I was worried about him. We broke away
from the parade and were zooming pretty quickly through
the streets. I looked back and saw our rescuer was still on the
back of the car. I told the driver and he slowed down and let
the guy off. I wanted to go to the team party, but my dad
insisted we go to the hospital so they could make sure I was
okay. After they checked me out, the three of us went home
[in Pittsburgh] and celebrated over scrambled eggs with ham
and cheese.*

After the stress and excitement of the World Series, it was time for
Danny to decide whether or not he would return to the dugout in 1972.
It would take more than a month, but on November 23 Danny
announced that he was retiring, mostly due to health concerns. "Although
the doctors have assured me that my health is good, each succeeding season seems to take that much more out of me," he said at the time.[30] Danny
said it helped knowing that he was leaving the team in the capable hands
of coach Bill Virdon, who was named the new manager.

At age 54, Murtaugh left behind a team that had some of the personnel from the 1960 World Champions and some fresher faces. They
were sorry to see him go. "He hinted pretty strongly near the end of the
season that he wouldn't return if he didn't feel better," said long-time
coach Frank Oceak. "I've never seen anything like him. He'll be a tough
act to follow. Just the other night, Richie Hebner asked me if he was coming back. He said he hoped so."[31]

Manny Sanguillen still recalls learning that Danny would not be back in 1972: "It really surprised me when he said he had to retire, but he said he couldn't manage anymore because of problems with his heart. After he retired, he said to me, 'I built this team. I built the foundation for you guys to keep it up. I want you to keep playing the same way.' He was the man who made me a big league player and I loved him."

News of Danny's retirement caused Arthur Daley of the *New York Times* to recall a line uttered by Cubs' Manager Leo Durocher twenty-five years earlier: "Nice guys finish last." Then Danny came along and proved Durocher wrong:

> *Danny is a nice guy. But Danny didn't finish last. He finished first. Are you paying attention, Leo? ... And what was the secret of his success? "Brilliant managerial thinking and dumb Irish luck," says this over-aged leprechaun with the map of Ireland features.*
>
> *If Danny ever started to get delusions of grandeur, his down-to-earth sense of humor would puncture every bubble before each was half inflated. There's no pretense to the man and therein lies his charm. He's honest and straightforward in dealings with his bosses, his ballplayers and the press among others. He won't lie. It seems a pity that he has been forced into early retirement [by his health] at the age of 54. ... "These games are tough on my boiler," he [has] said.*
>
> *That's where Danny fooled people. Although he had to be churning up inside, he never quite showed it. Outwardly he was a droll and whimsical guy with easy-going mannerisms. His clubhouse seemed happy and that was a reflection of a team spirit that flowed from him.*
>
> *[His retirement] is a shame because he was a quality man in a quality position. And if Leo Durocher will forgive the expression, Danny Murtaugh has always been a very nice guy.*[32]

# the offseason(s)

For Danny's family, life didn't revolve around four seasons; it revolved around two seasons: baseball season and the offseason. The extended family looked forward to the end of the baseball season. Danny's niece Gerrie recalls, "When Uncle Danny came home, everything was all right – it was like a big party with the player-piano going in his rec room. Even my mom [Danny's sister Eunice, who was a bit cantankerous] was happy, so that made us kids happy. He was St. Uncle Danny and his sisters all adored him."

Danny and Kate were both extremely close to their families. In the early years after the war, they lived in connecting row homes with Danny's sisters Mary and Eunice and his cousin Madge. Kate's parents and her brother and three sisters also lived in the Chester area. Madge remembers those as very happy times:

*The best thing I can say about Danny is that he was a great family man. He was always so family oriented, even when he could have been otherwise. His World Series wins, his league championships, nothing changed him. He was always happy to come home to his family and friends. Christmas was a very special time for Danny. From the first Christmas we were all together in the row on Kerlin Street, he and Kate never missed visiting the rest of the family on Christmas Eve.*

*We always put on a show every year when Danny came home from the baseball season. Our group of friends – the old 'gang' from our youth – would practice at each others' houses for months before he came home. We'd make up our own songs and my husband Art would play the ukulele. We always used popular songs, but we made up our own words using things that happened to him during the baseball season. We first started doing the shows when we all lived on Kerlin Street and Danny was with the Phillies. We continued with them through his managing days.*

After almost ten years of living side-by-side in row homes in Chester, Danny's extended family began migrating to nearby Woodlyn. First to go, in 1956, was Danny's sister Peggy, who had been living with Danny's family since her husband Dale died. In March 1957 Kate and the kids moved next door to Peggy into a modest new house on Kelly Avenue. Proving that he was indeed a master strategist, Danny was at spring training during the move. When school let out Kate and the kids met up with Danny in Pittsburgh like they always did. By the time he was named manager in August of that year, Kate said he had only been in the new house for a total of about three days.

Before too long, Mary and Bud, Madge and Art, and Eunice and George all moved to Kelly Avenue. Kate's sister Stashe also moved to the neighborhood. The kids – and adults – were thrilled to be able to walk to each other's houses again. As always, they all felt the absence of Danny and his family during the baseball season. Madge recalls Danny's homecomings fondly:

*When Danny and Kate would come home after the season, we all gave them their privacy. Even though we all lived so close together, we wouldn't go to their house when they first got back. Next thing you know, bright and early one morning after about two weeks, someone would be banging on your front door. It was Danny, saying, "Where have you been?" Then he'd grab a rocker, bring it out to the kitchen, and we'd have coffee and talk.*

Kate and the kids always went home earlier than Danny because of school. Danny would follow when the baseball season was over. Some years Danny coached in the Winter League in Florida, which would delay his return. He was always home for Thanksgiving, though, and they would host Kate's family for Thanksgiving dinner. The feast was held in the basement that Danny and his friends finished into a rec room – complete with partitions, paneling, a bar, and a tile floor. None of them had tackled a project like that before, so Danny was always proud of the room and liked to hold parties there.

Danny's rec room was also the "theater" for the Welcome Home shows that were a big highlight of the offseason. Kathy recalls that her aunts and uncles went all out for the productions – they had costumes, props, scenery, the works. Preparing for the shows was a great source of entertainment for the extended family throughout the summer. Every year the show was different, and Danny and Kate really looked forward to seeing what new skits their friends would think up. The 1960 World Series – and the debt the Chester "gang" incurred to go – provided much fodder for their show the next year.

## Lyrics from The Post-1960 World Series Show

TUNE: TELL ME WHY

Tell us why we're all so broke;
Tell us why we can't even joke;
Tell us why we eat dried beef;
Tell us why we're all on relief.

Because the Pirates went all the way;
the price of tickets we all had to pay.
Because Webster Hall rates were oh so high—
when we got that bill, we thought we would die.

Because God let the pirates win;
Becuase he let maz hit that run in.
Becuase god holds our dan so dear;
That's why he made him the Man of the Year.

TUNE: BE KIND TO YOUR WEB-FOOTED FRIENDS

Be kind to your ticketless friends

For some day we all may be loaded

Be kind to your friends from the sticks

Where the dollar seldom sticks

You may think that this is the end.

## WELL, IT IS!

In Danny's day baseball players didn't make the enormous salaries that today's players receive, so they often had other jobs during the off-season. Danny spent many winters working at McGovern's, an upscale men's clothing store in Chester. Owner John McGovern was a big sports fan and wanted to help Danny succeed, so he sometimes hired him even if the store didn't really need the extra hand. Danny never forgot that. In later years, when he no longer needed the money from an off-season job, Danny would still go in to McGovern's to help out before Christmas. He knew that people would come in just to see him, but he was a good enough salesman that they often walked out with some purchases.

Locals jokingly called McGovern's the "baseball school" because several employees became professional baseball players. In addition to Danny, McGovern's alumni included Mickey Vernon, major league pitchers Lew Krausse, Sr. and his son Lew Krausse, Jr., and Danny's son Tim, who spent ten years as a catcher and manager for Pittsburgh in the minor leagues. When asked which of the big leaguers was the best salesman, John McGovern was diplomatic, "They're all good ... They're as great as salesmen as they are on the playing field."[1]

Some years Danny worked as a salesman in the sporting goods department of the local Sears during the offseason. Sears took full advantage of having a successful baseball player in the ranks. In December they would run a big ad in the *Chester Times* with a picture of Danny and the caption "Meet Danny Murtaugh." During the Christmas season the store also ran a promotion that offered a "personally autographed picture of Danny with any purchase in the Sports Department."

When Christmas shopping time came around, Timmy, Danny Jr., Kathy, and their cousins would all go to Sears – although not for an autographed photo of the baseball star. The cousins liked to exchange Christmas gifts with each other, but none of their families had any money to speak of. Always generous – and loving to give Christmas gifts himself – Danny gladly gave them money for their Christmas shopping.

The Christmas season was one of Danny's favorite times of year. The family always put up their Christmas tree on Christmas Eve. When the kids were little, they would leave it undecorated and Santa Claus would decorate it during the night, adding extra excitement to Christmas morning. As they got older – and Santa Claus got busier – the family would decorate the tree and leave just the star for Santa. After dinner on Christmas Eve, Danny, Kate, and the kids would go visiting to all of Danny's family. When they lived in the row homes, of course, it was extremely easy to just pop in and out of houses. But even when Danny's family was in Woodlyn and some relatives were still in Chester, he never missed a Christmas Eve visit.

The kids especially looked forward to these visits because Uncle Danny was well known as the best gift giver of them all. His nephew Richard has many memories of Christmas with Uncle Danny, but two stand out in particular:

> Uncle Danny was the only one in the family with any money. One Christmas, when I was ten years old, my brother Sparky asked for a catcher's mitt and I asked for an infielder's glove. On Christmas Eve a big snow storm swept in and we didn't think Uncle Danny would make it. He got there a little late, but he made it. Sparky opened his present first, and he got his catcher's mitt. I opened mine and found a little baseball and bat soap set! I was mad, and I threw it against the wall and it broke. Uncle Danny laughed his butt off – it was just the reaction he was hoping for – and then he gave me my real present: an infielder's glove.
>
> Many years later, in 1973, I was laid off from my job. I had

*two kids at the time, and we didn't know what we were going to do for Christmas. Uncle Danny always walked around the neighborhood visiting people. He never knocked, he just walked in. One day he came walking in and we sat down talking. After an hour or so, he got up to leave and said, "Take this." It was $300 to buy Christmas gifts. He never said another word about it.*

Danny and Kate were devout Catholics, so Christmas Day always began with Mass – usually at 6 or 7 a.m. The kids had to cover their eyes as they walked through the living room so they wouldn't see what Santa Claus had left for them. After Mass they would hurry home to open their presents. The rest of the day would be spent visiting Kate's family. Danny always liked to see everyone's Christmas tree, so they formed something of a caravan. At each stop they'd have a bite to eat and that family would join them as they headed to the next house. They ended up at Danny and Kate's house for Christmas dinner.

One year Danny and his son Tim both received golf clubs for Christmas. Unlike baseball, golf was a game that was not exactly second nature to Danny. The *Daily Times'* Matt Zibitka discussed Danny's golf game in his Bull Pen column on January 29, 1962:

*Tim and Danny played several rounds at Springhaven Golf Club. Asked who won the matches between father and son, Mrs. Murtaugh laughed. "Truthfully, I can't tell you. I don't believe either of them when they tell me their scores."*

*Danny is a better than fair golfer, claims Springhaven pro Joe Hayes. "I remember the time when Danny looked down on golf," chuckled Hayes. "When asked to play he would always give the excuse that he had a trick knee. I used to tell him that golf would help to strengthen the knee. Reluctantly, he took up the game. At first, he was a typical weekend duffer. Then last October he took some lessons, and the improvement was immediate. I saw him get 36 for eight holes after he took lessons."*

*Danny was unavailable for comment. He was probably in some secret hideaway, drafting his speech for Wednesday's Old Timers' banquet.*

The Chester Old Timers' banquet honoring a local sports figure was another event that Danny looked forward to each offseason. Danny, you'll recall, was the 1961 honoree after his thrilling 1960 World Series victory. In 1962 his good friend Mickey Vernon was the guest of honor, and Danny was the main speaker. After the 1962 banquet most of the record six hundred attendees said he was the best speaker they'd ever had. Danny talked about growing up in one of Chester's poorest neighborhoods and how grateful he was to his Boys' Club baseball coach. When Danny paid tribute to Mickey, the place was absolutely silent only to erupt into one of the largest ovations in its history when he finished.[2]

Danny's family helped make sure he didn't get used to such adulation. While they loved and admired Danny, they were more than happy to tease and laugh at him when the occasion called for it. For Peggy's kids, Mary Ellen, Betsy, and Bennie, living so close to a character like Uncle Danny provided lots of laughs, as Betsy recalls:

*We used to have a talking Mynah bird named Mabel whose cage was in the dining room. We'd had a robbery in the area, so my mom started locking the door. No one locked their door then. One day Uncle Danny came over and knocked on the door and shouted, "Hey Peggy!"*

*Whenever anyone knocked, Mabel yelled, "Who's there?" So Uncle Danny yelled back, "It's Danny, let me in!" Every time*

*he pounded on the door, Mabel would just yell, "Who's there?"
Uncle Danny kept saying, "I know you're in there – let me in!"
Kathy and I had been playing outside and heard him hollering. It was only when he heard us laughing that he realized
he'd been yelling at a bird.*

Before her death in 2002, Mary Ellen wrote a personal memoire of
growing up in such a close extended family. Naturally, Uncle Danny was
a big part of her recollections "Every time the Pirates came to town, it was
party time in the family. After each game, which we would all attend (courtesy of Uncle Danny), we would gather at someone's house, order a bunch
of hoagies and soda, and sit around singing old songs for hours." Betsy
also remembers those games:

*Uncle Danny always got us tickets right behind home plate –
and we hated it because we couldn't catch any fly balls. Of
course, now we realize that they were the best seats in the
house. We'd complain about it later, and he'd say, 'I can bring
you a whole box of balls.' But it wasn't the same. We all took
our gloves to the game and we always wanted to catch a foul
ball. We got to meet the players and collect autographs after
the game. The girls would have to wait outside the locker
rooms, but the boys got to go right in.*

One of those boys, of course, was Bennie. Going to the baseball
games and meeting the players afterward was always very exciting. But
when Bennie thinks of Uncle Danny's summer visits, he recalls one
particular night – and it still makes him laugh:

*Uncle Danny used to stay at home instead of in the team hotel
when the Pirates played in Philadelphia and his family was
in Pittsburgh for the summer. One night, when I was around
11, everyone was out but me. I was in bed, and the phone rang.*

209

*It was Uncle Danny and he asked what I was doing. I said I
was in bed. He said, "Oh, I'm sorry. I just saw someone walk
past your dining room window and I wondered who it was."
Terrified, I flew across the driveway to his house. It turned out
he was just lonely and wanted some company.*

Baseball season, the offseason, it didn't matter – Danny was always
doing something special for his family. After college Eunice's daughter
Toodles entered a convent in Washington, DC. In 1966, when Danny was
scouting in Baltimore, he went to the convent to visit her. He wanted to
take her to a baseball game, but the Mother Superior wouldn't let her go
unless the whole convent went. Danny came back with a bus and took all
of the nuns up to Baltimore for the game – they were delighted!

Before she took her final vows, Toodles decided to leave the convent. She just showed up at home one day with no warning, and she was
a mess. According to her sister Gige, she looked like a plucked chicken.
Without being asked, Danny showed up the next day and took Toodles
shopping for a whole new wardrobe. Gige recalls other examples of
Danny's generosity:

*After my dad left my mom, Uncle Danny never came without
slipping her some money. He would just put it on the table as
he was leaving so you wouldn't see it right away and try to
give it back to him.*

*When our cousin Maureen [Mary's daughter] was getting
married, she wanted Toodles and me to be in her wedding. My
mother didn't have any money for a dress, so we didn't think
we could be in it. Uncle Danny showed up one day and told
us, "You're in the wedding, just shut up and go get measured
for your dresses."*

When it came down to it, nothing meant more to Danny than his family. When Danny was serving the Pirates in his "super scout" role, the Boston Red Sox approached Joe Brown to see if they could talk to Danny about becoming their General Manager. Joe Brown said, "Sure, you can talk to him, but he won't go. He won't move that far from his family." Joe was right. The Red Sox offered Danny a five year big money GM contract, but Danny was not interested in leaving Chester year round. He liked having the offseason back home with his family.

The feeling was mutual. In her memoire Mary Ellen summed up how she – and the whole family – felt about Danny: "I always knew I had touched greatness by having Uncle Danny in my life. He was the man who could make dreams come true … my dreams, the dreams of the Pirates, who won two World Series under his management, and the dreams of countless others. Uncle Danny was revered by his family and the baseball world. No one deserved that reverence more."

# the skipper
# returns...
# again

D irector of Player Acquisition and Development. While he took a great deal of ribbing from his friends for his fancy title, Danny was happy it enabled him to stay active in baseball following his 1971 retirement. He was even happier a few months later when his daughter Kathy presented him with his second grandson, Joey, on February 2, 1972. Two weeks later Danny headed south to attend the spring training camps for the Pirates' major and minor league teams. As a "super scout" or "troubleshooter," the former manager provided valuable insight with instruction and player evaluation in spring training.

There was – and still is – a custom in the Major Leagues that the managers who faced off in the World Series one year would match wits again the following year in the Summer Classic. However, since Danny was no longer the Buc skipper he wasn't sure if he would be the NL All Star manager in 1972. Thus he was quite flattered when NL President

# the skipper returns ... again

Chub Feeney asked him to lead the team. "I think I was paid the supreme compliment," Danny said. "It's the first time it has ever happened that somebody has been called back to manage the All-Star team after he has retired."[1] He had one 'condition' – that the clubhouse be equipped with a rocking chair, ever present in the clubhouse when he led the Pirates.

"I went into retirement because of games like that," said Danny after the game. "I didn't see anything out there tonight that makes me want to un-retire." Like the 1971 World Series, it was a hard-fought contest, and Danny admitted he was nervous the whole time. Danny's team prevailed again, as the National League team came away victorious after a tenth inning RBI single by Houston second baseman Joe Morgan. Danny praised his team: "It's hard to make a mistake managing a club like that. I always said that if anyone is lucky enough to manage Hank Aaron and fellows like that, then he's a very fortunate man."[2] When the game ended, Danny hung up his baseball cleats certain he'd never manage again.

Meanwhile, Danny's replacement, Bill Virdon, faced a daunting task – filling the shoes of the popular Irishman and leading the reigning World Champions. The Bucs got off to a rocky start, but by June 19 they staked their claim to first place in the NL East and didn't relinquish it the rest of the season. They lost the NL Championship Series 3-2 to Cincinnati, but Virdon's first year was certainly a success. It wasn't surprising when he was re-hired for the next year.

Tragedy struck during the offseason. In the wee hours of New Year's Eve the shocking news came that fan favorite and team leader Roberto Clemente lost his life. A great humanitarian, Clemente died in a plane crash as he led a relief mission to earthquake-stricken Nicaragua. The entire Pirate family – indeed, the entire country – was shocked and saddened by the news. Danny joined the rest of the Pirates, including Manager Bill Virdon, GM Joe Brown, team President Dan Galbreath, and the players, in Puerto Rico to pay his respects to Clemente's family. The

Pirate contingent attended a private Mass of Resurrection at the San Fernando Church in Clemente's hometown and offered their condolences to his widow, Vera, at the Clemente home.

Because of her husband's Navy assignment, Danny's daughter Kathy was living in Puerto Rico on the tragic night of the superstar's death. Kathy recalls, "The entire island was completely in mourning. Cars and houses were draped in black, there were silent parades, many stores were shut down, people were crying in the streets. It was amazing. They searched and searched for Clemente's remains but never found them. My Uncle John had died not long before that, and I remember my Dad saying, 'Anne knows John is dead; she buried him. Vera [Clemente] will just wonder and wonder because no body was found.'"

In February 1973 the New York Catholic Youth Organization wanted to present its Outstanding Athlete of the Year Award posthumously to Clemente and asked Danny to accept it on his behalf. Danny said it would be an honor. After a rocky start to their relationship, Danny and Clemente had grown very close in their later years together.[3] In fact, when Kathy and Joe first moved to Puerto Rico, Clemente gave Danny his home phone number and address. Clemente emphasized that Kathy should feel free to call if she ever needed anything.

In accepting the award for Roberto, Danny noted the incongruity of a lifetime .254 batter "pinch hitting" for a lifetime .317 batter. Speaking before a crowd that included New York Archbishop Terence Cardinal Cooke and Bob Hope, Danny thought back over his ten years managing Clemente:

> *You know what we used to call him? We called him "The Great One." He was the best ballplayer I've ever seen, and I say that with all due respect to Aaron, Musial, and Mays. ... Clemente to me was a compassionate man. He was a man of*

*two faces. In the clubhouse he was the center of all the funny stories. ... When the time came for the game, Roberto would put on his other face ... that determined face he always wore when he was concentrating completely on winning a baseball game. That's why I say the fans never really knew the real Roberto Clemente.*[4]

The 1973 Pirates suffered another leadership void because Bill Mazeroski, team captain since 1963, had retired at the end of the 1972 campaign. While Danny was not managing at this point, he was still a major influence on the team. As the 1973 spring training got underway, Danny asked Willie Stargell to take over Maz's post as team captain. In his autobiography Stargell recalls being shocked but flattered. "I'd be honored," he told Danny, "as long as you don't expect me to change." Danny chuckled and assured the slugger, "We like you just as you are."[5]

With Virdon as their skipper, the Pirates held onto first place for the first couple weeks of the 1973 season. But then they gradually began to slip until they were in sixth place for a week in late June. Stargell recalled that the team "didn't play like a championship club ... the spark, the efficient play, wasn't there." Despite a losing record the team stayed in the pennant race into August and September. If they could just put together a decent winning streak, they could win the division. But the team lacked a leader – as Stargell put it, "I think we needed Roberto to push us." Stargell tried to lead with his bat, and he and a few others had great personal seasons, but it wasn't enough.[6]

Joe Brown felt that Bill Virdon was not succeeding at getting the most out of the talented team. No one was more surprised than Danny when Joe Brown called him on Thursday, September 6, 1973, and asked him to return to the dugout. In fact, just a few weeks earlier Danny was in Pittsburgh visiting and urged Brown to renew Virdon's contract then as a vote of confidence. "I was shocked and flabbergasted that Joe was thinking of replacing Bill. The phone call was the first indication I had," Danny acknowledged.[7]

Danny initially protested the move, but Brown laid out a litany of reasons and brought their long-standing friendship into the equation. Danny told Joe he needed some time to think about it and discuss it with his family, but in the end he just couldn't say no to his old friend. "Joe Brown is the best friend I have … I couldn't turn him down," said Danny. "It's going to be difficult replacing someone I've thought so much of. After all, Bill Virdon was a protégé of mine. … No one feels as bad about Billy as I do."[8]

The team responded well to Danny, winning seven of the first nine games after he took over. A week into his tenure, the team was in first place by a game and a half. On September 14 the *McKeesport (PA) Daily News* noted that the new manager must be given at least some credit for the team's turnaround. In the same article Willie Stargell agreed, "Everything seems to be jelling now. We're playing the kind of baseball we were capable of doing right from the start. … Right now, we're playing fundamental baseball. And since things have been different on the club since Murtaugh took over, you have to feel he is the reason for it." In his autobiography, Stargell noted that the team didn't keep up the improved pace for long:

> *Unfortunately, Danny couldn't hit, run, pitch or play defense for us. His presence inspired us initially, but soon we were back to our old ways. We lost five of our next six and dropped into second place. From that point forward, we won only five of our next eleven games and finished the season with an 80-82 record, good for a third place. We weren't the same Buccos as we had been in '71 and '72. … We weren't as hungry. We weren't as competitive as we once were.*[9]

The offseason was a busy one for Danny as he prepared for a full year back at the helm of the Pirate ship. He was also preparing to welcome another grandchild into the family as Kathy was expecting again. Danny was at spring training by the time his first granddaughter, Colleen, was born. But he called daily before the big event to see if there was any news. A week before the new baby arrived, Danny called Kathy's house for a different reason – to sing Happy Birthday to Joey who was turning two. Later that day, Danny was on a Pittsburgh radio show to discuss the upcoming season.

Kathy, who now lived an hour north of Pittsburgh, called in to the show and told the call screener that she wanted to play a joke on her dad. They put her at the front of the line, and when it was her turn she said: "I have a really good prospect here in Greenville. He's two years old and I think he's got a lot of talent and could be good for the Pirates." Danny had what his family called "his interview voice" and started going on and on about how they like to develop local talent. As he continued, Kathy began interrupting "Dad, Dad." Finally, the host broke in and said, "Danny, it's your daughter." Danny laughed and said, "I didn't recognize her because she didn't call collect."

Joe Brown, meanwhile, had spent the off season acquiring new talent for the team. The Pirates of 1974 included several players who were either new or getting significantly more playing time than in the past. At first, it didn't look like the new team makeup was going to work. The Bucs spent most of the first two months in last place. Joe Brown wasn't worried, though, because he had tremendous faith in Danny. Stargell remembered this time in his autobiography:

> We began the season slowly, while all our new components
> nudged their way gently into place. Danny was the perfect
> manager for our rookies. As he had with me and dozens of
> others, he brought the newer players along slowly, exhibiting

*the patience and confidence of a saint. … Danny immediately hammered the problems out of our pitching staff.*[10]

Brown's confidence was well placed. The team climbed out of the basement with a pair of six-game winning streaks in mid June and early July. Then, in the second game of a double header on July 14, the Pirates launched an eight-game winning streak that would pull them to within three and a half games of the lead. Aided by what Stargell referred to as "Danny's crafty maneuvering and the confidence he instilled in his young team," the Pirates captured the NL East pennant again that year. Many others also credited Danny's managing for the Pirates' success:

> *There are those who believe that Murtaugh did the best job of his 13-year major league managing career with the 1974 Pirates. Pittsburgh was favored to win the National League East but got off to a horrendous start. They slipped into last place, trailing the leader by as many as nine games. They could have quit. But they didn't. Murtaugh wouldn't let them.*[11]

Unfortunately, the Bucs were not as successful in the 1974 NL Championships, which pitted Pittsburgh against the Los Angeles Dodgers in a best of five series. Despite playing at home, Danny's team got off to a bad start – dropping the first two games by scores of 3-0 and 5-2. As the Pirates headed to LA, the sportswriters were reminding fans that no team had ever come back from a 2-0 deficit in a best of five series. Game 3 was played on Danny's 57th birthday, and his team gave him quite a present: a 7-0 rout of the Dodgers. The Dodgers committed five errors in the game, causing manager Walt Aston to remark, "I doubt errors become contagious, but if they do, I hope the Pirates catch it."[12] Alas, the Dodgers paid the Pirates back the next day with a 12-1 drumming that ended Pittsburgh's season.

As the 1974 campaign drew to a close, the pundits widely expected

Danny to retire again. On October 14 the pundits learned they were wrong. As he did each season, he discussed the decision with Kate and the kids and put it up for a vote. He often claimed it was a very democratic process – other than the fact that the only vote he counted was his own. After consulting his family and being given the okay by his doctor, Danny realized there was nothing he wanted to do more than manage. If there had been a vote against Danny continuing as manager, it likely would have been from Tim, who was now a manager in the Pirate minor leagues. Local sportswriters liked to joke that Tim hoped his dad would retire for a fourth time so Joe Brown could call on a different Murtaugh to lead the Bucs.

In Bradenton for spring training in 1975, Danny referred to himself as a lucky man for being able to make a living doing what he loved. A March 26 AP story featured Danny as he discussed being a big league manager. The article noted, "He's recognized as a keen strategist, a man who always has the confidence and respect of his players":

> *"The most severe test of a manager," said the 57-year-old Murtaugh, "is the ability to keep the players contented and happy. After all, once you get to be a major league manager, you're supposed to be intelligent about the game. We all have the same rules. In fact, when it gets down to the close games the team with the most talent usually will win."*
>
> *Murtaugh said the big job is handling players who don't have regular jobs, the bench as it is described in baseball jargon. "You have to handle them in such a way that even though they're not playing, they're happy to be with the ball club. I don't say content. I don't want a contented bench. I want guys who are willing to bust their gut to show me they should play. I don't mind griping. No way you can fault a player who wants to play."*

*Murtaugh said he would advise a young manager that the job's greatest virtue is patience. "The more patient you are, the better manager you'll be. When I first came up as a manager I was too demanding. I had to learn never to expect a man to do something that he is not capable of doing. Now, I try to analyze and find out their capabilities and then never ask them to exceed them."*

Nearly 35 years later, Danny's players agree with his self-assessment. All-Star outfielder and occasional first baseman Al Oliver recalls, "Danny knew how to handle players. I thought he did an extremely good job keeping the players we had on that team happy. Because believe me, with our personalities – players who wanted to play every day – it was not an easy thing to do. But he did it." Relief pitcher Dave Giusti agrees, "One thing I learned from Danny was patience. Be patient with yourself as well as the rest of the club." Vernon Law, Danny's star pitcher from 1960, believes Danny had these qualities all along:

*He was a manager who knew his players, knew them well, and he would put them in situations most of the time where they couldn't fail or had a good opportunity to win. He knew the skills of each player and took advantage of their particular skills in game situations. … I think all the players that played under Danny had a lot of respect for Danny because of the way he handled us as individuals. … A manager who is able to do that with players, it makes you feel like you're on the same level. Then when you're out there playing for him, you're giving all you can, doing your very best.*

For the second year in a row, the Pirates took time during the 1975 spring training session to go to Puerto Rico and play an exhibition series to benefit the Roberto Clemente Sports City. Before his tragic death,

# the skipper returns...again

Clemente himself planned the complex as a place for Puerto Rican children to better themselves through sports. The 1975 series, which pitted the Bucs against the Yankees, coincided with a groundbreaking ceremony for the complex with Clemente's widow Vera. The ceremony was attended by Danny, Joe Brown, Willie Stargell, Al Oliver, Manny Sanguillen, and Yankee manager Bill Virdon (who, of course, as a Pirate had played with, coached, and managed Clemente).[13]

The Yankees swept the two-game exhibition series in 1975, but no one minded since their efforts raised almost $90,000 toward construction of the facility. Combined with the proceeds from the 1974 benefit series against the Montreal Expos, the Pirates had raised almost $160,000 of the estimated $500,000 - $1,000,000 construction cost of the complex. The Pirates planned similar exhibition series against the Mets, Phillies, and Red Sox in the following three years.[14]

It was back to business, though, when the Pirates returned to Florida to finish spring training. Leading up to spring training Danny had claimed, "We have the nucleus to have the best [pitching] staff in baseball."[15] Other managers, including the Mets' Yogi Berra and the Phillies' Danny Ozark, disagreed with Danny's assessment. On April 6 the *St. Petersburg Times* reported, "The big Pirate question mark once again appears to be pitching – and that old injury jinx that has plagued the mound staff the last few years." Before the season even began, one of those pitchers that Danny was counting on – Ken Brett – was on the disabled list.

Pitching worries aside, the season started on a positive note with the Pirates winning their first three games. By the beginning of May, the Pirates were in third place, three games behind the Cubs and one-half game behind the Mets. According to the *Post Gazette's* Charley Feeney, several of the new Pirates were amazed by their teammates' attitudes:

*"These are a remarkable bunch of guys," [Bill] Robinson said. "The mood never changes – win or lose. I've never seen anything like it with the Braves, the Yankees, the White Sox or the Phillies." … [With] the 1974 Phillies, "We used to get real high when we won, then we'd get down when we lost. Looking back, I think it hurt the team when things went bad last September. A lot of guys couldn't cope." …*

*[Former Met Duffy Dyer] noticed the low-key mood of the Pirates after they lost a few games. "It wasn't that way where I came from," Dyer said. "Around here, everything is the same – win or lose. I think it's a sign of confidence."*

*Sam McDowell, who has pitched for the Indians, Giants, and Yankees, says he has never been with such a cool club. "They know what they can do," he said. "They're not a bunch of kids. When they make a mistake, they know it. Nobody has to tell them about it."*[16]

Credit for the team's even keel was given to Danny and Willie Stargell, who was still serving as team captain. Stargell downplayed his role in the team's attitude, saying, "We're confident in ourselves. We're confident that when things go bad, we can come back. We expect to win, so maybe that's why we don't get excited about it." Danny acknowledged, "My philosophy of managing is to stay loose. I've always strived to get that across to my players. There are bound to be ups and downs in a season."[17]

As Danny well knew, there are bound to be ups and downs in life, too – and that May was no exception. On May 3 Danny missed a double-header with the Phillies to attend Danny Jr.'s wedding. It was a joyous occasion, marred only by the rapidly declining health of Danny's sister Peggy. They all knew she would not last much longer; on May 27 Peggy lost her years-long battle with cancer. Coach Bob Skinner filled in for Danny while he attended his sister's viewing and funeral. Peggy had lived either with or next door to Danny and his family for twenty two years. Her death was a major blow for the entire family, and it took a heavy personal toll on Danny.

On the baseball diamond, however, the 1975 Pirates had mostly ups. On June 6 they took up residence in first place and never left. Just two days earlier Danny and Joe Brown had met to discuss the team's pitching situation. They were about to enter a stretch of 45 games in 38 days without a break. With Dock Ellis and Ken Brett out with sore arms, Danny was going to need another pitcher. After looking at the situation, lefty John Candelaria, from the Pirate's AAA Charleston farm team, got the nod. Danny's daughter Kathy remembers when the Pirates first signed Candelaria back in 1972:

> We were living in Puerto Rico because my husband Joe was in the Navy. It was June and we were sitting in the living room when all of the sudden I saw a cab pull up. I said, "That's my parents!" The next day we got their telegram saying they were coming. John Candelaria was playing basketball for a Puerto Rican team and my dad was there to sign him. My mother came with him because our son Joey was four months old and she hadn't seen him for a while.

> Since we didn't have a phone, we had to keep driving my dad to a phone booth in our little Volkswagen bug that didn't have a back floor. Looking back, it seems almost unbelievable that this was how a two-time World Series Champion manager signed a future All-Star pitcher.

Any aggravations that Danny suffered in that trip would certainly prove worth it over the years. After a loss in his 1975 debut, the Candy

Man, as Candelaria became known, went 8-5 the rest of the season and posted a 2.76 ERA. In August, with Willie Stargell out because of a cracked rib, the team hit a slump that had some predicting their season was over. By August 17 the Phillies had crept within a half game of the Bucs. Three days later Danny reached a career milestone with his 1,000th victory as a Pirate manager. The Buccos were on their way back up. By the time October rolled around, the Pirates had a 92-69 record and won the NL East with a 6½ game lead over the Phillies.

The Pirates celebrated winning the division with the traditional champagne sprays. They knew it would be a tough matchup against the Cincinnati Reds to make it to the World Series, but they were confident they were up to the task. As Richie Zisk put it, "Every club has a slump ... I know Cincinnati is playing .700 baseball, but we're figuring the Reds' slump is coming in the playoffs."[18] Unfortunately, Zisk was wrong and the Reds cruised past the Bucs with three straight victories on their way to the World Series crown. After the Pirates won the NL East and then lost to the Reds for the NL Championship in 1970, 1972, and now 1975, Danny confided to his family, "If I knew who made up the divisions, I'd thank him for deciding that St. Louis was in the East and Cincinnati was in the West."

While Danny was obviously very disappointed with the outcome of the playoff series, there was one bright spot to the loss: He got to meet his fourth grandchild earlier than he would have otherwise. Tim's wife Janet had another son, Steven, on October 1, 1975. Tim had been managing at the Pirate farm team in Shreveport, LA, but they were back in the Chester area in time for Steven's birth. Shortly after the birth, Tim headed to the Dominican Republic to manage an independent team that had a loose relationship with the Pirates.

With the end of the Pirates' season came the annual tradition of sports writers discussing whether or not Danny would return the next year. *Post Gazette* columnist Charley Feeney noted that when Danny came aboard in 1973 he said he'd like to manage for three years. Add that to the fact that Joe Brown might retire when his five-year contract was up in 1976, and Feeney predicted one more year for the Irishman.

On October 15 Feeney learned that his prediction was correct. As the Pirates put it in a press release, "Danny Murtaugh today ended speculation as to who might be managing the Pirates in 1976 with the announcement that he would be back again ... As has been the case over the years in the long association between Murtaugh and General Manager Joe L. Brown, the decision was Danny's to make."

In December Willie Stargell discussed the upcoming season with the *Post Gazette's* Al Abrams. The Pirate slugger was optimistic: "Yes, we can win the pennant this year if we perform in certain areas. We have as good, if not better, pitching than any club. We can bomb away better than anybody. We'll have to cut down on the errors, and I think we're going to run a lot more." Citing Al Oliver, Dave Parker, Manny Sanguillen, and Rennie Stennett as potential base stealers, Stargell said he expected Danny to "cut 'em loose" when the situation calls for it.[19]

In February Danny previewed the season in the *St. Petersburg Times,* saying he was "really looking forward to the '76 season and the opportunity to improve on last year's performance."[20] He noted that the Pirates had won five division titles in the previous six years – something no other team could claim during the same period. Danny also pointed out that the 1975 Pirate pitching staff gave up fewer home runs than any other team in the majors and were second in hits allowed, runs, earned runs, earned run average, and complete games. Apparently Danny had been right in February 1975 when he predicted great things from his pitching staff that year. Not surprisingly, he was at least as optimistic in 1976 with his key pitchers set to return. Danny also highlighted the team's power hitters – including Stargell, Sanguillen, Oliver, Dave Parker, Richie Hebner, and Richie Zisk – a group who would become known as the Lumber Company for their prowess at the plate.

Heading into the 1976 season the Pirates and the Phillies were expected to duke it out for the NL East pennant. In a two-game season opening series in Philadelphia, the Pirates came away the victors. They had opened their season by beating the team everyone said they had to beat, but they knew it would be a long haul. Danny, characteristically, didn't get excited about the sweep, saying, "We never key in on one club. That's not our style."[21]

The Buccos may not have been focused on the Phillies in April, but by the end of August, they sure were. After winning their first five games inconsistent pitching and hitting put them in second place by mid-May, although they were still within two or three games of first. The Pirates had a solid May, but the Phillies won a team-record twenty two games that month and widened their lead to 6½ games. Same thing in June – the Pirates had a good month, but the Phillies were red hot and won 20 of 29 games and now had a nine-game lead.

The Pirates landed in Cincinnati for a four-game series leading into the All Star break. As manager of the 1975 World Series Champs, Reds Manager Sparky Anderson was heading up the National League All Star team. He planned to ask Danny to be one of his coaches, but NL President Chub Feeney told him that Danny wanted to take advantage of the break to await the birth of his fifth grandchild. Upon his arrival in Cincy, Danny took the opportunity to rib his fellow manager a little. "Hey Sparky," he chided, "how come you didn't ask me to be one of your coaches?" Sparky started to apologize and explain what happened but then realized he was being conned.

The All Star break came and went with no new grandchild for

Danny. On August 5 the Mets came to town for a four-game series. The next day, Kate called Danny at Three Rivers Stadium to let him know that Kathy had a new baby girl – named Katie after her proud grandmother. With a heavy baseball schedule stretching in front of him, Danny wasn't sure when he'd get to meet his new granddaughter. Luck smiled on the Irishman, though, and that night's game was rained out and re-scheduled as a doubleheader the next day. Kathy only lived around an hour north, so Danny headed up to see little Katie. It was past visiting hours by the time he arrived, but the nurses said they'd let him in ... if he signed autographs for them! Danny complied, of course, and then hurried back to Three Rivers the next day for the doubleheader.

By August 24 Pittsburgh was still in second place, but they were now fifteen games behind Philadelphia. *Post Gazette* sports writer Charley Feeney reported on August 30 that Danny charged the Phillies with being uncooperative: "We'd be right in the thick of it if the Phillies weren't such a bunch of bleeps," Murtaugh cracked. "In any other season, a team fourteen games over .500 would be close to first place, or in first place."

The Pirates were not a team prone to quitting, though, and they kept plugging away. Everything started to click, and from their low point on August 24 they won 18 of their next 22 games. By September 16 the Pirates had risen to just three games behind the Phils. It wasn't enough. Of the remaining sixteen games, the Pirates won just seven while the Phillies won thirteen. Thus it was the Phillies getting swept by the Reds in the 1976 NL Championship Series instead of the Pirates.

On September 29 Joe Brown held a news conference as the Pirates prepared for their last series. Most sports writers expected that Danny would be announcing his retirement – they'd been predicting it all season. They were in for a surprise, though – it was Brown himself who was ready to retire. After 26 years in the Pirate organization – including 21 years as

Pirate General Manager – Joe Brown was ready to slow down. Like Danny in previous years, Brown would stay on as a scout, but he was moving back to his native California.

Two days later Danny stepped up to the microphone at another news conference looking very happy. "I'm here to announce that I'll be back for two more years. I signed a contract with Joe [Brown] this morning." There was utter silence, until one of the reporters realized that Danny was playing one of his infamous pranks. When questioned about it, Danny acknowledged his health was a factor, "I think this year was one of the worst years I've had in the last three as far as my health is concerned. I was ill a few more times than anybody realized." Danny planned to stay involved with the Pirates, but said that this retirement was "for good."[22]

> I think that I've been around long enough. I'm approaching the age of 60 and also I've reached that point where I would like to spend some of the time with my grandchildren. I think that my own children were neglected a little bit when I was in the process of managing in my younger years and naturally I didn't spend as much time as I should have with them. So I'm going to try to make up for it by spending a little more time with the grandchildren.[23]

CHAPTER THIRTEEN

# the end of an era

The phone rang. Danny's daughter Kathy picked it up and heard her mother's voice on the line. "Your dad had a minor stroke," Kate said. It was Tuesday, November 30, 1976, less than a week after Thanksgiving. Throughout the day the phone continued to ring. Each call was a little worse. After hastily arranging for her sister-in-law Suzanne to watch their three kids, Kathy and her husband, Joe, left for Philly. "Mother told us not to come," Kathy recalls, "but the situation kept sounding worse, so we decided to go."

Everyone knew Danny wasn't in the best health – it was hard to look at him without realizing something was wrong. But he had been to the doctor for a checkup the morning of November 30, and everything looked pretty good. The doctor had taken blood to run tests on, but results took longer in those days than they do now. When the results came back a week or so later, they found out that his blood sugar had skyrocketed. By then, he was already gone.

Thus, when they arrived home from the checkup neither Danny nor Kate had any inkling tragedy was about to strike. Danny was relaxing in his favorite chair while Kate was in kitchen making scrambled eggs with ham and cheese. Kate heard a noise and went into living room to investigate. She found Danny slumped in his chair. She immediately called for an ambulance.

Danny's nephew-in-law heard the call on his scanner and told his mother-in-law (Danny's sister Mary) and Danny's cousin Madge. They lived just down the street, so they hurried to the house. Madge remembers arriving as the sirens wailed. Danny was lying on the floor with Kate at his side. Madge asked, "Danny where does it hurt?" and he pointed to his head. The ambulance arrived and took Danny to Chester's Crozier Hospital while Kate followed with Mary and Madge.

Danny's condition quickly deteriorated. By the time Wednesday's newspapers went out, a hospital spokesman called it a "serious stroke" and said a team of specialists was examining him. He was still conscious at the time – and still held onto his sense of humor. Madge remembers being in Danny's room with his sisters Mary and Eunice. They were all talking, trying to keep Danny's spirits up even though he wasn't able to talk back. At one point Eunice said something, and Danny used his hand to signal that he thought she was talking too much.

But "Little Danny Murtaugh" – the plucky Irishman, the peppery fighter, the born hustler, the sparkplug – was losing this battle. For Kathy, the memory is as clear as if it happened yesterday, "He was in a coma by the time we got there. There were a lot of people there – family, friends, and such. They said his fever was 106. I touched him and it was unbelievable how hot he was. I remember thinking, 'all that baseball knowledge, all that knowledge in his brain and it's never going to come out of there.' We knew as soon as we got to the hospital that he wasn't going to make it."

Danny's son Tim was managing in the Dominican Republic at the time. Joe Brown tracked him down so Kate could give him the news. "When I got the initial call, I asked if I should come home. My mother said he was doing fine and not to come. The next day I got fired, so I was on the way home anyway. While we were in a hotel near the airport waiting for our flight the next morning, I got a call from my brother Danny telling me that my dad had died."

Danny Jr. [now deceased] was in the room with his dad when he died. He told the family that his dad opened his eyes, "looked right at me, and squeezed my hand" right before he died. It was December 2, 1976. According to Kathy, "We went back to the house after he died – aunts, uncles, cousins, friends. Someone knocked over my dad's spittoon and I said, 'EEEWW!' Aunt Madge declared, 'That's precious spit now.' We went into the living room. On the TV was a vase of beautiful red roses with a card that said 'To Kathleen – Love, Daniel.' It was from their 35th wedding anniversary on November 29th."

The family didn't have time to process their loss before the newspapers started calling. Funeral plans had to be made. Kate took charge and handled everything. But, Kathy recalls, "She was a mess. She told me she felt like she lost half of herself." As funeral plans proceeded the house began to fill with flowers. Walking through at one point, Kathy said, "This smells like a funeral." Then she remembered: This is a funeral. It was still so unreal.

Kathy's husband Joe remembers that Danny connected with a lot of family members shortly before his death: "It was amazing. Danny retired October 1 and made the rounds at several family events. He was at a family reunion, came to our house in Greenville, PA, hosted Thanksgiving, went visiting his local family, and just managed to see numerous friends and family. Looking back, it was as if he was saying good-bye. I remember so many people at the funeral saying they'd just seen him."

Danny's cousin Madge was at the same family reunion with Danny. She remembers that Danny was walking very slowly down the steps – like someone much older than 59. She called out to him, "Danny, get back up here and go down the stairs right." He refused, saying, "Madge, my legs hurt." It wasn't long after that he died. Madge's 95-year-old mother-in-law also saw him at the reunion and mentioned to her son Art, "Danny looks so old." But even though he wasn't looking good, no one expected him to die any time soon. Everyone who knew him was shocked.

Former Pirate All Star Al Oliver, who played under Danny for five and a half years, agrees: "We all knew he had some heart problems, but still you don't expect that. It was a jolt. I was at the service. That was the least that I could do, to pay my respects by being there. I'm just glad that I was able to be there to show my respect to a man who led me to my only World Championship. That was a big hunk out of the Pittsburgh Pirate history that was lost that day. But he will always be remembered. That's the key. Memories can last for a lifetime and that's a good thing. The memories that I have of him were some funny [chuckles], but all of them were positive."

Danny's viewing and funeral were the largest ever in the city of Chester. People waited in a line that stretched around the block in 18 degree weather for the viewing. Steelers' owner Art Rooney, a fellow Irishman and good friend of Danny, was among those waiting outside in the cold. When Kate heard he was there, she said to her nephew Bennie, "Go out and get Art Rooney – he's waiting outside in the cold." Bennie went out but quickly came back and asked, "What does he look like?" A Philly boy, Bennie was an Eagles fan and had never seen the Steelers' owner.

On December 6, 1976, Danny was laid to rest at Sts. Peter and Paul Cemetery not far from Chester. That morning Danny's flag-draped coffin was wheeled past a Knights of Columbus Honor Guard paying tribute to a fellow Fourth Degree Knight. His longtime friend, pinochle partner, and pastor, Father Walter Nall, said the opening prayer at the Mass of Christian Burial at Our Lady of Peace Roman Catholic Church in Milmont Park, PA. Father Francis O'Reilly, who officiated at Danny and Kate's wedding 35 years earlier, celebrated the Mass and gave the eulogy:

> *Think how Danny influenced your life and what we can do to say "thank you." … When he took Kate for his wife, he had arrived at first base in his spiritual life. And so today, everyone in America and the civilized world is standing in adulation as Danny dashes across home plate.*[1]

The town that loved him, and that he loved, came out in full force to mourn Danny. One elderly neighbor recalled, "Everybody in Chester loved him. I remember him as a fun-loving, mischievous boy who played a lot of pranks but never hurt anyone in his life." *Pittsburgh Post Gazette* sports columnist Al Abrams observed, "The consensus here was that no baseball figure in history who 'has crossed the home plate of life' was more beloved and considered a friend by both neighbors and people afar than Danny Murtaugh."[2]

The team and players that Danny served so faithfully were present for Danny's final farewell. Among his former players in attendance at the funeral were Willie Stargell, Bill Robinson, Bruce Kison, Dave Giusti, Jim Rooker, Larry Demery, Bob Robertson, Al Oliver, Manny Sanguillen, and Steve Blass. The Pirates' front office was represented by team president Dan Galbreath; recently retired GM Joe Brown; his replacement, Harding "Pete" Peterson; part-owner Tom Johnson; and long-time Pirate announcer Bob Prince.

Danny's good friend and fellow local-boy-turned-major-league-player-and-manager Mickey Vernon was also at the funeral. Former Pirate player, coach, and manager Bill Virdon was managing the Houston Astros at the time, but he found his way to Chester to pay his respects to the man who was a mentor to him. Even the umpires, with whom Danny loved to tussle, paid their respects to the late manager. Retired ump Shag Crawford said that he and his fellow umpires had great respect for Danny, "He wore us out on occasion, but we wore him out too."[3]

The funeral procession included more than 70 cars and a flower-laden fire truck from the Franklin Fire house, where Danny volunteered for so many years. It seemed like every police officer in Chester was on duty to deal with the crowds – and to pay their own respects to the popular Irishman who never lost his roots. Police officers George Lauginiger and Rich Holmes typified those in attendance by remarking, "Danny never failed to say hello."[4] Officers in towns all along the 12-mile route directed traffic so the funeral procession would go smoothly.

Leaving the funeral, the funeral director took Kate, her kids, and their spouses back to Kelly Avenue. Kathy's husband Joe remembers arriving at the house: "The guy who drove the limo came around and opened the door for us. As we exited the car he said, 'Have a nice day.' I replied, 'Well it's been pretty shitty so far.' I was shocked that someone in the funeral business would make a slip like that."

Kathy stayed with Kate for around a week after the funeral, and then she had to get back to her three young children. Tim and Danny Jr. both offered to have their mother come and stay with them. But Kate figured she needed to face living alone eventually, so she decided to get on with it. It probably helped some that she was used to living alone since Danny traveled so much. However, that also made it harder to accept that he was really gone.

A few weeks later Kathy and Joe were back in Woodlyn with their kids for Christmas. It was tough. Christmas was Danny's favorite time of year – and he'd been really looking forward to having all five grandchildren with him that year. Tim bought Christmas corsages for the "girls" (Kate,

Tim's wife Janet, Kathy, and Danny Jr.'s wife Debbie) because that's what Danny had always done.

Due to his frequent speaking engagements Danny had a closet full of suits. His friends would often come "shopping" in Danny's closet. His cousin Madge recalls going to Danny's hotel suite after a game in New York and watching all the husbands try on his new suit jacket. With all her kids there for Christmas, Kate decided to start going through Danny's closets to sort out things to give away to his friends and to charity. Danny Jr. was looking for one item in particular and kept asking, "Where's that green suit? I really liked that green suit." Finally Kathy pulled him out into the hall and said, "They buried him in it."

Danny's grandchildren – the ones he retired to spend more time with – were too young to understand the enormity of their loss. They were forever robbed of the wit and wisdom, the guiding hand, and the love of the man who touched so many lives. Tim's son Timmy was the oldest, seven years old, and understood the most what had happened. He was devastated, of course. Timmy still remembers being in a hotel on the way home from the Dominican Republic and praying for Grandpop.

Kathy's son Joey was four when Danny died. The following spring Kathy was having work done on her roof and there was a ladder leaning against the house. She went outside one day and – to her horror – Joey was climbing the ladder. She managed to get him down and asked him what he was doing. His reply broke her heart, "I was trying to get to Heaven to visit Grandpop."

# Remembering Danny

Tributes to Danny began pouring in even before the funeral – both in newspapers and in Kate's mailbox. There were two men from Munhall who became friends with Danny when the family lived there during the baseball season. His son Tim remembers, "My dad would always joke about hiring them as coaches. Each year when he got back to Pittsburgh, they'd send him a note saying they were ready. After my dad died, they sent a message that said, 'We retire.'"

Danny's daughter Kathy recalls receiving a letter from a childhood friend who wrote, "Most people remember the World Series wins, the baseball stories, and all of that. I remember a man coming up to the attic and telling us silly stories at your sleepovers." Kate received thousands of letters, cards, and telegrams from fans all across the country expressing their shock and sorrow at Danny's passing. Sports pages were full of accolades for Danny – the man and the manager.

### JOE BROWN, Pirates General Manager who retired days before Danny

I haven't been as close to many men as I was to Danny. He was my very dear friend and I said when he was alive that he was like my brother. He was my brother. I loved him and I can't say any more than that. He was an unusual human being, a fine, fine fellow. I ache for his family.

### HARDING "PETE" PETERSON, Joe Brown's successor

I'm kind of in shock. We not only worked together. We were friends. We're all terribly shocked. We lost a tremendous friend. ... It's pretty hard at times like this.

### Baseball Commissioner BOWIE KUHN

I've always found Danny a wonderful mix of basic professional toughness and reverence. Reverence may seem like a strange word to use, but reverence is what I think of him. The toughness that went along with the goodness. He had a wonderful pixie quality about him.

### AL ABRAMS, *Pittsburgh Post Gazette*, December 4, 1976

Memories, one great man in the long ago said, are made up of mists. This could be true in some cases. But not in remembrance of Danny Murtaugh, a great man and a good friend who was called by his Maker Thursday night. The only mists I run into are those in my eyes as I recall some happy 30 years in which I got to know the "Smiling Irishman." ...

Danny Murtaugh was often described as a big Irish Leprechaun. Good description. A kind, good, humble man besides being a great manager, he had a devilish Irish witty streak that kept both friend and stranger wondering what he was saying or doing. ...

We could tell you a hundred or more incidents about Danny Murtaugh both on and off the field. For all his kidding, he was one of the best managers in the game's history. We won't go into that since his contributions will not be forgotten here or elsewhere.

The one thing I like to remember about Danny Murtaugh was his humble acceptance of his third *Post-Gazette* Dapper Dan Award in 1972. He shared honors with Roberto Clemente and Willie Stargell.

After he thanked his players for helping him win a second World Championship, Danny Murtaugh told the 2,200 men present: "I want to thank you for permitting me to walk through your Rose Garden."

Danny Murtaugh is walking through the greatest Rose Garden of all, looking impishly for someone to play a trick on.

## CHARLEY FEENEY, *Pittsburgh Post Gazette,* December 4, 1976

Danny Murtaugh would have been embarrassed by it all. He never wanted a fuss made about him. He never wanted to be center stage. There was always a little bit of a boy in Danny Murtaugh and that's the way he wanted it to be.

But he was all man. He didn't live and die with the outcome of Pirate games. He didn't curse after defeats and he didn't boast after victories. When he managed the Pirates, he put in longer hours than any player. Nobody insisted that Murtaugh show up at the park at one p.m. for a 7:30 game. This is the way he wanted it. ...

Murtaugh loved to tell baseball stories. He was a good listener, too. As a story-teller, Murtaugh rated with the best. He rarely told a story where he turned out to be the good guy, or the smart guy. ... Murtaugh loved to tell [about the truck crashing through his hotel room when he was in the minor leagues]. "Gambling," Murtaugh used to say, "saved my life. I was a lucky guy." The people who really are lucky are the people who got to know Danny Murtaugh. He was one of a kind.

**MATT ZIBITKA, former sports writer for the *Chester Times and Wilmington (DE) News-Journal,* December 4, 1976**

Three times voted manager of the year, Danny's success never spoiled him. The hat size never swelled for this product of the Depression, Franklin Fire Co. volunteer, Sun Shipyard worker, and World War II foot soldier, who trudged across Europe with the infantry and was ambushed by German snipers.

He was a deeply religious, quiet, conscientious and a patient man. A baseball manager who knew how to get the best out of his players without all the raucousness of a Billy Martin or the abuses of a Woody Hayes.

That's how I remember Daniel Edward Murtaugh.

When Danny stepped down as manger of the Bucs after the 1976 season in October, after managing 15 years during four different terms, he explained, "I think I've been around long enough. I'm approaching the age of 60 and I've also reached a point where I would like to spend some time with my grandchildren."

He admitted he neglected his own children a bit while in the process of playing and managing during his younger years. "So I'm going to try to make up for it by spending a little more time now with my grandchildren," he said. It's three weeks before Christmas and Danny never lived to watch his grandchildren greet Christmas Day.

**FRANK DOLSON, *Philadelphia Inquirer* Sports Editor, December 4, 1976**

There are men who take themselves so seriously in sports, managers and coaches who think the world revolves around them, who expect their every utterance to be treated as if it were something special and important.

And then there was Danny Murtaugh. Always playing harmless, little jokes. Always making people laugh. Never taking himself too seriously.

He proved you could do the job, you could manage a big league team, you could win pennants and world championships and be yourself. The real Danny Murtaugh was always sitting in that rocking chair in the Pirate clubhouse; it didn't matter if the team had won or lost, if his late-inning moves had worked or backfired, if the club was ten games ahead of the pack or twelve games behind. Nobody had to ask, "What's Danny Murtaugh really like?" He was what you saw – a very decent, very warm, very funny human being. "I don't think the fans ever knew how funny he was," Reds manager Sparky Anderson said after learning of Danny's death. ...

Some managers work overtime building up their images; Murtaugh seemed to take delight in knocking his down.

One time he sent up Dave Parker to pinch-hit with the bases loaded, and the kid hit a grand slam to wrap up the game. Pretty soon, the press gathered around his rocking chair, waiting to find out what brilliant thinking had led him to make the big move. Danny spoke first. "Thanks for calling me," he told a Pittsburgh writer. "I was going to put up Popovich until you told me to use Parker." Murtaugh would tell the story, and he'd laugh and say: "You know what? One guy believed me. He was writing it down. ... But there ARE some good sports writers. In Spartanburg. In Gastonia. ..."

And there was a good manager – and a beautiful human being – sitting in that rocking chair in Pittsburgh through four tours of duty, 1,115 victories, two World Series and four National League championship series.

"Hello, Mr. Brown," he would say to his boss and close friend, Joe Brown, the day after a tough defeat. "He lets me call him Joe if we win," Danny would explain.

"Sometimes," he said one night after a particularly galling defeat, "you think these games are pre-destined." And then the Irish eyes twinkled and he rocked back and forth a few times and added, "If they are, you wouldn't need managers, would you?"

The truth is, the game does need managers, and particularly men, like Danny Murtaugh.

"I think I'm a lucky man," he told me two springs ago. "I wanted to play baseball and I played in the big leagues … I would have been content to manage anywhere, but I was lucky enough to manage in the big leagues – a fulfillment of both dreams. Any time a man can do what he wants, he's lucky."

There are men who played for Danny Murtaugh who consider themselves lucky, too. "Danny was very, very instrumental in bringing me back to a position where I signed a nice, two-year contract, where I got a little security," Bill Robinson said yesterday. "Danny gave me a new lease on life, and I'm very appreciative. Because he gave me a chance, I'm happier now than I've ever been in baseball."

Naturally. Happiness and Danny Murtaugh went hand in hand.

## Bill Lyon, *Philadelphia Inquirer,* December 7, 1976

On the day they buried Danny Murtaugh, the sun was shining.

On the day they buried Danny Murtaugh, the sky was cloudless, and a wintery wind knifed through the cemetery and ruffled the flowers on a wreath of Pirates black and gold and made the tiny American flags on the other graves snap crisply to attention.

On the day they buried Danny Murtaugh, the Rev. Francis P. O'Reilly recited the Mass of Christian Burial and said: "Every person in the U.S., every person in every civilized country, is standing today as Danny Murtaugh crosses home plate."

On the day they buried Danny Murtaugh, Willie Stargell, a massive man, a slugger of prodigious home runs, hid his grief behind dark glasses and gently embraced Danny Murtaugh's widow.

They sprinkled holy water and ashes over Danny Murtaugh's casket and then Kate Murtaugh turned, wet-eyed but still strong, and buried her head in Willie Stargell's chest. Stargell enfolded her tenderly in his huge arms and whispered to her and the tears froze on his beard. Kate Murtaugh stepped back and smiled and nodded and got into the long, black limousine.

On the day they buried Danny Murtaugh, more than 700 mourners got down on their knees inside Our Lady of Peace Church.

"Listen," said Father O'Reilly, "the Lord is calling. He is saying, 'Daniel, come into your house.'" …

"Daniel Murtaugh," said Father O'Reilly, "was a man of baseball, but you see all of these priests here, all of these mourners, and you know that he must also have been a man of God, and that is the finest thing one can say of another human being. He lived a life of dedication and love and he is worthy of our admiration. We should all be inspired by him … inspired to try a little harder."

… Inspired to try a little harder. Ah yes, that was Danny Murtaugh's theme song. There were other players with more natural athletic gifts, but none who scraped and clawed and hustled as hard as the tough little Irishman.

… Inspired to try a little harder. Three [sic] times his heart forced Danny Murtaugh out of the dugout. Each time he came back to again manage the Pittsburgh Pirates.

… Inspired to try a little harder. In the blast furnace of a pennant race, Danny Murtaugh sat in his rocking chair, munching his cheese and crackers, and playing out the hand he had been dealt. He never complained about the cards they had given him.

So yesterday they buried Danny Murtaugh and the sun was shining and the sky was cloudless and the cold wind ruffled the floral wreaths and made the flags snap to attention, and the mourners stood, bundled in their great coats, and the trees were without leaves and Kate Murtaugh turned away from the grave and just before she got into the car she looked up … up into the cloudless sky, and she seemed to be searching it for something, and then she smiled just a little.

You had the feeling that she had found what she was looking for … that somewhere up there the Rocking Chair Irishman was looking down and that creased, craggy face was beaming and those leprechaun eyes were shining … and maybe, just maybe, Danny Murtaugh gave Kate Murtaugh a big wink.

### FURMAN BISHER, Sports Editor of *Atlanta Journal Constitution*

[Danny] was the little man's man. … He was always approachable … He never got far away from Chester even when he was out of town. … Born there, married Kathleen Patricia Clark there, had their kids there, and their kids had their kids there, always went home there, and died there. There was something so downright American about Danny Murtaugh it makes you want to cry to think that he's gone.

When Joe [Brown] tapped him to finish out a season that Bobby Bragan started, it was assumed Murtaugh was for the interim only. … He fit it so snugly that every time Joe Brown needed help, it was Murtaugh he turned to. By the time their little act was over, Murtaugh had set a record by managing the same club four different times. Brown kept calling and he kept answering.

The little guy won the championship in the improbable World Series of 1960, when the Yankees finally got taken down in a repetition of spectacles. It was looking like a fluke until [1971]. This time the Pirates beat Baltimore when Steve Blass and Roberto Clemente formed a heroic corporation.

The older he grew, the better Murtaugh managed. He was first in his division four of his last six seasons. …

When the Pirates made their last stop of the season in Atlanta, the final trouble was etched in Murtaugh's face. He was 59, but looking 70. He'd come back once too often and stayed too long [for his health].

He was always a little careless with his tobacco juice, and this time when he spat, he grinned. "See, I've lost my aim," he said. "I can't even hit your shoes anymore."

Soon as the season ended, he said that was his last run. He said he wanted to go home and spend time with the grandchildren. Dammit, they're the biggest losers. He had a stroke and died last week, and as he went, his grandchildren and American sport lost one genuine soul.

## POHLA SMITH, UPI Sports Writer, December 3, 1976

Few sports figures measure up in the flesh to the demanding, large-than-life images that children and fans have of them. Danny Murtaugh did. At least for me.

In the year that I knew him as a sportswriter covering the Pittsburgh Pirates, I learned that the Bucs' manager was everything everyone had ever told me about him. And more.

He was the pugnacious streetfighter of Irish-American lore, a practical jokester, a smart-mouth, a raconteur, a member of a dying breed who would have played the game for only the joy of locker room poker games and his teammates' camaraderie if the general manager had told him there was no money for salaries.

He was also a loving man who embraced all friends as family. He was more grandfather than manager to "the boys" on the team, their wives and children, and the younger members of the press corps and groundskeeping crew at Three Rivers Stadium.

**BOB BROEG, Sports Editor, *St. Louis Post-Dispatch,*
December 12, 1976**

As a man and as a manager, a wit and a wag, [Danny] was A-1, a winner. Although deadpanned, most of the time, fighting to remain expressionless behind sleepy, heavy-lidded eyes that betrayed him with a sparkle when he raised them, Murtaugh was a funny Irishman who became a bulging-bellied leprechaun when big league clubs went to two-way-stretch polyester uniforms. ...

The mind's eye and memory catch Murtaugh at the moment of his greatest triumph. In 1960, which was 33 years after Pittsburgh's last pennant and 35 seasons after the steel-mill center's last previous world championship, Danny Boy did it – and ridiculously.

Outhit by the New York Yankees, .338 to .256, and outscored by more than a 2-to-1 ratio (55 runs to 27), the underdog Pirates pulled a major upset in seven games ... Murtaugh retreated to his clubhouse, where, characteristically, he sat in his rocking chair, hands folded serenely in his lap like Whistler's Mother.

Incongruous, sure, but hardly more than Murtaugh's phiz or habits. He sat there chewing tobacco, smoking a cigar, and sipping milk. Although he looked like a whisky-head, Murtaugh was a teetotaler who manipulated milk around his chaw to placate an ulcer caused apparently by permitting patience to show on the outside and hiding gnawing competitiveness on the inside.

Behind his desk, framed just above his head, was a bit of verse written by Edgar Guest, longtime newspaper rhymester who put together once:

"There are nine men out on the field of play,

Nine men trying to win.

But if you are a star, as the paper says,

Who gets the run that brings you in?"

There was more under the verse entitled "Team Play," but, somehow, it typified the team-man manager and friend who was always good for a sly needle or a solemn-faced remark that masked his mirth.

But Daniel Edward Murtaugh was never his humble self more than that afternoon at Forbes Field in October 1960 when [Joe] Brown burst in, grabbed him, and said, "You're the greatest manager in the world."

"Not the greatest," said Danny Murtaugh, "but the most grateful."

## MICKEY FURFARI, *Charleston (WV) Daily Mail,* December 5, 1976

Danny Murtaugh loved baseball and he loved people. To him, those were dearest in a much-too-short life span which ended with his death last Thursday night in his native Chester, PA. The grand ol' gentleman made friends wherever he went with his twinkling Irish eyes, his wit, and his warmth. ...

In more serious moments Danny loved to talk about his wife, children, and grandchildren. While he dearly loved his work, he dearly loved his family even more. It was his desire to spend more time with his grandchildren that weighed heavily in his decision to retire as Pirate manager – for the [fourth] and last time – on October 1 of this year.

It is saddening that he never got the chance. He died two days after suffering a stroke, just two months from the day he retired.

He did have an opportunity to spend a brief vacation with wife Kate out in Las Vegas last month. And he did visit his grandchildren a few times. But the "make-up mission" was all much too short for the ailing 59-year-old Irishman. ...

Murtaugh appeared as jovial as ever during his visit to Morgantown about 11 months ago. He kidded area newsmen at a luncheon after dropping in on students at St. Francis High School and chatting with youngsters in the children's ward at University Hospital. He was late for the luncheon because he had stayed longer at the hospital than scheduled. He had a ball there talking to the young patients. They admittedly reminded him so much of his own grandchildren.

One little girl offered to "bake you a cake." He smiled his acceptance, then kept kidding her about "hurrying it along." That's the side of Danny Murtaugh I'll remember most – the love he had for people, particularly young people.

RICHIE ASHBURN, former Phillies' outfielder (Hall of Fame) and later radio-TV commentator, in *Philadelphia Evening Bulletin,* December 1976 (day unknown)

Danny was a ballplayer's manager. He always used the cliché, "I treat my players the way I wanted to be treated." A lot of managers have used that cliché and then have forgotten it, but Murtaugh lived by it. ...

Murtaugh was always low-key but very effective. He hardly ever raised his voice even when jawing with umpires, but he could get tough when he had to.

Murtaugh managed a lot of players who weren't that easy to handle and he did it successfully. Most managers have temperamental players but they don't win with them. Murtaugh did. ...

Murtaugh's Pirate teams won for two reasons. One, they had a lot of talent. And two, Danny didn't interfere with that talent. He wrote out the lineup and just turned it loose. If Danny had an ego, it wasn't apparent in the way he managed his teams.

The Pirates did reflect his personality though. Danny was happy and the Pirates were always a happy group of players. Danny was tough and so was his team. If they had to, they would fight at the drop of a hat. ...

Danny had been a sick man for quite a few years and probably should have retired earlier. It was apparent to those of us who saw him during the summer that his health was failing. Not in the way he acted because it was always a pleasure to be around him, but in the way he looked.

If there is a heaven and baseball players can somehow get there, that great general manager in the sky doesn't have to worry about a skipper.

**LES BIEDERMAN, longtime Sports Editor of *Pittsburgh Press*, writing in the *Sporting News*, December 18, 1976**

So long, Danny Murtaugh. Thanks for the memories. You were someone special on and off the field. You were kind, considerate, firm, loyal and above all, fair. And you were always modest. Your baseball cap always fit your Irish head.

## CHAPTER FIFTEEN

# Danny's Boys

### Dave Cash, Second Baseman (1969-73)

Danny was something special – he was a former infielder, a former second baseman. He not only helped me with my hitting, he and Maz helped me with my fielding in terms of turning the double play. When I signed with the Pirates in '66, I'd always been a shortstop. It was a few years later that I started playing second base. Danny gave me a lot of pointers in turning the double play because I'd never played that side of the infield before.

Danny was a good evaluator of talent. Even more important, in my opinion, he was a great communicator. He was a good reader of personalities. He never seemed to put a guy in a situation that he wasn't comfortable with or wasn't able to handle. He was always able to put the guy in the spot where he knew he was going to be successful. That's the sign of a good manager. Good managers acquire that quality over time. Danny had been in World Series before, he had managed before, and he was able to call on his experiences of the past to communicate to us what could happen in the future.

He was definitely the leader of our ball club. Most of the time, teams take on the personality of their manager. It was the same with our team. We never got too high when we won, and we never got too low when we lost. A lot of that came from Danny's experiences when he was younger, and he passed it on down to us, to the younger players. He'd experienced a lot of the things that we were experiencing at the time.

It was a sad day when Danny passed. We knew we lost a friend and a confidante, someone who really taught us how to play the game. I think that the things that he passed on to us, we've passed on to future generations.

## DAVE GUISTI, Pitcher (1970-76)

When I was traded to the Pirates, they were planning for me to have a good year as a starter. But when I got to spring training, I played poorly. And I continued to play poorly. Danny thought I just needed extra work in spring training. It ended up being true. In the last few games, I pitched a lot of innings. Even though I still did badly, I pitched a lot of innings and it really got me ready for the season. I think a lot of managers would've quit on me and thrown me back in the bullpen somewhere.

He was the kind of manager who let you either win or lose your position. In the early part of 1970, I earned my position and went on from there. I remember one time I was pitching poorly in a particular game and I'd given up a couple of runs, but we still had a little bit of a lead. Very seldom did Danny come out to the mound, but this time he did. He said, "Dave, look over my right shoulder. There are two guys warming up in the bullpen. I'm going to have to bring one of those guys in here unless you do something. You're much better than they are, but if you don't get someone out, I'm going to have to bring one of them in right away." And that was a psychological thing that helped me focus. …

Danny really was a psychologist in his own right. He tried to find out about you as an individual and how to handle situations within your relationship. In Game Four of the 1971 World Series, Luke Walker didn't have it. Danny knew it and he took him out early in the game and put in Bruce Kison. Kison was a young guy – just 20 or 21 – and everyone thought Danny was nuts. But Danny had this knowledge of individuals and how they would be in certain situations. Kison got the win and I got the save.

Danny wasn't overpowering, he didn't make statements he couldn't back up. He put everything on an even keel. When you did foul up, he didn't say anything in front of others; he'd take you into his office and work things out. He didn't say much, but when he did it was worth listening to because it made a lot of sense and applied well to whomever he was talking to.

### Nellie King, Pitcher (1954-57)

The first major league game I ever saw was in 1941 at Shibe Park in Philadelphia when Danny and Bobby Bragan were playing for the Phillies. At the time I didn't know who either of them were, but I ended up playing for both of them. In 1953, when I was returning to baseball after time in the Army, I met Danny in spring training. He was managing the New Orleans Pelicans at the time.

I had little personal contact with Danny that spring until "cut-down" day arrived. I was shagging fly balls during batting practice when I noticed Danny walking in the outfield. He would stop to have private conversations with various players. In a comforting way he would drape his arm around the player as he continued the conversation. A veteran of too many spring training "cut-down" days, I knew what was taking place. Danny finally worked his way to my side of the field, put his arm around me, and before he could say anything, I asked, "Where am I going Danny?" He laughed and said, "It's either Charleston, SC or Denver." I replied, "How about Denver? I've already seen Charleston."

To ease my disappointment he took me aside privately to inform me how difficult it was for him returning to baseball after his years in the army during World War II. He told me to be patient as it took him a month or more before he began to play with the confidence and consistency he had before the war. He was right on target, as I would experience the symptoms he described in the early months of the season at Denver in 1953. However I recovered and due to the advice and concern from Danny I had my most successful season in the minors [and eventually made it to the big leagues].

My conversation with Danny during cut-down day of spring training at New Orleans in 1953 indicated the sensitivity he had for players working their way up to the major leagues. Having played for Danny in 1954 at New Orleans, I knew he spoke only when he had something important to say. It didn't change when he took over as manager of the Pirates in August of 1957. He didn't hold his first team meeting until two weeks after being named manager. He watched and listened. I remember the first meeting; it was brief and to the point. He opened by saying, "I don't usually have a lot of meetings or have a lot to say. But I have been doing a lot of watching and listening, and I don't like what I'm seeing or hearing. And it's going to change." He then went on to lay down plain but simple things he expected.

Danny was very patient with players. His personal understanding of the struggles the average player has at the major league level was his strength. Some guys have to be bench players and Danny knew that. He described it well stating, "The longer you sit the more you doubt." Danny never allowed players to doubt. He consistently used them in starting or replacement roles, keeping them sharp and confident.

To confirm his opinions on their strengths and weaknesses, Danny spent the last week of spring training working with the players on game situations. He knew who could bunt successfully with runners on first and second, which pitchers could make the defensive play in this situation, which hitters could provide a sacrifice fly with a runner at third with one or none out. He never put players in situations where they were not capable of performing, which gave confidence to them and the team.

The 1960 and 1971 Pirate Championship teams believed they owned the final three innings of every game they played and proved it through the long season and two seven-game World Series Championships. Danny Murtaugh played a major role in developing the confident team attitude displayed by both of these teams.

## JOHNNY AND EDDIE O'BRIEN

The O'Briens were twin brothers who played for the Pirates in the 1950s. Johnny was primarily an infielder and Eddie an outfielder. However, on those struggling teams of the 1950s, the O'Brien brothers never knew where their manager would put them – as you'll soon learn:

JOHNNY: One time we were getting the heck beat out of us by the Phillies. Danny turned to me and said, "Do me a favor. Would you pitch tonight and then I'll save an arm?" I said, "Sure." I warmed up and went to the mound. Pretty soon I had two runners on base. We were already behind by 10 and there was no one in bullpen. I knew I was on my own. Danny came to the mound – he had no reason to be there – and I thought, "What's he doing out here?" He said to me, "If you're looking for help, there isn't any." He turned and walked back to the dugout. I said, "You buzzard. I'm doing you a favor and you're all over me!"

He came to me another day and said, "How would you like to be the starting pitcher at the Polo Grounds next Sunday?" I said, "Danny, I'm not a pitcher." He said, "Oh, don't get overconfident. I don't have any great thoughts that you'll win the game. But I want to show the rest of my pitchers that a guy with less than good talent who applies himself, works hard, and has some guts can play in this league." I said, "Okay." I pitched six innings and was behind 4-3. I threw the last pitch in the bottom of the sixth at the Polo Grounds and then I fell flat on my face. My legs just kind of went out from under me. I got up and went to the dugout. Danny came over and said, "Okay, you did what I wanted. Thanks." I said, "Wait a minute. I'm close enough to win this game. I want to go back out there again." He said, "Excuse me. I must have missed the press conference where they made you the manager of this team." So anyway, I was the losing pitcher.

He was something else. In 1958 our catcher, Hank Foiles, was chasing a pop fly when he tripped and hit his chin on a railing. He had about 37 stitches in his mouth, so he couldn't catch at all. We were down to one catcher, Danny Kravitz. I was taking batting practice the next day and when I finished Danny said, "Hey Sport, come here a minute." Whenever Danny said "Sport" it meant something was up. So I went over and said, "Yeah, Danny?" He said, "Sport, why don't you put the tools of ignorance on and catch batting practice?" I said, "You gotta be kidding me. I've got a wife and kids." He said, "Okay," and he walked around five steps away. Then he turned and said, "Oh, by the way, if Kravitz gets thrown out or hurt, you're it." The next day, I caught batting practice and I was getting hit by balls all over. Finally I learned how to catch a little bit, but I'd be down in the bullpen praying that Kravitz wouldn't get thrown out of the game or get hurt.

Another day we were standing near batting cage and Danny's there with his arms folded. One of the players said to Danny, "Skip, I want to play every day." Murtaugh quickly said, "Wonderful. I have an opening in Columbus [Pirate minor league team]." The guy said, "Disregard previous statement." Danny always had a quick retort.

But that was Murtaugh. He was very good with players. He never embarrassed a player in front of other players. He got his point across, but he didn't have to shout it. He was a players' manager. He knew how to say the right thing at the right time. When it was time to get something done that needed to be done, there he was doing it.

When Danny wanted to get his point across, he had his own unique style that never really agitated the player even though he was being admonished for something. He wouldn't say "Dammit, do this or that." He'd say, "Don't you think it's a little better if you try to do it this way?" He kind of led you into it nicely. Players always, always tried harder after he talked to them.

**EDDIE:** I would agree with John. You always knew where you stood with Danny.

I only started one game in majors [as pitcher], and that was in Chicago against the Cubs. I was sailing along, doing all right. I got to the sixth inning and had the bases loaded with nobody out. We were ahead 1-0. Danny came out to the mound and said, "I don't know why I ever put you out here to pitch today. You better get out of this." He turned and walked away. [Chuckles.] I did get out of it with no runs and went on to win that game.

Danny always used a motto that I still use for coach and player clinics. He would say to us, "All I want out of you is 100 percent [effort] every day. Some days your 100 percent is only 50 percent, sometimes it's like 120 percent. But all you have to do for me is try 100 percent and you'll never hear from me." That's a great philosophy on the game, especially when you're playing it day in and day out.

**JOHN:** He had a sign over the whirlpool in the trainer's room that said: No one makes my club if they spend any time in this tub. Nobody would go near it.

ED: Danny always treated families well, too. If he was in Seattle he would call and take my wife and me out for dinner. He did more than just manage – he had an interest in the player himself. In fact, my son Dan is named after Danny.

JOHN: Like Ed said, you knew where you stood with him. [Joe Brown] brought him back several times, but the key part is that the players were extremely happy when it happened. They really wanted to play for Danny Murtaugh. Everything I remember about Danny is good. It's been fifty years since I played and I still talk about him.

ED: To this day, people ask me who was the best manager I played for and I say, "No question. Danny Murtaugh."

## TOMMIE SISK, Pitcher (1962-68)

Danny was the best. I truly loved the man and felt he was the greatest manager I ever played for. Once while I was pitching in Forbes Field I threw a curve ball, which was probably my third or fourth best pitch, in a critical situation. The man got a hit off of it. Danny came to the mound and said, "Why the heck did you throw that pitch?" I said, "Well I thought" and he interrupted me and said "That's where you made your first mistake. You throw, I'll think." After the game several sports writers wondered why I would throw that pitch in that situation. Danny announced, "Because I told him to." He took the heat, and then took me to his office for a good butt chewing.

In spring training Danny had a conditioning game he used on pitchers. He would stand behind second base with a fungo bat and have the pitchers run from left field to right field. While you did this he would hit you a fly ball. After you caught it you would immediately turn around and run the other way. The exercise was over after you had caught three fly balls. Being observant I noticed how he would hit you two fly balls, followed by a ground ball. He then would have you timed where he could hit the ball a few feet in front of you and you would try hard but not quite get there. He would then say, "nice try, turn around and go back." This continued until he felt he had worked the person sufficiently.

So the next time he did this I ran about half speed across got my fly ball, back half speed got another fly ball, then of course the ground ball. When he threw the ball up to hit me my fourth ball I kicked it as hard as I could and was there waiting when it came down. Danny just looked at me, spit some tobacco on the ground and went to the next guy. The following day Danny announced we were going to play that game again. I knew I was in for it. After my two fly balls he hit me nine ground balls before he even gave me a chance for a fly. I was so tired I never did catch the last fly ball. I just fell on it while he yelled, "Did he catch it?" Everyone said yes, even though I didn't. I just crawled over under a tree for a long time. When I got the locker room Danny said, "Didn't have as much energy today did ya, kid?" I learned never to mess with him or show him up.

## AL OLIVER, Outfielder and First Baseman (1968-77)

As a manager the number one thing I always liked and respected about him was that he let the players play. He didn't put any stipulations on them. He filled out the lineup card and sent us out on the field. He allowed us to play ourselves out of the lineup. If we didn't hustle, if we went for a long period of time not hitting the ball well and not helping the team, then he would give us a day off and bring someone else in. ...

He had the respect of all the players. Even today when I travel around and give motivational speeches, I use him and how he handled the 1971 team. We were characters with character. In other words, he let us be who we were. I know he'd be back in his office and he would hear us out there talking a whole lot of trash. If we want to act the fool, fine. But when it came to game time, you better be ready to play. Some managers would cut that off.

We were a very positive team, a very confident team, and of course a very talented team. From the manager's standpoint, that had to be good for him to have a team that was loose. Because he was loose. It's always been said that a team kind of takes on the personality of its manager. He was laid back, but he could be aggressive if he had to be. With our ball club he didn't have to be aggressive except for a couple of times. We hustled because we knew deep down that if we didn't hustle, we wouldn't be playing.

Because of his patience and his ability to believe in our team, he brought together Latin American players, Afro American players, and Caucasian players for one common cause – to win and bring a World Championship back to Pittsburgh. He was able to do that, and that's not an easy task in this world due to cultural differences, religious differences. He was able to bind us together as a team. That's what I'm thankful for and that's the reason we were able to win in 1971. I will always remember that. Thanks to him and his leadership and Roberto's leadership.

At that time, as opposed to 1960, he had a better grip on Roberto. He knew his greatness, he knew Roberto as a player and as a person. Especially as a person as opposed to 1960 when even a lot of his teammates didn't know where he was coming from. But by 1971 he knew where Roberto was coming from, and that's why Roberto was able to lead us to a World Championship. Because his manager, in his own way, allowed him to be a true captain. But we all knew who the skipper was, the one who was guiding the ship. We just followed suit.

## MANNY SANGUILLEN, Catcher (1967, 1969-76)

Danny was my inspiration and my motivation. The first time I met him was in 1965. I was playing ball in Batavia, NY, with Manager Tom Saffell – he was rough. One night we played a long game and didn't get home until 3:40 a.m. The next day we had a double header and Saffell told us we had to be at the ball park at 10 a.m. I didn't even have a car. I got there 10 minutes late and he said he was going to fine me $50 for each minute. I was only making $250/month then.

I played the first game – we lost. In the second game he put me in as a pinch hitter for the other catcher and I got a hit. My next time up my leg started hurting and I couldn't run to first base. He started yelling at me, he called me everything in the world. ... I went crazy. I said, "I quit. I won't play for you anymore." Then he would have no catcher. He talked to my interpreter and had him tell me 'Please, forget about it – come in and play.' I finished the game and we won. After the game was over, Saffell, the interpreter, and I went in a room and he apologized. I said, "I don't like you. I'm leaving tomorrow morning at seven o'clock in the morning."

The next morning I got up at six o'clock to go to the train station. Bag in hand, I opened the hotel room door – and saw Danny Murtaugh standing there. He said, "Manny, I'm Danny Murtaugh. I'm a special scout for Joe Brown. We want to protect you in the 40-man roster." My interpreter came in to explain what he was saying because I didn't understand anything. From that time, I liked him. He said, "Don't go," so I stayed and finished the season. As soon as I saw him I knew he was a different kind of person.

By 1967, I was with the Pirates [AAA] team in Columbus. When Harry Walker was fired and they brought Danny back he called me up right away. We were in Toronto and I got called into the manager's office. He said, "Joe Brown is calling for you to go to the big league." The manager told Joe Brown I wasn't ready. Brown said to the manager, "You shut up. Danny Murtaugh wants him right now." From Toronto, I flew to Pittsburgh.

Danny was really smart in baseball. When he taught us in spring training it was unbelievable. Danny prepared each player in a different way to win the game. No matter what, he'd have the words and the way to motivate you. He motivated me so much. It was like a teacher with good kids who want to learn. He prepared us to go all the way.

He really didn't like to see me drop balls. I remember one day in San Diego I was really lazy. I dropped two balls. He called me and said, "Manny, come on over here and sit down beside me. Every ball you drop from now on you're going to pay $50. You already owe me $100 because you dropped two balls." I just said, "Okay sir." But I didn't drop anymore. I tried not paying the fine. Two weeks later he said, "Where's my money?" I had to give him the $100. He just wanted to make me better – make me concentrate 100 percent. I loved that.

He'd say to me, "Manny, the way we win the game, we have to make the routine plays. Because the big plays everybody is making. But if we don't make the routine plays we'll lose the game."

Danny was really my mentor and he helped me to develop a winning attitude. Never, never, never, never, never did I say anything back to him. He was like my second dad, and I didn't argue with my dad. If Danny said, "Manny, what happened?" I'd say, "Okay, I'll run." He'd say, "Okay."

Danny was always watching after us like we were something special. We really appreciated the love and the passion that he had for us and the game. Number one for him was to win. Play the right way – play like a big leaguer. He was tough. He really taught me because I wanted to learn.

When I get to Heaven, I'm going to look for Danny to shake hands with him. I'm really blessed and thank God that I met Danny. People like Danny don't come around every day.

# the prankster

Ask anyone who knew Danny Murtaugh what they remember most about him, and his pranks are probably high on the list. Whether you were a close family member, a good friend, a team member, a sports reporter, or his daughter's suitor … to Danny you were fair game for a practical joke. Share a laugh with Danny's friends, family, and players as they recall some of his more memorable pranks — and their own attempts to get back at the prankster.

## MICKEY VERNON, lifelong friend and baseball legend

Danny had a great sense of humor. We worked together at McGovern's [an upscale men's clothing store in Chester] around the Christmas holidays. One day Mr. McGovern had to go to the bank, which was just up the street. Danny and I were the only ones in the store. A little old guy came in to buy a suit. I think Danny knew him. Danny told the man he'd never sold a suit before and he'd have to measure him. So Danny had the man lay down on the floor, and Danny drew a white chalk outline around him. Mr. McGovern came back in and thought the man had a heart attack. Here Danny had him on the floor and was 'measuring' him.

## MADGE ROACH, cousin

Danny used to do this thing called doubletalk where he would talk in gibberish interspersed with a few recognizable words. One time Danny and a group of friends went to New Jersey to the race track. On the way back they stopped at a restaurant and they were all around the table. The waitress asked Danny what he wanted, and he gave her this doubletalk. The waitress couldn't understand him, and she kept asking him to repeat himself. He kept using the doubletalk. Finally the waitress said she'd bring her manager over to see if the manager could understand him. The manager said "I'm sorry, but the waitress couldn't understand what you said." Very clearly – enunciating each word – he answered, "Do you have chocolate cake and ice cream?" He used to love to use the doubletalk.

During spring training one year Danny was being interviewed by a sportswriter who was always looking for a hook – something negative to report. The man was shocked because he would ask the normally reticent Danny about different players and Danny kept saying uncomplimentary things about each one. Danny also leaked secret "inside" information that was going to shock everyone. The reporter thought this was huge – he couldn't believe what good stuff he was getting. But when he went to play it back, the tape was blank. He came back to Danny and explained that his recorder hadn't worked, could they do the interview again? Danny said, "What do you mean? We didn't talk about any of that stuff." It turned out that Danny had pulled the plug on the microphone before the interview – it was his turn to play "gotcha" with this sportswriter.

One of the sportswriters who frequently covered the Pirates wore a hearing aid. One day before a press conference, Danny set it up with the other reporters that he would pretend to talk and they would pretend to take notes. When Danny started "talking," the reporter took his hearing aid off and checked the batteries. He quickly realized that Danny was pulling a fast one on him.

# the prankster

**STEVE BLASS, former Pirate pitcher**

Danny and Pirate radio announcer Bob Prince were good friends. One time Prince was doing an interview on TV that just showed him from the waist up. Danny crawled on his hands and knees and lit Prince's shoes on fire. Prince was the consummate professional, and he just kept on doing the interview with the smoke billowing up.

Sometimes we played pranks on Danny. Once we were in New York heading to Shea Stadium to play the Mets. Before Danny got on the bus to leave the hotel, we told the driver that the game had been cancelled and we were heading back to Pittsburgh. Instead of going to Shea, he took us to the airport – Danny didn't know what the heck was going on. [Luckily] we made it to the game on time [or we would've been in for it].

During spring training we would sometimes go to a Latin country to play an exhibition game. One time we went to Mexico and for our bat boy we were assigned a 40-year-old midget who didn't speak any English. One afternoon during this series a bunch of us pitchers got bored. We signaled for the bat boy to come out to where we were on the field. So he got out there and we decided to teach him a little English. I knew some Spanish from when I played winter baseball. We pointed to Danny and said "jefe" which was Spanish for boss and "cuarenta" because he was number 40, so he knew we meant Danny. We said, "tú hablas," so he knew we wanted him to talk to jefe. Then we said "Kiss" and he said "keess;" we said "my" and he said "my;" and we said "ass" and he said "ass." We practiced for about 15 minutes. We'd point to Danny and say "Jefe – tú hablas – kiss – my – ass" and he'd say "keess my ass." Once he was ready, he ran across the field to Danny, tapped him on the shoulder and said "keess my ass." He was so proud of himself.

All Danny did was look around to where we were and nod his head. He didn't do anything else. But the next day he got all of us pitchers who

263

did that and for our exercises he ran us from one foul pole to the other foul pole, back and forth until we were ready to throw up. As we're lying on the ground, completely exhausted, he came over and said "Kiss – my – ass." I remember that vividly because I was one of the ones lying on the ground.

## CAROL McGINNIS BURK, Danny's cousin

When Danny was the Pirate manager, I went to a game against the Mets in New York. At the time I was a huge Richie Hebner fan. I was with Danny's sisters Eunice and Mary and some other people and we sat right behind the Pittsburgh dugout.

After the game we went to Danny's hotel and waited in the lobby for him. When he got there, he came over and we were chatting and I asked if I could meet Hebner. He told me, "Sure, Carol, no problem. Let's wait over by the counter for the bus to get here." Well he was leaning up against the counter and I had my back to the door and didn't see the players come in.

All of the sudden Danny started talking to me rather loudly (for him) and asked me why I disliked Hebner so much. I was stunned – I had no clue what he was talking about. Every time I tried to say something he just kept talking telling me, "That's not nice, cousin. If I knew you felt that way I wouldn't have brought you here." I was crushed. Little did I know that standing right behind me listening to it all was Richie Hebner. I wanted to kill Danny! Then he said to Hebner, "Gee, I'm so sorry. You talk to her. Maybe you can find out why she doesn't like you."

After a while we all got on the elevator to go to his room. At the last minute Willie Stargell got on and stood right in front of me. I am only 5 foot 2 inches, and Stargell was huge. As the elevator started to go up, Danny reached over and pinched Stargell on the butt. Stargell turned around and Danny said, "Carol, what the heck is wrong with you?" Then he told Willie, "I am so sorry. You will have to excuse my cousin – she doesn't get out much and now you know why."

## NELLIE KING (with additional details from Frank Bork and Steve Blass), all former Pirate pitchers

Jack Berger, the PR director of Pirates, was good friends with Danny and they often golfed together. Berger got very intense when he didn't play well – he'd throw the clubs in the bag and stomp around. Once they were playing golf in Ft. Myers and Jack hit his ball toward a pond on the left side of the hole. They parked the cart near the pond, but – unbeknownst to Jack – Danny put the cart in reverse. Danny said, "I'm going to go find my ball; you can bring the cart and pick me up." Berger hit a bad shot and got so mad that he threw his club in the bag, jumped in the cart and stomped on the pedal ... and went right into the pond. Berger got out of the cart and the water was waist deep. Everything from the cart was floating around in the pond – score card, tees, cigarettes, you name it. It was the talk of spring training for weeks.

## TOMMIE SISK, former Pirate pitcher

[Another time] during spring training, Danny was playing golf with Jack Berger. Danny always got one free shot in their matches. Before one game Danny said, "I don't want a shot today, I just want to pick up the ball and throw it once." Berger agreed. On the third hole, a par four around a lake, Danny announced he was taking his throw. He picked up Berger's ball and threw it in the lake. Never said which ball he was going to throw. It was hilarious.

## JOE WALTON, Danny's son-in-law

Growing up, I didn't pay a lot of attention to baseball, and what little attention I did pay was to the Cleveland Indians in the American League.

So when I met Kathy Murtaugh [Danny's daughter] in college I didn't recognize the name. It's kind of funny to think of now.

The first time I met Danny was when Kathy and I were dating in college and I went to visit her at their house near Philadelphia. I went to the front door and knocked – not realizing that no one used the front door. Everyone used the back door. If someone knocked on the front door, they automatically knew it wasn't a relative or close friend. So I knocked on the door and Danny opened it. I said I was here to see Kathy, and he said "Okay" and shut the door. I thought that was odd. I waited a little bit, and then a little longer – long enough that I was uncomfortable standing there and I didn't know whether to knock again or not. Looking back, I know that's exactly what he wanted me to feel.

So I knocked again. He opened the door back up, looked at me and said, "You still here?" At that point Kathy told him to let me in and to take my coat for me. So he took my coat, walked over, dropped it on the floor next to his chair, and sat down. I didn't know it at the time, but this was how he acted toward anyone who was a suitor.

Around a year later I called Danny and asked if I could meet with him the next time he was in Pittsburgh. He knew I wanted to talk to him about marrying Kathy. He said to come to his office at Forbes Field a few days before Thanksgiving in 1969. I went in, and he sat down and put his feet up on his desk – trying to act nonchalant. I said, "I've come to ask your permission to marry Kathy." He looked at me and said, "Why?" That totally threw me, of course. I think he was really as nervous as I was. So we had our conversation – the rest of it went more smoothly – and I went on my merry way.

At this point Kathy did not know that I had talked to her dad. She knew I was going to, but she didn't know I already had. I asked her to come to Cleveland, where my parents lived, for Christmas. She talked to her parents about it and asked to borrow some money toward her plane ticket. Danny decided to have some fun with her now, so he said he thought she was seeing too much of me and he was against the trip. He turned to Kate and said, "If you want her to go, you pay for it," and stormed out of the room. Kate said to Kathy, "I haven't worked in 30 years, where does he think I'm going to get the money?" Unknown to Kathy, he had already given his blessing to our engagement. He just constantly liked to play jokes. In the end they okayed the trip and helped her with the airfare. I proposed to her while she was in Cleveland that trip.

Years later Danny was visiting us in Greenville, PA. Kathy and the kids were in the car while Danny and I went into our neighborhood market. Danny checked out right in front of me, and as he was leaving he 'permitted gas to escape' ... silently. As he left and I moved to check out it hit me. The lady who was ringing me up almost passed out and she gave me the worst look in the world because she thought I did it. I knew exactly what had happened. When I got back in the car, I turned to him and said, "You SOB." Kathy was shocked because she'd never heard anyone talk to her dad that way. He just sat in the back giggling ... he'd got me again.

One time a friend of Danny's offered him a big load of firewood. The friend dropped off the load, and it was in huge logs – not cut like firewood. In order to use it, it had to be cut up. Danny sat out in the yard in his chair next to the wood with an ax, a sledgehammer, a wedge, a little hammer, and a screwdriver. Whenever he'd hear a car coming, he would take the hammer and screwdriver and whack at one of these logs. The driver would inevitably be a friend of Danny's, so the car would stop and the driver would ask what he was doing. Danny would say, "I'm splitting this wood."

The friend would say, "That's not how to split wood." Danny responded, "It's not?" "No, let me show you." The friend would get out and split some logs. Danny would thank him, and when the friend left Danny sat back down. When another car came along, Danny would do the same thing. Soon all of the wood was split into nice logs for the fireplace. Not long after that, Danny and Kate were at a party talking about the wood splitting. One of Danny's cousins was laughing hysterically at the story. Her husband – a local judge – told her not to laugh so hard because he [the judge] had split several of the logs himself.

Danny and Pirate Assistant GM Joe O'Toole loved going back and forth with pranks. One time Danny was meeting O'Toole at a restaurant in Pittsburgh. Danny arrived first and called the waitress over. He said, "I'll give you $5 to help me pull a prank. When this guy comes in and sits down, come over with the water. I want you to pour it as if you were going to pour it in his glass, but pour it in his lap instead. Just pretend you're talking to me." So the waitress takes the pitcher and pours the water on O'Toole's lap. O'Toole didn't say one word to the waitress. He just turned to Danny and said, "You SOB!" He knew right away that Danny set it up because they were always getting each other.

Another time Danny and Kate were at a hotel after being out with O'Toole and his wife and some other folks. Danny and Kate were back in their room for less than 5 minutes when there was a knock at the door. Danny said, "Don't answer it." Kate said, "What do you mean don't answer it?" A few minutes later there was another knock. Kate told Danny he had to answer it. Danny opened the door and there were two "ladies of the night" standing there. He said, "Ladies, you're welcome to come in but I've got to tell you that's my wife over there." O'Toole had paid the women to come knock on the door.

Danny and Kate were at the Media Inn (near Chester) for the Sunday buffet. Two lifelong friends, Doris and Joe Seber, came in when Danny and Kate were almost done eating. The Sebers sat down and chatted for a little while. When the Sebers went to the buffet, Danny took all kinds of silverware, salt and pepper shakers, and whatever else he could find off of other tables and put it in Doris' purse. When Danny and Kate were leaving, they waved goodbye to the Sebers. On the way out Danny pointed the Sebers out to the restaurant owner. Danny said he'd seen the wife put things in her purse and he thought they were going to steal them. The owner was heading to the Sebers' table as Danny and Kate left the restaurant.

*Delaware County (PA) Daily Times* **Sports Editor ED GEBHART, March 28, 1961 column**

Danny Murtaugh, it would appear, is up to his old tricks. And no one — veteran players, raw rookies or seasoned members of the press — is safe from the rare Murtaugh humor, as dry as the desert one time and uproarious as a Mack Sennett comedy the next. The trouble with Murtaugh's jokes many times is that you don't realize it's a joke until it's too late.

Take the case of Norman Housley, an 18-year-old rookie who is training with the Pirates in Fort Myers, Fla. When Housley was introduced to Murtaugh, Danny told him he would room with Bob Skinner, the veteran leftfielder. "The reason I'm putting you with 'Skins' is that you look like a strong fellow and we like to put our strongest men with Skinner," Murtaugh explained. "Why is that?" Housley asked nervously. "Well, you see, ordinarily this Skinner is a very nice guy," Murtaugh went on with a serious expression, "but he is subject to fits on occasion. He gets up in the middle of the night and it takes a strong man to pin him down."

The next day Skinner approached Murtaugh and protested. "What'd you do, Skip, put me in with some kind of a nut?" Skinner demanded. "I got up about 4 o'clock to go to the bathroom and this kid pounces on me. He threw me down and held me there until I convinced him nothing was wrong." Murtaugh, of course, had put it over on both Skinner and Housley and couldn't decide which was funnier — the kid sleeping with one eye open waiting for Skinner to make a move or Skinner being attacked en route to the bathroom.

Even the press is not safe from Murtaugh's sharp wit. We remember an incident after the first game of the 1960 World Series last fall when Murtaugh was being interviewed in his Forbes Field office by Joe Garagiola and Jack Lescoulie for a nationwide television program. The mikes, cameras and lights were all set up and the technician asked Danny so say a few words so he could get a "fix" on his voice. Murtaugh, dead-pan as usual, moved his lips in front of the mike but made no sound. The technician, with airtime scant seconds away, searched frantically to find out why Murtaugh's voice wasn't coming through. He'd still be looking if Garagiola, a great kidder himself, hadn't tipped him off.

## HARDING "PETE" PETERSON, former Pirates General Manager

Danny was always pulling jokes on us, so everyone was always trying to get him. One time I was managing in the minor leagues and we had spring training in Daytona Beach. The staff was staying in a motel fairly close to where the fields were. We were about ready to leave spring training to go to our respective clubs. I had noticed the night before that an elderly couple had checked into Room 10. So the morning that we were leaving Danny came around banging on the managers' doors saying "Get 'em up. Get 'em up." He banged on my door and I went out. He said to me, "Where's Ray Hathaway?" Ray was one of our other managers. I told him Ray was in Room 10. I kept my door open just a little bit and I watched him go a few doors down to Room 10. He pounded on the door and out came this little elderly man. Of course when he saw the elderly man he looked down the hall and saw me with my open door. He said, "You SOB!" So everyone pulled jokes on everyone else – it was a good time.

## CHAPTER SEVENTEEN

# Danny Murtaugh Memories

**W**hen Pittsburghers hear the name Danny Murtaugh, it instantly brings back great memories – of baseball, of childhood, of the "good ol' days." Fans of his era often say they felt like he was "part of the family." In December 2007, Danny was on the Veterans' Committee ballot for the Hall of Fame. He came up short in the voting (received six of 16 possible votes; he needed 12), but it prompted his granddaughter Colleen to write a tribute to him that ran in the *Pittsburgh Post Gazette*. Dozens of Danny's admirers contacted Colleen with stories about her grandfather. Those responses, some of which are reprinted below, prompted the book you are now reading. This walk down memory lane with the fans, the friends, and the family that loved Danny Murtaugh shows the enduring impact he had as a player, a manager, and – most of all – a man.

## *I Never Knew Your Granddad, But ...*

### DAVE BLAZEK, formerly of Baldwin Boro

I was born in 1950, so the 1960 World Series was special to me. I can remember listening to the game on a transistor radio full of static. My parents applied for a game ticket and were awarded the 7th game. When they received the tickets they thought they would never see a game; it wasn't going to go seven games against the mighty Yankees. I'm so glad they were wrong. The games we lost were by big scores and the games we won were by slight margins; but as you know the Pirates persevered.

I lived in a neighborhood in Baldwin that was very close knit. One man by the name of Jack always criticized Danny's managerial decisions. When the Pirates won the 7th game and the Series, some of the neighbors made a huge banner and placed it in Jack's front yard strung between badminton poles; it read:

*"Dear Lord, Let Jack Believe, Murtaugh for President"*

This was 47 years ago and I remember it as if it were yesterday. The entire neighborhood held a block party that went late into the night and I think we all skipped school the next day. Just wanted to share these memories about your grandfather and the Pirates, and I will be pulling for him to be inducted to the Baseball Hall of Fame some day soon. He deserves it.

### JOHN LAWLER, formerly of Pittsburgh (now living in Pace, FL)

Baseball has changed over the years. I liked it better when there were [fewer] teams in each of the two leagues. Players seemed to stay with their team and became recognizable as loyal members of the team. Those were the years I loved. I can still name the starting lineup for the 1960 Pittsburgh Pirates. I probably could not name nine baseball players these days if I used both leagues and all the divisions from which to choose.

# Danny Murtaugh Memories

I grew up in Pittsburgh and learned to love baseball listening to it as a youngster on my grandmother's radio situated on top of the refrigerator in her kitchen. I still have fond memories of those warm, summer, Pittsburgh days at my grandmother's home in Rankin listening to the vivid play-by-play descriptions of the action on the field. I even made the pilgrimage as a young boy to Forbes Field to see my beloved Pirates lose as they often did. As a Pirate fan, we got used to being in the cellar. We loved them anyways.

But, I also remember coming home from school one day with my transistor radio listening to the excitement of the final game of the 1960 World Series against the invincible New York Yankees. I still recall being in my kitchen listening to the final moments of that game. No one would have believed it if Hollywood had written this script. It was the bottom of the ninth with Bill Mazeroski at the plate. The pitch, the swing, and a home run out of the park. Pittsburgh erupted as a city in jubilation. I remember the celebration going on in neighborhoods all over the city that night.

And just who led them to that victory? It was the man in the newspaper photograph I saw with his two young grandchildren sitting on his lap. It was the man in the photograph whom I instantly recognized as our beloved Pirates manager, Danny Murtaugh.

A grandfather now myself with two young grandchildren of my own I am saddened by Danny Murtaugh's passing before he could enjoy his golden years. I am saddened that he did not get the opportunity to enjoy those grandchildren for more years than he did. I am also saddened that his grandchildren did not get the opportunity to spend more years with their grandfather and to experience more of his love for them. His grandchildren's memories may be vague or nonexistent, but now that they are grown, they can share in the memories of the fans who loved their grandfather and knew him as one who led the Pirates in both victory and defeat. We miss you, Danny boy.

## STEVE DOUGHERTY, formerly of Ford City (now living in Ft. Myers, FL)

I was disappointed that Danny did not receive sufficient votes to be enshrined in Cooperstown. He has certainly earned the right to be honored next to Clemente and Stargell, two guys who probably wouldn't be where they are without his leadership. Fans who didn't grow up in Danny's era have no idea what a tradition of excellence he fostered in the Pirates and what those traditions meant to all of us out there in the stands and listening on the radio. It's odd to say, but we all felt like we knew your grandfather. He gave the impression that he was approachable, kind and friendly and that he knew we liked him and most importantly, that he liked us back.

When Danny passed away in 1976, I was a veteran of the military and a young, tough cop in Reading Pa. I heard the news on duty from KYW radio, and I'm not ashamed to say that I shed a quiet tear. It was almost like I'd heard of the death of a favorite uncle. That is the kind of impact your grandfather had upon people he'd never met. That impact and his successful tenure as the Pirates manager is a legacy to be proud of whether the Hall of Fame voters recognize it or not. If he never gets into Cooperstown, I'd like to think that he would still be proud to know that even more than 30 years later, he is remembered with admiration, respect and genuine affection by Pirate fans everywhere.

I doubt that I'm unique among Pirate fans of that era – #40 held a special place in our hearts. He led the Pirates to victory and vindicated the city and fans after a long drought. He managed some of the most exciting teams and interesting ballplayers I've ever seen through the 60's and won another improbable victory against the Orioles in 1971.

# Danny Murtaugh Memories

## TERRY M. PHILLIPS formerly of Mt. Lebanon (now living in Katy, Texas)

Thanks for taking time to write about your Granddad Danny Murtaugh in the *Post-Gazette*. He was a great Manager and, as reiterated in your article, apparently a great man.

I never had the honor of meeting him, but ever since he took over from Bobby Bragan in the 50's, he has been one of the most admired men in my life. He made me a real Pirates fan, and I think the Pirates always were larger because of him.

On the day of his funeral in 1976, I was flying into Philadelphia from Pittsburgh for a job interview. On the same plane was the great Art Rooney. I overheard him say he was going to the Danny Murtaugh funeral. Now there were two quintessential Irishmen. Men that made me proud to be from Pittsburgh and Irish. I found myself later that day lost, asking for directions in Chester on my way to the interview.

Odd memories to have but between your Granddad being named the Pirates manager and my getting lost in Chester was a golden time for Pittsburghers in large part due to your Granddad. You're right - he is a Hall of Famer for reasons that some voters for the Hall may (unfortunately) never know. We were all truly blessed to have had him in our midst.

## ALFONSO L. TUSA C., Venezuela

I'm a native Venezuelan and a baseball fan. I listened to games on a short wave radio down here in Venezuela. I followed the Pirates because of Roberto Clemente.

My brothers told me about a baseball manager who as a player whistled a lot to motivate his teammates while he performed at second base, the short stop, or the hot corner. [Now in 1970] Danny Murtaugh had become the Pittsburgh Pirates manager [again]. I had seen in the paper that the Pirates with Dock Ellis would play against Don Sutton and the Los Angeles Dodgers. ... I turned on the short wave radio and searched for the ballgame. ...When I finally [found the game] the announcer was saying that the Dodgers were leading the Pirates 1-0 with an RBI double by Willie Davis. Mom came from the kitchen, "I need you to go to the bakery."

I just took the coin and left without looking at the radio. A pungent smell of garlic and fried potatoes escaped from the kitchen. I returned running as a great track and field athlete. I gave Mom the bread bag.

I couldn't find the radio in the backyard. Mom told me the radio was too delicate to be in the yard. I had to wait almost 40 minutes after we ate dinner. ...

[After dinner] I pushed the wooden table to the backyard and raised the volume. "...we're going into the bottom of the sixth inning with the Dodgers beating the Pirates 6-3." I didn't like that score. I wondered if Roberto Clemente was playing in that game. ...

The radio screen light opened a way through the backyard darkness. I took a chair in front of the wooden table. "...Danny Murtaugh trusts in his team until the last out. He's bringing Dave Giusti to pitch, one of his best relievers, when the Pirates trail 6-4 ..."

"...it's amazing folks Clemente scores the tying run on Bob Robertson's double to left. Here comes Manny Sanguillen to bat. It's a grounder to second base, Ted Sizemore takes it and makes the out at Wes Parker mitt. We're going to play extra innings..."

Three shouts from the front door made me run. Dad opened the door with his handkerchief on his head. "Hurry up Alfonsito. I need you to go to the pharmacy. I can't stand this bloody headache."

I turned back to the yard trying to hear the radio. Dad grabbed my hand and took me outside.

I began to walk faster and faster. At the middle of the distance I ran as the best Olympic athlete. All because I didn't want to miss what was going to happen on that extra inning. I didn't care about becoming breathless. I wondered if Danny Murtaugh would keep Dave Giusti on the mound.

I asked for the medicine and rushed back. One block away from home I realized I had forgotten the change. Because of my tiredness I walked one block and ran two. The guy at the pharmacy couldn't understand what I tried to say. I went outside, took a deep breath and told him about my change. After long minutes of remembering what type of bill I paid with he gave me my change back.

I lost some time by moving around people in the sidewalks. I almost collided with a woman who got mad at me but I continued my way. ...

[When I got home] I ran to the radio and raised the volume: "... Danny Murtaugh brings Jerry May as pinch hitter for Dave Giusti. The Pirates have Robertson on second and Billy Mazeroski at first base with two outs. Here it comes from Jose Pena. May connects a line drive to left... it's a base hit. Robertson scores. What a victory for the Pirates. What kind of skipper Murtaugh is. He knows how to handle his pitchers and when to bring the right batter to win the game..."

Dad whistled a song from the kitchen. I turned off the radio and pushed the table back to the living room. It was the first time I knew about an MLB manager who brought a pinch hitter to win the game in extra inning. I didn't remember anything about running to the pharmacy. Coming on time to listen the end of the game was like paradise for me.

### NICK FRANKART, formerly of Pittsburgh/Churchill (now living in Long Beach, CA)

What a wonderful tribute you have written to your beloved grandfather. Two of my uncles, Al Greenaway and Eddie Neary, worked many years as groundskeepers at Forbes Field. Al even sang the National Anthem regularly. Back in those days, there was much more interaction between those wearing the Pirates uniform and the media, groundskeepers, etc. Both of my uncles got to know and had a very special place in their hearts for your grandfather.

I always said that your grandfather literally gave his life for the Pirates, and I don't think I'm off base with that assessment. He was certainly a beloved icon in Pittsburgh (and baseball) history, and remains so to this day. Your grandfather (nicknamed "the Smiling Irishman" by the late Bob Prince) most definitely deserves his rightful place in the Baseball Hall of Fame, and I'm confident he will get there sooner rather than later. Thank you for sharing your story and tribute to your grandfather with those of us who practically considered him a member of our families in the 60's and 70's.

### MICHAEL BISHOP "BISH" RIEG, native of Southwest Pennsylvania, Pittsburgh Pirate fan since 1955

I have been a Pirates fan since I was a kid in the Fifties. I grew up with Roberto Clemente as my hero and would like nothing better than to see the Pirates restored to the glory years when your Granddad was manager. I always picture him in that rocking chair in the clubhouse. He always appeared to be a man who knew exactly who he was.

I am an amateur Pirates historian and we have a room in our house devoted to baseball, mostly the Pirates, Roberto Clemente and Babe Ruth. I have tons of biographies of Roberto. In reading about your grandfather one thing I can say: he did an amazing job handling Roberto Clemente as a player and person. I am sure Danny did not understand him all that well, and Roberto was a prickly, proud man. But Danny was able to manage him and help develop this very talented baseball player in what had to seem to Roberto like a very alien culture in the America of the 1950s. I sure hope Danny makes it to the Hall of Fame some day. He is very deserving.

## TOM LLOYD, Dormont, PA

Your Grandfather was one of my favorite Pirates of all time. I first became aware of him in 1948 when he teamed with Stan Rojek to form the double play combination. He played his position excellently. The Pirates of 1948 gave the National League a good race for the pennant. You could always hear Danny when he was on the field by his whistle. Of course Danny was and still is my all time favorite manager, not only because the Pirates won the Series twice, but the way he always handled the players during his time as manager. As you may have guessed by now I am a big admirer of Danny Murtaugh. I even named my youngest son after him. I share your hope that someday he will be selected for the Hall. He deserves it.

## GEOFF SANTOLIQUIDO, formerly of Pittsburgh
## (now lives in Cary, NC)

As a child in Pittsburgh in the 1960's and 1970's, Danny Murtaugh was an icon to me. My respect for him grew as I became an adult, long after your grandfather retired. I came to realize that he was a brave and fair man, willing to place players' ability ahead of political considerations. Pittsburgh had its share of prejudice-minded people at the time, yet he fielded a starting lineup of blacks and was rewarded by yet another World Series title. God bless him. I share your hope that he'll be inducted to the Hall of Fame and I believe that it will happen.

## Yvonne Francescon, Pittsburgh

Thanks so much for the article in the *Pittsburgh Post-Gazette* about your grandfather, Danny Murtaugh. It was so nice to remember one of my favorite players and managers from the "happy days" of baseball. We, as children, loved to listen to baseball on the radio, and were thrilled to be taken to old Forbes Field to sit in the bleachers to watch our favorite players, even if they seldom won the games! My favorites were Danny Murtaugh and Ralph Kiner. Your grandfather played well and hard and gave the fans many a thrill. He was a good second-baseman.

All the Pittsburgh fans – and there were many in those days – were extremely happy when he was named Manager. I certainly hope that he will be inducted into the Baseball Hall of Fame. Besides his talent, he represented everything wholesome and good that was baseball. You can be really proud of him.

I grew up at a time when there were many first- and second-generation ethnic neighborhoods in Pittsburgh. Ours was predominantly Irish, so Danny Murtaugh was claimed and admired by his name alone! And the fact that he was a great infielder AND a great Manager just made him a baseball legend.

It's been many a year since I went to a baseball game — not since the days of muddy fields, heavy bats and leaden balls, when getting on base was a challenge. There is no comparison today to past players who didn't have training programs (or drugs!) to enhance their performances. And the old-timers actually seemed to enjoy playing the game and interacting with the fans!

## Steve Stake, formerly of Pittsburgh
## (currently at Osan Air Base, South Korea)

I have been a Pirate fan all of my life. My first recollection of baseball is my father telling me that Bill Mazeroski hit a home run to win the 1960 World Series, which of course was your grandfather's first World Series victory. I know that your grandfather, throughout his career as a manager, consistently took a small market team and led them to compete often for the championship.

In 1976, I attended Thiel College in Greenville, PA and was a member of Phi Theta Phi fraternity. Once a year we do a major walkathon and fundraiser for the Children's Hospital in Pittsburgh. We always tried to get some of the local sports personalities to spend a few hours on the route with us.

I was always a MAJOR fan of Danny and one day on my way back to the fraternity house I saw Danny walking his grandchildren, which I assume were you and your brother. This was in October 1976, just a few months before he passed away. I got up enough nerve to knock on the door and asked if perhaps he would like to help us. He said he was actually aware of what we did, but he could not help as he would be in winter baseball meetings.

I asked about who he thought would replace him as manager (this was before Chuck Tanner was named). Even though I invaded his privacy that day, he took the time to chat with me, this young kid, and never let on that I was bothering him. When I learned that he died shortly after that, I was so sad that I bothered him that day, but of course I respected him even more because he was obviously in bad health at that time and he still treated me with so much respect. I will never forget that.

### Karen Brendlinger, Monroeville, PA

My older sister, Mary Beth, my younger brother, Jamie and myself were Pirate Fanatics from 1969 through the early 80's. We were obsessed with everything Pirates. We listened to or watched all of the games on our transistor radios or TV. We hated the last day of the season. We couldn't wait to see the first mention of spring training in the sports section of the old *Pittsburgh Press* and the *Post Gazette.* We even listened to rebroadcast games during the off season (played on a record player!). We loved going to the games at Three Rivers Stadium. We finally got old enough that our parents allowed us to take the bus on our own to see the games. Mom always said, "Don't let your brother out of your sight," since he was probably only 11 at the time.

We would be at the Stadium at least four hours before game time. We'd watch the players arriving, chase and hound them for autographs, and just relish their company ... yes we were pathetic. But we had so much fun! I'll never forget the day my brother spotted your Grandfather getting out of the car carrying his bags as the team was leaving on a road trip right after the game. Jamie ran up to him and said "Mr. Murtaugh, can I carry your bags?" Your Grandfather handed my brother a bag, put his arm around him and said, "Sure Sonny... come on with me into the clubhouse"!! My sister and I almost died. We were out of our minds. My brother walked away making faces at us over his shoulder, arm and arm with your Grandfather.

Two hours later, when the gates finally opened, we found Jamie sitting in the first row seat next to the Pirate dugout ... he was so excited. The first words out of his mouth were, "He let me sit in his rocking chair!!!" Through the eyes of an 11 year old brother, we shared the experience of the clubhouse and your Grandfather. Mary Beth and I were so jealous!! Jamie talked about this for years. Your Grandfather was in the heat of a pennant race and certainly had much more on his mind that day. He did not need an 11 year old kid bugging him. He chose to take time and give that 11 year old an experience of a lifetime ... one he never forgot. The baseball world would be a different place today if it still had the likes of Danny Murtaugh. Thanks, Danny, for the memories.

# Danny Murtaugh Memories

**JIM PONITZ** ["Jamie" from previous story], **Wilmerding, PA**

I understand my sister, Karen Brendlinger, submitted a memory about Danny and myself. I was the one who, after getting an autograph from him, saw his bag in his trunk and asked if he needed any help carrying it. He said "Sure." And to my two sisters' amazement, I proceeded to walk into the players' entrance under Gate A with him. My sister said I stuck my tongue out as I passed by them ... although I don't remember that. Danny took me into his office and I noticed his rocking chair. I asked if I could sit in it, and he said, "Sure." We chatted briefly. He then said for me to walk around. If anyone questioned me, I was to say "If there is a problem, call Danny Murtaugh." To this day, we still joke about it. It was a day I will always remember. I wanted to let you know how much him taking a few minutes out of his day meant to me.

**BOB IERADI, Mt. Laurel, NJ**

As a kid in Chester, I lived for baseball. One of my fondest baseball memories is of a time back in the 50's when I was about 11 years old – the day that Danny Murtaugh appeared at the Chester Central Little League field and showed us how a second baseman turns a double play. "Kick up the dust," he said. "If you miss the bag, the umpire will never know it." Well, I have taught that little tip to my sons and now my grandsons. I was totally in awe of Mr. Murtaugh, and I still respect him as a player and as a gentleman who took the time to teach a bunch of kids about a game we loved.

**JOHN APICE, Philadelphia, PA**

Since I was little I was always a baseball nut. When I was about six I found out that my uncle (Howard McGinnis) was a cousin of Danny's. I thought it was awesome that my uncle was related to someone in the major leagues. This started my lifelong love of the Pittsburgh Pirates.

When I would play baseball I would always dream that I was Roberto Clemente, Willie Stargell or Manny Sanguillen. Growing up in Philly in the late 1960's and early 70's, it was a great time for my Pirates and I let the local Phillies fans know how I felt by wearing everything black and gold that I could find.

I only met Danny one time after the Pirates were playing at the Vet. I was about 11 and waiting outside the Pirates door to get autographs. After trying to get a few of the players' autographs without much success I saw Danny and asked him for one. He said "You don't want mine, son. I'm no one special – you want the players." I told him who my uncle was and he said, "Well then, let's get you some of the players' autographs." And boy did he. He put his arm around me and we went from player to player. I was on cloud nine for about a month. My uncle got me an autographed picture of Danny that still proudly hangs on my wall 38 years later. I still remember the day that I met him like it was yesterday and appreciate that a great man like Danny took time out to be so kind to the biggest Pirates fan in Philadelphia. Thanks for a lifelong memory.

## JACK MYCKA, Philadelphia native

Both of my parents grew up in the Pittsburgh area, and their first four kids were born in Pittsburgh. They moved to Philadelphia a couple of years before I was born. But I was trained to be a Pirate fan and that was good with me. Around 1970 was when I was old enough to really follow the game. Of course the Pirates were a good team in 1970. In 1971, I was even more into it and I would pester my parents to take me to see the Pirates when they came to Philly.

My mother liked to support us in our interests, so she decided to figure out a way for me to meet Danny Murtaugh when he came to Philadelphia. She wrote a letter to him through the Pirates and told him about me. She asked if it would be possible for me to meet him when the

Pirates came to town. I can't remember if he called or wrote to her, but he responded and told her what game to attend and how to get in contact with him.

After the game, we went down to the visiting dugout per his instructions and told someone who we were. I was seven years old – of course I thought this was going to work. My mother wasn't quite as certain. Sure enough, there he was. He asked my parents to put me over the railing so I could sit on the dugout. He told me how happy he was to have such a strong fan in Philadelphia. I still have the picture of us both, my kid-sized baseball glove that he signed, and an autographed ball that he gave me. He couldn't have been nicer to a young fan like me.

### GEORGE SKORNICKEL, Tarentum, PA

As a young boy growing up on the North Side of Pittsburgh, I was a die-hard Pirate fan. If I wasn't at Forbes Field, I was listening to Bob Prince broadcasting the game on the radio. Going to Forbes Field meant not only seeing the game, but also getting autographs.

The prime spot was on the right field side of the dugout. There was a bar railing that projected out onto the field and allowed you to not only get closer to the field, but also gave you the ability to see who was sitting in and coming out of the dugout. If you showed up late the next best spot was lying on top of the dugout holding your scorecard or autograph book over the edge hoping that one of the players would take your book and sign it.

It was early in the 1961 season and I found myself lying on the dugout roof holding my autograph book and pen over the edge of the roof. Several players came into the dugout, but most of them entered at the side with the pipe railing. The field had cleared of players and I was about ready to give up when I felt my autograph book pulled roughly from my hand. After lying there for some time waiting to get my book returned by whatever player had taken it, I began to think it was a lost cause. I wasn't going to get my book back.

I just stood there, unhappy and wondering what to do. Standing there for what seemed like an hour, I finally saw Danny Murtaugh step out of the dugout. After spitting out some tobacco juice, he held up my book and said, "This belong to you, kid?" For a moment I was speechless. Then I shook my head and said, "Yes, Mr. Murtaugh." He spit some more tobacco juice, tossed the book to me and said, "Take care you don't lose this." I think I said, "Thank you," and I hurried to my seat.

It was then that I started looking through my book. To my surprise there were ten or twelve pages of autographs including my hero, Roberto Clemente. Apparently Danny had taken it into the locker room and passed it around to the players. I, unfortunately, no longer have the autograph book, but I'll never forget my brief encounter with Danny Murtaugh.

## *The Pirate Family*

### SALLY O'LEARY, former Administrative Assistant for Public Relations

I was treasurer of the Gus Fan Club, which was a local sports organization open to the general public. The Pirates and the visiting team always cooperated in sending players to our lunches. That's how I met a lot of the players and the media, and that's how I formed the contacts that enabled me to work for the Pirates. That's how I first met Danny.

I became good friends with him when I began working for the Pirates in 1964. You never knew when Danny would arrive in your office. He would announce his arrival with a whistle that would send you right through the wall. If you were on the phone talking to somebody, it didn't matter. He was the center of your attention. Danny was the boss. I used to keep a candy jar on my desk, and I always had to keep it full for when

Danny would stop by. If it was wrapped, he always put the wrapper back in the jar.

When he retired in 1971 there was a press conference to announce Bill Virdon as the new manager. Bill Guilfoile was the public relations director at the time. We got together as soon as Danny went down the hall to the press conference. I had a big, framed, autographed picture of Danny on the wall of my office. Guilefoile and I took the picture down and put it in the wastebasket facing the wall. In place of it, we put an 8x10 glossy of Bill Virdon. It looked like a postage stamp on the wall after that big picture. After the press conference, Danny came back and sat down. He looked up at the wall and said, "My word, the body isn't even cold yet." We said, "That's the way it works in baseball, Danny."

### MONICA NARR, former Pirate ticket office worker

I am a member of the Pirates Family and worked for them in the 70's and 80's. It is my extreme pleasure to say that I had the opportunity to know Danny Murtaugh as a close friend. He would often visit various offices on his way to the clubhouse at Three Rivers Stadium and I encountered him most frequently in Jeanie Donatelli's office. Assistant GM Joe O'Toole would often pop in the office and call him "The Lucky Leprechaun" and it was evident they had a long close history.

Your Grandfather's sparkling Irish eyes would twinkle just a little brighter as the corners of his mouth would turn up into a full broad smile whenever he spoke about his soul mate, Katie, or the lights of his life, his children. He freely shared knowledge and information about so much more than just baseball. Once when I asked him which was his favorite ballpark he did not hesitate and responded, "The ballpark that I am in today, where a ballgame would be played tonight."

God bless you and your wonderful family and for sharing your Grandpa with all of us here in Pittsburgh and around the country.

## JOSEPH CIRELLI, former batboy

My earliest recollection of Danny Murtaugh was in 1948, when I was 7 years old and Danny was the Pirates' second baseman. My father, Charles Cirelli, was an usher at Forbes Field and also worked in the visiting clubhouse. Consequently, I was hired as the visiting team bat boy at the beginning of the 1957 season. At the time, Bobby Bragan was the Pirate manager, and Danny was a coach. Because of Bragan's misbehavior and antics, on and off the field, he was fired in early August 1957, and Danny was named his replacement.

A couple weeks later, the team took the two bat boys on a road trip to Philadelphia and New York to play the Brooklyn Dodgers. It was my first airplane ride, and I was scared to death. I recall that Danny kept assuring me there was nothing to worry about as he had been flying for years, and he would be on the same plane with me. I sat with a pitcher, Luis Arroyo, and with his encouragement, I made it through the flight in one piece. I remember that when we arrived at the airport gate we were met by a large crowd from Chester, PA, and a high school band which was playing "O Danny Boy." They were celebrating the success of a "hometown boy."

After the final game in Philadelphia, we boarded a late night train for New York City, arriving after midnight. We played three games at Ebbets Field and one game at Roosevelt Stadium in Jersey City, NJ. Danny made me feel welcome to be traveling with the team, and initiated a collection from the team to provide me with spending money while on the road.

I returned for the 1958 season, which was very exciting because under Danny's leadership, he turned the team around, and they ended up with a winning record, and a second place finish behind the Milwaukee

Braves. In August, I was once again taken on a road trip to Philadelphia and then on to Cincinnati. The day we arrived in Cincinnati, Danny invited me to attend a cocktail reception hosted by Mr. John Galbreath, the owner of the Pirates, who resided in Columbus, Ohio. Danny made it a point to personally introduce me to Mr. Galbreath, and this was an impressionable experience for an 18 year old boy.

After the 1958 World Series, Danny was instrumental in having the team vote me a partial World Series share for ending up in second place. When the season ended, I enlisted in the U.S. Marine Corps, and was stationed in Adak, Alaska in 1960. It was at 7:30am on October 13, 1960, when Bill Mazeroski hit his famous home run to beat the Yankee's in the seventh game. I had listened to all the games on the armed forces radio and was thrilled for the team, and especially Danny, since he started the winning tradition of the Pirates.

Danny was a wonderful person and a real gentleman. His son Timmy, who was about my age, didn't let the fact that his father was the Pirate manager go to his head. This indicated to me that Danny was also a great father.

Danny was a great person, extremely popular with his players, and consequently created a winning tradition which had not existed for some 25 years or so.

### PAM RAHN, Bradenton, Florida

My mother was instrumental in developing the original Pirate City as part of the Bradenton City Council here in Bradenton, Florida. I was about six years old. I remember all of the Pirate Booster barbeques. I remember the 1971 World Series team very well. I spoke with players like Roberto Clemente, Manny Sanguillen, Willie Stargell, Gene Alley, and

Richie Hebner, but I was always excited when Danny came out. My grand-parents used to travel a lot and I used to refer to Danny as my "other" grandpa. He was so kind and funny to people. I loved having the opportunity to meet Danny Murtaugh. His name brings a smile to my face and tears to my eyes. Those were some great years. I was sad when he left for the last time and even sadder when he passed away.

## Branch Rickey III, Former Pirate Scout and Grandson of the late Pirate GM Branch Rickey

I have had two sides to many relationships that I've gone through in baseball. One side is that friendly, cordial, congenial side. And then when the pressure is there, when something went wrong, there are the angry exchanges, or those little betrayals, or those little unhappinesses. I cannot remember a single instance in which Danny was ever unkind, unfair, or not generous. I'm dead serious about that. And he was certainly under pressure at times where hard decisions had to be made or where he had been let down by a series of events or relationships or so forth. You don't find many people who have that capacity.

I remember being at spring training in 1972 or 1973 when Danny was no longer managing. He was there to help evaluate players as Joe Brown's special assistant. Danny came into breakfast in the cafeteria at Pirate City one morning and everyone started laughing. A player had just gone out the same door, and there had been some laughing outside. Now Danny came in and I've never seen a worse mess in my life. Everyone in the cafeteria turned as Danny came over to the table where Joe Brown, myself, and some others were sitting. The laughing got so hard that people had tears in their eyes. Danny was the object of the humor.

It turned out that [Danny's wife] Kate had left the day before – and that's a big part of the story. Up to that time I didn't know your grandfather was colorblind. As I recall, his socks were yellow, and didn't match his pants, which were green, his shirt was purple, and he had on a white belt. He was all colors of the rainbow. There was some tangerine somewhere, I don't remember where. It was the worst clash. He got to the table and said, "What?" I think it was Joe Brown who said to him, "Do you have any idea what you've done this morning?"

Danny said, "You know what? I just passed Dock Ellis coming out of the cafeteria, and he took one look at me and said, 'Real cool, man.' That was the point at which I wasn't sure I should come in through the door. I've never known Dock Ellis to think anything was cool that anyone else thought was cool." That's when we learned that Kate picked all his clothes out for him. He had no idea. It was brutal. I've never seen anybody so poorly coordinated.

Danny was a very contagious person in a wry way – it's an Irish thing, there's no doubt. That impishness was in him from sunup to sundown. Some people can go overboard, they're always at it. He just had a wonderful, laid back, clever, disruptive quality, and he laid traps for people in the most wonderful way. He was never hurtful; it was never at somebody else's expense.

Everything you've been told about him is true, but the truth is you haven't been told everything. You can't capture that man inside a book.

## EPILOGUE

**B**ranch Rickey was right. I couldn't fit my grandfather in a book. I was only two when my grandfather died, so I've been regaled with stories about him my whole life – but the stories never did him justice.

The grandfather that I met through writing his story was an amazing man. He grew up in a poverty that few of us can imagine, and he rose to become a two-time World Series Championship manager. He did it largely through hustle, determination, and strength of character. Despite his great successes, he remained a down-to-earth family man with an impish sense of humor. I would love to see the twinkle in his Irish eyes that so many people have mentioned to me.

There are countless stories that I wasn't able to fit into this book. Stories about his generosity, his pranks, his good-natured ribbing of baseball greats – and their ribbing of him in return. How people felt better just by being around him. How people who never met him felt like he was part of their family.

My grandfather was always available for sports banquets and charity events ... especially ones for kids ... especially around his hometown. He never accepted a penny for hometown appearances; he quietly donated out-of-town fees to charity (usually Children's Hospital). He seldom did endorsements, but when he did those earnings also went to charity. My mom didn't even know that until he died. He used to say that if you did a good deed and then talked about it, it was no longer a good deed.

My mom talks about how important my grandfather's Catholic faith was to him. She also remembers being embarrassed of the attention when the nuns would tell her whole elementary school, "Watch Danny Murtaugh when he goes to receive the Holy Eucharist. He's a famous baseball manager, and look how reverent he is. Look at how nicely his hands are folded. If he can be so devout, you can too."

My grandmother was truly his other half. She was the "wind beneath his wings," taking care of things on the home front so he could pursue his baseball career. She was also a great source of support to the wives of his players – serving as sort of a den mother, someone who knew exactly what they were going through.

Growing up, I always thought it was family bias when people would talk about my grandfather someday being in the Hall of Fame. After researching his career and the impact he had on the Pittsburgh Pirates, the fans, and baseball in general, I realize he truly does belong there. Whether he'll make it or not remains to be seen.

Regardless of whether the Hall of Fame voters recognize his accomplishments, Pirate fans around the country know what he meant to the team. Knowing my grandfather as well as I now do, I feel safe in saying that his place in fans' hearts would mean more to him than a place in Cooperstown.

The most rewarding part of this journey has been learning all of the wonderful sides of my grandfather. I miss him more now than I ever did before – because now I know what I missed out on growing up. I feel richer for knowing it, though.

Branch Rickey was right when he said I couldn't fit my grandfather in a book. But I'm sure glad I tried.

# INTERVIEWS CONDUCTED

**Multiple interviews with Danny's family:**

Gigi Mingis (Danny's niece, daughter of his sister Eunice)

Tim Murtaugh (Danny's son)

Timmy Murtaugh (Danny's grandson)

Madge Roche (Danny's first cousin)

Joe Walton (Danny's son-in-law, husband of Kathy)

Kathy Walton (Danny's daughter)

Bennie Wilson (Danny's nephew, Peggy's son)

Betsy Wojdylak (Danny's niece, Peggy's daughter)

**Interviews with friends, fans, and players:**

Gene Alley in Summer 2009

Tony Bartirome on April 14, 2008

Yogi Berra on August 6, 2009

Steve Blass on April 3, 2008

Frank Bork on August 6, 2008

Bobby Bragan on February 20, 2008

Joe Brown on August 4, 2009

Dave Cash on July 14, 2009

Bill Christine on August 6, 2009

Mary Christulides on February 22, 2008

Murray Cook on August 5, 2009

ElRoy Face on February 20, 2008

Ed Fitz Gerald on February 22, 2008

Bob Friend on July 10, 2009

Pat Friend on July 10, 2009

Joe Garagiola on March 26, 2008

Dave Giusti on March 13, 2008

Dick Groat on March 10, 2008

Merle Kalp in Spring 2008

Ralph Kiner on April 25, 2008

Nellie King on March 19, 2008

Vernon Law on February 26, 2008

VaNita Law on February 26, 2008

Bill Mazeroski on August 29, 2009

Jack Mycka on August 18, 2009

John O'Brien on July 16, 2009

Ed O'Brien on July 16, 2009

Sally O'Leary on February 22, 2008

Al Oliver on February 29, 2008

Dave Parker on August 18, 2009

John Podgajny on February 22, 2008

Sam Reich on February 22, 2008

Branch Rickey (III) on August 4, 2009

Manny Sanguillen on August 19, 2009

Martha Shanley on February 22, 2008

Herb Soltman on August 19, 2009

Ed Stevens on March 11, 2008

Frank Thomas on August 6, 2008

Ted van Deusen on April 24, 2008

Mickey Vernon on February 28, 2008

Wally Westlake on February 20, 2008

## END NOTES

### CHAPTER 1

1. Myron Cope, *Saturday Evening Post,* May 9, 1959, p. 77.
2. *Chester Times,* April 20, 1959, "The Danny Murtaugh Story — No. 1: Grit, Wit, Spit; Keys to Success" by Matt Zibitka.
3. Ibid.
4. Ibid.
5. *Chester Times,* September 9, 1931
6. *Chester Times,* April 21, 1959, "The Danny Murtaugh Story — No. 2: So Small, No Suit Could Fit Properly" by Matt Zibitka.
7. *Chester Times* July 25, 1933.
8. Current Biography 1961, New York : H. W. Wilson Co.
9. Myron Cope, *Saturday Evening Post,* May 9, 1959, p. 76.
10. McCollister, John. *The Good, The Bad, & The Ugly.* Triumph Books, Chicago, IL. 2008. P. 184.
11. *Pittsburgh Post Gazette,* May 11, 1955.
12. *Chester Times,* March 15, 1939
13. Ibid.
14. *Chester Times,* July 1, 1941.

### CHAPTER 2

1. *Pittsburgh Post Gazette*, March 18, 1958.
2. Philadelphia area newspaper sportswriter Bob French writing in offseason between 1941-1942.
3. *Delaware County* (PA) *Daily Times* (formerly *Chester Times*), May 16, 1961.

4. *Chester Times*, September 22, 1941
5. President Franklin Delano Roosevelt, *Green Light Letter*, January 15, 1942.
6. *New York World Telegram*, Dan Daniel, late June or early July 1942
7. Article by Frank Yeutter, *Philadelphia Evening Bulletin* May 12, 1942.
8. Hank Simmons, *Philadelphia Inquirer*, Spring 1943.

## CHAPTER 4

1. *Sporting News*, August 14, 1957.
2. *Chester Times*, September 21, 1951.

## CHAPTER 5

1. *Chester Times*, September 25, 1952.
2. *Chester Times*, October 25, 1952.
3. Reported by Dick Hudson, *Charleston Daily Mail*, Spring 1955 (date unknown).
4. *Charleston Gazette*, June 24, 1955.

## CHAPTER 6

1. *Chester Times*, August 5, 1957.
2. *Pittsburgh Sun Telegraph*, August 5, 1957.
3. *Pittsburgh Sun Telegraph*, August 10, 1957.
4. *Chester Times*, August 13, 1957.
5. *Chester Times*, December 13, 1957.
6. *The Bark*, St. James Catholic High School, February 13, 1958.
7. *Chester Times*, July 26, 1958.
8. *Pittsburgh Post Gazette*, October 24, 1958.
9. Ibid.
10. *New York Times*, September 28, 1958.
11. *St. Petersburg Times*, March 29, 1959.
12. *New Kensington (PA) Daily Dispatch;* October 3, 1959.

## CHAPTER 7

1. Reisler, Jim. *The Best Game Ever: Pirates vs. Yankees, October 13, 1960.* Perseus Publishing. p. 210.
2. Ibid. p. 51.
3. *The Fredericksburg (VA) Free Lance Star,* January 22, 1960.
4. *Pittsburgh Post Gazette,* May 28, 1960.
5. *New York Times,* July 11, 1960.
6. Ibid.
7. *Pittsburgh Post Gazette,* October 9, 1960.
8. Ibid.
9. *Pittsburgh Post Gazette,* October 11, 1960.
10. Ibid.
11. *Pittsburgh Post Gazette,* October 13, 1960.
12. *New York Times,* October 13, 1960.
13. Associated Press, October 14, 1960.
14. Reisler. p. 224.
15. *Pittsburgh Post-Gazette,* October 10, 2008.

## CHAPTER 8

1. *Delaware County (PA) Daily Times,* January 20, 1961.
2. Ibid.
3. *Milwaukee Sentinel,* January 23, 1961.
4. *Pittsburgh Post Gazette,* February 27, 1961.
5. *Ocala (FL) Star-Banner,* March 19, 1961.
6. Ibid.
7. *Pittsburgh Post Gazette,* January 31, 1961.
8. *Delaware County (PA) Daily Times,* May 24, 1961.
9. *Delaware County (PA) Daily Times,* May 31, 1961.
10. *Delaware County (PA) Daily Times,* June 21, 1961.
11. *Delaware County (PA) Daily Times,* July 11, 1961.
12. Ibid.

13. Associated Press, July 12, 1961.

14. *Pittsburgh Post Gazette,* August 3, 1961.

15. *Delaware County (PA) Daily Times,* September 16, 1961.

16. *Milwaukee Sentinel,* January 4, 1962.

**CHAPTER 9**

1. *The Bend Bulletin* (central OR), November 29, 1962.

2. *Pittsburgh Post Gazette,* October 2, 1964.

3. *Times-Express* (Monroeville, PA), July 27, 1967.

4. *Pittsburgh Post Gazette,* September 27, 1969.

5. Ibid.

**CHAPTER 10**

1. *Pittsburgh Post Gazette,* February 8, 1971.

2. United Press International, May 24, 1971.

3. *Delaware County Daily Times,* October 7, 1971.

4. Ibid.

5. *New York Times,* October 9, 1971.

6. Ibid.

7. *McKeesport (PA) Daily News,* October 16, 1971.

8. *New York Times,* October 10, 1971.

9. Ibid.

10. *New York Times,* October 13, 1971.

11. *Associated Press,* October 13, 1971.

12. Ibid.

13. Ibid.

14. *New York Times,* October 13, 1971.

15. Ibid.

16. *Pittsburgh Post-Gazette,* October 31, 2001.

17. Ibid.

18. Ibid.

19. Ibid.

20. *McKeesport (PA) Daily News,* October 15, 1971.

21. *Pittsburgh Post Gazette,* October 15, 1971.

22. *McKeesport (PA) Daily News,* October 16, 1971.

23. *Pittsburgh Post Gazette,* October 16, 1971.

24. Associated Press, October 18, 1971.

25. Ibid.

26. *New York Times,* October 18, 1971.

27. Ibid.

28. Associated Press, October 18, 1971.

29. Ibid.

30. Pittsburgh Pirates Press Release, November 23, 1971.

31. Associated Press, November 23, 1971.

32. *New York Times,* December 2, 1971.

## CHAPTER 11

1. Associated Press, July 20, 1972 (in Pennsylvania Mirror).

2. *McKeesport (PA) Daily News,* July 26, 1972.

3. *Rome (GA) News-Tribune,* February 18, 1973.

4. Ibid.

5. Stargell, Willie and Tom Bird. *Willie Stargell: An Autobiography.* New York : Harper & Row, 1984.

6. Ibid.

7. *Delaware County Daily Times,* September 7, 1973.

8. *Pittsburgh Post Gazette,* September 7, 1973.

9. Stargell autobiography.

10. Ibid.

11. Associated Press, March 26, 1975 (in *Penn State Daily Collegian*).

12. *Spokesman Review* (Spokane, WY), October 9, 1974.

13. *Boca Raton News,* March 19, 1975 (Fred Down, UPI Sport Writer).

14. *St. Petersburg Times,* May 4, 1975.

15. *St. Petersburg Times,* February 5, 1975

16. *Pittsburgh Post Gazette,* April 28, 1975.

17. Ibid.

18. *Pittsburgh Post Gazette,* September23, 1975.

19. *Pittsburgh Post Gazette,* December 24, 1975.

20. *St. Petersburg Times,* February 17, 1976.

21. Pittsburgh Post Gazette, April 12, 1976.

22. *Beaver County Times,* October 2, 1976
(Pohla Smith, UPI Sports Writer).

23. Ibid.

## CHAPTER 12

1. *Delaware County Daily Times,* June 14, 1961.

2. *Delaware County Daily Times,* February 2, 1962.

## CHAPTER 13

1. *Delaware County Daily Times,* December 7, 1976.

2. *Pittsburgh Post Gazette,* December 7, 1976.

3. *Philadelphia Evening Bulletin,* December 6, 1976.

4. *Penn State University Daily Collegian,* December 7, 1976.

# DANNY MURTAUGH LIFETIME STATS

| Year | Team | League | Level (Minors) | G | AB | R | H | 2B | 3B | HR | RBI | BA |
|------|------|--------|----------------|---|----|----|----|----|----|----|-----|-----|
| 1937 | Cambridge | Eastern Shore | D | 94 | 377 | 71 | 112 | 18 | 4 | 2 | 35 | 0.297 |
| 1938 | Cambridge | Eastern Shore | D | 112 | 429 | 87 | 134 | 21 | 5 | 3 | 52 | 0.312 |
| 1939 | Rochester | International | AA | 22 | 89 | 13 | 29 | 3 | 1 | 0 | 6 | 0.326 |
| 1939 | Columbus | AA | AA | 111 | 415 | 53 | 106 | 16 | 2 | 2 | 29 | 0.255 |
| 1940 | Houston | Texas | AA | 155 | 623 | 106 | 186 | 24 | 8 | 0 | 57 | 0.299 |
| 1941 | Houston | Texas | AA | 69 | 278 | 54 | 88 | 16 | 6 | 0 | 29 | 0.317 |
| 1941 | Philadelphia | National | | 85 | 347 | 34 | 76 | 8 | 1 | 0 | 11 | 0.219 |
| 1942 | Philadelphia | National | | 144 | 506 | 48 | 122 | 16 | 4 | 0 | 27 | 0.241 |
| 1943 | Philadelphia | National | | 113 | 451 | 65 | 123 | 17 | 4 | 1 | 35 | 0.273 |
| 1944-45 | Philadelphia | National | | (IN MILITARY SERVICE) | | | | | | | | |
| 1946 | Philadelphia | National | | 6 | 19 | 1 | 4 | 1 | 0 | 1 | 2 | 0.211 |
| 1946 | Rochester | International | AAA | 139 | 541 | | 174 | 23 | 4 | 0 | | 0.322 |
| 1947 | Boston | National | | 3 | 8 | 0 | 1 | 0 | 0 | 0 | 0 | 0.125 |
| 1947 | Milwaukee | Am. Assoc. | AAA | 119 | 444 | 96 | 134 | 15 | 5 | 7 | 49 | 0.302 |
| 1948 | Pittsburgh | National | | 146 | 514 | 56 | 149 | 21 | 5 | 1 | 71 | 0.290 |
| 1949 | Pittsburgh | National | | 75 | 236 | 16 | 48 | 7 | 2 | 2 | 24 | 0.203 |
| 1950 | Pittsburgh | National | | 118 | 367 | 34 | 108 | 20 | 5 | 2 | 37 | 0.294 |
| 1951 | Pittsburgh | National | | 77 | 151 | 9 | 30 | 7 | 0 | 1 | 11 | 0.199 |
| 1952 | New Orleans | Southern | AA | 57 | 156 | 14 | 33 | 2 | 3 | 2 | 19 | 0.212 |
| 1953 | New Orleans | Southern | AA | 3 | 4 | 0 | 0 | 0 | 0 | 0 | 0 | 0 |

# DANNY MURTAUGH MANAGING STATS

| Year | Team | Finish | W | L | WP |
|------|------|--------|-----|-----|-------|
| 1952 | New Orleans | Fifth | 80 | 75 | 0.516 |
| 1953 | New Orleans | Fifth | 76 | 78 | 0.494 |
| 1954 | New Orleans | Second | 92 | 62 | 0.597 |
| 1955 | Charleston | Eighth | 31 | 64 | 0.326 |
| 1957 | Pittsburgh | Seventh | 26 | 25 | 0.510 |
| 1958 | Pittsburgh | Second | 84 | 70 | 0.545 |
| 1959 | Pittsburgh | Fourth | 78 | 76 | 0.506 |
| 1960 | Pittsburgh | First | 95 | 59 | 0.617 |
| 1961 | Pittsburgh | Sixth | 75 | 79 | 0.487 |
| 1962 | Pittsburgh | Fourth | 93 | 68 | 0.578 |
| 1963 | Pittsburgh | Eighth | 74 | 88 | 0.457 |
| 1964 | Pittsburgh | Sixth | 80 | 82 | 0.494 |
| 1967 | Pittsburgh | Sixth | 39 | 39 | 0.500 |
| 1970 | Pittsburgh | First | 89 | 73 | 0.549 |
| 1971 | Pittsburgh | First | 97 | 65 | 0.599 |
| 1973 | Pittsburgh | Third | 13 | 13 | 0.500 |
| 1974 | Pittsburgh | First | 88 | 74 | 0.543 |
| 1975 | Pittsburgh | First | 92 | 69 | 0.571 |
| 1976 | Pittsburgh | Second | 92 | 70 | 0.568 |
| **Lifetime Major League Managing** | | | **1115** | **950** | **0.540** |